SERVICES MARKETING

Mrs. Samita Kher

Professor
M.A. (Economics), MBS (HR)
Sinhgad Institute of Management
Pune

Mr. Priyadarshan Patil

Lecturer
B.H.M.C.T., M.B.A. (Marketing),
Sinhgad Institute of Management
Pune

NIRALI PRAKASHAN

Pune | Mumbai | Nagpur | Chennai | Jalgaon | Bengaluru | Kolhapur

N1734

SERVICES MARKETING   **ISBN 978-93-82448-26-6**

First Edition   :   January, 2013

©   :   **Authors**

Published By :
NIRALI PRAKASHAN
Abhyudaya Pragati, 1312, Shivaji Nagar,
Off J.M. Road, PUNE – 411005
Tel - (020) 25512336/37/39, Fax - (020) 25511379
Email : niralipune@pragationline.com

DISTRIBUTION CENTRES

PUNE

Nirali Prakashan
119, Budhwar Peth, Jogeshwari Mandir Lane
Pune 411002, Maharashtra
Tel : (020) 2445 2044, 66022708
Fax : (020) 2445 1538
Email : bookorder@pragationline.com

MUMBAI

Nirali Prakashan
385, S.V.P. Road, Rasdhara Co-op. Hsg. Society Ltd.,
Girgaum, Mumbai 400004, Maharashtra
Tel : (022) 2385 6339 / 2386 9976,
Fax : (022) 2386 9976
Email : niralimumbai@pragationline.com

DISTRIBUTION BRANCHES

NAGPUR

Pratibha Book Distributors
Above Maratha Mandir, Shop No. 3, First Floor,
Rani Jhanshi Square, Sitabuldi, Nagpur 440012,
Maharashtra, Tel : (0712) 254 7129

JALGAON

Nirali Prakashan
34, V. V. Golani Market, Navi Peth, Jalgaon 425001,
Maharashtra, Tel : (0257) 222 0395
Mob : 94234 91860

BENGALURU

Pragati Book House
House No. 1, Sanjeevappa Lane, Avenue Road Cross,
Opp. Rice Church, Bengaluru – 560002.
Tel : (080) 64513344, 64513355,
Mob : 9880582331, 9845021552
Email:bharatsavla@yahoo.com

KOLHAPUR

Nirali Prakashan
New Mahadvar Road,
Kedar Plaza, 1st Floor Opp. IDBI Bank
Kolhapur 416 012, Maharashtra. Mob : 9855046155

CHENNAI
Pragati Books
9/1, Montieth Road, Behind Taas Mahal, Egmore,
Chennai 600008 Tamil Nadu, Tel : (044) 6518 3535,
Mob : 94440 01782 / 98450 21552 / 98805 82331
Email : bharatsavla@yahoo.com

RETAIL OUTLETS
PUNE

Pragati Book Centre
157, Budhwar Peth, Opp. Ratan Talkies,
Pune 411002, Maharashtra
Tel : (020) 2445 8887 / 6602 2707, Fax : (020) 2445 8887

Pragati Book Centre
Amber Chamber, 28/A, Budhwar Peth,
Appa Balwant Chowk, Pune : 411002, Maharashtra,
Tel : (020) 20240335 / 66281669
Email : pbcpune@pragationline.com

Pragati Book Centre
676/B, Budhwar Peth, Opp. Jogeshwari Mandir,
Pune 411002, Maharashtra
Tel : (020) 6601 7784 / 6602 0855

PBC Book Sellers & Stationers
152, Budhwar Peth, Pune 411002, Maharashtra
Tel : (020) 2445 2254 / 6609 2463

MUMBAI
Pragati Book Corner
Indira Niwas, 111 - A, Bhavani Shankar Road, Dadar (W), Mumbai 400028, Maharashtra
Tel : (022) 2422 3526 / 6662 5254
Email : pbcmumbai@pragationline.com

www.pragationline.com   info@pragationline.com

Preface ...

Today, people in the western world as well as the majority in India, earn a living from producing services rather than making manufactured goods or farming. For consumers, the increase in wealth has resulted in opportunities to consume services which were previously not possible or had to be produced at home by themselves. For businesses, services are essential as companies are concentrating on their core business activities and buy specialist services from outside for better quality and reliability.

The growth of the services sector in India contributing more than 50% of GDP, has lot of opportunities for budding managers to build their career in India as well as across the globe. With development of world economies, there is a growing need for services. Hospitality, health care, travel and tourism, e-commerce, e-business, airlines, education, insurance, banking are all part and parcel of this.

This book develops frameworks for understanding services and the effective marketing of them. The characteristics of intangibility, inseparability, inventory, inconsistency and ownership, have major implications for the marketing managers in the services sector to develop their service offer, promote it and then deliver it. Traditional marketing mix frameworks, which apply to manufactured goods, are inadequate for services. Services are about processes as much as outcomes and these processes often involve considerable interaction between customers and operations people. Hence, marketing cannot be seen as an isolated function. Successful service companies make sure that their front-line people can competently deliver the promises which marketing people make to customers. Services marketing cannot be separated from services management.

This book is intended to be a reference book for budding as well as practising managers. The benefits to the reader and user of this book are :

1. Dual coverage of services marketing.

2. An application oriented approach grounded with solid theory covering all the relevant facets in the Indian context.

3. Personal insights based on rich experience.

The objective of this book is to enable the student to acquire knowledge with deep insight into the concepts, tools and techniques of services marketing dovetailed with applications to real life problems in the global environment as well as in the Indian context.

The book has been streamlined and restructured to sharpen the students and reader's focus on the essentials of services marketing and coverage of new concepts and ideals especially the use of technology.

Particular attention has been paid to making this book stimulating and highly readable. The result is a text which is clear, focussed and designed to capture student interest. This text is equally suitable for courses directed at undergraduates and postgraduates and MBA students.

Although it's impossible to mention everyone who has like to helped in the publishing of the book, we would start with Dinesh Furia and Jignesh Furia our Publishers who gave us the opportunity to write. Special thanks are owed to Nirja Sharma for her research, valuable insights and editing of the text. We are also appreciative of all the hardwork put in by the editing and production staff in helping to transform our manuscript into a well finished published text. They include Akbar Shaikh and Prasad Chintakindi. It is hoped that the book will be of great help to the students. We welcome any suggestions for the improvement of book.

Authors

Contents ...

Chapter **1** *...*

Introduction to Services

Contents ...

1.1 Introduction

We as consumers use services every day. Getting a haircut, getting clothes cleaned from the dry cleaners, eating at a restaurant, taking a bus are all examples of service utilisation at the personal and individual level. The colleges and institutions at which students study, are themselves complex service organisations. These service organisations in addition to educational services provide services such as library, cafeteria, counselling, telephone services and many more. Businesses and other organisations are also dependent on an extensive range of services albeit on a much larger scale.

Services marketing concepts and strategies have developed in response to the tremendous growth of service industries. The economic importance of services can be seen by the fact that trade in services is growing worldwide. There is a growing market for services and an increasing dominance of services in economies worldwide. The tremendous growth and economic contributions of the service sector have drawn increasing attention to the issues and challenges of service sector industries all over the world.

Services have started to play an increasingly important role in the economy and in individual organisations. Services are particularly relevant in industries where competitive pressures are forcing companies to find ways to create competitive differentiation. However, there are significant differences between the marketing of services and the marketing of tangible products.

Although services marketing has been practiced by some enlightened professionals for decades, the concept of services marketing is still new to many marketing professionals. Many current marketing concepts and tools have simply been transferred from the manufacturing sector. There are common elements between services and products, yet there is a need for marketing methods, tools and concepts that are specific to services.

1.2 The Services Concept / The Nature of Services

Services define a huge diversity of activities and involve many intangible inputs and outputs. In services, the benefits are created by actions or performances. The term services covers a heterogeneous range of intangible products and activities that are difficult to encapsulate within a simple definition. Services are also often difficult to separate from goods with which they may be associated in varying degrees.

A service is the action of doing something for someone or something. It is largely intangible (i.e. not material). A product is tangible (i.e. material) since you can touch it and own it. A service tends to be an experience that is consumed at the point where it is purchased, and cannot be owned since it quickly perishes. A person could go to a café one day and have excellent service, and then return the next day and have a poor experience.

The 1993 SNA (System of National Accounts) use of the term services is defined as follows: "Services are not separate entities over which ownership rights can be established. They cannot be traded separately from their production. Services are heterogeneous outputs produced to order and typically consist of changes in the condition of the consuming units realised by the activities of the producers at the demand of the customers. By the time their production is completed they must have been provided to the consumers."

However, the 1993 SNA then qualifies this relatively simple definition as follows: "There is a group of industries, generally classified as service industries, that produce outputs that have many of the characteristics of goods, i.e., those concerned with the provision, storage, communication and dissemination of information, advice and entertainment in the broadest sense of those terms the production of general or specialised information, news, consultancy reports, computer programmes, movies, music, etc. The outputs of these industries, over which ownership rights may be established, are often stored on physical objects paper, tapes, disks, etc. that can be traded like ordinary goods. Whether characterised as goods or services, these products possess the essential characteristic that they can be produced by one unit and supplied to another, thus making possible division of labour and the emergence of markets."

Examples of service activities are wholesale, retail, certain kinds of repair, hotel, catering, transport, postal, telecommunication, financial, insurance, real estate, property rental, computer-related, research, professional, marketing and other business support, government, education, health, social, sanitation, community, audiovisual, recreational, cultural, personal, and domestic services.

- **Inseparable:** It is inseparable from the point where it is consumed, and from the provider of the service. For example, you cannot take a live theatre performance home to consume it (a DVD of the same performance would be a product, not a service).

- **Intangible:** A service cannot have a real, physical presence as does a product. For example, motor insurance may have a certificate, but the financial service itself cannot be touched i.e. it is intangible.

- **Perishable:** Here, the term perishable implies that once it has occurred it cannot be repeated in exactly the same way. For example, once a 100 metres Olympic final has been run, there will be no other for 4 more years, and even then it will be staged in a different place with many different finalists.

- **Variability:** The human involvement of service provision means that no two services will be completely identical. For example, returning to the same garage time and time again for a service on your car might see different levels of customer satisfaction, or speediness of work.

- **Right of Ownership:** Right of ownership is not taken to the service, since you merely experience it. For example, an engineer may service your air-conditioning, but you do not own the service, the engineer or his equipment. You cannot sell it once it has been consumed, and do not take ownership of it.

When one talks about product planning in marketing, a product is a package of benefits as perceived by the consumer. When one moves into the service concept, one is really talking about the same thing. The service concept is the bundle of goods and services that are sold to the consumer and their relative importance. We have to put ourselves in the minds of the consumer and understand how the consumer perceives the importance of each.

Definition of Services

Despite many authors having attempted to give a clear cut definition or description of a service no unanimous definition has yet emerged. In the simplest terms, services are deeds, processes and performances. A service is a set of benefits delivered from the accountable service provider, mostly in close co-actions with his services suppliers, generated by the functions of technical systems and/or by distinct activities of individuals, respectively, commissioned according to the needs of his service consumers by the service customer from the accountable service provider, rendered individually to the authorised service consumers on their dedicated request, and finally, utilised by the requesting service consumers for executing and/or supporting their day-to-day business tasks or private activities.

1. "A service is an activity or benefit that one party can offer to another that is essentially intangible and does not result in the ownership of anything. Its production may or may not be tied to a physical product".

    Kotler and Armstrong [1991)

2. "A Service as any primary or complimentary activity that does not directly produce a physical product, i.e., the non goods part of transaction between buyer (customer) and seller (provider)." **Service Industries Journal**

3. "Services are those separately identifiable, essentially intangible activities, which provide want satisfaction when marketed to consumers and/or industrial uses and which are not necessarily tied to the sale of a product or another service." **Stanton**

4. "Services include all economic activities whose output is not a physical product or construction, is generally consumed at the time it is produced, and provides added value in forms (such as convenience, amusement, timeliness, comfort or health) that are essentially intangible concerns of its first purchaser".

5. A service is an activity that has some element of intangibility associated with it, which involves some interaction with customers or with property in their possession and does not result in a transfer of ownership. A change in condition may occur and production of the service may or may not be loosely associated with a physical product.

To understand the concept and nature of services it is first essential to learn the basic differences between goods and services. A brief outline of the distinguishing factors is given below.

- Customers do not obtain ownership of services.
- Service products are ephemeral (transitory and perishable) and cannot be inventoried.
- Intangible elements dominate value creation.
- Customers may be involved in the production process.
- Many services are difficult for customers to evaluate.
- The time factor assumes great importance.
- Distribution channels take different forms.

The main distinction between goods and services is the fact that customers derive value from services without obtaining ownership of any tangible items except in food or repair services. A service is a deed or performance and thus ephemeral i.e. it is transitory and perishable. Intangible elements including labour and expertise of service personnel dominate the creation of value in service performances.

There are obvious differences between goods and services that are analysed based on characteristics of each. A good is a tangible object used either once or repeatedly. A service is intangible. The tangibility differentiator indicates the ability to touch, smell, taste and see which is absent in services. This can be a deterrent to the service receiver to gauge the quality and dependant on the service company reputation. In the case of goods the ownership of the product is transferable from sellers to buyers, whereas in services there is no ownership involved.

On the quality front, with goods it is homogeneous, once produced the quality is uniform across all line of products. They can be separated from the seller/ provider and not be dependant on the source for its delivery to the purchaser. With regard to service it is inseparable from the service provider and heterogeneous, where each time the service is offered it may vary in quality, output, and delivery. It cannot be controlled and is dependent on the human effort in achieving that quality, hence, is variable from producer, customer and daily basis.

Another key distinction is perishability of services and the non-perishability of goods. Goods will have a long storage life and are mostly non-perishable. Whereas services are delivered at that moment and do not have a long life or cannot be stored for repeat use. They do not bear the advantage of shelf life as in the case of goods like empty seats in airlines. With the production and consumption taking place simultaneously in services, it differs from goods on simultaneity and the provisions for quality control in the process.

The characteristics of services will be dealt with in greater detail later in the chapter.

1.3 Services Industry

Following the trade liberalisation in 1991, the Indian economy embarked on a path of rapid growth of aggregate output. In particular, it witnessed a high growth rate of service sector output while that of industry was relatively muted. As a result, the share of services in GDP has come to resemble that of a high income country while its per capita income still remains that of a low income country. Further, we also observe a sharp increase in the rate of growth of Services sector trade after liberalisation.

The Services industries (More formally termed: 'tertiary sector of industry' by economists) involve the provision of services to businesses as well as final consumers. Such sectors therefore, include accounting, tradesmanship (like mechanic or plumber services), computer services, restaurants, tourism, etc.

Hence, a Service Industry is one where no goods are produced whereas primary industries are those that extract minerals, oil etc. from the ground and secondary industries are those that manufacture products, including builders, but not remodelling contractors.

The tertiary sector of economy (also known as the service sector or the service industry) is one of the three economic sectors, the others being the secondary sector (approximately manufacturing) and the primary sector (extraction such as mining, agriculture and fishing). Sometimes an additional sector, the "quaternary sector", is defined for the sharing of information (which normally belongs to the tertiary sector)

Services Sector Growth Rate in Indian GDP has been very rapid in the last few years. The Services Sector contributes the most to the Indian GDP. The Growth Rate of the Services Sector in Indian GDP has risen due to several reasons and it has also given a major boost to the Indian economy.

Services Sector in India

India ranks fifteenth in the services output and it provides employment to around 23% of the total workforce in the country. The various sectors under the Services Sector in India are construction, trade, hotels, transport, restaurant, communication and storage, social and personal services, community, insurance, financing, business services, and real estate.

Services Sector Contribution to the Indian Economy

The Services Sector contributes the most to the Indian GDP. The Sector of Services in India has the biggest share in the country's GDP as can be seen from the following table. The contribution of the Services Sector in India, GDP has increased a lot in the last few years. The Services Sector contributed only 15% to the Indian GDP in 1950. Further, the Indian Services Sector's share in the country's GDP has increased from 43.695 in 1990- 1991 to around 51.16% in 1998- 1999. This shows that the Services Sector in India accounts for over half of the country's GDP.

Table 1.1: Real GDP Growth (%)

	Q1		Q2		Q3		April-December	
Sector	(April-June)		(July-September)		(October-December)			
	2007-08	2008-09	2007-08	2008-09	2007-08	2008-09	2007-08	2008-09
Agriculture	4.4	3.0	4.4	2.7	6.9	-2.2	5.5	0.6
Industry	8.5	5.2	7.5	4.7	7.6	0.8	7.9	3.5
Services	10.7	10.2	10.7	9.6	10.1	9.5	10.5	9.7
Overall	9.1	7.9	9.1	7.6	8.9	5.3	9.0	6.9

Source: Central Statistical Organisation (CSO).

The Reasons for the growth of the Services Sector contribution to the Indian GDP

The contribution of the Services Sector has increased very rapidly in the Indian GDP for many foreign consumers have shown interest in the country's services exports. This is due to the fact that India has a large pool of highly skilled, low cost, and educated workers in the country. This has made sure that the services that are available in the country are of the best quality. The foreign companies seeing this have started outsourcing their work to India especially in the area of business services which includes Business Process Outsourcing (BPO) and Information Technology (IT) services. This has given a major boost to the Services Sector in India, which in its turn has made the sector contribute more to the India in GDP.

Services Sector Growth Rate in Indian GDP registered a significant growth over the past few years. The Indian government must take steps in order to ensure that Services Sector Growth Rate in Indian GDP continues to rise. For this will ensure the growth and prosperity of the country's economy.

The most important services in the Indian economy have been health and education. They are one of the largest and most challenging sectors and hold a key to the country's overall progress. A strong and well-defined health care sector helps to build a healthy and productive workforce as well as stabilise population. The 'Ministry of Health and Family Welfare' is responsible for implementation of various programmes in the areas of health and family welfare, prevention and control of major communicable diseases as well as promotion of traditional and indigenous systems of medicines. Accordingly, it is carrying out measures like National health policy, implementing National Rural Health Mission (NRHM) in different States, conducting surveys and studies, etc. Education strongly influences improvement in health, hygiene and demographic profile. The 'Ministry of Human resource Development' is involved in eradicating illiteracy from the country. It is concerned with universalisation of elementary education, achieving full adult literacy, laying down of National Policy on Education, meeting needs of secondary and higher education for all, etc. India has achieved impressive demographic transition owing to the decline of crude birth rate, crude death rate, total fertility rate and infant mortality rate as well as gained high literacy rate in the country.

The era of economic liberalisation has ushered in a rapid change in the services industry. As a result, over the years, India is witnessing a transition from agriculture-based economy to a knowledge-based economy. The knowledge economy creates, disseminates, and uses knowledge to enhance its growth and development. One of the major functional pillars of this economy is Information Technology (IT) and IT-enabled services (ITeS) industry. The 'Department of Information Technology' has been making continuous efforts to make India a front-runner in the age of Information revolution. IT continues to be a dominating sector in the overall growth of the Indian industry. A large number of Indian software companies have acquired international quality certification. Several policies have also been framed on the key issues of IT infrastructure, electronic governance as well as IT education.

Another major and upcoming services industry has been media and entertainment. It is basically an intellectual property-driven sector with small to large players spread throughout the country. It covers film, music, radio, broadcast, television and live entertainment. It plays a significant role in creating people's awareness about national policies and programmes by providing information and education to all. The 'Ministry of Information and Broadcasting' is responsible for formulation and administration of the rules, regulations and laws relating to media industry. Besides, retailing has been one of the fastest growing services sectors both in terms of turnover and employment. Many national and global players have been investing in the retail segment and are making all efforts to further expand the sector. Out of the total retail outlets in the country, most of them are related to food items.

However, to supplement the achievements and meet the shortfalls in all the sub-sectors of the services industry, the travel and tourism sector has to be developed in a sustainable manner. Being one of the largest industries in terms of gross revenue and foreign exchange earnings, it stimulates growth and expansion in other economic sectors like agriculture, horticulture, poultry, handicrafts, transportation, construction, etc. as well as gives momentum to growth of services exports. It is a major contributor to the national integration process of the country as well as preserver of natural and cultural environments. The 'Ministry of Tourism' has been undertaking several policy measures and incentives so as to boost the sector such as the announcement of the National Tourism Policy.

All this shows that services hold immense potential to accelerate the growth of an economy and promote general well-being of the people. They offer innumerable business opportunities to the investors. They have the capacity to generate substantial employment opportunities in the economy as well as increase its per capita income. Without them, Indian economy would not have acquired a strong and dominating place on the world platform. Thus, service sector is considered to be an integral part of the economy and includes various sub-sectors spread all across the country.

1.4 Nature of Services

Services are a diverse group of economic activities that include high technology, knowledge-intensive sub-sectors, as well as labour-intensive, low skill areas. In many aspects, service sectors exhibit marked differences from manufacturing – although these distinctions may be blurring.

Simply defined, services are a diverse group of economic activities not directly associated with the manufacture of goods, mining or agriculture. They typically involve the provision of human value added in the form of labour, advice, managerial skill, entertainment, training, intermediation and the like. They differ from other types of economic activities in a number of ways. Many, for example, cannot be inventoried and must be consumed at the point of production. This would include trips to the doctor, enjoying a meal at a restaurant, flying from Tokyo to Paris, or attending a concert. This is in marked contrast with manufactured products, whose tangible character allows them to be stored, distributed widely and consumed without direct interaction with the entity that produced the good.

Technological advances are, however, narrowing the differences between services and other economic activities. While it has not reached the point where someone can enjoy the ambience of a good restaurant without physically going to one, information and communication technology (ICT) now enables people to participate in a growing number of service-related activities in real, or deferred, time, without having to be physically present. Copies of movies and most other performances can be recorded and mass-produced for future consumption, like manufactured products. Software is developed and boxed like any other manufactured product, and is considered, for all intents and purposes, a good – albeit with a high service-related content. In these instances services have, in a sense, taken on the characteristics of commodities – one provider is mass-producing a common product for many people. Service providers are thus increasingly able to benefit from economies of scale {Box 1}. The benefits have not, however, been restricted to large enterprises as small firms can achieve similar gains through increased networking.

The relationship between service providers and consumers is also changing in other ways that may have significant implications for economies. Technology now allows providers to produce a single product, which is not mass-produced, but which is capable of being mass-consumed, either on a standardised or customised basis. Such is the case with online Internet access to dictionaries, encyclopaedias, newspapers, museum collections, etc. It will also apparently be the case with key, basic operating software in the near future, as both Microsoft and Sun Microsystems have announced their intention to supplement distribution of "boxed" software with online versions (Taylor, 1999).

Box 1. Technological advances are transforming services

In the 1920s, Ford Motor Company built the River Rouge assembly plant in Michigan. Coal and iron ore were brought in one end and finished automobiles came out the other. Today, this would seem aberrant, some sort of bizarre theme park, but in fact, at that point in time, the technology of scale made it an entirely rational way of working. There is a great similarity between banks today and the automobile industry that built that plant nearly 80 years ago. And that is, today's banks, like Henry Ford in the 1920s, are learning the techniques of mass production for the first time. There was a time when a bank would lend to a business or provide a mortgage, would take the asset and put it on their books much the way a museum would place a piece of art on the wall or under glass – to be admired and valued for its security and constant return. Times have changed. Banks now take those assets, structure them into pools, and sell securities based on those pools to institutional investors and portfolio managers.

In effect, they use their balance sheets not as museums, but as parking lots – temporary holding spaces to bundle up assets and sell them to those investors who have a far greater interest in holding those assets for the long term. The bank has thus gone from being a

---

museum where it acquired only the finest assets and held and exhibited them in perpetuity into a manufacturing plant which provides a product for the secondary market. Just as Henry Ford did 80 years ago, banks today are focusing on producing a standardised product at a predictable rate, under standard norms of quality, and are teaching their workforces to produce that product as quickly and as efficiently as possible.

Technology has been the key to this process. The reason that we see a services economy today, and gather to talk about it and recognise its importance is because technology has allowed service industries to gain the operational leverage that manufacturing achieved 100 years ago. In addition to banks, health systems, telephone and telecommunications networks, and distribution and retailing firms are further examples of sectors that have been able to benefit from economies of scale. As a result, we are now living in a world where global-scale service companies exist for the first time, whereas we have seen global manufacturing companies for 50 years or more.

Source: Adapted from Ehrlich,1999.

Technology is also affecting the relationship between providers and consumers in areas previously unthinkable, such as health care, where the need for personal contact to diagnose and treat ailments is becoming less essential.

"Internet" banking, real estate, retail and financial services provide other examples where personal, or onsite, contact with service providers is no longer essential for the services to be performed; in many instances such services can, in fact, be provided far more efficiently via the Internet or through other remote communication modes.

Relationship to Manufacturing

The relative importance of manufacturing and services to economies, and the inter-relationship between the two have been the subject of much discussion through the years. Some have argued that the decline in manufacturing and the corresponding shift to services is unsupportable in the long run, since services depend critically on manufacturing for their existence. In the absence of manufacturing, service sectors are seen collapsing. On the other hand, a forceful case was made at the Forum that services have become a major driving force in the economic growth. Rather than services following and supporting manufacturing, manufacturing is seen as flowing to those countries and areas where the services infrastructure is efficient and well developed.

The discussion on this point ultimately underscored the close and symbiotic relationship between services and manufacturing, and the blurring, sometimes arbitrary, distinction between the two. Without demand for transportation, for example, the need for trucks, buses, ships and airplanes would collapse. Similarly, without demand for information and entertainment, there would be no need for printing presses, televisions and radios. The interrelationship between computers and software provides an example of the dynamic interplay between manufacturing and service activities, as software developments are pushing development of more powerful computers, and vice versa. At the same time, computers and software are totally dependent on each other in the sense that neither would have commercial value without the other (i.e. a computer without software would be as worthless as software without an operating platform).

Competitive Conditions

The service sector comprises some of the world's largest corporations, as well as a large number of small and medium-sized enterprises which, in many cases, consist of a sole person. While a number of sectors are still heavily regulated, others are relatively open, with low barriers to entry and keen competition.

The convergence of services and manufacturing in many areas is, however, making it increasingly difficult to classify firms uniquely under either category, particularly as manufacturers expand their businesses into service-related areas.

The firms General Electric (US) and IBM, for example, which are major manufacturers of goods, currently, generate more than half their revenues from services, reflecting a transition that can be found, to varying degrees, throughout industry (General Electric, 1998; IBM, 1998).

The provisions of services, and their cost structures, differ from other sectors in a number of key ways. In manufacturing, substantial costs – in the form of raw materials, labour and capital equipment – are typically incurred in mass-producing items for market. In the case of knowledge-based services, such costs can be negligible. In the case of electronically distributed items (such as software and Internet-based news sources), for example, virtually all costs are incurred in product development, the preparation of a single "master" product, marketing and technical support. This has important competitive implications.

Already, for example, sophisticated Internet browser software is being made freely available to consumers as is a wide range of other software and news products. This low-cost/no-cost accessibility, combined with the rapid development of the Internet and the World Wide Web, could be a catalyst for speeding the development and dissemination of a wide range of goods and services on a global basis.

Another distinguishing feature of services is the relatively high emphasis placed on intellectual capital, or "intangibles", in many service activities. While difficult to measure, "intangibles" can hold the key to value creation. However, because, unlike a piece of equipment, they cannot be valued in a concrete way, and because they represent a weak form of collateral for the purpose of securing debt finance, their contribution to companies and their intrinsic worth often goes unrecognised – a major drawback for obtaining finance. Until ways can be found to improve the reporting and understanding of the role played by intangibles, growth and investment in promising knowledge-based activities will be slowed, with start-ups remaining heavily dependent on venture capital.

Innovation

Innovation, in its broadest sense, is widespread in many service sectors, but far less evident in others. Financial services, distribution and retail trade, communication services and software are among the most active innovators, as evidenced by their heavy investment in ICT and the vast array of new products that are being developed and adapted to meet changing consumer demands and/or enhance competitiveness. Areas where innovation has lagged tend to be those where regulation has restricted competition, or those which, by their nature, are less inclined to be innovative. This latter group would include certain personal services where physical labour is a principal aspect, or services which are heavily rule-bound (e.g. certain sports or games).

Measurement of innovation in services, however, is not as straightforward as in manufacturing, which makes it difficult to evaluate the extent to which it is occurring. While research and development expenditures (an innovation indicator) tend to be relatively low, for example, some service sectors (as indicated above) are major buyers and users of advanced technology, which, in turn, can have a pronounced effect on innovation. Similarly, patenting (another innovation indicator) is common in manufacturing, whereas innovation in services is more likely to be protected by copyright and trademark procedures.

Moreover, there are many "intangible" forms of innovation associated, for example, with processes and procedures which are difficult to capture using established indicators.

In addition to being innovative themselves, services are spurring innovation elsewhere in the economy. Countries with advanced business services, for example, are likely to have stronger communication capabilities in terms of connectivity and receptivity and, as a result, higher innovative capacity. In this context, consultants and advisers can improve the connectivity between agents, sharing learning experiences and creating learning opportunities, thereby increasing receptivity. Similarly, advanced business services can improve the interaction between tacit and codified knowledge, helping to increase innovation (Hauknes, 1998). One of the more visible signs of this can be found in the field of electronic commerce (e-commerce), where the major advances being made by software and applications firms – like ICL, Oracle, Sun Microsystems, Microsoft, and many others – are facilitating a major re-engineering of a growing number of firms across all sectors of the economy.

Environment

Interest in promoting sustainable, environmentally sound, development is a high priority for most countries. Services provide a number of key challenges and opportunities in this area. Within services, transportation is a sector which is both a major energy consumer and a source of greenhouse gases. On the other hand, most of the fast-growing knowledge-based services are (relatively) environmentally benign. This is significant as it may mean that growth in these services could occur without aggravating environmental problems (such as greenhouse emissions). Although not conclusive, there is evidence that this could be occurring, albeit to a limited extent. During the 1990s, emissions of carbon dioxide in the United States were closely correlated to changes in economic activity. In 1998, however, emissions were only 0.4% above 1997 levels, despite weak energy prices and a 3.9% increase in GDP (Wright, 1999).

This de-linkage could play an important part in meeting longer-term objectives relating to sustainable development. In addition, the contribution that these services are making to increased efficiency in the production and distribution of other goods and services should have a beneficial effect on resource use, which, in turn, could have important environmental implications.

1.5 Characteristics of Services

The services literature highlights differences in the nature of services versus products which are believed to create special challenges for services marketers and for consumers buying services. To help understand these differences a number of characteristics that describe the unique nature of services have been proposed. These characteristics were first discussed in the early services marketing literature and are generally summarised as intangibility, inseparability, heterogeneity and perishability (Regan, 1963; Rathmell, 1966; Shostack, 1977; and Zeithaml et al 1985).

Although, there has been debate on the effectiveness of the four characteristics in distinguishing between products and services (e.g. Regan, 1963; Shostack, 1977; Onkvisit and Shaw, 1991) these are nevertheless widely accepted by scholars and marketers (e.g. Zeithaml, 1981, 1985; Levitt, 1981) and used both as the basis for examining services buyer behaviour and developing services marketing strategies. It is, therefore, important to establish the extent to which these characteristics reflect the perspective of the consumer. A US-based study by Hartman and Lindgren (1993) found that consumers did not use the four characteristics in distinguishing between products and services.

Bitner, Fisk and Brown (1993) suggest that the major output from the services marketing literature upto 1980 was the delineation of four services characteristics: intangibility, inseparability, heterogeneity and perishability. These characteristics underpinned the case for services marketing and made services a field of marketing that was distinct from the marketing of products.

4 I's OF SERVICES backed by an 0

Services have four distinct characteristics that need to be internalised by service professionals to create opportunities in the market place, to enhance both top and bottom line growth for the firm. Leading researchers have zeroed on Intangibility, Inseparability, Inconsistency, and Inventory while others mention Ownership as well. All these characteristics are providing opportunity as well as challenges to the service marketer.

Intangibility

It is one of the most important characteristics of service products. It has no physical dimension and attributes. Service is a deed, a performance, an effort. The customers buy performance as they cannot see, touch, hear, taste or smell a service before they decide to buy the product. This makes the perception of service quite subjective. For e.g. a buyer of health club package, for weight loss, cannot see what the outcome will be till the programme is over. Therefore, the customers for many services have to buy them on trust as they cannot be inspected before use. In case of goods, a consumer can touch, taste and sample the product. The intangible nature of services makes consumers concerned about their providers.

For e.g. in case of Global Trust Bank, a few years back, the investments made were not as per Regulatory norms, and when it was released in the press, it left many customers uneasy about the financial instability of GTB and their was a with drawal of deposits as investor's trust was shaken. Some customers lost total faith and stopped banking.

In fact some service providers like life insurance agents as per IRDA have to undergo 100 hours training to get a license to practice so that they are trained in their profession.

Service products are mostly intangible but are marketed with tangible evidence. This is referred to as **tangibilising the intangibles**. While services often are accompanied with physical evidence that enables the consumer to make the product less abstract and more tangible, but there will always be an intangible element to the service product.

The level of tangibility in the service offer is based on three criteria's:

1. Tangible goods which are included in the service offer and consumed by the user.
2. The physical environment in which the service production/consumption process takes place, and
3. Tangible evidence of service performance.

Where goods form an important component of a service offer, many of the practices in goods marketing can be applied to this part of the service offer. A firm's promotional efforts must state the benefits to be derived from a service rather than stressing on the service itself. It is used to communicate the nature and quality of service.

Take for instance an experience on a flight, the total service experience is an aggregate of many components such as experience at the airport, the nature of services on board, the in-flight entertainment. Here, there are some tangible elements but most are intangible elements.

Intangibility of services leads customers to have difficulty in evaluating competing services, perceiving and assessing high levels of risk placing more emphasis on personal information sources and often using price as the basis for assessing quality. Hence management responds by reducing service complexity, stressing more on tangible clues, focusing on service quality and facilitating word of mouth recommendation.

While some services are rich in such tangible cues like retail outlets, restaurants, other services provide relatively little tangible evidence like life insurance.

In case of restaurants, it represents a mix of tangibles and intangibles and in respect of the food element, few of the particular characteristics of services marketing are encountered. Therefore, production of the food can be separated from its consumption and the perishability of food is less significant than the perishability of an empty table which results in loss of business. The presence of a tangible component gives customers a visible basis to judge quality.

The tangible elements of the service offered comprise not just those goods which are exchanged but also the physical environment in which a service encounter takes place. Within this environment, the design of buildings, their cleanliness and the appearance of staff present important tangible evidence which may be the only basis on which a buyer is able to differentiate one service provider from another.

Tangibility is further provided by evidence of service production methods. Sore services provide many opportunities for customers to see the process of production, indeed the whole purpose of the service may be to see the production process like dramas or skits. Often this tangible evidence can be seen before a decision to purchase a service is made, either by direct observation of a service being performed on somebody else like watching the sculptor work on a statue or indirectly, through a description of the service production process by brochures which illustrate and detail the service process like education. On the other hand, some services provide very few tangible clues about the nature of the service production process.

The lack of physical evidence, which intangibility implies, increases the level of uncertainty which a consumer faces when choosing between competing services. The service marketers programme consists of reducing consumer uncertainty by adding physical evidence and the development of strong service brands, in contrast goods marketers augment their products by adding intangible elements such as after sales service and improved distribution.

Inseparability

Many services are created, delivered and consumed simultaneously through interaction between customers and service producers, where as goods generally, are produced first and consumed later on. As the customers are involved in the production process, the service quality becomes difficult to measure and control.

For e.g. a doctor creates, delivers all his services simultaneously but the consumer presence is required during the performance of the service. This means that in many cases, people are involved concurrently in the production and marketing efforts of the service organisations. In most of the cases, the customer receives and consumes the services at the service providers premises. Since inseparability characteristic generally means the direct interaction between the service provider and client, it is direct selling.

Inseparability leads customers to being co- producers of the service either alone or with other co-consumers and often they have to travel to the point of production service. The management has to respond to this by separating production and consumption, it has to monitor consumer producer interaction and focus on continuous improvement in service delivery system.

Production and consumption are separable for goods. On the other hand, the consumption of a service is said to be inseparable from its means of production. Producer and consumer must interact in order for the benefits of the service to be realised - both must normally meet at a time and a place which is mutually convenient in order that the producer can directly pass on service benefits.

For services, marketing becomes a means of facilitating complex producer-consumer interaction, rather than being merely an exchange medium.

Moreover, the service cannot be stocked by the distribution partners, as in case of goods. This poses as a major limitation for the service provider. For e.g. a car mechanic can only repair, say, four vehicles per day. Thus individual service seller's services cannot be sold in many markets or multi locations. This characteristics, limits the scale and reach of operation of a service firm.

There are other services which can be sold by a representative of the main service provider e.g. insurance agent, travel agent, but at the final point of service delivery the service provider presence is a must. Such services are generally sold by the institutions producing them.

The degree of involvement between transacting parties is dependent upon the extent to which the service, is 'equipment based 'or 'people based'.

THREE TYPES OF SERVICE PRODUCTION

1. **Self services:** Customer uses the equipment and services provided and maintained by the service provider, for e.g. ATM, Automatic vending machines for tea, coffee, cold drinks, etc. In case of ATM, machine service can only be realised if the producer and consumer interact.

2. **Co-production:** The service provider and customer work together to create the service and for the customer to maximise the benefit. In health club, the trainer guides his customer to get maximum from a weight loss programme. Health care services, coaching classes and dental services are some other examples.

3. **Isolated production:** It has been possible to separate service production and consumption, especially where there is a low level of personal contact. The part of the service is performed outside the service providers premises. For e.g. entertainment like cable viewing at homes, tele-banking from home or office, video conferencing are some other examples.

Inseparability has a number of important marketing implications for services. Firstly, whereas goods are generally first produced, then offered for sale and finally sold and consumed, inseparability causes the process to be different for services. They are generally sold first, then produced and consumed simultanously.Secondly, while the method of goods production is to a large extent of little importance to the consumer, production processes are critical to the enjoyment of services.

Inconsistency (Heterogeneity or Variability)

This characteristic of service also referred to as heterogeneity, is a function of human involvement in the delivery and consumption process. The inseparability of the production and consumption aspects of the service transaction refer to the fact that service is a performance, in real time, in which the customer cooperates with the service provider. Inseparability is a characteristic of a service indicating that it cannot be separated from service provider of the product. Therefore a great deal of effort has to go into standardisation of delivery. Since buyers and service providers interpersonal exchange is involved, there is opportunity for customisation, which can be the Unique Selling Proposition.

Inconsistency occurs largely because different service providers perform a given service on different occasions. The service performed by an individual provider may differ over a period of time. Interaction between customer and provider may vary. Every time a service is performed, the process and the customer experience are different. Services that are provided by individuals rather than equipment will vary, depending upon which individual performs the service, and these will even vary with the same service provider from one job to the next. The service will also vary according to the degree to which clients involved in the production of the service agree. The degree to which the service firm designs the service delivery system to control variability will influence the quality of the service experienced by the customer.

Customer uncertainty can be reduced by a combination of automation, standardisation and rationalisation. However, inseparability may be desired by those customers who want customised service, rather than standard approaches that are not appropriate for individual situation as in case of interiors for bungalows in exclusive schemes for high net worth individuals.

But it is not possible to standardise service industry output. In case of trips by the Shatabdi Express between Delhi - Agra, the consumer does not get the same quality of service day after day due to different service personnel, snacks, music etc.

The performance of a faculty in a lecture, is not of same standard in each performance, as it will depend on host of factors like preparation, mood, participation of the students, ambience etc. In case of an income tax consultant, he may provide a different service experience to a high net worth individual and a salaried class clerk because of varying needs and depends on his moods and pressures at the time of the day the interaction is taking place.

In order to provide consistent services, the firms should standardise staff performance through careful planning, control and automation. Firms which are automated have less people and hence they have lower inconsistency in services. A garage which has installed auto car wash facilities with mounting of the vehicle on the ramp, can provide consistent services. Banks have installed Automated Teller Machines to provide consistent services due to automation. Fountain, Cola and Pepsi vending machines are some other examples.

While these firms achieve high homogeneity in service delivery, they increase the risk of being inflexible and the staff reacts poorly to the unforeseen problem. Inconsistency is an opportunity and firms can strengthen their brands by customisation with greater empowerment to the staff.

For services, variability impacts upon customers not just in terms of outcomes but also in terms of processes of production. It is the latter point that causes variability to pose a much greater problem for services, compared to goods. Because the customer is usually involved in the production process for a service at the same time as they consume it, it can be difficult to carry out monitoring and control to ensure consistent standards. The opportunity for pre-delivery inspection and rejection which is open to the goods manufacturer is not normally possible with services - the service must normally be produced in the presence of the customer without the possibility of intervening quality control. Particular problems can occur where personnel are involved in providing services on a one-to-one basis - such as hairdressing - where no easy method of monitoring and control is possible.

There are two types of inconsistency:

1. The extent to which production standards vary from a norm, both in terms of outcomes and of production processes.

2. The extent to which a service can be deliberately varied to meet the specific needs of individual customers.

Variability in production standards is of greatest concern to services organisations where customers are highly involved in the production process, especially where production methods make it impractical to monitor service production. This is true of many labour intensive personal services provided in a one-to-one situation, such as personal healthcare.

Factors leading to the inconsistency of services because they are being produced live, often left to chance with no time to correct mistakes before consumption. It is sometimes difficult to blue print the service process. This results in difficulty of presenting an image of consistent quality, high level of perceived risk by the buyers and building a strong brand.

1. Services firms have tried to reduce inconsistency and build strong brands by automation. Replacing telephone operators with computerised voice systems and the automation of many banking services are typical of this trend. Sometimes reduced personnel inconsistency has been achieved by involving customers in the production process like self-service petrol filling stations.

2. The inconsistency is the extent to which a service can be strategically customised to meet the specific needs of individual customers. Because services are created as they are consumed, and because consumers are often a part of the production process, the potential for customisation of services is generally greater than for manufactured goods. The extent to which a service can be customised is dependent upon production methods employed. Services which are produced for large numbers of customers simultaneously may offer little scope for individual customisation like in case of mass transportation.

The extent to which services can be customised is dependent on management decisions on the level of authority to be delegated to front-line service personnel. While some service operations seek to give more authority to front-line staff, the tendency is for service firms to standardise their encounter with customers to minimise inconsistency. While industrialisation often reduces the flexibility of producers to meet customers' needs, it also has the effect of reducing inconsistency of processes and outcomes. The variability of service output can pose problems for brand building in services compared to goods. The service sector's attempts to reduce variability concentrate on methods used to select, train, motivate and control personnel or simplify service offers with reduced skill content of jobs, backed by automation.

Inventory (Perishability)

The perishability of services describes the real time nature of the product. Unlike goods, the consumer cannot store the service and the absence of the ability to build and maintain stocks of the product means that sudden demands cannot be accommodated as it can be done in case of goods. The buyer may decide to delay the consumption but may not consume more in advance than the requirements. For the buyer of services the time at which they choose to use the service may be critical to its performance and therefore to the consumer's experience, For e.g., in Pune Municipal Transport bus the experience in the rush hour is very different than in lean hours. Consumption of services is directly linked to the experience. In case of services, inventory costs are related to capacity utilisation. In idle service production environment, the inventory cost relates to reimbursing staff along with any needed equipment. E.g. If a lawyer is available but there is no customer during that period, the fixed cost of the idle lawyer's opportunity is the inventory carrying cost.

Some services have a characteristic that demand for them fluctuates, considerably by season and by day of the week and even hour of the day. An airline which offers seats on a 6.00 am flight from Mumbai to Delhi cannot sell any empty seats once the aircraft has left at 6.00 am. The service offer disappears and spare seats cannot be stored to meet a surge in demand which may occur at 8.00 am.

Few services have a constant pattern of demand over a period of time. Many show considerable variation like daily variation in cyber cafes towards the evening/night , weekends for travel by railways between Pune-Mumbai, seasonal for hotels, cyclical for mortgages or an unpredictable pattern of demand like emergency repair services like electricity after trees falling on electricity lines. For a travel agent, the demand fluctuates according to time and period and is linked to holidays in school and colleges in summer and winter coupled to festivals like Diwali, Durgapuja, Christmas etc., wherein the demand peaks.

The combination of perishability and fluctuating demand present challenges for marketers engaged in planning, pricing, promotion and distribution of services. The cellular companies try to spread out demand for their services by pricing off peak hours to make them more attractive to callers. They offer "happy hour" rates to increase traffic in lean periods of the day. The services providers focus on strategies for effective capacity management to reduce the inventory costs. Hence, even if volumes can be enhanced with a little margin over variable cost, the firm should push for it. An appointment with a dentist at a given time, on a given day, cannot be stored and if patient cancels the appointment last minute, the revenue is lost. The firms must monitor their capacity and review it periodically to ensure customers get better service as well as resources of the firm are optimally utilised.

Many services are bought even before they are experienced as in case of pension. Here the service firms have to tackle two issues: first, they have to develop image and reputation to attract customers. Secondly, they must retain customers, as competitors try to attract them away, even though they have yet to experience the service.

Perishability occurs because of inability to store services, inelasticity of short-term supply. This results in demand pattern being irregular with just in time production of services and if managed effectively congestion occurs at peak periods and loss of capacity at off-peak periods. Pricing and promotion are used extensively to encourage customers to utilise services at a time it is convenient to the service operator to have better capacity utilisation.

To manage these characteristics efficiently the Service Provider has to use the optimum strategies. The Problems and Strategies in Services Marketing adapted from Parasuramm, Berry and Zeithmal - Problem and Strategies in Services Marketing - Journal of Marketing are tabulated for ready reference.

Table 1.2

Characteristics	Problem	Marketing Strategy
Intangibility	Cannot be easily displayed	Provide tangible clues
	Cannot be patented	Stimulate word of mouth
		Use personnel sources
		Use post purchase communication
Inconsistency	Standardisation hard to achieve	Stress on Standardisation and performance
	Hard to set up quality control	Focus on employee training
	Can only predict quality or determine	Programmes, performance evaluation
	it after the service is performed	Licensing and other forms of credential requirement
Inseparability	Harder to mass produce	Need strong training programmes, incentives
	Less efficient than production goods	Focus on personal attention
Inventory	Customers must be present	Focus on convenience, saving time, faster service
		Extended hours
		Focus on competence and expertise
		Predict fluctuating demand
		Manage capacity to balance supply and demand

In addition to the 4I's of services, ownership has been identified as a distinguishing feature of services by some researchers including Kotler.

Ownership is another distinguishing feature of service. The inability to own a service is related to the characteristics of intangibility and perishability. In case of service, when it is performed, no ownership is transferred from buyer to seller. The buyer is merely buying the right to a service process such as the use of a car park or a solicitor's time. A distinction should be drawn between the inability to own the service act, and the rights which a buyer may acquire to have a service carried out at some time in the future. In case of service, the buyer has temporary access to or use of it. What is owned is the benefit of service, not the service itself, e.g. for a holiday tour package to picturesque Manali in Himachal, the buyer has access to hotel, mountains, snow, waterfalls, rivers etc. but doesn't own any of them.

The inability to own a service has implications for the design of distribution channels, so a wholesaler or retailer cannot take title, as is the case with goods. Instead, direct distribution methods are more common and where intermediaries are used, who generally act as a co-producer with the service provider.

1.6 Search, Experience and Credence Attributes

This section provides the preliminary elements in building a better measure for examining the differences in the consumer evaluation processes between goods and services that possess varying amounts of search, experience and credence (SEC) qualities. Such a classification schemata often represents a first key step in theoretical development (Hunt 1991).

Theoretical Foundation: The Economic Concept of Search, Experience, Credence Classification

Economics of Information theory (Nelson 1970, 1974; and Darby and Karni 1973) classifies products into three categories according to how consumers evaluate the product. This classification was initially developed to help explain the notion that consumer information about quality often has "profound effects upon the market structure of consumer goods" (Nelson 1970, p. 311). Economists examined the role of information and its links to advertising and search (Nelson, 1970, 1974; Stigler 1961) addressing the fact that advertising is frequently affected by consumer ignorance about quality differences among brands.

Nelson (1970) defined two types of qualities that had distinct characteristics in terms of consumer evaluation processes. Search qualities are those that can be fully evaluated prior to purchase, e.g. the style of a dress.

Experience qualities are those that must be first purchased and consumed before the consumer is able to evaluate. Nelson (1970) extended Stigler's (1961) information search theory to help explain "information by way of experience" (p.313). He argued that in addition to consumer search process as defined by Stigler, the consumer can also determine the quality of a good by purchasing and using it, i.e. experience. Among other predictions he argued that personal recommendations would be relied upon more for the purchase of experience goods than search goods, i.e. "guided sampling."

Darby and Karni (1973) introduced credence goods to extend the information acquisition classification into a more precise taxonomy. Credence qualities, they proposed, are those that the consumer can never fully evaluate even after purchase and consumption, i.e. those accepted on faith. Credence qualities are "expensive to judge even after purchase" (p.69). They claimed that when goods high in credence qualities are sold both branding and client relationships are used to help establish quality. Their paper focused on a unique feature of the service industry – joint provision of diagnosis and services, e.g. auto repair. In such situations, consumers can never be sure about the extent of the good they actually need; sellers act as experts in determining the customers' requirements (Emons 1997).

Sec Framework Introduced Into the Service Literature

Zeithaml (1981) introduced the three types of goods into marketing, via the service literature, as a theoretical framework to better conceptualize the proposed purchase evaluation differences between goods and services. Her classic piece placed goods and services on a continuum in which traditional consumer goods anchored one end of the spectrum (easy to evaluate) and pure services anchored the other end (difficult to evaluate). Goods, she proposed, have more search qualities while services exhibit more experience and credence qualities due to their unique characteristics -- intangibility, non-standardization and inseparability. Mitttal (1999) classifies the nonsearch ability of services, i.e. the experience and credence attributes, as one of the five properties of intangibility.

Those services bearing more credence qualities are harder to judge while services high in experience are in the middle of the continuum in terms of evaluation difficulty. Because services tend to have more experience and credence qualities, consumers may employ different evaluation processes than those high in search qualities. As services become more difficult to evaluate, there tends to be more uncertainty (i.e. more risk). In general, the greater the degree of perceived risk in a pre-purchase context, the greater the consumer's propensity to seek information about goods and services (Murray 1991; Guseman 1981; Murray and Schlacter 1990).

Search qualities, Zeithaml concluded, include attributes such as color, style, price, fit and smell while experience qualities include taste, wearability and purchase satisfaction. No credence qualities were mentioned in her paper - just examples of offerings high in credence qualities - appendix operations and brake relinings. Services provided by professionals and specialists are typically high in credence qualities, i.e. expert services (Emons 1997). Zeithaml discussed the SEC framework as she developed her hypotheses (goods versus services) but did not specifically hypothesise differences between search, experience and credence goods. However, almost implied in her hypotheses development is the further delineation of the service framework, i.e. extending the difference to include the three classifications – search/experience/credence.

Although useful both among goods and services, the SEC framework has the strongest appeal among service industry scholars. Ostrom and Iacobucci (1995) argue that this type of service industry distinction, i.e. experience and credence enhances theory development because the findings are not particular to some unique industry but are generalizable to other like type service situations Research in the services literature using the SEC framework can be loosely classified into four categories:

1. Conceptual (e.g. Zeithaml 1981),

2. Empirical (e.g. Iacobucci 1992, Ostrom and Iacobucci 1995; Ford, Swasy and Smith 1990; Maute and Forrester 1991),

3. Content analysis (e.g. Laband 1986; Ekelund, Mixon and Ressler 1995), and

4. Strategic (e.g. Mittal 1999; Klein 1998; Lieberman and Flint-Goor 1996; Bloom and Pailin 1995). There is dearth of services literature which addresses the measurement issues associated with search experience, and credence qualities.

1.7 Classification of Services

Goods and Services can be classified in several ways. To have a clear perspective some of the classification techniques for goods includes:

1. Market segment
2. Length of channel
3. Degree of durability
4. Customer contact
5. Value addition

Since 1980, many attempts have been made to classify the services. The service marketers have adopted different approaches and some more classifications are available in service literature. For services like in case of goods, can be classified and these are detailed below to enable professionals to broaden their vision while operating in service sector.

1. People Intensiveness

People are involved in performing services. The services differ according to extent of people involved, e.g. software versus manual, - versus semi automatic. People intensity will increase if a high volume/heavy weight equipment is to be installed at owner's premises as it will involve loading, transportation, unloading and other handling activities. Do it yourself services are performed by the consumers themselves.

The people intensive services categories are equipment based and people based. (a) Equipment based services are automated, monitored by relatively unskilled operators (b) automated tea vending machine.

People based services are those involving professionals like lawyers, doctors, professors, who are in continuous touch and their services are variable due to lack of standardisation and customisation.

2. Six Service Operating Dimensions

Silvestro et al. identified six service operating dimensions against any particular service to be viewed as under it.

1. Does the service have a people focus or an equipment focus? (People focus-Chartered accountant; Equipment focus ATM)
2. What is the length of customer contact time in a typical service encounter?
3. What is the extent of customisation of the service? Is it tailored to the specific needs of individual clients like in case of management consultancy?
4. To what extent are the customer contact personnel empowered to exercise judgement in meeting customer needs?
5. Is the source of value added mainly 'front office' or 'back office'? Front office in case of hairdresser while back office in case of Insurance.
6. Does the service have a product focus or a process focus?
   Car for mechanic has product focus while mangement education has process focus.

The classification of services into three broad categories: Professional/ service shop/ and mass services was done by comparing the six dimensions with a ranking of services according to volume of customers handled per day by a unit.

Several experts argue that the service strategy, control and performance measurements differ significantly between the three classes of service process. As such the classification is of value. However, there are services which do not fit well into any of the classes like with other classification system. For e.g. World Cup Cricket final 2003, which by virtue of volume of customers should be mass services. It has low customisation to the six typical characteristics of a mass service.

Table 1.3

Class of Service Process	Volume of Customers	Characteristics
Professionals e.g. Accountant, Lawyer	Low	People focus High contact time High Customisation High Level of Empowerment Front office value added Process focus
Service Shop e.g. Bank, Hotel	Medium	People and Equipment Focus Medium contact time Medium Customisation Medium level of empowerment Front and Back office value added Process and product focus
Mass service e.g. Railways	High	Process and product focus Equipment focus Low contact time Low customisation Low level of empowerment

(Source: Adopted from Silverstro et al.)

3. Level of Tangibility

G.L. Shostack has used level of tangibility as a way of classifying services on a goods services spectrum. From the consumers viewpoint, the more tangible the product i.e. good, the easier it is to evaluate in terms of quality, suitability whereas in intangible product the opposite is true.

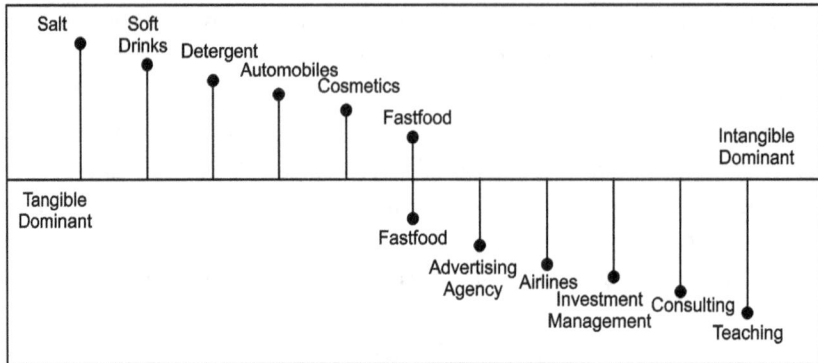

Fig. 1.1: Levels of tangibility as a way of classifying services

For services dominated products, the provider may need to focus more attention to the consumer's concern about the product.

4. Customer-Employees Contact

During the Service the buyers often rely on tangible clues or physical evidence, to evaluate the service before purchase and to assess their satisfaction with the service during and after consumption.

Table 1.4

Elements of Physical Evidence		
Servicescape (Physical facility)		**Other tangibles**
Facility exterior	Facility interior	Business cards
Exterior design	Interior design	Stationary
Signage	Equipment	Billing statements
Parking	Signage	Employee dress
Landscape	Layout	Uniforms
Surrounding Environment	Ambience Air quality / Temperature	Brochures
		Internet / Web pages

Mary Jo Bitner classified service organisations into three types of services;

Self-service by customer where the complexity of servicescape is elaborate like Golf course, Surf and Splash while lean like ATM, Automatic vending machines. Internet services etc.

Interpersonal services in which both customer and employee interaction is high, where the complexity of servicescape is elaborate like hotel, restaurant, health clinic. hospital, bank, airline, school, while it is lean for dry cleaner, hair salon etc.

Remote service in which employees participate once in a while like insurance, telephones, utility and many professional services while it is lean for call centers, automated voice messaging service.

This three-way classification can aid the focus of management activity on either operations efficiency or marketing effectiveness in addition to the consideration of physical surroundings.

5. Customisation / Empowerment

The pioneering work by Lovelock classifies services on two-dimensional classification of services. This is combined with Silvestro et al. classifications and outcome is tabulated below.

Table 1.5

		Level of Customisation	
		Low	High
Empowerment By Employees	Low	Retailing superstore e.g. Food World	Telephone Banking
	High	Dental Services	Accountant Lawyer

(*Source:* Adopted from Lovelock)

Here the comparison is between customisation of services with the extent of empowerment and the customer contact personnel. Such a classification, may provide insights into the positioning and the operational strategy of a service organisation. For e.g. a restaurant chain is different from a fast food chain. Categorisations image by offering a higher level of customisation (or vice versa).

6. Drama Analogy of Services

Classification based on Drama Analogy of Services by Grove and Fisk provide analogy by considering service as drama. (1) The service contact personnel are-the 'actors'. (2) The customers are the 'audience', (3) The service setting is the 'stage'(4)The process is the 'performance'. The two-dimensional classification of service is contact measured by the rate of front-of-house activities to back-of-house and the size of the audience. According to Berry and Parasuraman state that the performance is the product which the customers buy in service.

7. Classification by Market Segmentation

The firm has to understand the consumers needs and analyse to identify segments based on reasons for purchase of service, frequency and the complexity of the service performed so that the key reasons of segmentation are clearly identified.

Table 1.6

Types of Services		
Communication	**Transportation Services**	**Real Estate Services**
1. Telephone 2. Postal 3. Courier 4. Radio Broadcasting 5. Telecommunication 6. Satellite	1. Railway 2. Airlines 3. Road transportation 4. Water transportation 5. Helicopter services 6. Private aircraft	1. Rental 2. Investment consultants 3. Property consultants 4. Building and real estate management
Entertainment Services	**Marketing Related Services**	**Financial and Insurance Services**
1. Motion picture 2. Video parlour 3. Party 4. Event management 5. Disco 6. Club	1. Marketing Consultancy 2. Market research 3. Advertising 4. Sales promotion 5. New product testing	1. Banking 2. Leasing and hire purchase 3. Investment banking 4. Security and brokerage 5. Retailing 6. Insurance
Government Services	**Public Utility Services**	**Hospitality Services**
1. Infrastructural 2. Defence 3. Police 4. Broadcasting 5. Education 6. Medical	1. Water supply 2. Electric supply 3. Gas supply	1. Hotels and restaurants 2. Catering 3. Home delivery
Trading Services		
1. Wholesaling		2. Retailing
Other Services		
1. Public relations 2. Repair and maintenance 3. Security 4. Landscaping 5. Printing 6. Speech writing	7. Professional grooming 8. Educational – classes 9. Training 10. Courier 11. Health care	12. Interior designing 13. Laundry/dry cleaning 14. Old age homes 15. Warehousing 16. Equipment rental

Types of Service Industries

The representative listing of service businesses in a range of commercial sectors that could conceivably be launched by an enterprising entrepreneur is as follows:

- Professional services (physicians, pharmacists, dentists, attorneys, architects, civil engineers)
- Business services (advertising, financial planning, mailing services, computer and data processing, consulting, training, recruiting)
- Counselling services (marriage, weight loss, career planning, pastoral, psychiatric)
- Transportation services (trucking, busing, taxicab service, limousine service, car rental)
- Personal services (pet grooming, health clubs, catering, beauticians, barbers, hairdressers, tailors and seamstresses, photography studios, realtors, funeral parlours, wedding planning)
- Restaurants and lodging (diners, family restaurants, taverns, hotels, cottages)
- Social services (individual and family services, child day care, residential care)
- Maintenance services (landscaping, plumbing and electrical, appliance, equipment, automobile, bicycle)

In addition, many service-oriented businesses are, by their very nature, slanted toward meeting the needs of one of two markets: individual consumers or other businesses/ organisations. Of course, some service establishments, like carpet cleaning companies, can market their services to both client categories. But the majority of service businesses place their emphasis on meeting the needs of one market segment or the other. For example, a pet grooming establishment will not waste its advertising money trying to reach other businesses; its primary clients are going to be individual consumers simply because of the nature of the services they offer. Conversely, the primary target of a company that provides security personnel is going to be commercial establishments. Entrepreneurs that hope to market their services primarily to organisations rather than individuals should note that, on the whole, such businesses require greater capital investment at the outset.

1.8 What is Services Marketing?

Marketing a service differs from marketing physical goods. Goods provide benefits because of their physical characteristics. In contrast, services are actions and are:

- Performed, not produced
- Experienced - the result of a deed or action
- Intangible - cannot be seen, felt, tasted or touched
- Cannot be stocked
- Once performed, the service cannot be returned
- Highly dependent on the human element
- Typically, the customer is a participant in the service delivery process
- Service delivery quality is dependent on the individual service provider

Services can be tangible acts directed at people's bodies, for example medical procedures, or beauty salons. Or services can be directed at goods and other physical possessions, for example maintenance services. Services can also be intangible acts, for example education, or consulting services.

When a company is considering creating a new service for its customers the starting point is to determine:

- What should be done?
- To whom?
- How the service will be performed?
- With which resources?
- Why there is a customer need?
- Which benefits are provided to customers?

It takes a managed approach to creating, assessing and developing a new service concept to ensure the company offers the right things, to the right customers, and for the right reasons.

Traditionally, marketers have used a product marketing approach to services, focusing on a careful balance of the well-known four P's of the Marketing Mix: Product, Place, Price, and Promotion. The right mix of these is still critical. However, because of the nature of services, the additional P's of "People," "Process," and "Physical Evidence" take on a greater importance. The intangible nature of services requires a special approach at the strategic stage of service offer development.

The following factors need to be addressed through the P's of "People," "Process" and "Physical Evidence":

- Services do not have physical properties to shape a customer's perception. Because of this, services need to be defined so customers can understand and value the service, and therefore will buy the service. In other words, service descriptions need to emphasise "benefits." Also important is recognising the value that service personnel provide because of their interaction with customers ("People" considerations).

- People, processes, tools, methods and management capability need to be in place ready to respond to a market opportunity. Processes need to enable a consistent level of service delivery. These factors are of importance for the service provider organisation for efficiency and for quality management in the customer's eyes ("Process" & "People" considerations).

- Service needs to become more tangible so they can be charged for and perceived as something to be purchased ("Physical Evidence" considerations).

Services marketing is marketing based on relationship and value. It is used to market a service. The major difference in the education of services marketing versus regular marketing is that apart from the traditional "4 P's," Product, Price, Place, Promotion, there are three additional "P's" consisting of People, Physical evidence, and Process. Service Marketing has been relatively gaining ground in the overall spectrum of educational marketing as developed economies move farther away from industrial importance to service oriented economies.

The dynamic environment of services makes effective marketing a necessity. Service firms have traditionally been weak in marketing strategy and execution which makes marketing strategy and execution the keys to compete effectively in this continually evolving and challenging environment. According to Christian Gronroos, the services marketing function is much broader than the activities and output of the traditional marketing department. It has become essential for service organisations to tailor their service product to customer needs, price them realistically, distribute them through suitable channels, and actively promote them to customers. Service organisations must also be aware of trends of the markets their services compete in.

Developing a marketing strategy is much the same for products and services, in that it involves selecting target markets and formulating a marketing mix. Thus, Theodore Levitt suggested that "instead of talking of 'goods' and of 'services', it is better to talk of 'tangibles' and 'intangibles'". Levitt also went on to suggest that marketing a physical product is often more concerned with intangible aspects (frequently the 'product service' elements of the total package) than with its physical aspect. Charles Revson made a famous comment regarding the business of Revlon Inc.: 'In the factory we make cosmetics. In the store we sell hope.' Arguably, service industry marketing merely approaches the problems from the opposite end of the same spectrum.

Instruments in the Marketing of Services

Product Policy

Specific to the service sector is the need to free the potential necessary for service delivery (process management). This implies exact quantitative and qualitative capacity planning. But further to this, service providers need to think about standardisation options. These relate to standardisation within capacity potentials, processes and outcomes. Within any standardisation process the cost advantages are less important than how the standardisation is perceived by the customer. A standardised offer can reduce uncertainty. The same is true of branding. The uniform appearance and product range available at Burger King or McDonalds, for instance, make the customer feel he is getting a service at a generally acceptable level. Trust in the service provider is strengthened when the consumer is confronted with an atmosphere he knows and feels comfortable with, and this in turn raises the level of test characteristics.

Product differentiation also plays a considerable role within the service sector. On the one hand, many services are tailor-made to meet the customer's needs. On the other hand, the marginal costs involved in product differentiation are lower than with physical products due to the high level of fixed costs (maintaining the capacity needed for service delivery).

Communication Policy

The personal approach to sales is paramount within service industry, given there is always a need to explain the service. Classic advertising finds it difficult dealing with the essential immateriality of service provision. Services have no "want appeal" whatsoever, whereas physical products can arouse desire by simply being on display. A substitute is needed in the case of service advertising (materialisation via visualisation). This is why building societies, for example, feature material goods in their advertising campaigns, showing family dream homes in order to motivate customers to sign up for a building loan agreement. Other examples of visualisation are:

- Before and after dramatisations.
- Dramatisation of internal production factors such as employees, machines or premises.
- Testimonials from satisfied customers and opinion leaders.

In the service sector, the communication objective is often risk minimisation via building an image and conveying competence. The risk is perceived to be higher because of a lack of test characteristics but also because of an absence of standardisation. Even consumers who have bought into a specific service many times cannot be sure they will receive the same result and the same quality the next time they access the service.

Uncertainty prior to purchase can be reduced by close "branded" designation of the service provided or by communication of a concrete service benefit. Seen this way, marketing communication within the service industry aims to create an image which the consumer can then use to make his choice.

Services marketing has the problem that a close "branded" designation of the service is not possible because of the immaterial nature of service delivery. To offset this, internal and external reference subjects need to be "branded" instead. These can be all the material production factors which the consumer is confronted with. Customer contact staff serve as a good example.

Pricing Policy

Price setting in advance is only possible in the case of standardised services. The costs of service provision are often dependent on external factors, as is the case with piano lessons. Here, it is advisable to fix the price according to the time needed to provide the service. But this means the consumer agrees to buy a service without knowing exactly what the final price will be (e. g. services provided by tradesmen).

The common practice of price bundling (price fixing for a complete service package) leads to a reduction in market transparency. It may be advantageous for the service provider (price comparisons are more difficult), but it can at times prove detrimental to the customer.

Price is often regarded as an indication of quality due to the complex evaluation process needed to gauge real quality within service provision. This leads to the price quality effect (it's only good if it's expensive).

Price differentiation assumes a crucial role in capacity management. The fact that a service cannot be stored and transported implies that a service must be supplied at a particular point in time, at a particular place and to a particular customer and/or object. If these imperatives are not met, the service can lose its entire value in a worst-case scenario.

An unoccupied seat on a flight has no value whatsoever for the airline. For the passenger who arrives too late, the promise of a flight the next day or to another destination is also worthless. Therefore, the service provider must predict exactly how his supply matches demand. However, a peak load approach in a situation of low demand leads to poor utilisation of available capacity. But offering too little contributes to customer dissatisfaction.

A service provider can adapt demand to available supply by implementing a skilful price differentiation policy. Examples of this are lower off-season tariffs in the hotel industry, happy hours in bars or special reductions at cinemas at the beginning of the week.

Distribution Policy

The fact that services are not transportable or storable also influences the distribution policy within the sector. Service providers and users need to be brought together so that the service can be supplied to the customer or his object (safeguarding capacity potential). This happens via support points (branches of a restaurant chain or a bank, railway stations, taxi stands, doctors' practices), via the service provider finding service recipients (meals on wheels, insurance policy advice, management consultancy, air conditioning system maintenance) or by using different media (legal advice on the telephone, dispatching an appliance which needs repaired by post, remote maintenance of IT systems via modem). The nature of the product supplied can limit the possibilities in this regard (meals on wheels), as can the service user's preferences (a home visit by the insurance salesperson). Waiting time procedures and reservation systems are two further management tools. Decisions must also be made on the distribution channels and the number of intermediate steps.

IMPLEMENTING SERVICES MARKETING

When implementing service marketing, internal marketing should not be overlooked because the employees are the interface with the customer. Internal marketing refers to measures employed by the company to motivate its staff. This is important because they constitute an important element within the value creation chain. The relationship between customer contact personnel and the customer is fostered by interactive marketing. Marketing of the service company to the customer is defined as external marketing.

Management within the service sector is based on profiling the service offered, on providing differentiated service offers, on the quality of the service provided (service quality) and on the productivity while the service is being performed.

There are many definitions for the basic concept of service. However, they all have one thing in common: services are not physical products. As was clearly shown, service delivery is different to physical product delivery in terms of both production and distribution/sales. The basic constituent characteristics of a service are of the utmost importance as they have a considerable bearing on management decisions. Services are of vital importance to the national economy and they already make a major contribution to the gross value added. We can assume this will increase in the future.

Marketing within the service sector will face many challenges in the future. The opportunities and risks associated with future developments within the sector should be taken into consideration.

FACTORS IN SERVICES INDUSTRY GROWTH

Researchers point to a number of factors that have accounted for the surge in service business start-ups over the last few decades. Many of these factors reflect fundamental changes in societal structure and character. W. F. Schoell and J. T. Ivy, authors of "Marketing: Contemporary Concepts and Practices", cited the following as major reasons for service industry expansion globally:

- **Increased Affluence:** As consumers have raised their standard of living, they have increasingly chosen to purchase services such as lawn maintenance and carpet cleaning that they previously took care of themselves.
- **Increased Leisure Time:** Some segments of the population have been able to garner larger chunks of free time; this trend, coupled with increased wealth, has spurred a higher demand for certain service businesses such as travel agencies and resorts, adult education courses, guide services, golf courses, health clubs, etc.
- **Changing Work Force Demographics:** Over the past few decades, increasing numbers of women have entered the work force. This has spurred greater demand for services in such realms as child care, housekeeping, dry-cleaning, etc.
- **Greater Life Expectancy:** Another development that has had a particular impact on certain service sectors, particularly in the health care industries.
- Increased complexity of products/technological advancement—High-tech products have created a corresponding increase in demand for specialists who can fix and maintain those products (computers, cars, electronic equipment, etc.).
- **Increased Complexity of Life:** Many service sectors have enjoyed tremendous growth because of their orientation toward helping individuals and businesses stay on top of the many facets of today's fast-paced society. Tax preparers, psychiatrists and counsellors, and legal advisors are good examples.

- **Increased Environmental Awareness:** General trends toward increased ecological sensitivity and enlightened natural resource management practices have spurred growth in environmental service sectors (waste management, recycling, environmental advocacy).
- **Increased number of Available Products:** Technological advances have spurred development of service industries in such areas as programming.

KEYS TO SERVICE BUSINESS SUCCESS

"Service supplier skill should be distinguished on atleast two levels," wrote Glenn Bassett, author of Operations Management for Service Industries. "The first is the technical product/service knowledge level. The service giver is expected to know the offering in depth and detail so that information about its utility and application can be provided on demand. He or she must also be technically competent to deliver the service expected, adapting as needed to varied or changing customer need. The second level of skill pertains to customer relationship. Here it is often as simple as whether the service-giver treats the customer as an object to be controlled and used, or as a unique, important individual to be served."

Entrepreneurs engaged in service businesses also need to recognise how service marketing differs from product marketing. "Service marketing," said Burstiner, "can be far more challenging than the marketing of products because of these three distinctive characteristics of service offerings: 1) Services are intangible; 2) Services are perishable; 3) Services cannot be separated from the service providers." Finally, service businesses need to consider the way in which they distribute their services. Most service businesses can be grouped according to the methodology with which they deliver their services. In other words, does the company bring its service to the customer, or does the customer go to the firm to receive the service? "In some cases," wrote Bateman and Zeithaml in "Management: Function and Strategy", "there is no choice. The plumber or house painter has to go to the work. Conversely, the customer goes to the restaurant, and the patient has to go to the hospital for the operation. Some services have options. Either the TV repairperson can go to the customer or the customer delivers the TV to the back room (the repair shop). A service that has traditionally required the customer to come to its facility has a strategic advantage in changing that tradition." Indeed, owners of service businesses should examine this facet of their business closely to look for ways of realising an advantage over competitors. In fact, customer convenience is—next to quality of service rendered—perhaps the single most important factor in securing and retaining new customers.

The boom in the services sector has been relatively "jobless". The rise in services share in GDP is not accompanied by proportionate increase in the sector's share of national employment. Some economists have also cautioned that service sector growth must be supported by proportionate growth of the industrial sector, otherwise the services sector grown will not be sustainable. In the current economic scenario it looks that the boom in the services sector is here to stay as India is fast emerging as global services hub.

For any developing nation development of services and infrastructure segment is very important to reach its economic goals. India is successful in improving its services and infrastructure areas. It is very evident that the role of services sector in Indian economic development has increased by several notches from the fact that this sector which was contributing only around 20 percent during independence is contributing over 43 percent currently to India's GDP.

To understand the services industry in greater depth the section below covers the two main services sectors in India i.e. the banking and insurance sectors.

The Banking Sector

Performance of the banking sector is considered as a proxy for the economy as a whole, due to banks' wide spectrum of exposure across industries. Unfortunately for India, the banking sector has historically remained under the impact of non-competitiveness, poor technology integration, high NPAs and grossly under productive manpower.

Banking sector in India has a wide mix, comprising joint sector (scheduled and non-scheduled banks), nationalised sector (Reserve Bank of India, State Bank of India and all other nationalised commercial banks and post office savings bank), specialised corporate financial institutions (specific industrial finance corporations and state finance corporations), co-operative sector (co-operative banks and land development banks) and foreign sector (foreign commercial banks and exchange banks).

Keeping in mind the socio-economic goals of the country, banks were under strict control of the regulatory bank - Reserve Bank of India. For instance, during mid-1969, 14 major Indian commercial banks were nationalised. One of the major criticism against nationalisation of commercial banks was with respect to efficiency. And the critics were right. Since nationalisation, the operational efficiency of the commercial banks have come down, thanks to the 'public-sector working' attitude of the bank work force. Since, their pay is not linked to performance, there is no inducement for the banking staff to perform well. This has been further, deteriorated by the poor quality to man power planning which is linked to selection of inefficient staff on the basis of social reservations.

Earlier profitability gained only secondary importance, since banks lived in the comfort of a controlled environment. However, today banks cannot survive only with government support. They have to set goals of profitability along with service and set targets and evolve strategies to reach them.

There is certainly a paradigm shift in banking in India in the recent past. At present profitability, capital restructuring and transparency are considered important and significant for banks. Also, banks in India have started realising the need to be 'customer focused' that in turn leads to 'customer appreciation' which is imperative for survival and growth.

The first change along this line was brought in by the foreign banks with their emphasis on high quality and efficient service combined with the technological advantages like satellite banking and tele-banking manned by skeletal staff and lesser number of branches.

Further, development of special manpower, innovative products, technology exploitation and personalised services play a crucial role in the banking industry today, since the customer has more options in choosing a bank thus, leading to consumerism in the banking sector. Also, since customers are becoming more sophisticated and educated, their expectations from the neighbourhood bank are increasing.

The private banks wisely chose to use this opportunity to prepare for the future rather than scramble for current business. Many of them refocused their activities, seeking clearly defined identities in terms of services and customer segments.

To sum up, the new private sector banks are poised to redefine banking in India. Though they do not pose a threat to the existing private banks they will certainly force them to gear up their strategies to remain in the field. This will lead to intense competition among the new banks, that would also serve as a challenge to the foreign banks.

The last five years saw a sea-change in banking strategies, with more focus on quality.

The adoption of a specialised customer-oriented focus is fast getting wider acceptability. In a market that keeps growing in depth and diversity, niche banking is the new mantra adopted by all. Thus, instead of targeting an entire market segment, banks have adopted a specific business focus to clearly reach their target audience.

The best banks' strategies:

1. Increase volumes to compensate for declining interest rate spreads;
2. Trim expenditure on provisions and contingencies, thus narrowing the gap between operating profits and net profits;
3. Pare down operating expenses through organisational restructuring; and
4. Adopt a clearly focused communication plan.

Thus, today focus is more important than size in achieving success in the banking industry. The latest technology, innovative retail products and personalised services are vital to carve out a niche in banking sector.

Over the last few years, the communication style too has changed with respect to the banking industry.

Communication has shifted from branding the bank to branding banking products, highlighting service commitment, convenience, etc. Further, branding of banking products, such as home loans, consumer durable loans, tele-banking, ATM's, net banking, etc. have started taking place, especially after the entry of foreign banks and private sector banks which had the advantage of the latest technology.

Insurance

Insurance sector in India has been enjoying a state-monopoly status in India for decades. Under Indian conditions there are two broad classifications of insurance companies: life and non-life insurance. The life insurance activities are solely managed by Life Insurance Corporation of India and the rest is handled by General Insurance Corporation of India.

Life insurance business was started in India during the British rule. Prior to independence, there were several insurance companies: Oriental Life Insurance Company, Bombay Life Assurance, The Madras Equitable Life Insurance Society, Oriental Government Security Life Assurance Company, etc. Most of the insurance companies were charging a very high extra premium of 15 to 20 percent, since they considered Indian lives as sub-standard.

These insurance companies prevailed during the time of independence failed to sustain on a long term basis. As many as 25 companies were liquidated and another 25 companies had to merge with other companies at a lost to the policy holders. This has forced the Government of India in 1956 to nationalise all the 245 life insurance companies (154 Indian and 16 foreign), and form the Life Insurance Corporation of India.

Financial Performance of Life Insurance Corporation of India, 1997 (figures in ₹ crore)

Table 1.7

Total premium	16240
Investment income	9396
Total income	25921
Management expenses	3504
Total outgo	10843
Total assets	91448
Life fund	87760

Till December 1972, the Indian general insurance market was overcrowded with as many as 107 companies. However, as in the case of commercial banks, all these insurance companies were nationalised under an act in 1972 which has yielded the state-monopoly General Insurance Corporation of India. General Insurance Corporation of India operates through four of its subsidiary companies which are spread geographically. They are: National Insurance Company (Kolkata-based), New India Assurance Company (Mumbai-based), Oriental Insurance Company (New Delhi-based) and United India Insurance Company (Chennai-based). The paid up capital of General Insurance Company is fully subscribed by the Indian Government.

1.9 Consumer VS Industrial Services

INDUSTRIAL SERVICES

Industrial goods and services are categorised in different ways. A typical categorisation involves construction, heavy equipment, light equipment, components and subassemblies, raw materials, processed materials, maintenance, repair and operating supplies and industrial services. A customer may buy a product or product with services.

For example, a civil contractor may buy an excavator or a crane only. Alternatively he may buy an excavator or a crane along with an annual maintenance contract. In the latter case the customer is buying a product and a service for maintaining the equipment. In industrial environment the types of services purchased are:

- Property insurance.
- Banking and financial services.
- Chartered accountancy and auditing services.
- Consulting services including architectural, engineering, supervision and co-ordination services.
- Transportation services.
- Advertising and market research services.
- Data processing services.

The portion of expenditure on services in case of industrial market is not as large as in case or consumer markets. The consumer spends more than half of his disposable personal income on services in consumer markets. You may imagine that out of the total earning, how much your expenditure is on procuring goods and how much on services like transportation, medical, education, tutoring, health clubs, out-of-home eating, entertainment and servicing the society. The organisational/institutional purchases involves high value/high volume, and the services portion in term of value is considerably high. So it becomes very important expense item of most organisations.

The core industrial products being of same quality the industrial marketers are now competing on the basis of services only. They are differentiating themselves from the competitors with the type of support services they are providing with the product.

Thus, services are fundamental to the economic health of the organisation as the tangible goods. The intangible nature of services complicates their manufacturing and procurement. For example, the purchase specifications to buy a 'gas based turbine' or 'tower crane' may be difficult to create and marketers may find it hard to develop and maintain standard of quality for this product.

Quality of services is often determined by:

- Skills of persons who delivers it.
- Attitude of the person towards their job.

People play a key role in industrial services marketing and they are major sources of differentiation amongst service providers. Therefore, their training, supervision and control is important. The astute purchaser always assesses above elements with great care before buying services.

Industrial services which can be provided to customers can be categorised as given in Table 1.8.

Table 1.8: Category of Services

Category	Illustration / Example
Equipment based services	Services associated with erection, and commissioning • Utility services • Project management services • Erection supervision services • Equipment testing services • Instrument calibration services.
Facilitating services	Services offered to facilitate the production operations of the organisation. • Transportation services • Financial services • Insurance services
Advisory and Consultative Services	Services offering general or specific technical expertise and intelligence • Enterprise Resource Planning • Market Research • Engineering Services.

Though this taxonomy provides a guideline for categorising the services but it will be more practical to identify the services by the function they perform. It is not possible to generate a list applicable to all type of industries but the list given below in table 1.9 can perhaps be used to consider and think about the type of industrial services a firm requires.

Table 1.9: Type of Services: A Firm's Product/Service Back-up

Types of Services	Illustrations
1. Design and engineering services	• Facilities planning services • Engineering consultancy services • Pilot plant fabrication services • Equipment design services • Plant re-engineering services.

contd. ...

2. Product enhancement services	<ul><li>Non destructive testing services</li><li>TQM services</li><li>Equipment calibration services</li><li>Heat treatment services</li><li>Finishing/polishing services</li></ul>
3. Pre-start-up	<ul><li>Construction management services</li><li>Project Co-ordination services</li><li>Installation and Commissioning services</li><li>Equipment assembly services</li><li>Project start-up services</li></ul>
4. Negotiation Services	<ul><li>Arbitration services</li><li>Legal services</li><li>Liaison services</li><li>Warranty adjustment including exchange of products services.</li></ul>
5. Education services	<ul><li>On-site demonstration, instruction, training and in-plant lecture services</li><li>Handling and safety advice</li><li>Library services</li><li>Technical literature services</li><li>General industrial advice services</li><li>Guidance on application, use and adaptation of products to customer needs services</li></ul>
6. Visiting services	<ul><li>General and specific purpose visits to customer's plants</li><li>Customer visits to service and production facilities/departments</li><li>On site supervision.</li></ul>
7. Maintenance and repair services	<ul><li>Periodic tests and adjustments services</li><li>Reconditioning and repair services</li><li>Part stock and repair services</li><li>Equipment rental services</li></ul>

contd. ...

8. Product adaptation services	• Retrofitting services • Applications research • Modification services
9. Emergency services	• Fire fighting services • Flood control services
10. Stand-by services	• Stand by diesel generated power • Stand by water supply services
11. Operating services	• Online stock and delivery services • Consumable supplies and stock services • Packaging services.
12. Delivery services	• Transit quality control services • Post delivery inspection services • Loading and offloading services • Online information services.
13. Marketing services	• New product development services • Merchandising aids • Marketing research • Product promotion services.
14. Financial services	• Credit services • Leasing services • Renting services • Discounting services • Factoring services
15. Disposal services	• Removal services • Trade-in services • Dismantling services • Recycling services

• adapted from new directions in marketing by Aubrey Wilson.

The industrial services differ from the consumer service in many respects.

Table 1.10 presents a contrast between the consumer services and industrial services.

Table 1.10: Difference between Consumer and Industrial Services

Characteristics	Consumer services	Industrial services
1. Role in service delivery	Individual's involvement in service delivery (Contact employee interaction)	Team interaction
2. Service type	Specialty services	Convenience services
3. Participative nature	High employee-customer participation in service production	Low employee-customer participation in service production
4. Risk Level	Maximum	Minimum
5. Pre-purchase Activities	Several	Nil
6. Problem Issues	Customer problem solving is key to satisfaction.	Problem solving is a routine affair.
7. Commitment	Relatively high	Relatively low
8. Decision Process	Long Decision Process	Short Decision Process

Source: Service Marketing, Concepts, Applications and Cases: M.K. Rampal and S.L. Gupta, Galgotia Publishing Company

ANNEXURE

THE GENERAL AGREEMENT ON TRADE IN SERVICES (GATS)

PART: BACKGROUND

WHAT ARE SERVICES?

Services are often described as things you can buy and sell but can't drop on your foot – i.e. not a tangible commodity. The list of services which are covered by this agreement include:

- Business services
- Communication services
- Construction and engineering services
- Distribution services
- Educational services
- Environmental services
- Financial services
- Health related and social services
- Tourism and travel related services
- Recreational, cultural and sporting services
- Transport services

(see the attached list for a more detailed breakdown)

At present the agreement only applies to those services which a government has agreed to have covered.

WHAT IS THE GOAL OF THE AGREEMENT?

To get access for one country's suppliers of those services to the services markets in other countries.

To prevent governments from discriminating in favour of their domestic services suppliers and against foreign suppliers of those services.

To prevent governments from giving services suppliers from some foreign countries better treatment than those from other foreign countries

To prevent governments from structuring their services markets in ways that reduce access for foreign service suppliers.

WHO ARE THE MAJOR PROMOTERS OF THIS AGREEMENT?

The services agreement is especially important for the big transnational enterprises operating in all these sectors. The major push has come from the US and EU, plus the more ideologically driven free trade countries.

WHEN WAS IT SIGNED?

It was an outcome of the Uruguay Round of GATT negotiations and came into effect in January 1995. However, the agreement built in another round of negotiations to extend its scope. That began in January this year and the initial proposals for extending it are expected to be tabled by the end of the year. Like all such negotiations, they take place in secret.

WHO RUNS IT?

The agreement is administered by the World Trade Organisation. The WTO has a special Council on Trade in Services whose job is to oversee the operation of the agreement and expand its scope.

WHAT COUNTRIES DOES IT APPLY TO?

All WTO members, which covers almost all countries in the world. China will join shortly, as will a number of South Pacific countries.

WHAT ACTIONS OF GOVERNMENT DOES IT APPLY TO?

It applies to anything a government does that can be defined as a 'measure' – i.e. policies, laws, regulations, administrative practices, subsidies and grants, licensing requirements, national interest tests, quality controls and standards, etc. The reason for adopting these measures is irrelevant. If they breach the agreement they are not allowed.

WHAT LEVELS OF GOVERNMENT DOES IT COVER?

All levels from central to local government, including states in federal systems such as Australia.

WHY IS IT IMPORTANT?

The agreement effectively sets the boundaries on what policies a government can adopt on these services. If a government is found to have breached the agreement, a dispute panel can authorise a country whose service suppliers have lost out to impose serious financial sanctions.

HOW DOES GATS RELATE TO REGIONAL AND BILATERAL AGREEMENTS?

All such agreements are required to be consistent with the WTO. That means they can only go further than GATS; they can't wind parts of it back. Hence, the Singapore Agreement made more commitments than New Zealand has made at the WTO, although they only apply to Singapore. CER also makes more extensive commitments in relation to Australia.

PART B: THE BASICS OF THE AGREEMENT

WHAT KIND OF TRANSACTIONS DOES 'TRADE IN SERVICES' COVER?

It covers four ways of supplying services, which are pretty comprehensive:

1. **Supply Across the Border**: For example, allowing people to access foreign-supplied medical advice, offshore financial services, distance education services, entertainment services, etc, especially through the internet.

2. **Consumption Abroad**: Citizens physically moving offshore to consume services, such as tourism, education, health services, rather than being required to use local services or limits on offshore travel and expenditure for balance of payments reasons.

3. **Establishing a Commercial Presence**: Allowing a foreign service provider to set up a local business, such as a retail chain or cleaning company franchise, banks and insurance companies, schools and universities, waste disposal companies, media corporations, bus and rail companies.

4. **Movement of Personnel:** Supply of a service by specialist personnel travelling to the country, such as consultants, professionals, specialist teachers or researchers, entertainers, specialist tourism operators (note: this doesn't apply to ordinary workers in the services sector)

WHAT RULES APPLY TO THESE TRANSACTIONS?

Some rules apply across the board.

The most important of these is the rule that says you can't treat the service suppliers from one WTO member better than the rest. (That's known as 'Most Favoured Nation' treatment.)

Other rules only apply to particular services a country has agreed to have covered by the agreement, which are set out in each country's schedule.

These are far more intrusive because they require non-discrimination between domestic and foreign service suppliers (this is called 'national treatment'). They also prohibit a number of measures which would limit foreign access to domestic services markets (known as 'market access' restrictions). These are:

- Limits on the ***number of service suppliers*** through numerical quotas, monopolies, licensing exclusive suppliers or applying an economic needs test; (e.g. television broadcasters or universities)

- Limits on the **total value of service transactions or assets**, through numerical quotas or applying an economic needs test; (e.g. banks)

- Limits on the **total number of service operations or quantity of services** provided, through numerical quotas or applying an economic needs test; (e.g. medical schools and medical students)

- Limits on the **total number of people who can be employed** in a particular sector or by a supplier, through numerical quotas or applying an economic needs test; (e.g. licensed health providers)

- Measures which restrict or require certain **types of legal entity or joint venture** as the means for supplying the service (e.g. fishing companies);

- Limits on the **level of foreign capital** involved in a particular services enterprise or in total for a sector (e.g. media ownership).

Some services sectors have their own <u>special annexes</u>.

These are the ones which weren't finalised when the first negotiations were completed, and cover areas like financial services and telecommunications.

HOW DO YOU FIND OUT IF A COUNTRY HAS AGREED TO HAVE A PARTICULAR SERVICE COVERED?

Each government's schedule of its commitments can be found on the WTO website. These are quite difficult to interpret. They indicate which services are covered. But they also say whether the government has retained are any restrictions within those services on national treatment or market access and in relation to any of the four 'modes of supply'. The New Zealand government made amongst the most extensive commitments of any.

CAN SERVICES BE TAKEN OUT OF THESE SCHEDULES IN THE FUTURE?

The agreement is meant to be a one-way street – governments are required to remove their existing restrictions over time, not add to them. Although it is possible to withdraw a commitment, the government would have to open up another service area to an equivalent value. New Zealand hasn't left many to trade off in that way. No government has tried to do this yet.

IS THERE ANY SPECIAL PROTECTION FOR PUBLIC SERVICES?

In theory 'services supplied in the exercise of government authority' are excluded. But only if those services (a) don't have a commercial element and (b) are not provided in competition with another supplier. There are very few public services that meet those conditions today.

PART C: MOBILISATION AGAINST THE GATS

WHAT IS HAPPENING WITH THE NEW GATS NEGOTIATIONS?

Negotiations to extend the GATS are now well underway in Geneva. These are moving secretly, and most documents released by New Zealand government officials have any information relating to these negotiations deleted. Despite claims that progress is slow, governments are supposed to put their new offers on the table by the end of this year.

WHAT ARE THE MAIN ISSUES?

The transnational services exporters and their governments (mainly US and EU) are trying to expand the agreement as far as possible, especially in growth areas of information technology, and public services which are being privatised or opened to competition (postal, transport, health, education, broadcasting, etc). Poorer countries are very concerned about the effects of existing and future commitments on them. Proposals on the table include:

- applying the agreement to all services except those opted out, rather than only the services that are opted in;
- extending the list of services that might be covered and regrouping them in ways that ensure the widest possible coverage;
- getting governments to extend their existing commitments substantially;
- make it clear that subsidies are covered;
- restricting the kind of domestic regulations governments can use;
- extending non-discrimination to government procurement or purchase of services (as now applies with Singapore for contracts over $125,000)

(A) SERVICES SECTORAL CLASSIFICATION LIST

1. BUSINESS SERVICES

   A. Professional Services
   B. Computer and Related Services
   C. Research and Development Services
   D. Real Estate Services
   E. Rental/Leasing Services without Operators
   F. Other Business Services

2. COMMUNICATION SERVICES

   A. Postal services
   B. Courier services
   C. Telecommunication services
   D. Audiovisual services
   E. Other

3. **CONSTRUCTION AND RELATED ENGINEERING SERVICES**

   A. General construction work for buildings

   B. General construction work for civil engineering

   C. Installation and assembly work

   D. Building completion and finishing work

   E. Other

4. **DISTRIBUTION SERVICES**

   A. Commission agents' services

   B. Wholesale trade services

   C. Retailing services

   D. Franchising

   E. Other

5. **EDUCATIONAL SERVICES**

   A. Primary education services

   B. Secondary education services

   C. Higher education services

   D. Adult education

   E. Other education services

6. **ENVIRONMENTAL SERVICES**

   A. Sewage services

   B. Refuse disposal services

   C. Sanitation and similar services

   D. Other

7. **FINANCIAL SERVICES**

   A. All insurance and insurance-related services

   B. Banking and other financial services

8. **HEALTH RELATED AND SOCIAL SERVICES**

   Hospital services

(B) **OTHER HUMAN HEALTH SERVICES**

   A. Social Services

   B. Other

9. TOURISM AND TRAVEL RELATED SERVICES

   A. Hotels and restaurants

   B. Travel agencies and tour operators services

   C. Tourist guides services

   D. Other

10. RECREATIONAL, CULTURAL AND SPORTING SERVICES

   A. Entertainment services

   B. News agency services

   C. Libraries, archives, museums and other cultural services

   D. Sporting and other recreational services

   E. Other

11. TRANSPORT SERVICES

   A. Maritime Transport Services

   B. Internal Waterways Transport

   C. Air Transport Services

   D. Space Transport

   E. Rail Transport Services

   F. Road Transport Services

   G. Pipeline Transport

   H. Services auxiliary to all modes of transport

Questions for Discussion

1. Define and explain the term 'Services'. State the Broad classification of Services.
2. What is 'Services'? State its various forms.
3. Explain the various characteristics of services.
4. Describe the various important services.
5. Describe the importance of services marketing.
6. State the impact of services on daily life.
7. State the nature of demand and supply in services.
8. State the nature of services.
9. Explain 4I's of services.
10. Explain the growing importance of services in the society.

11. State the various demographic, social, economical, political and legal changes affecting the services marketing economy.

12. Describe the four characteristics of services which distinguish the marketing of services from marketing of physical products. Justify your answer with suitable examples.

13. Define services indicating the salient characteristics. Elaborate how does services marketing mix differ from marketing mix of goods.

14. What are search, experience and credence attributes of services?

15. Differentiate between Consumer and Industrial Services.

■■■

Chapter **2**...

Global and Indian Scenario in Services Sector

Contents ...

2.1 Introduction

The service industry forms a backbone of social and economic development of a region. It has emerged as the largest and fastest-growing sectors in the world economy, making higher contributions to the global output and employment. Its growth rate has been higher than that of agriculture and manufacturing sectors. It is a large and most dynamic part of the Indian economy both in terms of employment potential and contribution to national income. It covers a wide range of activities, such as trading, transportation and communication, financial, real estate and business services, as well as community, social and personal services. In India, services sector, as a whole, contributed as much as 68.6 percent of the overall average growth in gross domestic product (GDP) between the years 2002-03 and 2006-07.

Services play a central role in the economies of both developed and developing countries. They account for over half of the gross domestic product of all developed economies and constitute the single largest sector in most developing economies. Main reasons behind the growth of services include rapid urbanisation, the expansion of the public sector and increased demand for intermediate and final consumer services. Access to efficient services has become crucial for the productivity and competitiveness of the entire economy. The successful growth of the primary and secondary activities in the economy, to a large extent, dependent on services offered by banking, insurance, trade, commerce, entertainment, maintenance of machinery and equipment and numerous other services categorised as tertiary activities.

THE GLOBAL SCENARIO

The real reason for the growth of the service sector is due to the increase in urbanisation, privatisation and more demand for intermediate and final consumer services. Availability of quality services is vital for the well being of the economy.

In advanced economies the growth in the primary and secondary sectors are directly dependent on the growth of services like banking, insurance, trade, commerce, entertainment etc.

Service businesses boomed through much of the 1990s and early 2000s, as companies brought in outside consultants to handle matters ranging from branding to human resources. But companies that primarily sell services are now struggling, according to a new report released by Sageworks, a company that tracks the financial data of private businesses. The report's authors note that businesses are behaving much like the average consumer these days, often choosing to forgo some basic services or to handle them in house. "People are cutting back on the things that they normally would spend on growing the business," says Drew White, the chief financial officer of Sageworks.

Drawn from responses of 950 private businesses, the report analyses data from December 2007 through October 2009. Among the service industries with the sharpest decline in sales were legal counsel and advertising and marketing services providers. The rate of annual growth in billings at law firms contracted 18 percentage points from 5 percent growth in 2007 to negative 13 percent growth in 2009. At advertising and marketing services, the rate of growth of annual billings dropped 21 percentage points from 9 percent in 2007 to negative 12 percent in 2009. Computer systems and website design services companies saw a decline in revenue growth of nearly 15 percent in that same period, while automotive repair companies saw revenue growth fall off by 8 percent.

In the case of marketing, for example, many companies are turning to viral campaigns on social media sites like Facebook and Twitter, and managing them primarily with existing staff members, rather than contracting out the work to a public relations firm or a marketing agency. "Privately-held companies are being more frugal, more disciplined, and less impulsive," says White. "They're spending a little more time thinking, 'I could hire the firm, or I could do it myself.'"

The offices of physicians were one of the few areas in the service sector to continue to prosper, with the rate of annual revenue growth rising from 7.6 percent in 2007 to 10 percent in 2009. The fact that this industry stands out could be attributed to the presence of the insurance company as a third-party payer, White says. "It's one of the only industries where you're not paying for the service directly," he notes.

The size of the service sector is increasing in almost all economies around the world. Services make up the bulk of today's economy and also account for most of the growth in new jobs. Even in emerging economies, service output is growing rapidly and often accounts for half or more of GDP.

Future Trends

- Globally outsourcing industry would continue to grow.
- Following the success of US and UK, more countries in the European Union would outsource their business.
- Technological power shift from the West to the East as India and China emerge as major players.

Political backlash over outsourcing would come down as companies reap the benefit of outsourcing.

THE INDIAN SCENARIO

There has been a structural change in the Indian economy since Independence. This is reflected in the change in the sector-wise composition of income and workforce over the years. The last decade of the twentieth century witnessed major policy changes in the Indian economy and its constituent sub-national economies. The emergence of India as one of the fastest growing economies in the world during the 1990s is attributable to a significant extent to the rapid growth of its services sector. During the last decade, the Indian service sector grew at an average annual rate of nine percent, contributing to nearly sixty percent of the overall growth rate of the economy (World Bank, 2004). Most of the growth in services has been in information technology (IT), business process outsourcing (BPO) services and knowledge based activities; other sectors like telecommunications, financial services, community services and hotels and restaurants, have also grown considerably. Access to external markets and domestic reforms have played an important role in creating a dynamic services sector in India.

The phenomenon of the growth of tertiary sector is reflected also in the changing composition of incomes in the state economies. Each state of the Indian union is different in terms of its natural, social, political and economic features. Therefore, the pattern of growth of each sub-national unit is unique.

At the time of Independence, the Indian economy was overwhelmingly rural and agricultural in character, as nearly 85 percent of the population lived in villages and 70 percent of the working population was engaged in agriculture. The growth and development of all sectors of the economy led to an increase in the share of the non-agricultural sector and a decrease in the share of the agriculture sector in both output and employment.

At the beginning of the plan period, i.e., in 1950-51, the share of agriculture in GDP was nearly 60 percent and that of secondary and tertiary sectors was 13 percent and 28 percent respectively. Over a period of time, there have been changes in the contribution of various sectors to GDP in India. In the beginning of the nineties, i.e., in 1990-91, the share of the primary sector declined to nearly 35 percent and that of the secondary sector increased to 25 percent and tertiary sector accounted for nearly 40 percent of the GDP.

The decadal growth rates for each of the three sectors show that the rate of growth of the income originating in the primary sector was the least in all the five decades from the 1950s to the 1990s in the Indian economy. The contribution of the secondary sector to GDP grew at the fastest rate during the first two decades after the process of planning was started and the growth of income originating in the tertiary sector surpassed the growth of the secondary sector during the decades of the 1970s, 1980s and 1990s.

Though, the share of non-agriculture sector has increased and the improvement in the growth has taken place both as a result of growth in industrial and services sectors there are marked differences in the sector-wise composition of growth as between these two major sectors. The generally held view (Seema Joshi, 2004) is as compared to the industrial sector, the services sector has experienced a higher growth rate in a more uniform and consistent manner. But the results of the compound annual growth rate of GDP over the entire period of five decades show that the share of secondary sector in GDP has grown faster than the share of the services sector (Amrita Shergil, 2003). Nevertheless, the development experience of India has been different from that of developed countries, as the share of services sector in GDP has surpassed that of the agriculture and industrial sector in relatively short span of time.

There have been variations in the pace and pattern of economic growth of different states in India. These differences are also evident in the case of the tertiary sector. The share of the services sector in Net State Domestic Product was the highest in Tamil Nadu (40.5 percent) followed by Jammu and Kashmir (40.1 percent), Assam (39.9 percent), West Bengal (39.8 percent) and Maharashtra (38.5 percent) in the early 1980s. The share of services sector was the lowest in the states of Madhya Pradesh (26.7 percent), Haryana (28.5 percent), Bihar (28.8 percent) and Rajasthan (29.4 percent). Punjab's share was 30.9 percent for the same period. The mean share of services sector in 17 major states was 33.9 percent. The ranking of the states changed in the early 1990s with Jammu and Kashmir (45 percent) followed by Assam (44.6 percent), Maharashtra (45 percent) and Tamil Nadu (44.6 percent). The share of the services sector was the lowest in Punjab (28.5 percent), Haryana (31.9 percent), Madhya

Pradesh (32.5 percent) and Bihar (32.3 percent). The service sector had emerged as the largest sector in terms of its contribution to NSDP in Gujarat, Maharashtra, Karnataka, Kerala, Tamil Nadu, Andhra Pradesh, West Bengal, Assam and Jammu and Kashmir (Shergil, 2003).

The most important services in the Indian economy have been health and education. They are one of the largest and most challenging sectors and hold a key to the country's overall progress. A strong and well-defined health care sector helps to build a healthy and productive workforce as well as stabilise population. The 'Ministry of Health and Family Welfare' is responsible for implementation of various programmes in the areas of health and family welfare, prevention and control of major communicable diseases as well as promotion of traditional and indigenous systems of medicines. Accordingly, it is carrying out measures like National health policy, implementing National Rural Health Mission (NRHM) in different States, conducting surveys and studies, etc., while, education strongly influences improvement in health, hygiene and demographic profile. The 'Ministry of Human Resource Development' is involved in eradicating illiteracy from the country. It is concerned with universalisation of elementary education, achieving full adult literacy, laying down of National Policy on Education, meeting needs of secondary and higher education for all, etc. India has achieved impressive demographic transition owing to the decline of crude birth rate, crude death rate, total fertility rate and infant mortality rate as well as gained high literacy rate in the country.

The era of economic liberalisation has ushered in a rapid change in the service industry. As a result, over the years, India is witnessing a transition from agriculture-based economy to a knowledge-based economy. The knowledge economy creates, disseminates, and uses knowledge to enhance its growth and development. One of the major functional pillars of this economy is Information Technology (IT) and IT-enabled services (ITeS) industry. The 'Department of Information Technology' has been making continuous efforts to make India a front-runner in the age of Information revolution. IT continues to be a dominating sector in the overall growth of the Indian industry. A large number of Indian software companies have acquired international quality certification. Several policies have also been framed on the key issues of IT infrastructure, electronic governance as well as IT education.

Post Liberalisation, the Indian economy has moved from agriculture based economy to a knowledge based economy. Today, the IT industry and ITES industry are the dominant industry in the service sector. Media and entertainment have also seen tremendous growth in the past few years.

2.2 Importance of Services Marketing

The following points highlight the growing importance of services:

- There has been an increase in demand for the services of professionally qualified technicians with establishment of technical institutes.

- Communication services like entertainment, education and the right to information by the public is more important.

- Due to increasing standards in education there is an increasing demand for educational services. Primary, secondary, higher secondary schools, junior degree colleges are the institutes which are in great demand. As the number of students goes up the demand for private classes, tuitions, etc. also increases.

- Banking services have become necessary to meet financial requirements of the public and the national industrial sector.

- Personal care services are essential to develop potentiality of an individual for a perfect personality and positive image.

- Electricity services are required for the benefit of society, industry and so on.

- With the increasing amount of trade and business, done by road there has been a demand for transport services which benefits various automobile manufacturers. Large sections of population prefer having their own vehicles, proving a good business proposition for automobile industry.

- Tourism has geared itself to make the tourists enjoy the holiday seasons in the places of their choice and take them away from monotonous existence of cities.

- Adequate hospital services are essential for the well being of the society.

- Hospitality services work on the strategies to satisfy the business class through their service in terms of comfort and satisfaction. The above activities have left the management scientists, professionals and socio-economic thinkers to analyse and understand that managing services need attention, to stay in business.

- As the natural resources are depleting and need for conservation is increasing we see the coming of service providers like pollution control agencies, car pools etc.

- The development in information technology has given rise to services like pager service PCOs, world wide web etc. Professional requirements need a change when technology develops and evolves. This necessitates proficiency in the management level by giving a boost to abilities.

2.3 Every Business a Service Business

Services Marketing is that sector which is used in all the business processes. Various sectors wherein Services Marketing is used is explained as follows:

Information Technology Industry

The Information Technology industry has achieved phenomenal growth after liberalisation. The industry has performed exceedingly well amidst tough global competition. Being a knowledge based industry; India has been able to leverage the global markets, because of the huge pool of engineering talent available and the proficiency in English language among the middle class.

ITES sector

The ITES sector has also leveraged the global changes positively to emerge as one of the prominent industries. Some of the services covered by the ITES industry would be:

- Customer interaction services -Non voice and Voice.
- Back office, revenue accounting, data entry, data conversion, HR services.
- Medical Transcription.
- Content development and animation.
- Remote education, market research and GIS

Retailing

Prior to liberalisation, India was one of the most underdeveloped retail sectors in the world. After liberalisation the scenario changed dramatically. Organised retailing with prominence on self service and chain stores has changed the dynamics of retailing. In most of the tier I and tier II cities supermarket chains mushroomed, catering to the needs of vibrant middle class. This indirectly contributed to the growth of the packaged food industry and other consumer goods.

Financial Services-Banking and Insurance

Prior to liberalisation, these two sectors were controlled and regulated by the government. Nationalised banks and insurance companies had a firm grip over the market. After liberalisation the banking and insurance domain opened up for private participation.

Banking Sector

The three major changes in the banking sector after liberalisation are:

- Step to increase the cash outflow through reduction in the statutory liquidity and cash reserve ratio.
- Nationalised banks including SBI were allowed to sell stakes to private sector and private investors were allowed to enter the banking domain. Foreign banks were given greater access to the domestic market, both as subsidiaries and branches, provided the foreign banks maintained a minimum assigned capital and would be governed by the same rules and regulations governing domestic banks.

- Banks were given greater freedom to leverage the capital markets and determine their asset portfolios. The banks were allowed to provide advances against equity provided as collateral and provide bank guarantees to the broking community.

Insurance Sector

The Insurance Regulatory and Development Authority Act 1999 (IRDA Act) allowed the participation of private insurance companies in the insurance sector. The primary role of IRDA was to safeguard the interest of insurance policy holders, to regulate, promote and ensure orderly growth of the insurance industry. The insurance sector could invest in the capital markets and other than traditional insurance products, various market link insurance products were available to the end customer to choose from.

Some of the prominent insurance companies are:

- Bajaj Allianz Insurance Corporation.
- Birla Sun Insurance Co Ltd.
- HDFC Standard Insurance Co Ltd.
- ICICI Prudential Insurance Co Ltd.
- Max New York Insurance Co Ltd.
- Tata AIG Insurance Co Ltd.

Another major and upcoming service industry has been media and entertainment. It is basically an intellectual property-driven sector with small to large players spread throughout the country. It covers film, music, radio, broadcast, television and live entertainment. It plays a significant role in creating people's awareness about national policies and programmes by providing information and education to all. The 'Ministry of Information and Broadcasting' is responsible for formulation and administration of the rules, regulations and laws relating to media industry. Besides, retailing has been one of the fastest growing Services sector both in terms of turnover and employment. Many national and global players have been investing in the retail segment and are making all efforts to further expand the sector. Out of the total retail outlets in the country, most of them are related to food items.

However, to supplement the achievements and meet the shortfalls in all the sub-sectors of the service industry, travel and tourism sector has to be developed in a sustainable manner. Being one of the largest industry in terms of gross revenue and foreign exchange earnings, it stimulates growth and expansion in other economic sectors like agriculture, horticulture, poultry, handicrafts, transportation, construction, etc. as well as gives momentum to growth of service exports. It is a major contributor to the national integration process of the country as well as preserver of natural and cultural environments. The 'Ministry of Tourism' has been undertaking several policy measures and incentives so as to boost the sector such as the announcement of the National Tourism Policy.

Today in India, service sector alone contributes more than half of its GDP. According to financial year 2007-08, share of service sector is about 55.1% i.e. more than industry sector (26.4%) and agriculture sector (18.5%). The service sector now accounts for more than half the GDP marks a turning point in the evolution of the Indian economy and takes it closer to the essentials of a developed economy.

India has young population of nearly 37% among the total population. Using them in service sectors where immense opportunities are present can be better rewarded. The government should step forward for availing these facilities for the enhancement of services sector, which will act as a boost to Indian economy.

There was marked increase in rate of services sector's growth in the eighties and nineties. While the share of services in India's GDP increased by 21 percent points in the 50 years between 1950 and 2000, nearly 40 percent of that increase was concentrated in the nineties. One of the reasons for the sudden growth in the services sector in India in the nineties was the liberalisation and globalization in the regulatory framework that gave rise to innovation and higher exports from the services sector.

Service sector accounts more than half of India's Gross Domestic Product. The rise in service sector's share in GDP marks a structural change. Reason for high growth rate in service sector in India is liberalisation in regulatory framework. That gives rise to innovation and high export earnings. The growth rate of India's service exports in 2002 was 8% with regards to 5% Worldwide. India is ranked 21st among exporters of services.

India is also a signatory to the General Agreement on Trade in Services (WTO-1995) and is actively engaged in seeking full opportunities for free movement of services across borders.

Keeping in view the growing dimensions with structural shifts the Government of India has given special status to the services sector in its Export-Import Policy 2002-2007 announced on 31st March, 2002. It included all the 161 tradable services covered under the head "Services" where payment for them is received in free foreign exchange.

A "Service Provider", according to the EXIM Policy, means a person providing:

(i)   'Service' from India to any other country;

(ii)   'Service' from India to the service consumer of any other country in India;

(iii) 'Service' from India through commercial or physical presence in the territory of any other country; and

(iv)   Supply of a 'service' in India relating to exports paid in free foreign exchange or in Indian currency, which are otherwise considered as having been paid for in free foreign exchange by RBI.

The contribution of some of the major Services sectors and sub-sectors in India are summarised below:

Important Services Sectors in India

India's IT Market reached a turnover of US$ 16.2 billion in 2004-05. The IT Sector employs 697,000 people and this is likely to reach 2 million by 2014. IT Companies are expected to account for 8-10% of GDP by 2008 from 1.4% in 2001. India is considered as a global player in Information Technology with software exports of US Dollars 12 billion in 2003-2004 and $ 17.2 billion in 2004-2005. The revenue from exports of IT and related services is expected to reach US$ 57 billion by 2008.

Outsourcing Industry has changed the image of India. Western companies are continuing to eye India as their top destination for outsourcing work. Rapid increase in the profits of several Indian outsource service providers including two of top companies like Tata consultancy services and Infosys Technology. Mumbai based TCS has risen by 20.5% and Bangalore based Infosys recorded a 36% rise.

The **BPO Sector** has been growing at 60-70% annually and its turnover in 2004-05 reached US$5.8 billion from US$565 million in 1999-00. It is projected to increase to US$ 12.3 billion by 2006 and create employment opportunities for a million people from its current level of 200,000.

India's **Consultancy Professionals** possess capability and capacity to provide expertise especially suitable for developing countries. In addition, it also offers consultancy in sophisticated areas like information technology, advanced financial and banking services etc. to developed countries like USA, UK, France, West Germany and Australia. Expertise offered by Indian consultancy professionals covers areas like infrastructure, Economic & Social Sector, Water Resource Dam, Flood Control, Irrigation, Rural Development, Environment, Industries, Computer, Training of personnel and transfer technology etc.

India's **health services** (with highly qualified and experienced personnel), super-speciality hospitals specialising in both modern and traditional Indian medical systems (like Ayurveda, Unani, Siddha and nature- cure) supported by state-of-the-art equipment, are attracting patients from across the world, and constitute a larger portion in India's services sector.

Education is another field which is not only a huge segment of the services sector within the country, but also a foreign exchange earner by way of NRIs and foreign students enrolled in major medical, technological and other institutions in India. We also export manpower even to the western world. The demand for teachers from India has started growing in the United States and England in recent times.

Tourism: India is a subcontinent with varied geographical, climatic, ethnic, cultural, religious and social condition. So it is a top destination for any tourist. The tourism industry in the country is well equipped and also growing very fast to offer tourists all the services needed for making their visit memorable.

All this shows that services hold immense potential to accelerate the growth of an economy and promote general well-being of the people. They offer innumerable business opportunities to the investors. They have the capacity to generate substantial employment opportunities in the economy as well as increase its per capita income. Without them, Indian economy would not have acquired a strong and dominating place on the world platform. Thus, service sector is considered to be an integral part of the economy and includes various sub-sectors spread all across the country.

2.4 Service as a Key Differentiator for Manufacturing Industries

"A business absolutely devoted to service will have only one worry about profits. They will be embarrassingly large," Henry Ford, founder of one of the world's largest manufacturing companies, once said. Decades later, however, companies are still struggling to heed this advice. Manufacturers are looking for growth and profits in all corners of the globe, but they often neglect the very large opportunities much closer to home—in their own service businesses.

Across the manufacturing companies, services revenues today represent an average of more than 25 percent of the total business. In many companies, as for Rolls-Royce plc and Xerox Corporation, the service business contributes 50 percent or more of total revenues. Even more importantly, the average profitability of the service businesses benchmarked is more than 75 percent higher than overall business unit profitability, and accounts for an estimated 46 percent of total profits generated today. In fact, in many manufacturing companies there would be little or no profitability without the service business.

Analysis suggests the untapped potential for growing profits through the service business is immense. But most companies fail to grow their service business. More than two-thirds (67 percent) of companies are growing their service businesses at the same rate or slower than their overall business. In essence, they are managing a high growth potential "star" business as a slow-growth "cash cow." The median company benchmarked secures only 40 percent of the after-sales service market and 75 percent of the aftersales spare parts market in servicing its own installed base of products (the "captive market"). For many companies, such as automotive original equipment manufacturers (OEMs), these shares are often much lower.

In addition, only a few OEMs have made significant inroads in servicing "non-captive" customers—a market that is typically 2 to 10 times larger than the captive market. The challenges are many:

- In strategy and business design, most companies struggle to build the foundation for service excellence. Few have sufficient insight into the barriers and opportunities for driving profitable growth through services, which makes it difficult, at best, to develop the right strategies, identify the right priorities and invest sufficiently in the service business. Yet some companies, such as Siemens AG Medical Solutions, make the service business central to their corporate strategy: they design the service business around customer requirements in order to drive customer satisfaction, loyalty and business performance.

- In operations planning and management, companies with complex service operations those with thousands or hundreds of thousands of parts, services that need to be delivered around the clock and often in remote parts of the world, and service lifecycles that can stretch for decades often lack the capabilities to realise service excellence. The experiences of some of the world's leading manufacturing companies, show that persistent investment in, and focus on, improving the service and logistics operations can drive outstanding customer service, resulting in enhanced customer loyalty and a foundation for profitable growth.

- In execution, the "last mile" to the customer where battles for customer loyalty are won or lost, the majority of companies are still unable to provide customers with excellent and cost-effective service. Overall, results suggest that customers are likely to get exactly what they want, at the right time and place, less than 75 percent of the time—a dismal performance in a global economy where customers have more options and more information than ever before to prompt a switch to competitors' products and services.

Ensuring service excellence, however, is core to the business model for many companies, such as Hyundai Motor Company, where service guarantees, such as extended warranties, are an essential part of the value provided to the consumer.

There are great opportunities for companies to improve what should be an engine for profitable growth in many or most manufacturing organisations. Some companies are championing the service revolution to drive performance. Twenty five percent of the benchmarked companies report an on-time delivery performance to customers of 96 percent or higher. A US company Caterpillar—with more than 600,000 spare parts, and an installed base of equipment that often needs service for 40 years or longer—is able to ship its customers exactly what they want, within just 24 hours, 99.7 percent of the time.

While the challenges are numerous, research suggests that companies can make strategic and operational investments in processes and technologies that will enable them to leapfrog the competition and drive continuous improvement in the operational and financial performance of their global service businesses.

- First, companies can adopt collaborative processes across the service supply chain, from suppliers to customers that are well-documented, proven, and ready for implementation. Indeed, analysis indicates a strong relationship between the level of implementation of processes—such as collaborative planning, forecasting, and replenishment with customers—with the benefits achieved from the implementation. Across the service businesses benchmarked, the more extensive the level of implementation, the higher the benefits reported from adoption of key processes. Volkswagen AG experienced first-hand in its North American operations the benefits of implementing robust processes for service parts management. It drove dramatic improvements in customer order fill rates over just six months while reducing annual cost by over US$25 million.

- Second, information systems for designing, planning, managing and executing the service and parts business are maturing rapidly and can now support most of the requirements of even the world's largest and most complex service businesses. These systems are no longer the weak links on the road to service excellence that they were 5, 10 or 20 years ago. In fact, without sufficient technology support it will be increasingly difficult, if not impossible, to manage and optimise the service business as customer requirements increase and the service business grows more complex. While adoption rates are still abysmally low in many areas, analysis points toward a strong correlation between information systems implementation and benefits achieved. Some companies, such as Rolls Royce, are capitalising on improved technology, sometimes going beyond what would have been thought possible just a few years back.

In diversified manufacturing and industrial products companies, such as General Electric, the service business is an integral part of the business in the eyes of the customers. According to Jeffrey Immelt, chairman and chief executive officer of GE, "Services represent about 30 percent of our industrial sales and have the potential to grow at double-digit rates for the foreseeable future. Services are a powerful growth engine because our technology is long-lived and we focus on making the customer more profitable." In industrial automation, customers are under pressure to reduce costs and time to market, and to increase quality and safety.

With profitability and growth levels in many cases far exceeding the main business, it is abundantly clear that the service revolution in global manufacturing is well underway. For most manufacturers, it is now a matter of effectively embracing the service revolution or risking being left behind.

Questions for Discussion

1. Explain: every business is a service business.
2. Explain Globalisation of the Indian service sector.
3. Write a short note on:

    (a) Service as a key differentiator for manufacturing industries.
4. Explain the global and Indian scenario in the services sector.
5. Explain the importance of services marketing.

■■■

Chapter **3**...

Services Market Segmentation

Contents ...

3.1 Introduction

Market segmentation is a strategy that involves dividing a larger market into subsets of consumers who have common needs and applications for the goods and services offered in the market. These subgroups of consumers can be identified by a number of different demographics, depending on the purposes behind identifying the groups. Marketing campaigns are often designed and implemented based on this type of customer segmentation.

One of the main reasons for engaging in market segmentation is to help the company understand the needs of the customer base. Often the task of segregating consumers by specific criteria will help the company identify other applications for their products that may or may not have been self evident before. Uncovering these other ideas for use of goods and services may help the company target a larger audience in that same demographic classification and thus increase market share among a specific sub-market base.

Market segmentation strategies can be developed over a wide range of characteristics found among consumers. One group within the market may be identified by gender, while another group may be composed of consumers within a given age group. Location is another common component in market segmentation, as is income level and education level. Generally, there will be atleast a few established customers who fall into more than one category, but marketing strategists normally allow for this phenomenon.

Along with playing a role in the development of new marketing approaches to attract a certain demographic within the market base, market segmentation can also help a company understand ways to enhance customer loyalty with existing customers. As a part of the process of identifying specific groups within the larger client base, the company will often ask questions that lead to practical suggestions on how to make the products more desirable to customers. This activity may lead to changes in packaging or other similar changes that do not impact the core product. However, making a few simple changes in the appearance of the product sends a clear message to consumers that the company does listen to customers. This demonstration of good will can go a long way to strengthen the ties between a consumer and a vendor.

3.2 Meaning and Concept of Market Segmentation

"Market segmentation consists of taking the total heterogeneous market for a product and dividing it into several sub markets or segments, each of which tends to be homogenous in all significant aspects"

William Stanton

"The process of classifying customers into group exhibiting different needs, characteristics or behaviour, is called market segmentation. Every market is made up of market segments".

Philip Kotler

The Need for Market Segmentation

The marketing concept calls for understanding customers and satisfying their needs better than the competition. But different customers have different needs, and it rarely is possible to satisfy all customers by treating them alike. The underlying principle of market segmentation is that individual customers have different product and service needs. Mass marketing, the marketing of a single product to everyone, is rarely a viable strategy, just as it is to customise products to an individual.

Market Segmentation provides fresh perspectives for increased customer identification, selection, profitability, and retention and helps to answer the following questions:

➢ What are the customers' needs, wants and motivations?

➢ Who are the most and least profitable customers?

➢ Where are the best opportunities?

➢ What are the customers' hidden or untapped needs?

Why Segment a Market?

Consumer diversity is rapidly increasing and firms are seeking to differentiate their products relative to competitors. When the focus is specifically on the desires and needs of a niche group, there is a greater probability that the company's marketing can match the needs of that group. Target marketing and market segmentation allows firms to focus their resources more effectively, with a greater chance of success.

The purpose of market segmentation is to focus on the subset of prospects that have the greatest potential of becoming customers. When segmentation is done correctly, it helps a company realise the highest return for its marketing expenditures.

Market segmentation is a proven way of improving profitability. By focusing the company's offerings to different groups, the company is able to meet their needs precisely and gain higher market share and profits.

Companies who segment their markets match their strengths and offerings to the groups of customers most likely to respond to them. By selecting and focusing on some segments to the exclusion of others, marketing can be specifically created to fit those customers.

The Segmentation Process

Segmentation is the term given to the grouping of customers with similar needs by a number of different variables. Once this has been done, segments can be targeted by a number of targeting strategies. The stage that then follows is known as positioning which is the place that services occupy in the marketplace in relation to the competition, as perceived by the target market. The segmentation process comprises three stages; segmentation, targeting and positioning.

Implementing a segmentation strategy has three components:

Identifying the market segments,

- Targeting desirable segments to focus on and
- Positioning the organisation to take advantage of those choices.

The first stage of the segmentation process involves the selection of suitable variables for grouping customers. These are also referred to as base variables or the segmentation basis. There is rarely one best way of segmenting a market and more than one variable can be used. There are a number of segmentation variables that can be used for consumer and business-to-business markets.

Research plays an important role in segmentation as segmentation analysis requires a range of data from a wide variety of sources on markets, customers' attitudes, motives and behaviour as well as competitor information.

Targeting is the next step in the sequential process and involves business making choices about segment(s) on which resources are to be focused. There are three major targeting strategies: undifferentiated, concentrated and differentiated. During this process, the business must balance its resources and capabilities against the attractiveness of different segments.

Positioning follows on logically from the segmentation and targeting stages. Customer perceptions are central to the product position especially in relation to the competition's offering. The service has to satisfy key customer requirements and this has to be clearly communicated to the customers. A tool that helps marketers understand customer perceptions of their brand is perceptual mapping and a simple 7-step approach can be used to develop a clear positioning strategy.

However, a number of positioning problems can arise.

Market segmentation, targeting and positioning are not always easy to apply and problems can arise for a number of reasons. There are a number of steps that can be taken to avoid these problems and, in addition, there are a set of segmentation criteria that can help.

The two key factors that will affect segmentation in the future are competitive and technological forces. In addition, there is a rising trend towards one-to-one marketing.

Market Segments

A **market segment** is a group of people or organisations sharing one or more characteristics that cause them to have similar service needs. A true market segment meets all of the following criteria: it is distinct from other segments (different segments have different needs), it is homogeneous within the segment (exhibits common needs); it responds similarly to a market stimulus, and it can be reached by a market intervention.

The term is also used when consumers with identical service needs are divided up into groups so they can be charged different amounts.

Requirements of Market Segments

In addition to having different needs, for segments to be practical they should be evaluated against the following criteria:

➢ **Identifiable:** The differentiating attributes of the segments must be measurable so that they can be identified.

➢ **Accessible:** The segments must be reachable through communication and distribution channels.

➢ **Substantial:** The segments should be sufficiently large to justify the resources required to target them.

➢ **Unique needs:** To justify separate offerings, the segments must respond differently to the different marketing mixes.

➢ **Durable:** The segments should be relatively stable to minimise the cost of frequent changes.

➢ A good market segmentation will result in segment members that are internally homogenous and externally heterogeneous; that is, as similar as possible within the segment, and as different as possible between segments.

"Know your market" is a mantra for marketing professionals. Sellers and advertisers want to be able to determine what the potential market is for their service, as well as the best ways to reach potential consumers. In order to know the potential market they must identify the characteristics of individuals likely to be interested in that particular Service, establish how many such individuals there are, as well as study how these people behave and respond to particular advertising approaches. In short, demographic characteristics as well as behaviour patterns are essential to niche marketing.

Market segmentation and targeting for services are the same as those for manufactured goods. There are differences, however. The most powerful involves the need for **compatibility in market segments.** Service provider must therefore recognise the need to choose compatible segments or to ensure that incompatible segments are not receiving service at the same time. One more factor to be taken into consideration is that service provider has the better ability to customise service offerings than manufacturing firms have. Consequently, a service marketer can choose a broader set of segments or sub segments to service than can manufacture firms, particularly if they can keep these segments separate.

Two broad categories of variables are useful in describing the difference between the segments. The first have to do with user characteristics-the second, with usage behaviour.

User characteristics may vary from one person to another, reflecting demographic (For instance, age, income And education) geographic location, and psychographic (the attitude, values lifestyle and opinions of decision makers and users). E.g. Specific benefit that individual and corporate purchasers seek from particular services.

Usage behaviour relates to how a service is purchased, delivered and used. Among such variables are when and where consumption takes place, the quantities consumed (heavy users), frequency and purpose of use, the occasion under which consumption takes place (occasion segmentation-grouping people according to product use occasion), e.g. Airline passenger flying for business, pleasure or emergency reasons**.**

Characteristics of Segmentation

1. It is a customer oriented Philosophy.
2. Since services marketing is highly customer oriented (more than manufacturing firms) it offers wider scope to service providers to bring flexible compatibility in their segmentation.
3. Multi segment approach is easier. Within a same organisation different segments or clients can be served at different operational levels. E.g. Variety of rooms offered to different guests according to their affordability.
4. Proportion of tangibility and intangibility plays a significant role for segmentation.

Steps or Process for the selection of segments:

1. **Research:** Collecting responses, to research on needs, attitudes, behaviours, demographics.

2. **Analysis:** Identifying customer segments that appears similar.

3. **Segment Profiling:** Defining and describing demographic and other information useful for target marketing.

4. **Segment Sizing:** Estimating the size of each segment by percentage of population and revenue potential.

5. **Segment Selection:** Applying criteria and selecting most attractive segments.

6. **Reaching the Segments:** Developing strategies for reaching segments using various tools.

3.3 Segmentation Strategies

Segmentation of consumer markets become more complex or difficult. Three broad bases are conventionally used to segment consumer markets:

1. Customer-based segmentation.
2. Product-related segmentation
3. Competition-related segmentation

Customer-based segmentation can be divided into three major groups:

1. Geographic segmentation
2. Demographic segmentation
3. Psychographic segmentation

Geographic Segmentation

Geographic segmentation is the starting point of all market segmentation strategies. Common bases for geographic segmentation are metro and non-metro markets, urban, semi-urban and rural markets and any other intermediate classification. It can be divided into units such as countries, regions, states, cities, towns and neighborhoods. The reason for such segmentation is that consumers in a particular geographical location have identical tastes, preferences and consumption behaviour; and these are distinct from patterns in another location. A firm may decide to market different products or services in certain areas and not in other local variations.

The most distinctive location for classification is rural-urban and most of the companies have clearly differentiated strategies for urban and rural marketing, although, for many companies, rural marketing is more at a developmental stage. Even with introduction of TV, video and satellite TV, the distinction between rural and urban markets is not disappearing as fast as many had predicted and this will take its own time.

For locating ATM's, bank use geographic segmentation to decide on the location based on traffic flow and concentration of customer base in a pocket which has high usage frequency to reduce the load in the branch. The breakeven point for ATM in the Indian context is 250 transactions per day and where such volume are envisaged, the bank must allocate its resources to meet its objectives.

Demographic Segmentation

The most commonly used basis for market segmentation is demographic characteristics like age, gender, income, education, occupation, social class, family size, marital status, family life cycle, etc. These factors are used singly or in combination to segment the market.

Age is a major segmenting factor, which is also strategic. Based on the age factor, the market can have many useful segments:

1. Infants market   upto 1 year
2. Child market   1-11 years
3. Teens market   12-15 years
4. Adolescent market   16-19 years
5. Youth market   20-35 years
6. Middle market   36-50 years
7. Elders market   51-65 years
8. Senior citizens market   66 years onwards

Income is an important factor of segmenting because people in different income levels are likely to have different consumption patterns mostly because of income differences.

Gender is also another important segmenting factor. The male market for many products, particularly textiles, garment, cosmetics and toiletries is different from the female market.

Educational levels, occupational profiles, marital status, family size and structure are also used by many companies as an important criteria for segmentation.

In case of The Economic Times, the paper is being targeted to some of these age groups like Youth market the ET, Middle market with ET and ET bucks, and the Elders market with The Complete ET which also has a relationship to levels of income.

Bank of India has a special attractive interest rate scheme for doctors to buy equipments, hence it is segmenting on the basis of social class. A bank that develops equity credit line aimed at house owners with income more than Rs. 2,00,000/- is targeting income segment.

Demographic segmentation is used extensively in banking, tourism etc. Many tourism marketing efforts are built on demographic segmentation. For tours to Far East, Australia and New Zealand we are seeing Couple tours being marketed in rainy season with shopping as additional focus for the wife and sight-seeing for the husband. The families aspect of demographic has always been significant and there has been a few that you can determine people's desires and needs in relation to their position in the 'Family Life-Cycle'. Children mature more quickly now and are becoming more independent of their parents at an early age. Many people never become part of a couple and many couples now do not have children. A significant proportion of families are single-parent families with different needs from the traditional two-parent family. The nuclear family is the model which is gradually phasing out joint family.

Youths have a tendency to visit in groups, whose members are often not related and who visit attractions either as friends or as members of educational party. There are also senior citizens, who visit attractions as part of travel tours, rather than in family groups especially to holy destinations.

Marketers have generally focused on demographic variables such as age, gender and family situation, but opportunities exist for variables such as race, religion, language and nationality.

Psychographic Segmentation

Many-a-times, it has been found that consumers with the same demographic characteristics may act in a different manner in making purchase decisions. This is because, personality and life style differences are referred to as psychographic variables. Many marketers therefore, use psychographic variables to segment their markets. In case of the Pune Golf Club they have segmented the market for leisure and health loving people on the basis of life style.

A women's magazine "Savvy" has used psychographic variables to segment its market and distance itself from Femina. The Saavy woman is identified as the modern, highly liberated, independent, strong woman as compared to the Femina's the woman of substance.

Life Style

Psychographic segmentation is the process of dividing markets into segments on the basis of consumer life styles, personality or values. It is a technique that classifies life styles by investigating how people live, what interests them and what they like, their activities, interests and opinions.

ICICI Bank identifies the MBA students as young professionals on fast track and hence offers its credit cards with no joining fees at campuses so as to catch this youth with similar lifestyle.

Study reveals that regionwise the east emerged as liberal, most modern and socially integrated, the west as self indulgent and confident, the south as conservative and introverted, the north as hospitable and most dominating.

Marketers use the results of such studies to understand consumer life styles and how product or service fits within and what type of promotional themes might appeal to the life style segment. Interestingly people's lifestyle influence all their decisions as consumers, as they try to develop a lifestyle which reflects their idea of how they want to be seen and which reinforces the way they see themselves.

Customer's decisions on which tourist spot to go are just as much part of this as the clothes they buy, car they drive and the newspapers they read and internet they access. Some key changes in lifestyle types are health and environment segments.

Marketers have to position their organisation or its offerings suiting the life styles of customers. If the offering is health club or fitness centre or sport centre you have to target health conscious members of the segment. Many people are now shifting their life style very fast. The advertisements whether related to product or services are focusing on this. Fashion marketers rely heavily on life style marketing.

Social Class

Social class is a status ranking by which groups and individuals are classified on the basis of esteem and prestige. It is a division of or ranking within, society based education, occupation and type of neighbourhood. Here the income is not the classification factor. Social class can be categorised as the upper class, the upper middle class, the lower-middle class, the upper-lower class, and lower-lower class on the basis of income.

A young lawyer's monthly income may be equal to that of a middle aged professor, but they may have different family backgrounds, tastes, aspirations and outlook.

Personality

Personality is an aggregate total of an individual's internal psychological traits that make the person unique. 'Personality type' determines how consumers can be grouped. Key personality traits are self confidence, dominant, autonomy, sociability, adaptability and emotional stability. Individual can be segmented on the basis of shared personality traits which influence decisions of the consumers in relation to service offerings.

One kind of grouping may be adventurous people going for snow-trekking, skating and they are fun loving and risk taking.

The segmentation based on personality type gives enough information about personality traits of an individual and how they take a decision. But the market should also give due consideration to the fact that it is not always an individual who takes a decision, but opts to go along with decision of others in group settings.

The Market Research Society of India has suggested an important empirical basis for segmenting the Indian consumers. According to them, the consumption behaviour of consumers is determined by their social and economic class. The social class is determined by the occupation of the earning member of the family and the economic class by income. As per the study, there are socio-economic groups of consumers in the Indian market which are detailed as below:

1. Graduates, White Collared workers and professionals.
2. High School or 40% graduates with occupation as clerk /shopkeeper.
3. Skilled workers, clerks and salespersons with graduations.
4. Skilled workers, clerks and salespersons with high school qualification.
5. Unskilled labour.

Consumer-based market classification is the more commonly used basis for segmentation. But a marketer can also make product-related segments and competition-based or customer loyalty-based segments for targeting the customer groups more effectively.

Product-related segmentation can be of three forms:

A. Volume segmentation
B. Benefit segmentation
C. Use situation segmentation

Volume Segmentation

Marketers have attempted to segment the customers based on usage frequency, value and brand loyalty. The users can be segmented on the basis of volume as,

(i) Heavy users
(ii) Medium users
(iii) Light users

Differentiation between the categories of users is based on benchmark volume determined for each segment.

Heavy user segment is a consumer group that accounts for a large proportion of the sales relative to size of the market. In many businesses, 20% customers generate 80% of sales. It is crucial to concentrate on retaining these customers, who make up for heavy half for the brand. Moreover the strategy on how to rope the competition heavy, half users to switch their brand must be a priority.

For the light users the approach should be caring as well as some incentives must be given to ensure that their usage frequency increases to progressively shift the category.

Benefit Segmentation

The marketer identifies the benefits which a customer looks at while buying a product. The buyers can be classified into groups according to the benefits they seek. Consumers vary considerably in the benefits that they seek from the same product.

ICICI Bank in Pune, recently introduced a scheme for the lowest rate of home loan, booking on spot in approved properties of Builders in a loan mela. The scheme met with success as 1600 customers with home loans worth Rs.175 Crores got their loans sanctioned within four days. The benefits derived by the customers were speed and convenience.

Yahoo is not charging any fees-joining or yearly subscription to have a large e-mail client base.

In life insurance, LIC gave high assured returns and a lot of individuals opted for the same last year. A bank may offer the benefit of 'Happy hours on Sunday' for the working class.

For tax saving bonds, it is observed that every year an early bird incentive is given to give more returns to investors flushed with funds.

Competition-based segmentation is loyalty-based segmentation. As we know, customer loyalty is an important factor for determining the competitive position of a firm. This can also be used as a basis for segmenting the market for evolving a marketing strategy. Based on loyalty, we can have three segments:

(i) Hard core loyals-commonly seen among newspaper readers, cigarette smokers and tea drinkers;

(ii) Soft core loyalists-loyal to two or three brands in a product group; and

(iii) Switchers-customers who do not stick to a particular brand.

The various bases of segmentation are not mutually exclusive and in many cases they help each other in segmenting and market targeting. In case of a particular market, it can be segmented initially by an auto finance firm for 150 cc and above motor cycles, first basis of segmentation is geographic - metro, urban, rural; then segmented on a psychographic basis, based on lifestyles of males and targeting can be done on the basis of benefit segmentation with Zero percent finance scheme and two additional free service coupons by the dealer.

It should be consistent with the firm's goal. Kesari Travels, a tourism firm, catering to families / groups in international tours cannot suddenly target individuals effectively.

A firm should look for markets that are consistent with the resources. A computer hardware firm cannot suddenly start catering to software in ERP Package where it has no skillsets available.

A firm should generate not only volumes but also profits. A firm should look for a target market where the number and size of competition is small.

Issues in Segmentation

1. There can be many more bases or ways depending on the market situation. Segments keep evolving and changing overtime, the marketer has to continuously look for new segments or sub-segments.

2. Another challenge lies in ensuring that a particular segment is operationally attractive. This can be gauged from the following:

- **Accessible:** The segment can be reached and serviced with no constraints, controls or regulations.
- **Measurable:** The size and characteristics of the segment should be measurable.
- **Differentiable:** The segment should be conceptually distinguishable and this should be spelt out.
- **Profitable:** It should be profit making segment with good growth rate.

3. There are a number of behavioural parameters which dilute the accessibility or measurability or viability of a segment because of the ability or the intention to pay. In auto financing, we have seen that willful defaulters are those, who have the ability but are not willing to pay because they want their car seized as they know it is very difficult as yet in our country, for the finance company to recover the money.

4. Exposure levels of different consumer groups to the particular brand would determine the actual target group.

5. Cultural factors can also become differentiators or inhibitors for particular brands of products. If all or some of these factors come into play, the original or planned segmentation may get diluted to a large extent and the final operative segment can be different.

6. Depending on the product or brand, a multidimensional segmenting can be done, to give proper representation to all key variables or factors including the behavioural or propensity factors.

Market Targeting Strategies

The formulation of a market targeting strategy involves three steps:

(a) Evaluating the market segments

(b) Selecting the market segments

(c) Deciding the targeting strategy

For evaluating various market segments, a company has to consider two factors: the attractiveness of the segment coupled with the company's objectives and resources. The attractiveness of the segment can be determined by the firm based on size, accessibility and/or profitability. Based on these criteria, ranking is done and only the top ranked segments are retained for targeting and implementation.

The firm should consider its financial as well as managerial resources and also its long-term objectives. A segment may be attractive if the Internal Rate of Return is attractive. Once the evaluation of the segment is completed, the company is better equipped to decide which segments to target and draws out appropriate targeting strategies.

Six different patterns of market selection and targeting are as follows:

(a) **Single Segment Concentration:** The company selects a single segment and concentrates on that.

(b) **Product Specialisation:** A company specialises in marketing a single product which it sells to several segments. This is a good strategy with brand equity. This helps the company to build a strong market reputation in a particular product area.

(c) **Market Specialisation:** The company concentrates on serving many product needs of a particular customer group-a company selling a range of equipments / gadgets to the same laboratories will include microscopes, oscilloscopes, burners, chemical flasks etc.

(d) **Product Market Specialisation:** The company selects a number of segments for a number of products. The multi-segment, multi-product strategy gives the company the advantage of diversifying or diffusing its marketing risks. This is a common targeting strategy used by software training firms.

(e) **Full Market Coverage:** The company aims to serve all customer groups with all the products they might need. In reality, only very large companies can undertake a full market coverage strategy. Education by institutions, which have now become Deemed Universities have used this strategy.

(f) Kotler suggests four more considerations for evaluating and selecting market segments; (i) ethical choice of target market; (ii) segment interelationships and super segments; (iii) segment-by-segment invasion; and (iv) inter-segment cooperation.

In ethical market targeting, the issue is not so much as to who is targeted, but how and for what. Market targeting sometimes generates controversy because marketers take undue advantage of certain vulnerable groups such as children to promote potentially harmful products. McDonald's and other chains have invited criticism for pitching their high-fat, salt-laden food to consumers. Ethical marketing calls for segmentation and targeting that serve, not just the markets of the company, but also the social interests of those targeted.

If a company is targeting more than one segment, it should pay attention to segment interrelationships in terms of cost, product, performance, etc., to achieve certain economies. Companies should also try to identify and target super segments rather than operate in isolated segments. Arthur Andersen, like most other public accounting firms, operates three divisions: auditing, taxes and business consulting. The auditing staff are not keen and dislike giving leads to the consulting staff for fear that clients may change auditors, if they do a poor job.

Super segment is a set of segments sharing some exploitable similarity. Mega marketing involves strategic coordination of economic, psychological, political and public relations skills to gain the cooperation of a number of parties in order to enter and/or operate in a given market.

Approaches to Target Market

Service providers use any one of the following strategies to reach its target market:

1. **Undifferentiated Marketing:** A firm appeals to the whole market with one basic marketing strategy intended to reach the masses by using mass media.
2. **Differentiated Marketing:** A firm operates simultaneously in several market segments. It designs products to appeal to a specific segment and the marketing strategy is tailored to each segment to get maximum result with suitable media.
3. **Concentrated Marketing:** A firm focuses on a target market segment with a tailor - made marketing strategy for results with niche media.

Using Segmentation in Customer Retention

Segmentation is commonly used by organisations to improve their customer retention programmes and help to ensure that they are:

➤ Focused on retaining their most profitable customers.
➤ Employing those tactics most likely to retain these customers.

The basic approach to retention-based segmentation is that a company tags each of its active customers with 3 values:

Tag #1: Is this customer at high risk of cancelling the company's service? (Or becoming a non-user)

One of the most common indicators of high-risk customers is a drop off in usage of the company's service. For example, in the credit card industry this could be signaled through a customer's decline in spending on his card.

Tag #2: Is this customer worth retaining?

This determination boils down to whether the post-retention profit generated from the customer is predicted to be greater than the cost incurred to retain the customer.

Tag #3: What retention tactics should be used to retain this customer?

For customers who are deemed "save-worthy", it's essential for the company to know which save tactics are most likely to be successful. Tactics commonly used range from providing "special" customer discounts to sending customers communications that reinforce the value proposition of the given service.

Advantages of Market segmentation

1. More precise definition of market.
2. Maximum customer satisfaction
3. An aid to formulate effective marketing strategies.
4. Improved Profitability.
5. Optimum use of productive resources.
6. Benefits of niche marketing competitiveness.
7. Benefits of multi segment approach.

3.4 Positioning

Positioning is a process that companies use in business marketing to create an image in the mind of the consumer. With all of the media and the mass marketing we have in today's society, everyone is over powered with advertising messages. We have advertisements on the Internet, television, stores and even before a movie at the theatre. With the correct positioning a company can bring its product to the front of the consumers mind and make their product a stand out brand.

Jack Trout and Al Ries are two men who brought the positioning process to the forefront of the marketing world in the early 1970's. They said that the idea of positioning *"was to occupy a unique position in the consumer's mind to cut through all of the confusion caused by brand proliferation and advertising clutter."*

This "positioning" is part of an over-all marketing strategy in which the marketing specialists choose who they want to target for their product and then "position" their product to that market. There are many different types of strategies for this style of advertising. "There are broad, price segment, usage segment, geographical segments, psychological segments and channel distribution marketing strategies."

"To succeed in our over-communicated society, a company must create a position in the prospects mind, a position that takes into consideration not only a company's own strength and weaknesses, but those of its competitors as well."

Al Reis And Jack Trout

"Positioning is the act of designing the company's product and image so that they occupy a meaningful and distinct competitive position in the target consumer's mind".

Philip Kotler

Positioning is the act of communicating company's offer so that it occupies a distinct and valued place in the customers mind.

Positioning is not what you do to a product. But what you do to the mind of the prospect. In general understanding positioning and differentiation can be mixed but it can be differentiated. Differentiation is actually making technical and physical change in the offering. Positioning, however, is very much related to perception. Trying to fit in the same product with different perception is positioning. It is all about creating an image of the same product in a different manner, may be in the same segment.

Positioning is simply acquiring a place in the mind of the customer, which is also called as "Battle for my mind".

Positioning the Service

The idea of positioning relates to the way consumers perceive and evaluate the service being provided. Specially, it relates to the way in which a consumer ranks the features and attributes of services against those of the competitors. The way in which service provider differentiates their offering impacts on its positioning in the customers mind. Different attributes of a service reflects different values, which can be attached to that service in the consumer's perception. E.g. high price can reflect an idea of quality or luxury when other features also reflect these values.

Positioning is very important in services marketing as it involves careful tailoring of service offering to the needs of the target market, which underpins marketing success.

Developing the Value Proposition

No company can be good at everything. First, companies have limited funds and must decide where to concentrate them. Second, choosing to be good at one thing may reduce the possibility of being good at some thing else.

Choosing a broad Positioning

Professor Michael Porter, in his competitive strategy, proposed three broad alternatives. Broad positioning revolves around the alternatives; like the business unit should focus on being the product differentiator, the low cost leader or niches. He reiterates that if they tried to be good in all three ways, but not superior in any way, they would lose out to firms that would be superior in one way. This frame work is based on the notion that in every market there are three types of customers. Some customers favour the firm that is advancing the technological frontier (Product leadership). Another customer group does not need the latest product but wants highly reliable and dependable performance (operational excellence). A final customer group prefers the form that is most responsive and flexible in meeting individual needs (customer intimacy)

Choosing a specific positioning

Companies need to go beyond positioning to express a more concrete benefit and reason to buy. Many companies advertise a *single major benefit positioning,* drawing from such possibilities as: best quality, best performance, most reliable, most durable, safest, fastest, convenient and so on.

Services can be positioned in six different ways. They can be positioned by service attributes, user application, price/quality relationship, service class, service user or competitor. Price quality relationship can also be used for positioning a firm. E.g. Air indigo positions itself as a low fair airline. In hotels, Shangri La positions itself at the high end of price quality relationship. The steps in determining a positioning strategy are:

1. Identify the competition.
2. Assess consumer perception of each firm in the industry.

3. Determine the position of each firm

4. Analyse consumer preference.

5. Make a position decision.

6. Develop a strategy to implement the new position or to reinforce the current position.

Benefits/Importance of Positioning

1. To make the entire organisation market oriented.

2. To cope with market changes.

3. To meet the expectation of buyers.

4. To promote consumer's goodwill and loyalty.

5. To win attention and interest of consumers.

6. To communicate new and varied features added later on.

7. It improves competitive strength.

3.5 Differentiation

A sustainable competitive advantage is built on firms providing either superior resources or distinctive skill. Sustainable competitive advantage can be achieved through a unique or different operational position. Service companies are unique- marketing and managing an intangible experience is different. Service companies must differentiate their business and the benefits customer receive, bring out the intangible aspects of the service experience lead their company into a different direction from the competitors by addressing new, intense, unmet customer needs and adopt market leadership strategies that get service companies differentiated.

To gain a competitive advantage, a company should differentiate itself from its competitors based on the attributes that are important, distinct, communicable, superior, pre-emptive, affordable and profitable to the customers. Further, companies should understand the importance of positioning in developing a marketing strategy and its influence on the profit margins of a particular company.

In business terms, to differentiate means to create a benefit that customers perceive as being of greater value to them than what they can get elsewhere. It's not enough for you to be different – a potential customer has to take note of the difference and must feel that the difference somehow fits their need better. (Other words that mean virtually the same thing: Competitive Advantage; Unique Selling Proposition; or Value Proposition.)   Unique   Value Proposition (UVP) is customer focused, differentiation of services is product focused.

In sales and marketing, to introduce a service to a potential customer most effectively, one has to create a perception of "differential advantage". That means one has to describe it in a way that;

1. Differentiates it from others,

2. Builds positive perception of value. Part (1) is differentiation of services, part (2) is unique value proposition. Rolling (1) and (2) together effectively in a word or phrase is what branding is all about.

An UVP is essentially a description or encapsulation of the value to the customer of doing business with the company rather than anyone else. The focus is on the value of the benefits that the company brings to that customer's situation, rather than on the benefits themselves. Differentiation of services is more about the branding of that UVP. If the UVP is the unique "WHAT" that my customers gain from this, differentiation of services is the unique "HOW" my services deliver that "what". The focus is on the features and benefits of the SERVICE itself that are different from the features/benefits offered by competing products. And it is the "personality" that you want your product/service to be remembered for. The label or tag or mental short-cut that you associate with your product (the brand, your name) that makes it stand out from others in the field.

A company can use differentiation to attract more customers. Once they have momentum, differentiation allows the company to charge a higher price because they are delivering more value to their customers.

The various methods of differentiating businesses fall into four general categories:

➢ Price Differentiation

➢ Focus Differentiation

➢ Product/Service Differentiation

➢ Customer Service Differentiation

In marketing, product differentiation is the modification of a product to make it more attractive to the target market. This involves differentiating it from competitors' products as well as your own product offerings.

The changes are usually minor; they can be merely a change in packaging or also include a change in advertising theme. The physical product need not change, but it could. The major sources of product differentiation are as follows. Advertising, generally speaking, is the promotion of goods, services, companies and ideas, usually performed by an identified sponsor.

➢ Differences in quality or design among output (product).

➢ Ignorance of buyers regarding the essential characteristics and qualities of goods they are purchasing.

➢ Pervasive sales promotion activities of sellers and , in particular, advertising.

➢ Possibility of developing significant product differentiation through advertising is greatly enhanced for so called "gift goods" or "prestige goods".

➢ Differentiation in the locations of sellers of the same good. Where product fills no technical function, but rather, can satisfy many different sort of personal needs or uses, psychic or physical.

The objective of this strategy is to develop a position that potential customers will see as unique. If the target market sees a product as different from the competitors', the company will have more flexibility in developing its marketing mix. A successful product differentiation strategy will move the product from competing based primarily on price to competing on non-price factors (such as product characteristics, distribution strategy, or promotional variables).

Differentiation has been shown to impact a company's performance positively both theoretically and empirically. Differentiation primarily impacts performance through two mechanisms:

➢ **Reduced price sensitivity:** Consumers may become willing to pay a premium price for the differentiating factor/s.

➢ **Reducing directness of competition:** As the product becomes more different, Categorisation becomes more difficult and hence draws fewer comparisons with its competition.

While most people would say that the implication of differentiation is the possibility of charging a price premium, this is a gross simplification. Customers, if they value the firm's offer will be less sensitive to aspects of competing offers, and price may not be one of these aspects. Differentiation makes customers in a given segment have a lower sensitivity to other features (non price) of the product

The disadvantage of this repositioning is that it usually requires large advertising and production expenditures.

Why Differentiate?

The concept of being unique or different is far more important today than it was ten years ago. The key to successful marketing and competing is differentiation.

Hypercompetition is a key feature of the new economy. What used to be national markets with local companies competing for business has now become a global market with everyone competing for everyone's business everywhere. With the enormous competition markets today are driven by choice - targeted customers have too many choices, all of which can be fulfilled instantly. Choosing among multiple options is always based on differences, implicit or explicit, so one ought to differentiate in order to give the customer a reason to chose a product or service. Thus, "differentiation is one of the most important strategic and tactical activities in which companies must constantly engage. It is not discretionary".

Means of Differentiation

In order to be different, the intangible market should be developing and delivering intangibles that make the service unique which is a critical challenge for service companies.

1. **Product:** Features, performance, conformance, durability, reliability, reparability, style and design.
2. **Service:** Delivery, installation, customer training, consulting and repair.
3. **Personnel:** Competence, courtesy, credibility, reliability, responsiveness and communication skill.
4. **Image:** Symbol, return and audio/video media, atmosphere and event.

The Concept of Differentiation

As explained above differentiation is a marketing process that showcases the differences between products. Differentiation looks to make a product more attractive by contrasting its unique qualities with other competing products. Successful differentiation creates a competitive advantage for the seller, as customers view these products as unique or superior.

Differentiation can be achieved in many ways. It may be as simple as packaging the goods in a creative way or as elaborate as incorporating new functional features. Sometimes differentiation does not involve changing the product at all, but creating a new advertising campaign or other sales promotions instead.

Offered under different brands by competing firms, products fulfilling the same need typically do not have identical features. The differentiation of goods along key features and minor details is an important strategy for firms to defend their price from levelling down to the bottom part of the price spectrum.

Within firms, product differentiation is the way multi-product firms build their own supplied products' range.

At market level, differentiation is the way through which the quality of goods is improved over time thanks to innovation. Launching new goods with entirely new performances is a radical change, often leading to changes in market shares and industry structures.

In an evolutionary sense, differentiation is a strategy to adapt to a moving environment and its social groups.

With differentiation, each producer gains a bit of market control and is able to charge a slightly (or even a significantly) higher price for their product. While some product differences are only in the minds of the buyers, others are very real and let consumers satisfy the hidden nooks and crannies of their desires. In fact, product differentiation adds the variety that spices up the lives of consumers. Product differentiation is usually achieved through advertising.

Three Differences:

Differentiation is usually achieved in one of three ways: (1) physical differences, (2) perceived differences, (3) support services.

> **Physical Differences:** Physical differences arise when the product of one firm is physically different from the product of other firms. These differences can exist due to materials used, chemical composition, shape, size, taste or colour.
>
> For example the Fleet Foot 30 running shoe produced by the Master Foot Company in USA. The Fleet Foot 30 has ankle stabilizers and an extra thick cushioned insole. Other running shoes, such as the OmniFast 9000 sold by OmniRun lack both of these features, but it is available in five different colour schemes and uses Velcro fasteners rather than shoestrings.

> **Perceived Differences:** Product differentiation can also result from differences perceived by buyers, even though no physical differences exist. Such perceived differences are usually accomplished through advertising, especially by establishing brand names. Brand names, in fact, are a common way to create the perception of differences among products, even if none physically exist.
>
> However, as far as a demand is concerned, perceived differences work just as well as physical differences. It matters not whether the differences are real or perceived, so long as buyers are willing to pay different prices.

> **Support Services:** Products that are physically identical and perceived to be identical can also be differentiated by support services. This is quite common in retail trade. One store offers "service with a smile," while another provides convenient parking, and a third has a 90-day money back guarantee. Even though the products are identical, differences exist in the "overall package" of product and support services.

Vertical differentiation

Vertical differentiation occurs in a market where the several goods that are present can be ordered according to their objective quality from the highest to the lowest. It's possible to say in this case that one good is "better" than another.

Vertical differentiation can be obtained:

> Along one decisive feature;

> Along a few features, each of which has a wide possible range of (continuous or discrete) values;

> Across a large number of features, each of which has only a presence/absence "flag".

In the second and third cases, it is possible to find out a product that is better than another one according to one criteria but worse than it in respect to another feature.

Vertical differentiation is a property of the supplied goods but, as it is maybe needless to say, the perceived difference in quality by different consumer will play a crucial role in the purchase decisions.

In particular, potential consumers can have a biased perception of the features of the good (say because of advertising or social pressure).

When evaluating a real market, a good starting point is a top-down grid of interpretation, we shall present in 3 segments.

Class	Price	Crucial feature
Low	Low	The price is low, the product simply works
Middle	Middle	Use of the good is comfortable. Most people use it. Mass market brand.
High	High	Quality, exclusivity, durability (= low life-long price),

To this basic classification, one should add two intermediate classes:

Class	Price	Crucial feature
Middle-low	Low	The cheapest nation-wide brand
Middle-high	Middle	The cheapest product of high quality

Two extreme classes should finally be added:

Class	Price	Crucial feature
Extremely low	Low	It usually does not work, it does not last, and it has important defects
Extremely High	High	Exclusivity, non practical, status symbol

In this way, one can vertically position different brands and product versions, also using clues from advertising campaigns.

If one compares widely different goods fulfilling the same (highly-relevant) need, one may distinguish at the extreme of one's spectrum necessity goods and at the other luxury goods. In other cases, what makes this difference is, instead, the nature of the need fulfilled.

As a general rule, better products have a higher price, both because of higher production costs (more noble materials, longer production, more selective tests for throughput,...) and bigger expected advantages for clients, partly reflected in higher margins.

Thus, the quality-price relationship is typically upwards sloped. This means that consumers without their own opinion or the capability of directly judging quality may rely on the price to infer quality. They will prefer to pay a higher price because they expect quality to be better.

This important flaw in knowledge and information processing capability - an instance of bounded rationality - can be purposefully exploited by the seller, with the result that not all highly priced products are of good quality.

Through this mechanism, the demand curve - that in the neoclassical model - is always downward sloped, can instead turn out to be in the opposite direction.

Horizontal differentiation

When products are different according to features that can't be ordered, a horizontal differentiation emerges in the market.

A typical example is the ice-cream offered in different tastes. Chocolate is lot "better" than lemon.

Horizontal differentiation can be linked to differentiation in colours (different colour version for the same good), in styles (e.g. modern / antique), in tastes.

This does not prevent specific consumers to have a stable preference for one or the other version, since you should always distinguish what belongs to the supply structure and what is due to consumers' subjectivity.

It is quite common that, in horizontal differentiation, the supplier of many versions decide a unique price for all of them. Chocolate ice-creams cost as much as lemon ones.

When consumers don't have strong stable preferences, a rule of behaviour can be to change often the chosen good, looking for variety itself. An example is when you go to a fast food joint and ask for what you haven't eaten the previous time.

Fashion waves often emerge in horizontally-differentiated markets with imitation behaviours among consumers and specific styles going "in" and "out".

Impact on other variables

Differentiated versions of a good can have widely different costs of production. Upstream, they may be produced using different raw materials and semi-manufactured parts, thus referring to diverse suppliers and their relative market power. Import of exotic substances can be the effect of the attempt to introduce new goods on the market (think for instance to cosmetics).

Downstream, the supply of different and better goods allows for deeper fulfilment of consumption needs, for production processes at higher productivity as well as for the opening of export opportunities to other countries.

For the firms introducing the new version of the product, the expected results are mainly improvements of profits (thanks to lower elasticity of consumption to price and higher mark-up on costs), sales, and market shares.

For the consumer, product differentiation can increase the satisfaction from its consumption. At the same time, he will be confronted with a wider spectrum of prices. When faced with the burgeoning choice spectrum at supermarket premises among product varieties of the same category, the consumer can react with several rules of selection; retailers take them into account to assure profits and profitability, as you can experiment with this spreadsheet.

At the same time, product differentiation can lead to the exploration of the product space by disloyal customers, who use the repurchase occasions to try new versions.

A product differentiation strategy must meet the VRIO criteria...

➤ Is it *Valuable*?

➤ Is it *Rare*?

➤ Is it costly to *Imitate*

➤ Is the firm *Organised* to exploit it?

Questions for Discussion

1. What is market segmentation?
2. What are the segmentation strategies?
3. What is positioning?
4. What is differentiation?
5. Explain vertical and horizontal differentiation.

■■■

Chapter **4**...

Services Marketing Mix

Contents ...

4.1 Introduction

The marketing mix is probably the most famous marketing term. Its elements are the basic, tactical components of a marketing plan. Also known as the Four P's, the marketing mix elements are price, place, product, and promotion. The concept is simple like another common mix - a cake mix. All cakes contain eggs, milk, flour, and sugar. However, one can alter the final cake by altering the amounts of mix elements contained in it.

It is the same with the marketing mix. The offer one makes to the customer can be altered by varying the mix elements. So for a high profile brand, one can increase the focus on promotion and desensitise the weight given to price. Another way to think about the marketing mix is to use the image of an artist's palette. The marketer mixes the prime colours (mix elements) in different quantities to deliver a particular final colour. Every hand painted picture is original in some way, as is every marketing mix.

The term was coined by Neil H. Borden in his article The Concept of the Marketing Mix in 1965. The major difference in the services marketing versus regular marketing mix is that apart from the traditional "4 P's," Product, Price, Place, Promotion, there are three additional "P's" consisting of People, Physical evidence, and Process. Services marketing also includes the servicewomen referring to but not limited to the aesthetic appearance of the business from the outside, the inside, and the general appearance of the employees themselves.

All principles of marketing apply to Services

By their very nature, services impact customers more directly than products do. A customer walks into a restaurant and realises immediately whether the ambience is pleasant or not. Few minutes into the facility, and most customers have already decided whether they have the right choice of the service provider or not. Some of the services are more urgently needed than products. And again due to its very nature, service providers come in more frequent and intimate contact with customers, and therefore providers have more opportunities to please customers, or put them off. For these reasons marketing of services has become more deliberate and to be essential.

A service provider has to carefully audit his resources and competencies, and then conduct market research to locate the segment which can serve best. And when it comes to positioning, the provider for long periods has more chances of discovering discrepancies and inconsistencies in the provider's positioning plank and also most of them are very clear about the quality of service that they want. They walk into the premises expecting a certain level of service and are disappointed if these expectations are not met, because such expectations are very precise. So positioning of services has to be razor sharp.

Services are more intractable than products because they come in various shades and hues. The provider has to define his service very precisely and also design the appropriate service-product mix. The basic services, like eating at a restaurant, is just one part of the entire service offering. The ambience, the music and the behaviour of the employees are other vital components of the service. And decisions have to be made very precisely as to how and in what degree will the ancillary elements be incorporated into the main service.

Representing services in promotional methods like advertising is extremely challenging due to its intangible and variable nature.

Services need more creativity and focus to get the positioning plank depicted accurately. Service providers are in frequent touch with customers. A doctor has to be good at his primary task and he also has to be a good marketer, besides his ability to cure. The employees of service industry come in contact with customers frequently, who make them important in promotion and brand building exercise of the company. The service provider has to be an expert both in operations and marketing.

The same basic service, like surgery, can be provided in vastly different service facilities offering different levels of amenities and luxuries. Service offerings lend themselves to differentiation easily and the same basic service can be combined with other auxiliary services and priced differently. The service provider has huge price flexibility and charging the right price becomes an important decision.

The same service can be delivered in various ways. With a proliferation of new technologies, the different ways that a service can be availed is only increasing. A customer can go to the bank and withdraw money, he can use ATM to do the same job, he can use phone, or engage in internet banking. Even medical services will see a revolution with the establishment of new channels of delivery. Even a critical patient can stay at home, the equipments attached to their bodies would transmit vital information about the functioning of their organs to doctors in hospital who can prescribe suitable remedies.

Marketing mix conveys the positioning of a service or a product. In case of services all the 4 Ps are very flexible, i.e. many number of combination of the 4Ps are possible to arrive at a marketing mix. But the segmentation criteria has to be very well defined and the positioning has to be very sharp, because a customer is impacted instantly and very perceptibly as soon as he comes into contact with a service provider or enters a service facility. Service marketers face tremendous challenges in getting the marketing mix right to be able to convey their positioning plank because the marketing mix is flexible but the positioning has to be very pointed.

The marketer carefully plans these factors in an attempt to conceive the customers to buy their products. These are the basic ingredients of the marketing mix, which we will be considering in this unit.

Although the elements of marketing mix are detailed individually, like individual music score for each instrument of the orchestra, it is their service combination and right blend that skill of the marketing professional should show. If the organisation is not customer oriented, marketing will have only limited effect over most of the mix elements.

Some Facts about Services Marketing Mix

- Concept marketing mix was first coined by Neil Borden in his Article in 1962.
- Companies marketing mix as the basis of designing strategy of sketching marketing plan.
- Traditionally – Product, Price, Place and Promotion are 4 elements of a mix.
- An organisation should analyse which element is important at a given point of time. (hotel-focus on promotion during peak demand and on pricing in off season)
- Four P's fall short while designing marketing strategy for services three more P's – People, Process and Physical evidence have been added.

4.2 Introduction to the 7P's of the Services Marketing Mix

INADEQUACY OF FOUR P'S

- Product involves only tangible aspects.
- Services are produced and consumed simultaneously—hence promotion before buying not possible.
- If services are provided by public sector units-prices are standardised, control over prices of private sector units.
- Customer's participation in production of services goes unnoticed.
- Perceiving quality standards of services is very difficult.
- Above problems have led to addition of three more P's — People, Process, Physical evidence.

In order for any business to sell its products and services as successfully as possible, one needs to look at what products are being sold in detail to ensure they will be attractive and needed; the price to ensure it is not too cheap or too expensive; where it is best to distribute the product; and finally, how can interest and awareness for the products be created. All these elements need to be targeted at the right people at the right time. In order for your business to tackle this correctly, you need to get the right type of mix (marketing mix), the mix should include four main elements: Product, Price, Place and Promotion, by examining each carefully and adapting them to your customer's needs, you will continue to produce and needed products and services

One who buys a service offering probably takes the decision.

A way to address the challenges of services marketing is to think creatively about the marketing mix by expanded marketing mix for services.

Traditional Marketing Mix

One of the most basic concepts in marketing is the marketing mix elements, an organisation controls, that can be used to satisfy or communicate with customers. The traditional marketing mix is composed of the four P's: Product, Price, Place and Promotion. These elements are the core decision variables in any marketing plan. The notion of a mix implies that all of the variables are interrelated and depend on each other to some extent. Further, the marketing mix implies that there is an optimal mix of the four factors for a given market segment at a given point in time.

Careful management of these 4 P's will, clearly, also be essential to the successful marketing of services. However, the strategies for the four P's require some modifications when applied to services. For example, traditionally promotion is thought of as involving decisions related to sales, advertising, sales promotions, and publicity. In services, these factors are also important, but because services are produced and consumed simultaneously, service delivery people like delivery boys, clerks, conductors, doctors, cleaners, are involved in promotion of the service, even if their jobs are being carried out in terms of the operational function they perform. Pricing also becomes very complex in services where unit costs needed to calculate prices may be difficult to determine, and where the customer frequently uses price as a cue to quality.

1. **Products** are the means by which firms seek to satisfy consumer needs. A product in this sense is anything which the firm offers to potential customers, whether it be tangible or intangible. After initial hesitation, most marketers talk about an intangible service as a product. Thus bank accounts, insurance policies and holidays are frequently referred to as products including stars or even politicians are referred to as a product to be marketed. Product mix decisions facing a services marketer can be very different from those dealing with goods. Fundamentally pure services can only be defined using process descriptions rather than tangible descriptions of outcomes. Quality becomes a key element defining a product. Other elements of the product mix such as design, reliability, brand image, and product range may sound familiar to a goods marketer. There is a significant difference with goods in that new service developments cannot be protected by patent.

2. **Price:** Price mix decisions include strategic and tactical decisions about, the average level of prices to be charged, discount structures, terms of payment and the extent to which price discrimination between different groups of customers is to take place. Differences do however occur where the intangible nature of a service can mean that price in itself can become a very significant indicator of quality. The personal and non-transferable nature of many services presents additional opportunities for price discrimination within service markets, while the fact that many services are marketed by the public sector at a subsidized or no price can complicate price setting.

3. **Promotion:** The traditional promotion mix includes various methods of communicating the benefits of a service to potential consumers. The mix has been traditionally consisting of advertising, sales promotion, personal selling and public relations. The promotion of services often needs to place particular emphasis on increasing the apparent tangibility of a service. Also, in the case of services marketing, production personnel can themselves become an important element of the promotion mix.

4. **Place** refers to the ease of access which potential customers have to a service. Place decisions can involve physical location deCisios-6, decisions about which intermediaries to use in making a service accessible to a consumer and non-locational-decisions which are used to make services available. For pure services,

decisions about how to physically move a good are of little strategic relevance. However, most services involve movement of goods of some form. These can either be materials necessary to produce a service or the service can have as its whole purpose the movement of goods.

Expanded Mix For Services: Because services are usually produced and consumed simultaneously, customers are often present in the firm's location, interact directly with the firm's personnel and are actually part of the service production process. As services are intangible, customers will often be looking for any tangible cue to help them understand the nature of the service experience. These facts have led marketers to conclude that they can use additional variables to communicate with and satisfy their customers. For e.g. in the banks the design, layout and decor of the branch as well as the appearance and attitudes of its employees will influence customer perceptions and experiences.

Acknowledgment of the importance of these additional variables has led services marketers to adopt the concept of an expanded marketing mix for services to include Process, Physical evidence and People.

5. **People:** For most services, people are a vital element of the marketing mix. All of the participants who play a part in service delivery and thus influence the buyer's perceptions, namely, the firm's personnel, the customer and other customers in the service environment.

The participants in the delivery of a service provide cues to the customer regarding the nature of the service itself. How these people are dressed, their personal appearance, and their attitudes and behaviors all influence the customer's perceptions of the service. Gummeson calls everyone as a **'part-time marketer'** in that their actions have a direct effect on the output received by customers. In fact for services like consulting, counseling, training, teaching and other professional relationship based services, the provider is the service. In other cases, the contact person plays what appears to be a relatively small part in service delivery like a courier delivery boy. Even these providers may be the focal point of service encounters that can prove critical for the firm.

In many service situations, customers themselves can also influence service delivery thus affecting service quality and their own satisfaction. In case of weight loss customers it greatly affects the quality of service they receive when they either comply or don't comply with health regimens prescribed by the service provider.

Customers not only influence their own service outcomes, but they can influence other customers as well. In a classroom, customers students influence the quality of service received by others-either enhancing or detracting from other customers' experiences.

People management in improving quality people planning assumes greater importance within the service sector. This is especially true for those services where staff have a high level of contact with customers. For this reason, it is therefore essential that services firms clearly specify what is expected from personnel in their interaction with customers. To achieve these specified standard, methods of recruiting, training, motivating and rewarding staff are not personnel decisions but they are important marketing mix decisions. People planning within the marketing mix also involves developing a pattern of interaction between customers themselves, which can be very important where service consumption takes place in public. An important way in which a corporate executive will judge a club might be the kind of people who frequent it. An empty club may convey no atmosphere while a bubbly one may convey, that this is just the place. Marketers must also develop strategies for producing favourable interaction between its customers - for example by excluding certain groups and developing a physical environment which affects customers' behaviour.

Given the strong influence they can have on service quality and service delivery employees, the customer and other customers are included within the people element of the services marketing mix.

6. **Physical evidence:** The intangible nature of a service means that customers are unable to judge a service before it is consumed, increasing the risk inherent in a purchase decision. An important element of marketing planning is therefore to reduce this level of risk by offering tangible evidence of the nature of the service. At its simplest, a brochure can describe and give pictures of important elements of the service product - a pictorial evidence of students, faculty, infrastructure, in which the service is delivered and where the firm and students interact, and any tangible components that facilitate performance or communication of the service. The physical evidence of service includes all of the tangible representations of the service such as letterhead, business cards, report formats, signage etc. also tangablize service.

In some cases it includes the physical facility where the service is offered e.g. the retail bank branch facility while in telecommunication services, the physical facility may be irrelevant. In case of repairs, tangibles such as billing statements and appearance of the car after repair may be important indicators of quality.

Since consumers have little on which to judge the actual quality of service, they will rely on these cues or they rely on the cues provided by the people and the service process.

A clean and bright environment used in a service outlet can help reassure potential customers at the point where they make a service purchase decision. Hence, fast food and photo processing outlets use red and yellow colour schemes to convey an image of speedy service.

Physical evidence cues provide excellent opportunities for the firm to send consistent and strong messages regarding the organisation's purpose, the intended market segments and the nature of the service.

7. **Process:** The actual procedures, mechanisms, and flow of activities by which the service is delivered comprise the service delivery and operating systems. The actual delivery steps the customer experiences, or the operational flow of the service, will also provide customers with evidence on which to judge the service.

Some services are very complex, requiring the customer to follow a complicated and extensive series of actions to complete the process.

Highly bureaucratized services frequently follow this pattern, and the logic of the steps involved often escapes the customer. Another distinguishing characteristic of the process that can provide evidence to the customer is whether the service follows a production line, standardized approach or whether the process is an empowered or customized one. None of these characteristics of the service is inherently better or worse than another but these process characteristics are another form of evidence used by the consumer to judge service.

Processes are often of critical concern to consumers of high contact services where the consumers can be seen as a co-producer of the service. A customer of a fast food joint is affected by the manner in which staff serve them and the amount of waiting which is involved during the production process. The boundary between the producer and consumer in terms of the production functions like customer to collect their meal from a counter, or to deposit their own rubbish; it is not specific and varies as per service provider. Hence, with services, a clear distinction cannot be made between marketing and operations management.

Within the service sector, customer service is the total quality of the service as perceived by the customer. This element of the marketing mix cannot be isolated within a narrowly defined customer services department, but becomes a concern of all production personnel, both those directly employed by the organisation and those employed by suppliers. Managing the quality of the service offered to the customer becomes closely identified with policy on the related marketing mix elements of product design and personnel.

Expanded Marketing Mix For Services			
Product	**Place**	**Promotion**	**Price**
Product	Outlet Location	Advertising	Flexibility
Range	Accessibility	Personal selling	Level
Features	Channels	Sales promotion	Payment terms
Quality level	Coverage	Publicity	Differentiation
Accessories	Transportation	Public relations	Discounts
Warranties	Storage		Allowances
Branding	Managing channels		Quality/price
Service line			
After sales service			
People			
People	**Physical Evidence**	**Process**	
Employees	**External**	Policies	
Recruitment	Signage	Procedures	
Training	Parking	Mechanization	
Motivation	Environment	Employee discretion	
Reward	Location	Customer	
Team work	Noise level	involvement	
Appearance	Clean, cool air	Customer direction	
Interpersonal	Facilitating goods	Flow of activities	
behaviour	Tangible clues		
Customer contact	Brochure		
	Documents		
	Notices for dues		
	Statements		
	Reports		
Customers			
Education			
Training			

(**Source:** Derived from Booms, B H and Bitner, M J` Marketing Strategies and Organisation Structures for Service Firms')

Expanded Marketing Mix For Services		
7 P's of Services Marketing		Measurement
1. Product 2. Price 3. Promotion 4. Place 5. People	6. Physical evidence Customers 7. Process	Quality Satisfaction Loyalty Profitability
	Service Characteristic's Control	
Intangibility Inconsistency	Inseparability Inventory	 Ownership

To use this screen just mark the area where problems exist in a service firm, formulate a plan and then action the activities to ensure resolution. This screen is useful to solve case studies and monitor the operations of the service firm.

4.3 Product / Goods-Services Continuum

Products and services are the outputs offered by businesses to satisfy the demands of consumer and industrial markets. They are differentiated on the basis of four characteristics:

1. **Tangibility:** Goods are tangible products such as cars, clothing, and machinery. They have shape and can be seen and touched. Services are intangible. Hair styling, pest control and equipment repair, for example, do not have a physical presence.

2. **Perishability:** All goods have some degree of durability beyond the time of purchase. Services do not; they perish as they are delivered.

3. **Separability:** Goods can be stored for later use. Thus, production and consumption are typically separate. Because the production and consumption of services are simultaneous, services and the service provider cannot be separated.

4. **Standardisation:** The quality of goods can be controlled through standardisation and grading in the production process. The quality of services, however, is different each time they are delivered.

For the purpose of developing marketing strategies, particularly product planning and promotion, goods and services are categorised in two ways. One is to designate their position on a goods and services continuum. The second is to place them into a classification system.

The products or goods and services continuum enables marketers to see the relative goods/services composition of total products. A product's position on the continuum, in turn, enables marketers to spot opportunities. At the pure goods end of the continuum, goods that have no related services are positioned. At the pure services end are services that are not associated with physical products. Products that are a combination of goods and services fall between the two ends. For example, goods such as furnaces, which require accompanying services such as delivery and installation, are situated toward the pure goods end. Products that involve the sale of both goods and services, such as auto repair, are near the center. Products that are primarily services but rely on physical equipment, such as taxis, are located toward the pure services end.

The second approach to categorising products is to classify them on the basis of their uses. This organisation facilitates the identification of prospective users and the design of strategies to reach them. The major distinction in this system is between consumer and industrial products. Consumer goods and services are those that are purchased for personal, family or household use. Industrial goods and services are products that companies buy to make the products they sell.

Two major changes have affected the marketing and production of goods and services since about 1950. The first was a shift in marketing philosophy from the belief that consumers could be convinced to buy whatever was produced to the marketing concept, in which consumer expectations became the driving force in deter mining what was to be produced and marketed. This change in orientation has resulted in increases in both lines of products and choices within the lines.

The second change was an increased demand for services. The growth in demand for services—and resulting production—continues to increase at a faster rate than the demand for manufactured goods.

As per Theodore Levitt "There is no such thing as the service industry. There are some service industries whose service components are greater (or less) than those of other industries". Everybody is in service. The point that Levitt was trying to put across is that with almost every tangible physical product an intangible service component is associated. Therefore every body is in service. He has further put that goods can be put into two categories.

Search goods are tangible goods and the experienced goods are intangible.

Experienced Goods : Goods which one can see or evaluate after the purchase like (holidays, travel etc.)

Fig. 4.1

Experienced goods: Goods which one can see or evaluate after the purchase like (holidays, travel etc.)

Search Goods are tangible goods and the experienced goods are intangible.

Fig. 4.2

Philip Kotler suggests 4 categories

1. Pure tangible (salt)
2. Major tangible with minor intangibles (soap)
3. Minor tangible with major intangibles (consultancy)
4. Pure service (teaching)

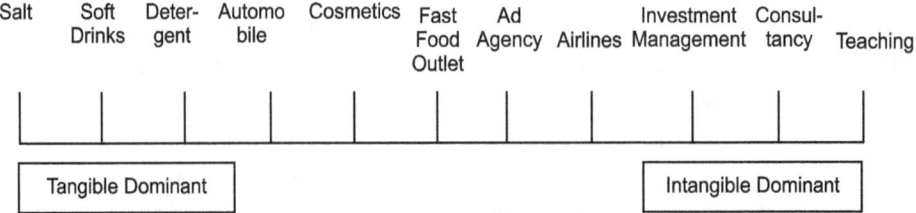

Fig. 4.3

The above diagram shows the Service – goods continuum – some goods being tangible dominant others being service dominant. The fast food outlets has almost 50/50 of tangible and intangible parts i.e. in this case both tangible (such as food) and intangible factors (such as services) are important. Due to this importance they attain the centre position.

In case of other products like salt there the services won't play any important role so it is more towards tangible and in case of teaching profession it is purely service dominated. We never known about service without experiencing and in this manner various goods fall in place according to its category i.e. less service oriented or more service oriented.

4.4 The Nature of Service Products

Service Products are of a very complex nature and are mostly intangible. While manufactured products may be offered with or without customer service elements, nearly all service products involve close interaction with customers. The implication of this is that service suppliers must design the interaction with customers in addition to developing the service product itself.

Service products are predominantly processes rather than objects. Thus, the development of a new service is often more complex than that for a new manufactured product.

Service products represent the wide range of intangible product offerings that customers value and pay for. Service products are sold by service companies and by non-service companies such as manufacturers and technology companies. For example, Departmental stores like *More* or *Reliance Fresh* which sell services like gift wrapping or parceling etc.

Given the intangible nature of services, the decisions regarding the tangible/physical service aim at reducing the inherent intangibility of services, and thus, help customers perceive the service more easily. In general, this effort is assigned to marketers and it is considered so critical that it is recognised as the fifth p of the marketing mix (namely, physical evidence), along with product, price, place and promotion. Physical evidence includes the following elements (Hoffman and Bateson, 1997):

- Facility exterior (for example, car park, signing);
- Facility interior (for example, lighting, temperature, interior design);
- Tangibles (for example, brochures, business documents, personnel uniforms).

The pertinent decisions a service company has to make include:

1. How tangible should the service be?
2. What elements should be used to make a service more tangible?
3. Should service providers make decisions relating to service quality?

4.5 Service Products Bundled with Tangible Products

Services marketing is selling relationships and values rather than the capabilities of products. While a product is tangible in nature, services are intangible. It doesn't provide a physical presence that one can touch and feel. For example, health insurance provides a certificate or policy as a physical evidence but the insurance itself is based upon a good faith relationship between insurers and the insured. Moreover, services are perishable in the sense that they can be here today and gone tomorrow. Finally, you do not get ownership with a service, since it is just an experience. And you cannot sell it once you have used it. Western economies have experienced a decline in their manufacturing industries (products) while, at the same time, services have replaced them. Thus, the marketing mix has seen an extension and an adoption into the mix referred to as physical evidence, people and process.

To ensure successful business, services marketing executives and managers must understand these characteristics thoroughly. They must be clear about how they affect the behaviour of their clients and also how their businesses can respond to minimise engagement risk, enhance customer perceptions of their services and increase market opportunities for a greater share of market. They must be able to determine ways to communicate the services process to customers effectively and to convey details about the deliverables and benefits in order to instill client confidence in their offerings. These tangible signals of the quality and value of their services are achieved through personal interaction with clients, clear communications, recommendations from others, pricing and the businesses physical operating environment.

Creating Tangibility for the Intangible

A degree of tangibility can be provided to intangible services marketing through solid corporate identities such as logos, the quality of descriptive sales materials and the confidence and honesty projected by sales and marketing people. Pricing can also be used as an indicator of quality where high-end prices suggest quality and low-end prices have the opposite aura. Nevertheless, any sense of tangibility must extend well past pricing and promotions. The client usually measures quality of a service in terms of the 'chemistry' that develops in personal relations with the company's representatives. If trust and reliability are conveyed through services marketing, this is a successful first step. Then, if the provider delivers on brand promises, the message is fully delivered.

(**Source:** MarketingProfs.com 2006)

In services marketing, clients often anticipates that the service will be provided in a certain way or by a certain individual. This is a challenge for service marketers in assigning the appropriate staff, process management and making certain that representatives in relationships with customers and prospects have displayed the proper knowledge, attitude and appearance when providing the requested service. Services marketing professionals should therefore encourage the client's participation during the service delivery process by engaging him in interviews, testing, strategy discussions, testing and updates when required. These interactions build customer confidence and build his commitment to the company. They go far toward ensuring repeat business.

Goods	Services	Resulting Implication
Tangible Goods are objects, which can be seen, felt, sensed easily.	**Intangible** Services are performance or actions, which cannot be tasted, felt, touched. e.g. health care services. (Treatment, surgery)	Services cannot be inventoried. It cannot be patented nor readily displayed or communicated. Pricing of services is very difficult.
Homogenous/ Standardised Goods have their own standards and many goods are alike.	**Heterogeneous** Services are frequently produced by human beings so no two services will be alike. e.g. two different clients have different service experience from the same tax accountant.	Service delivery and customer satisfaction depends on employee actions. Service quality depends on many uncontrollable factors. There is no sure knowledge that the service delivered matches what is planned.

contd. ...

Production and Distribution are separated from consumption	Simultaneous Production and Consumption	
Goods are produced first, then sold, then consumed.	Most services are sold first and then produced and consumed simultaneously. e.g. restaurant services are sold first dinning experience is produced and consumed.	Customers participate in and affect the transaction. Customers affect each other. Employees affect the service outcome. Decentralisation may be essential. Mass production is difficult.
Non-perisable Goods can be stored in inventory or resold or even returned.	Services cannot be saved, stored or returned. e.g. bad haircut.	It is difficult to synchronise supply and demand in services. Right quality has to be delivered in the first instance.
Core value produced in factory	**Core value produced in buyer seller interactions**	
Customers do not participate in production process	**Customers participate in the production**	
Transfer of ownership a thin	**No transfer of ownership an activity/process**	

4.6 Service Lifecycle

The concept of service lifecycle is very similar to the proud lifecycle concept. It is on the premise that total sales and profitability of products fluctuate according to some pattern during the product's life. This concept can be used for individual product items, product classes and whole industries.

The service life cycle is the sum of a customer's interaction with a product and the company that sells it, from the presale evaluation through maintenance and even to the purchase of a new product. The customer who buys a product today spends between five and twenty times the initial sale price on subsequent services and consumables.

Phase I-Introduction: New products are expensive to produce and launch, and may have teething problems. Customers may be wary of trying something new, especially a new service whose intangibility prevents prior evaluation. Sales are slow and restricted to those who like trying out new products or who believe they can gain status or benefits by having it.

Phase II-Growth: Product has been tested and teething problems have been resolved. The product is now more reliable and more readily available. People see the benefits that can be gained by using the product. Sales start to increase greatly, signally competitors to start entering the market.

Phase III-Maturity: Almost everyone who wants to acquire the product has done so although some people may now be updating the product having purchased it earlier in the lifecycle. The number of competitors has risen.

Phase IV-Saturation: There are too many competitors and no further growth in the market. Competitors compete with each other on the basis of price.

Phase V-Decline: With falling demand and new substitute products appearing, organisations drop out of the market.

Marketing activity for a service should be closely related to the stage in the lifecycle that a service has reached. Promotional planning is closely related to the lifecycle, with emphasis placed in the launch phase on raising awareness through public relations activity; building on this through the growth phase with advertising; resorting to sales promotion incentives as the market matures and becomes more competitive; and finally allowing promotional activity to fall as the service is allowed to decline. Distribution and pricing decisions are also related to the stage which a service has reached in its lifecycle.

Research has reinforced the existence of lifecycle among services (for instance, air transportation). Instead of speaking of the lifecycle of a product, the inseparability of services make it more appropriate to discuss the lifecycle of services.

Stage I-Entrepreneurial: An individual identifies a market need and offers a service to a small number of people usually operating from one location. Most entrepreneurs stay at this stage but some move to large and/or additional sites.

Stage II-Multi-stage rationalisation: Successful entrepreneurs start to add to the limited number of facilities. Skills required for being a multi-site operator begin to be developed. -Franchising is considered.

Stage III-Growth: The concept has been accepted as a profitable business idea. Expansion is through purchase of competitors, franchising/licensing, developing new company operated facilities, or a combination of the three. Growth is influenced by the founder's desire to succeed and financial pressures placed upon the company.

Stage IV-Maturity: The number of new outlets decline and revenues of individual facilities stabilise and in some cases also decline. This may be due to changing demographics within the firm's market, changing needs and tastes of consumers, increased competition and cannibalisation of older services by firm's newer products.

Stage V-Decline/Regeneration: Firms can become complacent and unless a new concept is developed or new markets found, decline follows.

Difficulties in Applying the Lifecycle concept

The service lifecycle concept is more useful for strategic planning and control than for developing short-term forecasts. In reality, lifecycle patterns are too variable in both shape and duration for any realistic predictions to be made. Marketers are unable to predict accurately where in the lifecycle a product actually is at any time. For instance, a stabilisation of sales may be a movement into maturity or simply a temporary plateau due to external causes. It is also possible that the shape of the lifecycle is a result of an organisation's marketing activity rather than an indication of environmental factors to which the organisation should respond.

Duration of the stages will depend upon whether it is a product class, form or brand which is being considered. Most service organisations have only a very small number of core services and there is need for caution in using the lifecycle concept for services.

New Service Development

In the following circumstances, new services development may become necessary:

(i)   If a major service has reached the maturity stage and may be moving towards decline, new services may be sought to preserve sales levels.

(ii) New services may be developed as a means of utilising space capacity.

(iii) New services can help to balance an organisation's existing sales portfolio and thus reduce dependency on a few services offered within a range

In order to retain and develop a relationship with its customers, an organisation may be forced to introduce new products to allow it to offer a comprehensive portfolio of services. An opportunity may arise for an organisation to satisfy unmet needs with new services as a result of the competitor leaving the market.

The intangible nature of services means that it is easy to produce slight variants of an existing service, with the result that the term new services can mean anything from minor style change to major innovation.

Five types of new services are:

1. **Style changes:** These include change in decor, logo.

2. **Service improvements:** These involve an actual change to a feature of the service already on offer to an established market, for instance, computerization of travel agency information.

3. **Service Line Extensions:** These are additions to the existing service product range.

4. **New Services:** These are new services that are offered by an organisation to its existing customers although these may be currently available from its competitors.

5. **Major Innovation:** These are entirely new services for new markets.

The distinctive features of services as compared to tangible goods raise a number of special issues:

(i)   The intangibility of services leads to proliferation of slightly different service products. New services are easy to develop and variety of different services causes confusion.

(ii) inseparability between service production and consumption means that front line operational staff has greater opportunity to identify new service ideas that are likely to be successful.

(iii) As services are more likely than goods to be customised to the needs to individual customers, there are greater opportunities for marginally different new services each having its own selling proposition.

To aid companies in maximising existing service profits and creating new sources of revenue, tools that handle the comprehensive management of the service life cycle can deploy, measure, and analyse business practices for service delivery, as well as create more flexible, customer-driven business processes in ways that niche solutions cannot. Extending and synchronising the flow of automation across divisional and corporate boundaries transforms an organisation's ability to manage the customer from lead through product sale and finally to product retirement. Service life-cycle management comprises nine core elements: service sales and marketing, service contract management, customer service and support, installed-base management, warranty and claims management, field service, depot repair, service parts management, and financial management. These functionalities provide true service life-cycle management, which not only reduces costs and increases revenue, but also increases customer retention, a critical competitive differentiator in today's fast-changing marketplace.

Questions for Discussion

1. State the extended Marketing Mix for services.
2. What is Marketing Mix? Explain the 7P's of marketing mix.
3. Explain service life cycle.
4. Explain services marketing mix.
5. What is the Product – Services Continuum?
6. Explain the nature of service products?

■■■

Chapter **5**...

Distribution

Contents ...

5.1 Introduction

Delivery of services differs significantly from that of the manufactured goods. It involves decisions about where, when and how. The rapid growth of internet and now also broadband mobile communications means that service marketing strategy must address issues of place, cyberspace and time, paying at least as much attention to speed, scheduling and electronic access as to the more traditional notion of physical location. The production of goods is followed by distribution whereas services usually cannot be separated from the service provider. Because of this inseparability characteristic the channels for most services are short and simple. The place or distribution of services refers to availability of a service, i.e., when and where it can be purchased. The place or distribution of services is discussed in light of:

- Location
- Accessibility
- Channels of Distribution
- Distribution facilities
- Service Inventory / Shortage
- Managing Channels

5.2 Distribution of Services

The special characteristics of services e.g., intangibility, inventory, inconsistency and inseparability have led to specific form of distribution. Service products are mostly those where no transfer of ownership takes place and the service is simply rented or consumed. But it is essential that it must be available and accessible before its consumption. This needs a distribution system. The distribution system may be defined as the channels or means using which the services provider gains access to potential buyer of the service product. Before the formulation of channel structure following aspects of service distribution must be taken into consideration:

- There is no actual tangible product which is being distributed.
- It involves consumer's movement to the service location. As consumer is part of the service operation, the method of selling and environment within which service product purchase is made becomes part of service experience.
- The intermediaries/agents play a key role in recommending services to consumers.
- The service organisation have to devise promotional/distribution strategies suiting customer coming directly, through agents or other modes.

5.2.1 Location

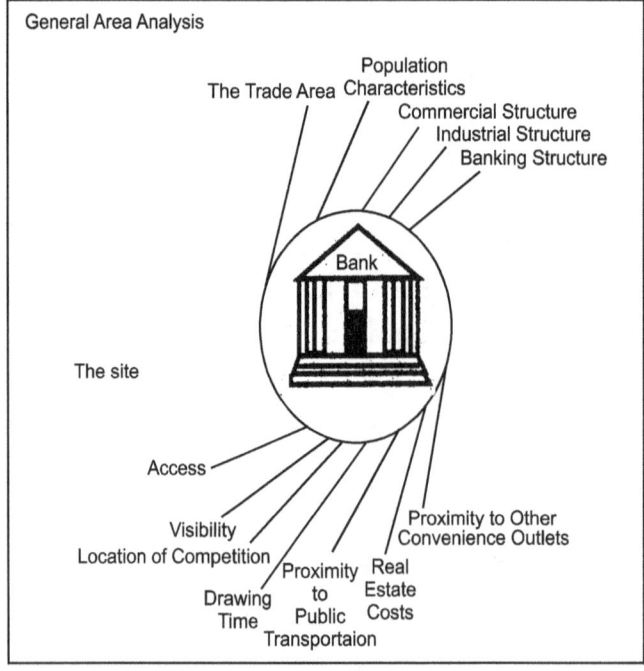

Fig. 5.1: Elements of Branch Location Analysis

Location involves considering where to deliver the service to the customer and whether the service organisation should be single location or multi-locations. A well located restaurant will be able to pick up passing demand because the consumer will locate the service product easily and quickly. Thus, a well located hotel/restaurant/travel agent may not need any distribution channel.

The importance of location varies with the type of service and marketers should address following issues regarding location of the service. Fig. 5.1 highlights the considerations for branch location analysis.

- **Need of the market:** If the market requires accessibility and convenience to make a choice of service, poor location will lead to either postponement or delay in service operation or the customer will look for a service available at arm's length.

- **Technological innovation:** Number of service sector are finding that they gain considerable competitive edge through changes of distribution. Technology has facilitated telephone banking and at home shopping. The banks are now expanding their distribution network through ATMs or electronic fund transfer facilities. For example, cinema tickets can be booked electronically.

- **Convenience:** Is it obligatory to locate the services at the convenient place? Government hospitals, health care services are located accordingly. The concept of convenience has created services like home delivery, advance reservation of air tickets and train tickets etc.

In service operations the following three situations are generally faced regarding service locations refer table 5.1.

Table 5.1: Service Location: Situations and their Impact

Situation	Impact
Customer goes to service provider	Service providers have to select an appropriate location or multi-locations.
Service provider goes to customer	Location becomes less important because the service provider either provides service at customer's place e.g. janitorial services, lawn care service, lift repair service or provides service at customer's place or decides to do at his premises e.g., some mechanics repair the car at owner's premises or they bring car to garage for repairs
Service provider and customer transact at arm's length	Location becomes insignificant e.g., in case of e-mail, no interaction is required where as at ATM. Customer is using a service without interacting with people but he may choose to go to bank for another transaction personally.

5.2.2 Accessibility

While designing the service distribution channels accessibility should clearly be given special attention. In addition to convenient location, following factors play a significant role in influencing the customer.

- Accessibility to range and choice of service literature and brochures.
- Accessibility to components such as visas, traveller cheques, insurance and cards.
- Accessibility to booking points in every main town and cities.
- Accessibility to alternative brands.
- Accessibility to alternative agents.

For example, Electronic distribution has created opportunity to have access to a wide network and now travel agents located at distant locations can make the services accessible at the convenience of the customer.

5.2.3 Channels of Distribution

All the organisations or people participating in distribution process are known as channels of distributions. These are three types of participants:

- The service provider
- Intermediaries
- Customers

It has already been explained that the channel for many services is simple and short because services cannot be separated from its providers. Therefore, it has been argued that the most appropriate form of distribution for services is direct selling. While the direct selling channel of distribution is common for some of the services firms in other areas of services are looking for additional channels to achieve the better growth and to fill the unutilized capacity. Intermediaries are now playing an important role in delivering the services. Some typical examples of channels of distribution are given below:

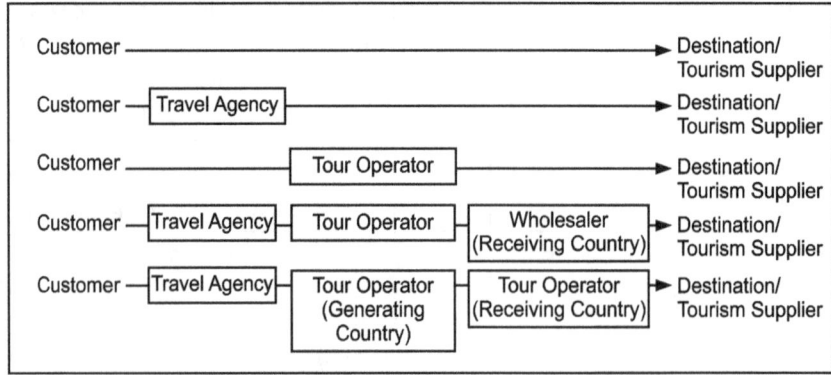

Fig. 5.2: Channels of Distribution – Destination/Tourism supplier (Typical)

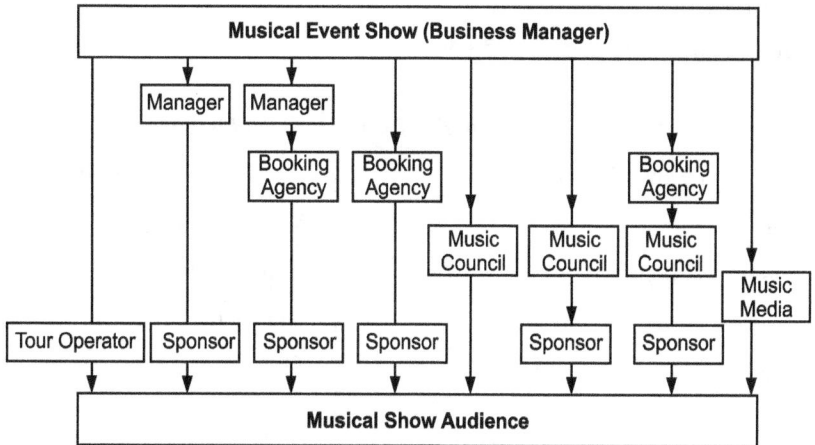

Fig. 5.3: Channels of distribution for Airlines service

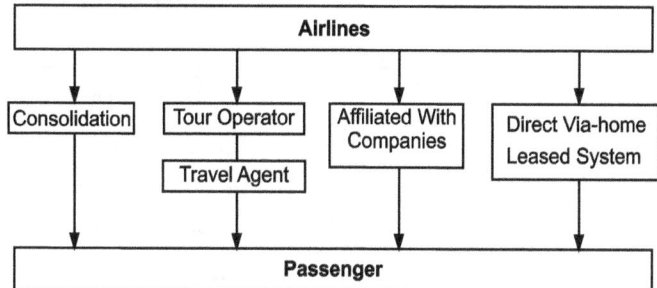

Fig. 5.4: Channels of distribution for bank services

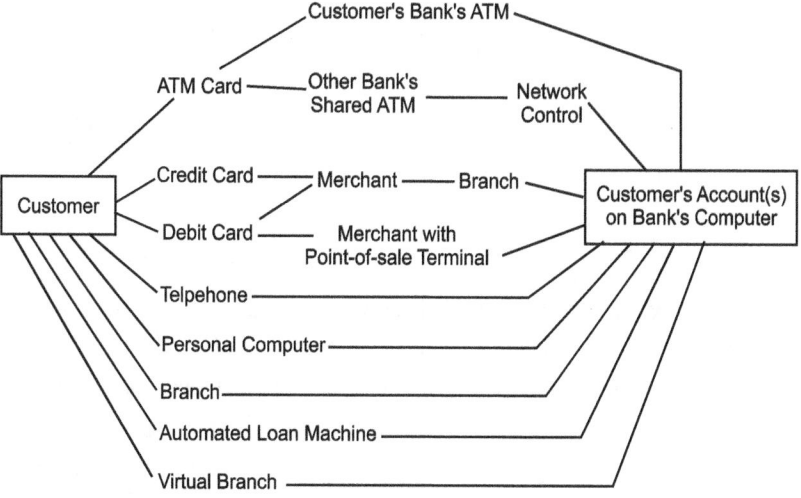

Fig. 5.5: Channels of distribution for bank services typical

Channel Options

Marketers have following broad option for the forms of channels refer the table 5.2 below:

Table 5.2: Broad Obtains for the form of Channel

Forms of Channel	Type of Service
Direct Sales	Accounting Services
Producer → Consumers	Management Consulting Services
	Design and Technical Services
	Dieting Services
	Eyecare Services
	Hair Fashioning Services
	Healthcare Services
	Legal Services
Agents or Brokers	Insurance Services
Producers → Agents → Consumer	Tour and Travel Services
	Hotel Reservation Services
	Ticketing Services
	Advertising Services
Seller and Buyer Agent or Broker	Stocks and Shares Brokers
	Commodity Brokers
	Real Estate
Agent → Consumer	Holding and Investment
Franchises and Contracted Services deliveries	Fast Food Services
	Car Rental Services
	Dry Cleaning Services

Today is an increasingly competitive marketing environment. It has become necessary for most of the service firms to think and consider different forms of distribution. Firms are able to sell direct either from their place of location or through direct marketing methods.

For example, several hotels are organizing weekend breaks to improve weekend occupancy levels and these are promoted through print media and booked directly with the hotel.

5.3 Distribution Facilities

Since today's consumer is convenience oriented, a good location is essential when the service is distributed directly from producer or originator or service principal to consumer. Some service marketers in an attempt to reduce inseparability factor have broadened their distribution base by extending their locations. Mobile banking may be a good example if a bank designs an armoured mobile van to provide banking services street to street. ATM's are located at various places at convenient locations, away from the main bank to facilitate service delivery. Many courier companies have opened distribution and collection centres at different parts of the city.

In non-profit marketing, health care organisation provide mobile units for X-rays blood examination. Delhi Public Library has set up a mobile library which is covering various parts of Delhi.

The physical surroundings, ambience in the distribution of services play important role in influencing the customers perception of that service and its originator. As the services are intangible, the customer look to the service facility and the people providing that service before making a purchase. Because of this, many firms which are facing competition are redesigning or revamping their facilities to reflect a more caring and trusting atmosphere. Service facilities are being upgraded by improvements in interior designs, lighting, music and even the smell in the service facility.

For example, hotels are providing small fountains with perfumed water to give a fragrance. Indian Oil Corporation is redesigning its petrol pumps by changing layout, providing soothing colour schemes and also retrofitting the gas delivery systems.

5.3.1 Managing Channels

Channel selection is the difficult decision. While choosing a distribution channel, the firms need to consider intensity of market coverage. Market coverage can be achieved by one of three major types of distribution.

1. **Intensive distribution:** It is a strategy in which a producer sells product and services at retail and wholesale levels in a particular territory. The objectives are volume sales and corresponding profits, channel acceptance and wide market coverage. The intermediaries services are all types of firms many number of outlets. Organisational consumer focuses on all types of accounts. Many number of customer. Services expected from intermediaries. Marketing focus on final consumers, mass advertising, convenient outlets, items in inventory, organisational consumer availability, continuous communication superior service. The disadvantage is limited channel control. For example, routine service like fast foods, courier services, home delivery services.

2. **Selective distribution:** It is a strategy in which a producer sells its goods and service through multiple, but not all possible, wholesaler and retailers in a market where a consumer might reasonably look for it. The objectives are best image, good profit margins, reasonable channel control and loyalty, moderate market coverage. Intermediaries services include well established firms, moderate number of outlets only. Customers are brand conscious. Moderate number of customers. Marketing focus on final consumers, promotion mix, pleasant ambience, good service, organisational consumer availability, continous communication and superior service. The disadvantage is difficult to carve out a niche. For example, industrialized services, repair and maintenance, electrical appliances, air-conditioners, refrigerators.

3. **Exclusive distribution:** It is a strategy in which a supplier agrees to sell its products and services only to a single wholesaling middleman and/or retailer in a given market. The objectives are exclusive image, high profit margins, price stability and loyalty. Intermediaries services are well established sound and reputed firms, few outlets. Customers are brand loyal, few customers and final customers. Marketing focus is on final consumers, personal selling, pleasant ambience, good service, organisational consumer availability, continuous communication and superior service. Disadvantage is limited sales. For example, complex, services, designer's hair style, specialised training and designers fashioning.

Many producers for achieving broad market coverage employ multiple distribution channels which are sometimes called dual distribution channels. The producers use multiple distribution channels to:

- Reach different types of markets
- Reach different segments within a single market
- Life Insurance Corporation of India may directly sell group health insurance policies to large business houses and individual life insurance policies indirectly to final consumers through independent insurance agents.

5.4 Delivering Service through Intermediaries

Due to the inseparability of production and consumption in services, providers must either be present themselves when customers receive service or find ways to involve others in distribution. Involving others can be problematic, because quality in service occurs in the service encounter between company and customer. Unless the service distributor is willing and able to perform in the service encounter as the service principal would, the value of the offering decreases and the reputation of the original provider damaged.

The reputation of the original provider damaged. Most services companies face a formidable task of attaining service excellence and consistency when intermediaries represent themselves to customers. Two service marketers are involved in delivering service through intermediaries; the service principal or originator and the service deliverer or intermediary.

The service principal is the entity that creates the service concept and the service deliverer is the entity that interacts with the customer in the actual execution of the service. Service intermediaries perform many important functions for the service principal; namely

1. They often co-produce the service, fulfilling service principal's promises to customers. Franchise services such as hair cutting, dry cleaning are produced by the intermediary using the process developed by the principal.

2. Service intermediaries also make services available locally, providing time and place convenience for the customers.

3. They offer choice to the customer in one place e.g. travel agents.

In contrast to channels for products channels for services are almost always direct, if not to the customer then to the intermediary that sells to the customer. As services cannot be owned, there are no titles or rights to most services that can be passed along a delivery channel. Because services are intangible and perishable inventories cannot making warehousing a dispensable function. Many channels available to goods producer are not feasible for service firms. The focus in service distribution is on identifying ways to bring the customer and principal or its representative together. The options for doing so are limited to franchisees, brokers and electronic channels.

Service principals depend on their intermediaries to deliver service to their specifications. It is in the execution by the intermediary that the customer evaluates the quality of the company. Unless service intermediaries ensure that the intermediaries goals, incentives and motives are consistent with their own, they lose control over the service encounters between the service intermediary and the customer.

Intermediaries are a force in the service performance gap, the difference between service quality standards (as set by management of the company) and delivery to the customers(as executed by employees, franchisees, agents etc.).

As intermediaries are contact person they have a strong role in facilitating communication between the customer and the service principal to ensure that policy about service meets customer expectations.

Issues related to delivery

- channel conflict over objectives and performance
- channel conflict over costs and rewards
- difficulty controlling quality and consistency across outlets
- tension between empowerment and control
- channel ambiguity.

Services can be distributed to the end customer through franchisees, electronic channels, and agents and brokers.

Franchisees are service outlets licensed by a principal to deliver an unique service concept it has created or popularised, e.g. McDonalds, Holiday inn.

Electronic media include all forms of service provision through TV, telephone, interactive multimedia, computers

Agents are representatives who distribute and sell the service.

1. Franchising

A contractual relationship between the 2 parties in which the franchiser offers or is obliged to maintain a continuing interest in the business of the franchisee in such areas as know how and training; wherein the franchise operates under a common trade name, format or procedure owned by or controlled by the franchiser and in which the franchisee has made or will make a substantial capital investment in his business from his own resources. The franchise system is the combination of franchisor and franchisee. For example, in fast food-franchises are McDonald's, Domino's and Wimpy. In courier, Overnite Express, DHL, Fedex. In hotels, Holiday Inn and Radission so on.

There are two types of franchising:

Product or Trade Name Franchising: It is a distribution contract under which franchisor (supplier) authorises the franchisee (dealer/distributor) to sell a product line using the franchisor firm's (parent organisation) trade name for purposes of promotion. The key element in product and trade name franchising focuses on 'what is sold'. The franchisee agrees to buy from franchisor and also in bound by the specific policies.

Business Format Franchising: For the past three decades, franchising growth has taken place over the business format franchising. This format covers the entire method for the business operations. A successful retail business sells right to operator the same business in different geographical locations.

McDonald's are the examples of business format franchising. The franchisee in this type of format expects to receive from the parent company a proven method of operating the business including policies and procedures, standards of consumption, marketing policies etc and in return, receives from each business owner payment and conformance of policy and procedures to maintain business standards. The focus in this format is 'how the business is run'?

Some well known commercial business format franchising arrangements are car rentals, market research, copy shops, industrial cleaning, security services and hotels and restaurants.

Benefits of Franchising

- Leverages the business format to gain expansion and revenues.
- Maintains consistency in outlets.
- Gains knowledge of local markets.
- Shares financial risk and frees up capital.

Challenges of Franchising

- Difficulty in maintaining and motivating franchisees.
- Highly publicized disputes between franchisees and franchisers.
- Inconsistent quality that can undermine the company's name.
- Customer relationship controlled by the intermediary rather than the service principal.

Benefits of franchising for the Franchisees

- Obtaining an established business format on which to base a business.
- Receiving national or regional marketing.
- Minimising the risk of starting a business.

Challenges of Franchising for Franchisees

- Disappointing profits and revenues.
- Encroachment and franchise saturation.
- High failure rates and unfair terminations.
- Lack of perceived control.
- High fees and rigid contracts.
- Unrealistic expectations.

2. Agents and Brokers

The major part of services business is still transacted through agents and brokers. These channels of distribution are discussed here. Unlike merchant wholesaler, agents and brokers do not take title to the merchandise. In service environment, their primary function is to sell services, in return for which they get a commission from the service provider.

Agents are wholesalers that do not take title of products. They work for commission or fees as payment for their services and are comprised of manufacturers/service provider's agents, selling agents and commission merchants. **Service provider agents** work for the two or more related services from non-competing service creators in a specific geographic territory. For example, a travel agent represent Indian Airlines and does the banking for passengers traveling by Indian Airlines for a fee or commission and may also provide booking for tour related services for a tour operator. A service firm may employ many agents (LIC agents) each with a unique product territory mix. Agents have limited association with the marketing programme or price structure of the service.

Selling agents sell full range of service provider and are responsible for all aspect of marketing of those services under a contractual agreement. In fact they are empowered to negotiate on behalf of the service providers. They perform the function of wholesaling without taking the title of the product. They mostly work for small firms. For example, a travel agent who is authorised selling agent of a hotel may negotiate a block booking on behalf of the hotel under contractual obligation.

Brokers do not have any affiliation with any particular service provider. They specialise in certain areas and bring buyers and seller together to negotiate the contract. For example real estate broker does not have the title of the property but brings, property owner who wants to sell and a customer who wants to buy, together for negotiations. He gets a fee/commission for this deal. A broker may represent many non-competing brands in a metropolitan area. Brokers are very common in food and financial services industries. For example, commercial stock broker are licensed sales representatives who advise business clients, take orders and then acquire stocks for the clients. For these services they get the brokerage/commission. Brokers are well informed about market conditions, prices, potential buyers an sellers, terms of business an possess the negotiating skills. They do not take the title and usually are not allowed to complete the transaction without the approval of the parties involved in negotiations.

Benefits

- Reduced selling and distributing costs.
- Possession of special skills and knowledge.
- Wide representation.
- Knowledge of local markets.
- Customer choice.

Challenges

- Loss of control over pricing and other aspects of marketing.
- Representation of multiple service principals.

3. Electronic Channels

Number of technological advances have taken place due to immense use of EDI (Electronic Data Interchange). These advances have led to:

- Increased use of self-service operations e.g., many marketing firms have put their services on website and those who need get it by self servicing e.g., Tata Mcgraw Publishing Company has a website giving details of the books published.

- Providing data bank services e.g., a service provider may require information to make a mailing list to target a specific audience.

- Electronic banking

- E-mail and many more.

Distribution of services through electronic channel is without any direct human interaction because services are distributed through a service distribution system. This channel requires a pre-designed service and a system to deliver it. Delivery of services through alternate channels like ATMs, call centres, Internet and Kiosks is growing at an ever—increasing pace. For example, Electronic banking involves ATMs, Cards for instant delivery services through electronic processing of data. The electronic banking services enable customer 24 hours banking, seven days a week at convenient locations. Mobile banking is an example of electronic distribution system.

Benefits

- **Quality control:** The service delivery by electronic channel is to be of the same quality. For example, the service provided by a bank employee sitting at the cheque counter will not be of same quality everytime whereas same service provided by ATM will be same everytime in each transaction.

- **Low cost:** Reaching a customer through personal selling is quite expensive compared to electronic media. Also the delivery is more efficient as electronic media has introduced the element of speed of service (SOS). The interactive media approach has added credibility to remote encounters. For example, e-banking, electronic fund transfer.

- **Customer convenience:** Customer can have access to services at convenient location, are on a convenient day and marketers have access to those customers who otherwise are not accessible at the service outlets. For example, 24 hours, 7 days, 365 days.

- **Wide distribution:** The electronic media allows simultaneous interaction directly or through number of intermediaries, thereby resulting in wide distribution. For example, installation of electronic terminals at agents/brokers premises or ATMs at different locations has added wide spectrum to distribution.

- **Customer choice:** The electronic media explosion has made option available with the customer. For example, the service provided by bank employee sitting at the cheque counter will not be of same quality every time whereas same service provided by ATM will be same every time in each transaction.

- Electronic media no doubt, has brought in fast revolution in the service business environment but security of data, customer involvement in service delivery, customisation of services is lacking.

Challenges

- Lack of control of the electronic environment.

- Inability to customise.

- Customer involvement.

- Security.

E.g Smart cards, selling online, education online, business to business video conferencing.

Electronic Channels examples

- Plastic money

- Selling through online services

- Buying through online services

- Video conferences

- Electronic marketing/E-banking

- Education through satellite/ E-MBA

5.4.1 Strategies for effective Service Delivery through Intermediaries

- **Empowerment strategies** help the intermediary develop customer oriented service process, provide needed support systems, develop intermediaries to deliver service quality, change to a cooperative management structure.

- **Partnering strategies** alignment of goals, consultation and cooperation.

5.5 Challenges in Distribution of Services (Especially with Intermediaries)

The firm has to handle issues which typically arise with the intermediaries which include conflict over vision, objectives and performance, costs and rewards, difficulty controlling, service quality and consistency across outlets as per firm's norms, balance between empowerment and control and channel ambiguity.

- **Conflict Over Objectives and Performance**

  All the parties involved in delivering services are not always in agreement about the way the channel should operate. Multiple channel conflict can occur like between the service provider and the service intermediary, among intermediaries in a given city and between different types of channels used by a service provider in the same area due to overlap. The conflict arise as the parties involved have different goals, competing roles, with different rights. They give conflicting views of the way the channel is performing and complaint of poorer service quality by the other channel intermediary. The conflict occurs when the one of the intermediaries becomes dominant and begins to dictate to the service provider.

- **Controlling Quality and Consistency Across Outlets**

  Both principals and their intermediaries face problem of the inconsistency and lack of quality which arises because multiple outlets deliver services with different levels of quality. When the performance drops below standards, even at a single outlet on any given day the entire reputation is at stake. Other intermediaries have negative impact at their outlets, which results in big blow to the service provider in terms of image and revenue. The cost increases disproportionately as the service provider has to exercise care and diligence in setting this right once and for all.

- **Conflict Over Costs and Rewards**

  The financial arrangement between those who create the service and those who deliver it is a major issue of contention. The discounts range from quantity, turnover, special and one time. This results in conflict because one intermediary gets the advantage and is able to gain significantly in the market place. The costs go up due to inflation and technology up-gradation and intermediary want compensation. Moreover, they want recognition in midst of their breathen annually.

- **Empowerment and Control a Fine Balance**

  McDonald's business is a trend setter for performance consistency in which the intermediaries have attained profits and long term relationship even with the company controlling every aspect of their intermediaries businesses. McDonald's do this as its brand name is on the line in each outlet with care and understanding. Controls must be balanced as many service franchisees have entrepreneurial nature and select this because they can own and operate their own businesses. The independent ideas given by franchisees must be integrated into their plan, practices and policies if they are advantageous to the firm.

- **Channel Ambiguity**

  The service provider in its agreement must clarify issues pertaining to who would conduct surveys, assess changes in needs, norms for service delivery, training etc. so that confusion and conflict is minimized later on.

5.6 Role of Internet in Distribution of Services

Technological developments and advances have had a major impact on the way in which services are produced and delivered. Computer technology developments have resulted in many innovations in service distribution and delivery.

While the recent meltdown of the dot-com sector has raised concerns about Internet business models in general, there is little doubt that "channel power" the use of electronic distribution channels – will continue to have a significant impact on the e-commerce business landscape.

The adoption of channel power has meant a seismic shift in the relationships between consumers, retailers, distributors, manufacturers and service providers. It presents many companies with the option of reducing or eliminating the role of intermediaries and lets those providers transact directly with their customers.

Direct distribution offers a company significant opportunities, but it also can present "numerous strategic uncertainties". Before launching an e-commerce effort and bypassing its traditional distribution channels, a business should analyse which products are appropriate for electronic distribution, which consumer activities will be supported by which channel participants, and which segments or groups of consumers are likely to adopt electronic distribution.

As a distribution channel the internet facilitates information flow, negotiation flow, service flow, transaction flow and promotion flow. When compared to the traditional channels the net is much better for research purposes, for gaining an insight into the consumer's behaviour through search behaviours and getting feedback form consumers and for creating communities online to market services.

There are many factors that attract consumers into virtual stores. These are,

- Convenience
- Ease of Research
- Better prices
- Broad selection

Consumers can enjoy 24-hour service with prompt delivery especially in today's world where everyone is so short of time.

Companies however should recognise that adding an internet channel to an already established physical channel is a double edged strategy which requires high capital setup. No one can be sure whether the investment will definitely lead to long-term profits and high growth potential.

Websites have become very sophisticated and user friendly. They often simulate the services of a sales assistant to steer customers towards items of likely interest. Some even provide the opportunity of interactive dialogue through email with customer service personnel. Facilitating searches is another useful service on many sites. These could range from looking at the book titles by a particular author to displaying flight schedules between two cities on a specific date.

The recent developments that link websites, customer relationship management (CRM) systems and mobile telephony provide even more exciting applications. Integrating mobile devices into the service delivery infrastructure can be used for increasing the accessibility of services, alerting by delivering the right information or interaction at the right time and updating to create and maintain up to date real time information. For example, customers can get stock alerts on their brokers' web site and get an email or SMS alert when a certain price or transaction has been conducted (alerting service) or they can obtain real time information on stock prices (updating service). With this information the customers can then respond by directly trading using their mobile phones as an interface (accessing service). Another interesting example is that of Singapore International Airlines (SIA). Some time back they introduced a departure time alert service. Through this the service, the customers could specify on the SIA website whether they want an SMS or email to be sent to them should their flight departure time be delayed. With this service now they could adjust their own schedule accordingly.

Questions for Discussion

1. What are the 'Challenges' in distribution of services?

2. Describe the various methods of distribution of services.

3. Describe the various factors affecting the 'channel of distribution of services'.

4. Explain the role of internet in distribution of services.

5. Explain the concept of 'Place' in distribution of services.

6. What is location in distribution of services? State the factors affecting the location selection in the distribution of services.

7. Services firm critically determine the channel for delivery of services e.g. LIC uses the network of agents. McDonald's has chosen Franchising. Explain the advantages and also the problems faced for using these 2 methods for distribution of services.

■■■

Chapter **6**...

Promotion

Contents ...

6.1 Introduction

Promotion is a key element of firm's marketing mix that informs, persuades and reminds customers about the services, image and ideas the firm has a value proposition for. Promotion helps in influencing the receivers from the target market for their feelings, beliefs or behaviour through ideal communication mix. The promotion campaign has to be planned, executed and monitored. For every promotion the target life has to be identified. In case of Life Insurance Corporation, he target markets comprise current and potential customers, competitors, agents, corporate agents, other channel partners tike banks and professional associations.

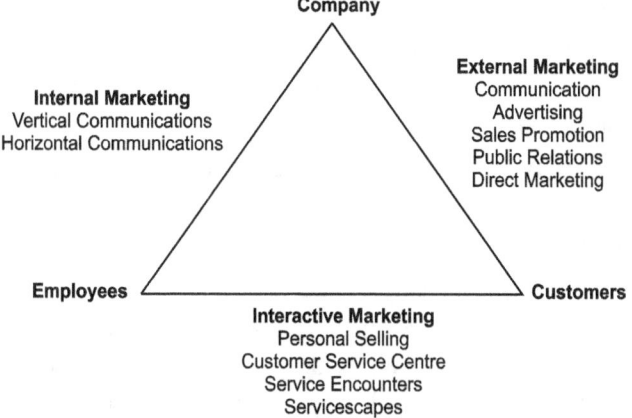

Fig. 6.1

(Adapted from Kotler's, Marketing Management: Analysis, Planning Implementation and Control)

A mix of the following promotional tools is used for promotion of services as each has unique characteristic and cost:

1. Advertising
2. Personal selling
3. Sales promotion
4. Publicity and Public relations
5. Direct Marketing includes direct mail, telemarketing, internet marketing which share four characteristics:
   - The message is addressed to a specific person.
   - The message is customised.
   - A message can be prepared quickly.
   - The message can be changed on the response.

6.2 Promotion Objectives for Services

(a) It creates brand of the firm or its services with proposition of value for money, prestige or innovation. Promotions symbolise added values associated with purchase. By branding, awareness of the firms is established which may results in premium prices. In case of Le Meridian, it has established the image that it is the destination to stay in Pune with value for money proposition.

(b) Promotions reduce perceived risk. For the established products or services, brand image increases the consumers confidence resulting in more purchases by reducing consumer's risk of buying the product or service. Brands like HDFC, SBI, LIC, ICICI are safe and reliable. Customers have got confidence in dealing with these brands.

(c) Communicates features of goods and services which creates awareness for new goods and services.

(d) Enhances recall of existing goods and services for existing customers.

(e) Pushes channel members to enhance sales with different offerings.

(f) Helps in repositioning of brands when required.

(g) Explains channels where goods and services can be purchased with their availability.

(h) Can persuade consumers to trade up from one good or service to more expensive one by explaining the benefits.

(i) Answers consumer queries with justification.

(j) Some elements of promotional activity add direct value as they are also functional. In case of hand bags, to keep tools provided by service providers like authorised service centers of Honda, when the vehicle owner signs an annual maintenance contract. Gifts and prizes on purchase of European tour tickets when the season is ending.

(k) Post purchase promotion helps to reassure buyers that they made a right decision which keeps them satisfied and earns customer loyalty which enables a higher life time value.

Six Steps in Developing Effective Communication

1. **Select the target market,** including potential buyers, current users, and possibly others who influence the buying decision.

   Target market is a group of consumers for a service. These are analyzed and decision is taken for the segments to be targeted. The market segments are identified by research with the reasons of opting for that segment. The product must be then aligned with the client profile. The product can be a composite product catering to more than one segment. In particular, careful distinction must be made between the tourist and the intermediaries, who is influencing the decision.

2. **Determining the communication objectives,** typically involving such goals as awareness, knowledge, liking, preference, conviction and purchase. State the objectives clearly and quantify them.

3. **Deciding on a budget,** deciding how much to spend on the total campaign as well as allocation to various promotion types.

4. **Creating a message,** capturing what to say, how to say it and who will deliver the message. The message is an instrument of converting a suspect into a prospect. To achieve the most effective response from the target market there is a need to plan an effective message such that promotional efforts achieve the objectives planned.

   Promotional message should aim to provide knowledge of the product or service to ensure that the consumer attitude will be favourable towards the product/service to build up preference for the product/ service offered. The promotional message is significant because the promotional campaign effectiveness depends upon it. Any promotional campaign has to sell the benefits that a customer is seeking in a credible way so that the potential customer is more likely to make a purchase. In marketing services use persuasive words in using promotion elements of the mix.

5. **Choosing media,** among them personal communication channels such as personal selling or nonpersonal communication channels such as television and newspapers. We also need to distinguish between mass media such as television and targeted media such as specialised magazines and direct mail.

   There should be careful blend of promotion mix with the marketing strategy of the firm and the situation should be examined for its merits and demerits.

The criteria to be considered for using different promotional techniques to achieve success are:

1. Overall marketing objectives

2. Nature of the service

3. Characteristics of target market

4. Type of intermediaries

5. Activities of competitors

6. Implementation plan

7. Legal and ethical considerations

8. Cost effectiveness

6. **Collecting feedback,** which includes researching how effective the communication was in meeting the objectives.

6.3 Personal Selling

Personal selling involves communication with one or more prospective buyers by a representative from a firm to make sales in face to face interaction and builds customer relationship. The objectives of the personal selling is informing, persuading and reminding the customer about the market offering, which could be based on demand or image. It plays a significant role in the promotional plans for services marketing.

Must have Sales Professionalism

Selling is a means that you use to persuade someone to buy from you where initially, your desire to supply products is greater than his desire to buy them. Customer oriented approach is listening, questioning, identifying needs and addressing the problems to have a win- win scenario.

Selling Process

Neil Rackham trains sales people for four questions to deal with the prospect.

(a) Situation questions ask for facts to explore the services attributes.

(b) Problem questions, to provide answers to questions and queries

(c) Implications questions to investigate for any further probing, questioning related to problems, concerns or dissatisfaction.

(d) Need pay off questions ask for details about the value or usefulness of a proposed solution.

Feature is fact or description of the product or service we sell while benefit is what the product or service will do for the customer whereas positioning is a skill that helps the salesperson to talk about products or services from customers viewpoint rather than from your own. Therefore, features give credibility while benefits give marketability while positioning is required to close the sales as it helps to differentiate customers having a generic mindset. Hence service sellers will have to master this.

The objectives of Personal Selling can be demand oriented or image oriented or a combination of both but it must make the customer buy the service. The sales person can tangabilise the service, which the customer can identify the firm. The image impact is due to knowledge, skills, pleasing disposition and dress code.

Table 6.1

I	Demand Oriented	Details
(A)	Informing	Explain goods and service attributes
		Provide answers to questions and queries
		Investigate and further probing
(B)	Persuading	Convert a suspect into a prospect to point dissatisfied customers
		Differentiation with an USP
		Sell complimentary items
(C)	Reminding	Post purchase follow-up. To follow up when repeat buying is near.
		To ensure promised delivery of products/services
II.	Image Oriented with positive impact	Good appearance by all executives in client interface. Selling practices accepted by the environment.

The sales force is well aware of 80/20 customer pyramid in which 20% customers produce 80% of the profit while 80% customers produce 20%.Going further the extended customer pyramid consists of the following:

Table 6.2

Factors					
Tier of Pyramid	Profitable	Volume	Price sensitive	Added range	Loyalty
Platinum	High	High	Low	Buy	Highest
Gold	Medium	Medium	Medium	May buy	Medium
Silver	Low	Low	High	Will not buy	Low
Lead	Low	Very low	Very high	Will not buy	In doubt

The sales force keeps this in mind while achieving its sales objectives.

To enhance motivation and get the best from the employees the sales force can have major promotion efforts directed at their own sales force to boost sales and loyalty of the employee.

Sales Promotions measures directed at firm's sales force

Table 6.3

Methods	Features	Examples
Training	To provide job enlargement enrichment to the performing executives	Hands on training at the joint venture partners firm Bajaj Allianz. Short training with premier training institutions in India and across the Globe.
Contests	For being number one performer in a category	Photograph in the house journal and facilatation in Annual gathering with Film Stars and Foreign Posting - Bank of India.
Conferences	Motivating the sales force	Resort trips for achievers - DSA of Citi Bank.
Awards	Motivating outstanding performers.	Certificates/Trophies/Cash prizes by Kinetic Fincap.

6.4 Advertising

Advertising is a paid form of nonpersonal presentation and promotion of ideas, services or goods by an identified sponsor. The advertising programme covers all the 5 M i.e. Mission, Money, Message, Media and Measurement. The mission of the firm must be stated in terms of specific goals.

The advertising objectives can be classified according to their aim as informative, persuasive, reminder and reinforcement.

- Informative advertising to create awareness of service with benefits.
- Persuasive advertising focuses on liking, preference, conviction and purchase of a service. To generate outstanding results you need to be seen over and over again. By using this method you are creating a change of the mind set. Repetition is what implants your service firmly in the prospect's mind.
- Reminder advertising stimulates repurchase of services.
- Reinforcement advertisement aims to convince the customers that they have made the right choice.

Advertising is used to achieve objectives which may include building image or brand, changing attitude and achieve sales.

The media may include various types such as newspapers, direct mail, magazines, exhibitions, television, radio, outdoor, telephone and internet. Advertising uses a combination of media to get the message across to the potential customers. For each media chosen the reach, frequency and impact along with timing and geographic allocation have to be taken into account. The impact of the advertisements can be obtained by measuring its effectiveness. Marketers choose the relevant media depending on the nature of the target to be reached, complexity of the message together with other factors such as proportion of the audience reached that is not the target market. This is very high in case of television advertising, but much lower in direct mail. Television advertising is quite expensive in terms of total cost but is quite reasonable in terms of the cost per person reached; where direct mail is low in total cost but high in terms of cost per person. Reach means total number of persons reached by the advertisement. This is estimated by examining the published data that gives this information. Regularity means how often the advertising can be used. Press advertising can be used quite often and outdoor not so often. Television advertising has shown to have highest persuasion on the consumer. If there is a lot going on around the advertisement attention will be diverted away from the advertising message due to high advertising clutter in breaks. Lead time is the duration of time from deciding the place of the advertisement to getting it shown. Television has long lead time and newspapers have a short lead time.

Various approaches are used by advertisers to promote services. Because services are intangible, they tend to be more difficult to advertise than goods.

1. Focus on tangibles

Tangible clues help the customers to understand and evaluate services and are emphasised in the message. These clues are the things that a customer can see as in case of an institute, the brochure, physical facilities like class room, library, internet, computer facilities, placement cell, seminar hall are clues to tangibilise this service.

As the services are intangible, marketers can use tangible attributes of the service to help the customer to understand better the service offered. In case of ICICI, the umbrella has been used to symbolise that the bonds issued have protection of ICICI.

Another way that advertisers can increase the effectiveness of services communications is to feature the tangibles associated with the service, such as showing a bank's operations with granite columns, automation backed with excellent illumination. Because services are abstract, they are often difficult to communicate clearly.

An advertisement for Merill Lynch that appeared in newspapers immediately before financial year closure urged customers to invest with them and avoid paying more in taxes. Using vivid information cues is particularly desirable when services are highly intangible and complex, as are the financial services featured in this advertisement.

Use interactive imagery-One type of vividness involves what is called interactive imagery. Imagery is a mental event that involves the visualisation of a concept or relationship which can enhance recall of names and facts about a service. Interactive imagery integrates two or more items in some mutual action, resulting in improved recall. Some service companies effectively integrate their logos or symbols with an expression of what they do.

2. **Feature service employees in communication.**

   Customer-contact personnel are an important second audience for services advertising. Featuring actual employees doing their jobs or explaining their services in advertising is effective both for the customers and the employees because it communicates to employees that they are important. Furthermore, when employees who perform a service well are featured in advertising, they become standards for other employees' behaviours and it becomes a factor of motivation. This is frequently accomplished by featuring the professors and management team in brochures with the toppers of their institute.

3. **Promise what is possible**

   All service communications should promise only what is possible and not attempt to make services more attractive than they actually are. Many companies hope to create good service by leading with good advertising, but this strategy can backfire when the actual service does not live up to the promises in advertising. In case of Dominos Pizza, if pizza is not delivered within thirty minutes it shall be free. Hence the service provider is aware of the probability of failure and focuses on minimising this failure even though there are many uncontrollable factors like weather, traffic, vehicle failure, delivery boy shortage etc.

4. **Encourage word of mouth communication**

   Since services are often high in experience and credence properties, people frequently turn to others for information rather than to traditional marketing channels. For professional services like tutors, lawyers, consultants, doctors, accountants, we seek personal recommendations about them. As the service is variable in nature, the word-of-mouth plays an important role in decision making of the buyer.

5. **Focus on benefits**

   Many private life insurance players are focussing on the benefits to the customers. To target high networth individuals they promise benefits like quick approval, higher returns and tie up of their Joint Venture foreign partner for safety and trust. Benefits are always very powerful in financial services wherein specific returns in the past can be tabled to justify the higher returns.

   If you are managing a massage centre, explain to the executive customers that their blood circulation will improve and they will feel more fresh and relaxed, to take on to the pressures of the corporate world.

6. **Direct communication to employees**

   In services which have high customer contact, the promotion should be directed at employees to motivate them to deliver the promise and also excite them to work towards zero defection of customers. High contact services like air travel, hotels concentrate on development of customer care attitude of their employees.

7. **Communication continuity**

   For achieving differentiation and presenting a unifying and consistent theme over a period there should be a continuous communication with the target audience. Firms keep in touch with their consumer through the use of logos/ signs/ packaging. Advertising makes use of these tools frequently to communicate with customers continuously. As an example McDonld's in their advertisement use yellow arched M throughout the world.

8. **Feature service customers in communication.**

   Advertisement testimonials featuring actual service customers simulate personal communications between people and enhances credibility.

6.5 Sales Promotion

Sales promotion is a key ingredient of a marketing campaign, which consists of short-term incentives such as coupons, premiums or discounts that stimulate quicker or greater purchase of particular products/services by consumers or trade. It is paid marketing communication activities that are intended to stimulate consumer purchases and dealer effectiveness. Demand stimulating devices like trade shows, incentives, give aways, demonstrations, contests etc. are used to supplement advertising activities. The objective of sales promotion is to induce a desired result from the trade intermediaries or the sales force. Sales promotion campaigns are intended to add value to the product because the incentives ordinarily will not accompany the product like in case of welcome drink when you check into the hotel. A ship offer for a night with a weeks stay in Goa. The incentive planned are short term and the duration of the scheme is spelt out.

Promotional Methods-Aimed at Channel Members

Objectives of sales promotion methods aimed at channel members:

(a) Defend shelf space against competition

(b) Improve the product knowledge

(c) Smoothen the capacity against peak and toughs

(d) A Provide sales support

(e) Motivates channel partners to stock more and push the brand on promotion.

The type of schemes, their characteristics with examples related to service sector are tabulated below with special focus to Auto-financing:

Table 6.4

Type	Characteristic	Examples
Advertising allowance	Advertising promotes products of two or more firms, which share its cost.	Dealers and finance firm share the cost 50-50 basis.
Conventions Trade shows Meetings	The firm invites the channel members for conventions, trade shows, meetings and their products are displayed with discussions.	When a new brand is being launched, dealers are called for a meeting where the new product with a new finance scheme is introduced to make a success in launch.
Display allowance	The channel members are provided with free product for demonstration.	The dealers are reimbursed the cost of free demonstration including the podium for display as well for leaflets, banners which they use for closing the sale.
Gifts	Gifts are given to the channel members for performing specified functions.	For product display steel stands are gifted to the dealer.
Push strategy	For pushing a particular brand of the firm, dealer and the sales team are given incentives.	Reputed companies are giving dealers Rs.100 for a case and to the staff they are giving Rs.50.

contd. ...

Special discounts	Channel partners are given a reduction from the price list that is offered by a seller to buyer in payment for purchasing during certain period.	In December, on the vehicle sales the dealers are given 1.5% discount, which is passed to the consumer via the finance company, to ensure that sales occur as the customers have marked preference for a registration with next year number plate on it.
Sales Contests	For achieving certain level of sales performance, prizes are distributed to dealers.	For coming first in all India finance sales, the dealer gets a trip to Far East for a week and if he repeats the performance the next year a trip to a destination of his choice, anywhere in the world.
Training	The members of the channel are provided training to improve knowledge about the product.	To tackle difficult and knowledgeable customers the financial products IRR training is imparted.

Promotional Methods - Aimed at Customers

Objectives of a sales promotion programme aimed at customers:

(a) Generate trial order

(b) Generate enquiries from target group

(c) Repurchase

(d) Increases traffic building

(e) Enhanced rate of purchase

The type of schemes, their characteristics with examples related to service sector are tabulated below:

Table 6.5

Type	Characteristic	Examples
Contest for prizes	Consumers participate in contests for prizes by answering question or by filling forms with slogan.	ESPN asking questions on sports and give away exciting prizes.
Contest for sales force	For achieving sales target prizes are distributed quarterly and annually.	Bajaj Allianz for life insurance gives cash award with a trip to Singapore.

contd. ...

Coupons	Services provider offer special discounts to the customers and shareholders, who redeem coupons.	Offer made by Oberoi and Taj group on special days.
Demos	Live demonstration of goods and services.	HCL displays use of photoshop to software photographers
Gifts	A gift to consumer for opening a new account	Global Trust Bank gave hot case lunch box to the first hundred account holder in every city in their first year of operation.
Rebate	Consumers get discount or rebate.	The insurance agents offer rebate to close the sales even though it is not allowed by IRDA.
Referral Gifts	Gifts to customers for referring the services to friends.	Le Meridian gives exquisite gifts to customers if their referral take annual membership.
Samples	Customers are given the offering, free of charge	ICICI Bill Junction provided its ESC scheme for bill payment absolutely free at the initial stage.
Gifts for relationship	The consumers get free gifts/special discounts based on frequent purchases.	Jet Airways frequent flyer programme for milage.
Bulk Discount	Buying services in bulk by consumers	Corporates get bulk discounts for food for seminars.

6.6 Relationship Marketing

The emphasis on relationship is now a key to successful business and the traditional concept of making sales is being replaced by making long time win – win relationship with customers. It is emerging as the core marketing activity for businesses operating in fiercely competitive environments. On an average, a business spends six times more to acquire customers than they do to keep them (Gruen, 1997). Therefore most of the firms are now paying more attention to their relationships with existing customers to retain them and increase their share of customers' purchases.

Relationship marketing can be defined as "process of attracting, maintaining, and in multi service organisations, enhancing customer relationship" – Berry (1983).

The underlying concept is to keep the loyal customer retained within the company and to honour their long term performance.

Shani and Chalsani (1992) viewed relationship marketing as ' an integrated effort to identify, maintain and build up a network with individual customers and to continuously strengthen the network for mutual benefits of both the sides, through interactive, individualised and value added contracts over a long period of time.

Intensifying competition and technological developments made businesses look for ways to reduce cost and improve their effectiveness. The practice of relationship marketing has the potential to improve marketing productivity through marketing efficiencies and effectiveness (Sheth and Parvatiyar, 1995).

The benefits of relationship marketing and CRM come through lower costs of retention and increased profits due to longer defection rates (Reichheld & Sasser, 1990).

Relationship marketing is a paradigm shift within marketing from an acquisition or transaction focus toward a retention or relationship focus. Relationship marketing is a way of doing business with a strategic orientation, that focuses on, keeping and enhancing business with current customers, rather than on acquiring new customers. This way assumes that consumers prefer to have an ongoing relationship with one organisation than to switch continually among providers in their search for value. Based on this assumption and the fact that it is much cheaper to keep a current customer than to attract a new one, successful marketers are working on effective strategies for retaining customers.

Customers have become partners with the firms taking long term commitments to maintaining those relationship with quality, service and innovations.

Pathmarajah defines relationship marketing as "the process where by the seller and the buyer join in a strong personal, professional and mutually profitable relationship over a time."

Relationship Marketing is marketing with the conscious aim to develop and manage long term and/or trusting relationship with customers, distributors, suppliers or other parties in the marketing environment. The building and management of relationship with customers has always been a key approach to marketing practices and some firms market on a relationship basis without calling it by that name. However, use of the term "relationship marketing" suggests that deliberate efforts are being made to retain customers and provide effective communication with them and use different approaches to marketing that it based on development of two way communication between suppliers and customers. It is affordable by technology and guided by analysis of customer purchasing and profitability.

Relationship Marketing there is a rationale for, benefits of and strategies for developing long-term relationships with customers. It is obvious that firms focusing only on getting new customers may fail to understand their current customers and thus may be bringing customers through the front door while equal or greater numbers are exiting through the back door. Estimates of lifetime value, support logically the importance of current customers and relationships.

The building of good personal relationship with customer is usually integral to small business management, for example our garage mechanic for vehicle repairs can easily illustrate the essence of relationship marketing. The mechanic in the small shop has direct knowledge of all regular customers and becomes familiar with their needs and their likes and dislikes. This enables the mechanic to provide services tailored to individual needs/ planned on the basis of known customer requirements. Over a period of time a bond of loyalty is likely to develop between the mechanic and the regular customer based on satisfaction.

Fig. 6.2

The particular strategy a firm uses to retain its current customers can and should be customised to fit the industry, the culture and the customer needs of the firm.

The criteria of a good relationship strategy require:

1. Effective market segmentation to identify whom to have relationships with.
2. Continuous development of services that evolve to suit the needs of these customers, and
3. Monitoring of current customer relationships through surveys and an updated customer database. By working with current customers in these ways, the organisation has a good chance of accurately understanding current customer expectations and of narrowing service quality gap. Based on this, the specific retention strategies offering increasing levels of competitive advantage can be

implemented. Each strategic approach focuses on a different type of bond between the customer and the firm: financial bonds, social and interpersonal bonds, customisation bonds and structural bonds. Although long-term customer relationships are critical and can be extremely profitable, firms should not attempt to build relationships with just any customer. In other words **'the customer isn't always right.'**

It has been suggested that firms frequently focus on attracting customers but pay little attention to what they should do to keep them. A senior executive of marketing at Holiday Inn, in an interview stated the bucket theory of marketing. The executive considered that marketing can be conceptualised as a big bucket: sales, advertising and promotion programs do pour business into the top of the bucket. As long as these programmes are effective, the bucket stays full but the problem arises if there's a hole in the bucket. When the business is running well and the hotel is delivering on its promises, the hole is small and few customers are leaving but when the operation is not upto the mark, customers are not satisfied with what they get, however, people start falling out of the bucket through the holes faster than they can be poured in through the top. The bucket theory highlights why a relationship strategy that focuses on plugging the holes in the bucket makes so much sense.

Historically, marketers have been more concerned with acquisition of customers, so a shift to a relationship strategy often represents changes in mind set, firms culture and employee reward systems. The sales incentive systems in many firms is based on bringing in new customers; but often no rewards for retaining current accounts. Thus, even when people see the logic of customer retention, the existing firms systems may not support its implementation.

As per Groonroos, marketing is to establish, maintain, and enhance relationships with customers and other partners profitably, so that the objectives of the buyer and service provider are met. This is achieved by a mutual exchange and fulfillment of promises. Groonroos highlighted that relationship and transaction marketing are opposed on a marketing strategy continuum and equated with the marketing of services and consumer goods respectively. Transaction marketing is common in the consumer goods sector and services marketing performance is purely the type of relationship with the consumer

TRANSACTIONAL MARKETING VS RELATIONSHIP MARKETING

Transaction Marketing	Relationship Marketing
1. Orientation to single sales	Orientation to customer retention
2. Discontinuous customer contact	Continuous customer contact
3. Focus on product features	Focus on customer value

contd. ...

4. Reducing price based on sensitivity analysis with right promotional measure	Promote Value and explain the benefits
5. No measures to build the on-going business	Measures like membership, clubs like frequent flyer to build on the going business
6. After sales support is poor as it is seen as cost	After sales support is excellent as it is seen as investment
7. Do the deal and disappear	Negotiate win-win and stay around to benefit later on from the same customer in terms of revenue and profitability.
8. Adding new customers with the existing customer	Data mining to develop and enhance relationship
9. Limited emphasis on customer service	High emphasis on customer service

Six market model in relationship marketing

In relationship marketing there is a wider view to build and sustain real customer value. It is important to recognise that relationships must be built with a number of important constituents:

1. Internal market
2. Referral market
3. Influence market
4. Employee market
5. Supplier market
6. Customer market

The cumulative effect of this shows how they differ from traditional marketing which has a narrow focus.

Reasons for Relationship Marketing

Liberalisation, Privatisation and Globalisation has increased the intensity of competition and many firms are trying to adapt to this environment.

1. The need to keep existing customers has became a priority in the face of intense competition and the high marketing costs for acquiring new customers.
2. For survival and growth, the ability, to produce physical products at lower costs, to compete with domestic and international players is required. This encouraged many

manufacturers to augment their physical products with services in order to compete and even to survive. Many large firms have been transformed from predominantly manufacturing organisations into service firms by bundling services with products. e.g. Kinetic Engineering - Auto financing to enhance sales and sustain competition by having group company for financing.

3. Increased competition and deregulation in many service dominated industries resulted in concentration on service quality as a means of achieving a competitive advantage. E.g. In Life Insurance, LIC of India was the only player but with 12 other private players it has ensured that automation and better trained employees has resulted in reducing the rate of complaints as well as faster service.

5 E'S of Relationship Marketing

1. Effective
2. Efficient
3. Enjoyable
4. Enthusiastic
5. Ethical

Very few firms can effectively implement 5E's but those who are aiming to offer the most value, professionally become a unique source in helping the buyer to become a partner with long term caring and trusting relationship.

Firms with transactional marketing approach constantly search for new customers because they fail to satisfy existing customers rather than retaining the existing customers base by demonstrating an unequivocal commitment to total quality customer care. Transactional marketing leads quickly to decline of the firm. The most expensive customer is the new customer you have probably had to advertise to get. You have no relationship as yet. Getting an order from a new customer can be five to six time more costly than getting one from the existing one, who contributes to firms profitability. The value of the customer sharply rises with each subsequent order because there are no promotion costs as well as the buyer buys more quantity with enhanced frequency and also recommends your firm to other friends.

Three Types of Customers

Jackson identified three types of customers based on the 'time horizon' within which a customer makes a commitment to a buyer and also the actual pattern of relationship builds overtime. The three types of customer pattern are:

1. Lost for good customers
2. Always a share customer
3. Intermediate type customer.

1. Lost for Good Customer

At one end of the customer behaviour spectrum, the buyer faces a high switching cost for high involvement products like life insurance, hence they look for a long-term relationship with the seller. The seller needs to make up-front investment to win new or enhance commitments from such a customer. Relationship marketing is apt, since the buyer maybe lost for good. If you can win this account, customer loyalty can be expected but if you lose you are never likely to get it.

2. Always a Share Customer

At the other end of the customer behaviour spectrum, lies the 'always a share customer' who purchases regularly low involvement products and has little or no loyalty to a supplier and can switch easily from one service provider to another. This is a short term relationship. In case you wish to get your house painted, you call in the nearest operator or the name of supplier you recall in your locality. Hence any service provider, who can offer immediately the best package of the service marketing mix, has a realistic chance of getting business from the always a share customer. Thus, transaction marketing emphasises on the individual transaction and is most appropriate for the 'always a share customer'. The typical characteristics of customers at the end points of the behaviour spectrum are detailed below:

Table 6.6

Type of customer	Always a share customer	Lost for good customers
Type of marketing	Transaction based	Relationship based
Time Horizon	Short	Long
Switching cost	Low	High
Investment	Smaller	Higher
Perceived exposure	Lower	Higher
Importance in strategic and operational	Lower	Higher
Focus	Service provider	Technology or vendor

3. Intermediate Type Customer

Most of the customers fall in this category. Factors like product category, the customer's pattern of product usage, the actions of the customer and the supplier affect the relationship. This pattern is exhibited by organisational buyer and not by a consumer who buys products regularly.

Aims of Relationship Marketing

The primary aim of relationship marketing is to build and maintain a base of customers who are profitable to the firm. To achieve this goal, the firm will focus on the attraction, retention and enhancement of customer relationships.

1. The firm will seek to attract customers who are likely to become long-term relationship customers.

2. Through market segmentation, the firm can understand the best target markets for building lasting customer relationships.

3. As the number of these relationships grows, the loyal customers themselves will frequently help to attract new customers by word of mouth with similar relationship potential.

4. Once they are attracted to begin a relationship with the company, customers will be more likely to stay in the relationship when they are consistently provided with quality products and services and good value overtime.

5. They are less likely to be pulled away by competitors, if they feel the company understands their changing needs and seems willing to invest in the relationship by constantly improving and evolving its product and service mix.

6. The aim of customer enhancement is that loyal customers can be even better customers if they buy more products and services from the firm over time. Loyal customers provide a base for the firm and have latent potential for growth.

Example, A bank customer becomes a better customer when a savings account is followed by an auto and home finance loan, keeps a good deposit and also buys insurance on the financial advise of the bank. Moreover, it is not only in the best interest of the firm to build and maintain a loyal customer base, but benefit from long-term associations.

Benefits for Customers in Customer Relationship

(a) Customers Benefits for those who will remain loyal to a firm when they receive greater value relative to what they expect from competing firms. Perceived value is the consumer's overall assessment of the utility of a product based on perceptions of what is received and what is given. Value is a trade-off for the consumer between the quality, satisfaction, and specific benefits exceed the monetary and non-monetary costs. When firms can consistently deliver, value the customer benefits and has an incentive to stay in the relationship,

(b) Trust Benefits comprise feelings of trust in the provider, along with a sense of reduced anxiety and comfort in knowing what to expect.

(c) Special Treatment Benefits include special pricing or preferential treatment.

(d) Social Benefits.

Benefits for Firm in Customer Relationship

(a) Higher value and volume of purchases with each passing year.

(b) Lower costs in operation, as many initial costs are not incurred as well as lower promotional spending.

(c) Enhanced employee retention as customers loyalty base leads to more satisfied employees.

(d) The marketing costs associated are higher with generating interest in new customers as opposed to already informed existing customers. The marketing costs involved in the creation of interest in an uninformed new customer, far outweigh those involved in maintaining the relationship necessary to continue exchanges, between buyer and seller. It has been estimated that the cost of attracting new customers can be as high as six times that of retaining existing customers.

(e) Close and long-term relationships with customers imply continuing exchange opportunities with existing customers at a lower marketing cost per customer. Across a wide range of businesses, the pattern is the same the longer a firm keeps a customer, the more money it tends to make.

(f) Viewing customer exchanges as a revenue stream, as opposed to a compendium of isolated transactions, enables cross-selling of related services overtime and premium pricing, for the customer's confidence in the business.

(g) Strong customer relationships with a high degree of familiarity and communications on both sides can generate, more practical new product ideas from customers and contact personnel.

(h) Good relationships with customers can result in good word-of-mouth from successful exchanges and minimal bad word-of-mouth in the event of unsuccessful exchanges. Service quality cracks can often be plugged easily where good relationships have existed.

Lifetime Value of a Customer (LTV)

Lifetime value of a customer is a calculation that looks at customers from the point of view of their lifetime revenue and profitability contribution to a firm. This homework is needed when firm start conceptualizing of building long-term relationships with their customers overtime and computing the financial value.

Factors That Influence Lifetime Value

1. The length of an average lifetime

2. The average revenues generated per relevant time period over the lifetime

3. Sales of additional products and services over time

4. Referrals generated by the customer overtime.

Table 6.7

Life Time Value for a BSNL Customer	Option 1	Option 2
Services availed	Landline	Landline, Mobile, Cable
Monthly bill	600	1500
Land line	600	600
Mobile	0	400
Cable	0	500
Cost	400	750
Land line	400	400
Mobile	0	150
Cable	0	200
Profit Monthly	200	750
No. of bills per year	12	12
Yearly profitability	2400	9000
Average customer life	40	40
Profit	96000	360000
Referrals	1	4
Referral profitability	96000	144000
Total Profitability	**192000**	**1800000**

Lifetime value should not be lifetime revenue stream but the costs are considered the lifetime value means lifetime profitability. For BSNL, providing communication service with land lines now offers, mobile telephony can also provide cable service. For a typical customer the lifetime value of a customer has been estimated:

Thus, LTV is an excellent opportunity to the marketer to concentrate and you can see that Option 2 is far more profitable and a strategy for same needs to be built in.

Market Segmentation and Targeting

1. **Identify basis for Segmenting the Market:** Market segments are identified by clubbing customers with common characteristics that are meaningful either to the product, pricing, promotion or place of the service. The segmentation for consumer markets can be demographic, geographic, psychographic, benefit, volume and behavioural segmentation. Segments may be identified on the basis of one of these or a combination.

2. **Develop profiles of Segments Identified:** These profiles usually involve demographic variables or psychographics or usage pattern. In a nutshell, understand how and whether the segments differ from each other in their profiles.

3. **Develop Measures of Segment Attractiveness:** The firm will select the target segment or segments for the service. Estimate the market size and determine share. Analyse competition using Porter's model of 5 forces. The firm must decide whether serving the segment is in line with firms' objectives and resources. Rank the segment on the basis of attractiveness.

4. **Select the Target Segments** for the service on the basis that it is large with good growth potential and the segment fits in line with firms mission. The firm must decide if the segment is large enough and has good growth potential.
5. **Ensure that the Target Segments are Compatible:** This step is the most critical for service firms than for goods companies, as services are often performed in the presence of the customer, the services marketer must be certain that the customers are compatible with each other.

Retention Strategies

The successful retention strategies will be built on foundations of quality service, market segmentation, monitoring of changing relationship needs over a period of time. Leonard Berry and A. Parasuraman have developed a framework for understanding four types of retention strategies. Retention marketing can occur at different levels and that each successive level of strategy results in ties that bind the customer a little closer to the firm. At each successive level, the potential for sustained competitive advantage is also increased.

Level 1 - Financial Bonds

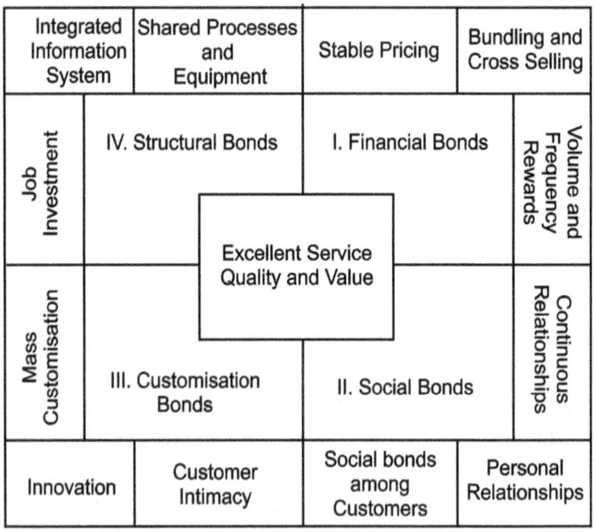

Integrated Information System	Shared Processes and Equipment	Stable Pricing	Bundling and Cross Selling
Job Investment	IV. Structural Bonds	I. Financial Bonds	Volume and Frequency Rewards
Mass Customisation	III. Customisation Bonds	II. Social Bonds	Continuous Relationships
Innovation	Customer Intimacy	Social bonds among Customers	Personal Relationships

(center box: Excellent Service Quality and Value)

Fig. 6.3

The customer is bonded to the firm with financial incentives like lower prices based on volume or lower prices for customers, who have been with the firm for a long time. BSNL has recently changed the billing to monthly and have offered volume discounts, linked to price incentives to retain market share and build a loyal customer base. Jet Airways has a frequent flyer programme, based on the mileage logged by the customer and they are entitled to a free flight to any one destination, any where in the globe. The financial incentive programmes are common as they are easy to initiate and result in immediate gains. Financial incentives provide long-term advantages to a firm only, when they are coupled with other relationship strategies. Their is considerable customer switching every month among the mobile operators from BPL to Idea to Airtel to BSNL and so on and so forth. Currently their churn rate is hovering around 7-8%. While price lowered is important to customers, it can be duplicated in no time by competitors. Bundling and cross selling of services like ICICI Bank for the home loans is given accident insurance for an equivalent amount as well as free credit card membership for a period of one year. Financial bonds reduce loyalty and the chances for customer retention reduces, as customer is on lookout for similar programme from the other players.

Level II - Social Bonds

Social Bonds bind the customers more with the firm than financial incentives and focus is on building long-term relationships, through social and interpersonal as well as financial bonds. Customers are viewed as clients and their needs and wants are understood by the firm. Services are dovetailed to fit individual needs, and marketers find ways of staying in touch with their customers, thereby developing social bonds with them. During a study of Customer Satisfaction Survey by a market research firm, for Tata Engineering Company in automobile sector, it was found that staying in touch with clients helped in assessing their changing needs, sharing personal information with clients and discussing changes in the sector all served to increase the likelihood, that the client would stay with the firm due to better relationship.

Interpersonal bonds are common among professional service providers like accountants, doctors, lawyers, professors and their clients as well as among personal care providers like counselors, hair dressers, health care providers and their clients. A dentist friend of mine, Dr. Shirish Pradhan, has the fact file before meeting the patient with personal facts about the patient like occupation, interests and dental health. By bringing some of these personal details into the conversation, the dentist shows genuine interest in the patient as an individual and builds social bonds.

Interpersonal bonds are common in business-to-business relationships where customers develop relationships with salespeople and/or relationship managers working with their firms. Recognising the value of continuous relationships in building loyalty, KSB Pumps Limited credits much of its success to its extensive distribution network in India.

KSB is a global leader in submersible and horizontal pumps. While its engineering and product quality are superior due to inflow of technology from its parent, the success is due to its strong dealer network and product support services offered. The dealers are businessmen who offer excellent service in their territories, do social projects related to drinking water in rural areas and keep the visibility of KSB in the area. This has resulted in excellent customer relationship.

Sometimes, relationships are formed with the firm due to the social bonds that develop between customers themselves due to meeting in the service provider premises. In case of Pune club, members interact with each other. Over time, the social relationships they have with other members are important factors that keep them from switching to another club. Firms that encourage bonding among customers are using social retention strategy.

While social bonds are difficult for competitors to imitate than price incentives due to absence of strong reasons to shift to another provider, interpersonal bonds can encourage customers to stay in a relationship.

Level III - Customisation Bonds

Customisation strategies involve a combination of social ties, financial incentives which are encompassed within a customisation strategy and vice versa. For e.g. in the KSB dealership strategy, dealers make good personal commitments to customers. Dealers also provide information back into the system to help KSB customise services to meet the customer needs. Customer loyalty can be enhanced through intimate knowledge of individual customers and through the development of one-to-one solution that fits in with the individual customers' needs. Mass customisation is the use of flexible processes to produce individually customised products and services at the price of standardised, mass-produced options. The financial consultant or investment advisor uses a strategy of building relationships with its customers with one solution at a time based on details of the customer based on his profile and current financial status.

Level IV - Structural Bonds

Structural strategies are the most difficult to copy and are a composite mix of structural, financial, social, interpersonal, customisation bonds between the customer and the firm. Structural bonds focus on providing services to the client that are frequently designed right into the service system for that client. Often structural bonds are created by technology based solutions that make client more profitable.

In case of Federal Express as they attempt to tie their clients closer to them by providing them with free computers-Federal Express, Power Ships store address, shipping data, print labels for mailing and track the status of packages around the globe. With this arrangement, a firm can save time and keep better track of shipping records. The customer's have a negation that the arrangement with one provider may not allow them to take advantage of price savings with other providers in the future if the competition offers a better option; which is what must be protected contractually while getting into this arrangement.

6.7 Role of Relationship Marketing in Promoting Services

The developing economies are now very dependent on service industries. There is a shift to service economy from the industrial economy. In this labour intensive sector relationship plays an important role. The major service organisations like banks, hospitals, hotels, IT and telecoms require regular interaction of marketers and customers, so that the bond and understanding between both will become strong.

According to market Line Associates, the top 20% of typical bank customers produce as much as 150% of overall profit, while the bottom 20% drain about 50% from bank's bottom line and the revenues from the rest just meeting their expenses.

Berry (1993) recommended the following five strategies for practicing relationship marketing:

- Developing a core service around which to build a customer relationship.
- Customizing relationship to the individual customer.
- Augmenting the core service with extra benefits.
- Pricing service to encourage customer loyalty.
- Marketing to employees so that they will perform well for customers.

Development of relationship orientation of marketing in the post industrial era is the rebirth of direct marketing between producers and consumers. Several environmental and organisational development factors are responsible for their rebirth. Development in information technology, data warehousing, data mining have made it possible for firms to maintain a one to one relationship with their customers.

Service firms are always been relationship oriented. The nature of service business is relationship based. A service is a process or performance where the customer is involved, sometimes for a long period of time, sometime only for a short time, and sometime on a regular basis. There is always a direct contact between a customer and the service firms. This contact makes it possible to create a relationship between the service provider and customer. In growing service businesses, the customer was turned from a relationship partner into market share statistics.

There are certain important issues for understanding customers and maintain a long term mutually trusted relationship with them. These issues are as follows –

- CRM initiatives undertaken by firms
- Development of those programmes
- Identifying important (key) customers
- Measurement of effectiveness

CRM Initiatives

IT and Telecom, Banking, Hotel, Hospital sectors are adopting various CRM initiatives. In case of IT and telecom the customer care centres are the initial receiver of customer complaints and processor for the other levels of management for solutions. In case of Banking, Hotels and Hospital sectors the feed back opportunity is one of the forms of getting customer satisfaction and dissatisfaction level. In customer centric marketing, marketers assess each customer individually to determine whether to serve that customer directly or indirectly. Also customer centric marketers determine whether to create an offering that customises the product or service of the marketing mix or standardise the offering.

Process

Information from customers is collected systematically over a period of time. This can be done through regular surveys and during customer interaction noting down the important points. This information has to be combined with the organisations experiences with customers to build rich customer profiles, buying behaviours, preferences and usage patterns.

Identifying Key Customers

When it comes to combining customer information with experiences, service firms seem to be economising. Most of them seem to be doing it for selected customers. Hotels do it for their regular guests specially those who have enrolled for their membership schemes. Financial service providers selectively do it for their high net worth individuals who typically use multiple offerings of the service provider.

Measurement of Effectiveness

Most service firms rely on periodic surveys to understand their customers' expectations and also understand and anticipate the behaviour of customers. Many service firms have indicated that they work with their customers as a team to ensure that their expectations are met. Research has constantly indicated that one of the major reasons for poor quality service is the gap between perception of managers about the customer expectations and customers' real or actual expectations (Parasuraman, Zeithaml & Berry, 1985). Roger and Dorf (1999) have recommended a four stage process of Identification, Differentiation, Interaction, and Customisation for implementing one to one relationship with customers. After analysing the information and findings company must go for implementing those key elements and again they need to follow up the result.

Questions for Discussion

1. What is promotion of services? Explain sales promotion in the services industry.
2. Explain 'Advertising' in services industry/sector.
3. What is personal selling in services industry?
4. Define advertising. Explain the elements and objectives of advertising.
5. What do you mean by sales promotion? State the objectives and advantages of sales promotion.
6. What is 'direct marketing'? State its importance.
7. Explain the role and implications of relationship marketing.
8. State the process of relationship marketing.
9. State the importance of relationship marketing (in services marketing) for attaining customer value.
10. Explain the various promotion objectives of services.
11. Explain the role of relationship marketing in promotion of services.
12. Write a short note on: internal marketing.
13. Explain how to gain sustainable competitive advantage in services marketing.

■■■

Chapter **7** ...

Pricing

Contents ...

7.1 Introduction

A key goal of effective pricing strategy is to manage revenues in ways that support the firm's profitability objectives. To do this, the firm has to have a good understanding of its costs, the value created for customers and competitor's pricing. Value to customers usually varies widely between segments and even within the same segment across time. To complicate matters, demand fluctuates widely, whereas capacity tends to be relatively fixed. Marketing is the only function that brings revenues into the organisation. All other management functions incur costs. Pricing is the mechanism by which sales are transformed into revenues. Pricing is typically more complex in services than in manufacturing. Because there is no ownership of services, it is usually more difficult for managers to determine the financial costs of creating a process or performance for a customer than to identify the costs associated with creating and distributing a physical good.

7.2 Price an Indicator of Service Quality

One of the intriguing aspects of pricing is that buyers are likely to use price as an indicator of both service costs and service quality-price is at once an attraction variable and a repellent. Customers' use of price as an indicator of quality depends on several factors, one of which is the other information available to them. When service cues to quality are readily accessible, when brand names provide evidence of a company's reputation, or when the level of advertising communicates the company's belief in the brand, customers may prefer to use those cues instead of price. In other situations, however, such as when quality is hard to detect or when quality or price varies a great deal within a class of services, consumers may believe that price is the best indicator of quality. Many of these conditions typify situations that face consumers when purchasing services. Another factor that increases the dependence on price as a quality indicator is the risk associated with the service purchase. In high-risk situations, many of which involve credence services such as medical treatment or management consulting, the customer will look to price as a surrogate for quality.

Because customers depend on price as a cue to quality and because price sets expectations of quality, service prices must be determined carefully. In addition to being chosen to cover costs or match competitors, prices must be selected to convey the appropriate quality signal. Pricing too low can lead to inaccurate inferences about the quality of the service. Pricing too high can set expectations that may be difficult to match in service delivery.

7.3 Approaches to Pricing Services

This chapter's Strategy Insight briefly reviews key strategic concepts about pricing that apply equally to goods and services. Rather than repeating what you learned about pricing in your marketing principles class, we want to emphasise in this chapter the way that services prices and pricing differ from both the customer's and the company's perspective. We discuss these differences in the context of the three pricing structures typically used to set prices: (1) cost-based, (2) competition-based, and (3) demand based pricing. These categories, as shown in Fig. 7.1, are the same bases on which goods prices are set, but adaptations must be made in services. The figure shows the three structures interrelating, because companies need to consider each of the three to some extent in setting prices. In the following sections we describe in general each basis for pricing and discuss challenges that occur when the approach is used in services pricing. Fig. 7.1 summarises those challenges.

BOX: 7.1. STRATEGY INSIGHT: STRATEGIC DECISIONS IN PRICING

Many of the strategic aspects of pricing of services are the same as pricing of goods. A summary of the basics is provided here. For more details, return to your basic marketing textbook or to Marketing Management by Philip Kotler, the text from which we excerpted these fundamental points about pricing.

1. The firm must consider many factors in setting its pricing policy: selecting the pricing objective, determining demand, estimating costs, analysing competitors' prices and offers, selecting a pricing method, and selecting the final price.

2. Companies do not always seek to maximize profits through pricing. Other objectives they may have include survival, maximising current revenue, maximising sales growth, maximising market skimming, and product/quality leadership.

---

3. Marketers need to understand how responsive demand would be to a change in price. To evaluate this important criterion of price sensitivity, marketers can calculate the price elasticity of demand, which is expressed as:

$$\text{Elasticity} = \frac{\text{Percentage change in quantity purchased}}{\text{Percentage change in price}}$$

4. Various types of costs must be considered in setting prices, including direct and indirect costs, fixed and variable costs, indirect traceable costs, and allocated costs. If a product or service is to be profitable for company, price must cover all costs and include a markup as well.

5. Competitors' prices will affect the desirability of a company's offerings and must be considered in establishing prices.

6. A variety of pricing methods exist including markup, target return, perceived-value, going-rate, sealed-bid, and psychological.

7. After setting a price structure, companies adapt prices using geographic pricing, price discounts and allowances, promotional pricing, discriminatory pricing, and product-mix pricing.

Source: Kotler, Philip, Marketing Management, 11th Edition, © 2003. Reprinted by permission of Pearson Education, Inc., Upper Saddle River, NJ.

Challenges:
1. Small firms may charge too little to be viable.
2. Heterogeneity of services limits comparability.
3. Prices may not reflect customer value.

Challenges:
1. Costs are difficult to trace.
2. Labour is more difficult to price than materials.
3. Costs may not equal the value that customers perceive the services are worth.

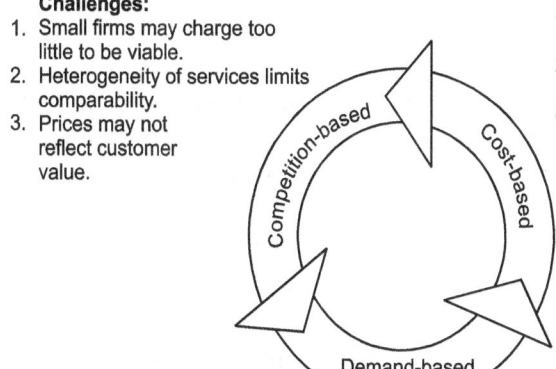

Challenges:
1. Monetary price must be adjusted to reflect the value of nonmonetary costs.
2. Information on service costs is less available to customers; hence, price may not be a central factor.

Fig. 7.1: Three Basic Marketing Price Structures and Challenges Associated with Their Use for Services

1. Cost-Based Pricing

In cost-based pricing, a company determines expenses from raw materials and labour, adds amounts or percentages for overhead and profit, and thereby arrives at the price. This method is widely used by industries such as utilities, contracting, wholesaling, and advertising. The basic formula for cost-based pricing is

$$Price = Direct\ costs + Overhead\ costs + Profit\ margin$$

Direct costs involve materials and labour that are associated with delivering the service, overhead costs are a share of fixed costs, and the profit margin is a percentage of full costs (direct + overhead).

Special Challenges in Cost-Based Pricing for Services

One of the major difficulties in cost-based pricing involves defining the units in which a service is purchased. Thus the price per unit a well-understood concept in pricing of manufactured goods-is a vague entity. For this reason many services are sold in terms of input units rather than units of measured output. For example, most professional services (such as consulting, engineering, architecture, psychotherapy, and tutoring) are sold by the hour.

What is unique about services when using cost-based approaches to pricing? First, costs are difficult to trace or calculate in services businesses, particularly where multiple services are provided by the firm. Consider how difficult it must be for a bank to allocate teller time accurately across its checking, savings, and money market accounts in order to decide what to charge for the services. Second, a major component of cost is employee time rather than materials, and the value of people's time, particularly non-professional time, is not easy to calculate or estimate.

An added difficulty is that actual service costs may under-represent the value of the service to the customer. A local tailor charges $10 for taking in a seam on a$350 ladies' suit jacket and an equal $10 for taking in a seam on a pair of $14 sweat shorts. The tailor's rationale is that both jobs require the same amount of time. What she neglects to see is that the customer would pay a higher price and might even be happier about the alterations-for the expensive suit jacket, and that $10 is too high a price for the sweat shorts.

Examples of Cost-Based Pricing Strategies Used in Services

Cost-plus pricing is a commonly used approach in which component costs are calculated and a markup is added. In product pricing, this approach is quite simple; in service industries, however, it is complicated because the tracking and identification of costs are difficult. The approach is typically used in industries in which cost must be estimated in advance, such as Construction, engineering, and advertising. In construction or engineering, bids are solicited by clients on the basis of the description of the service desired. Using their knowledge of the costs of the components of the service (including the raw material's such as masonry and lumber), labour (including both professional and unskilled), and margin, the company estimates and presents to the client a price for the finished service. A contingency amount-to cover the possibility that costs may be higher than estimated is also stated because in large projects specifications can change as the service is provided.

7.4

Fee for service is the pricing strategy used by professionals; it represents the cost of the time involved in providing the service. Consultants, psychologists, accountants, and lawyers, among other professionals, charge for their services on an hourly basis. Virtually all psychologists and social workers have a set hourly rate they charge to their clients, and most structure their time in increments of an hour.

In the early 1900s, lawyers typically billed clients a certain fee for services rendered regardless of the amount of time they spent delivering them. Then in the 1970s, law firms began to bill on an hourly rate, in part because this approach offered accountability to clients and an internal budgeting system for the firm. One of the most difficult aspects of this approach is that recordkeeping is tedious for professionals. Lawyers and accountants must keep track of the time they spend for a given client, often down to 10 minute increments. For this reason the method has been criticised because it does not promote efficiency and sometimes ignores the expertise of the lawyers (those who are very experienced can accomplish much more than novices in a given time period, yet billings do not always reflect this). Clients also feared padding of their legal bills, and began to audit them. Despite these concerns, the hourly bill dominates the industry, with the majority of revenues billed this way.

2. Competition-Based Pricing

The competition-based pricing approach focuses on the prices charged by other firms in the same industry or market. Competition-based pricing does not always imply charging the identical rate others charge but rather using others' prices as an anchor for the firm's price. This approach is used predominantly in two situations: (1) when services are standard across providers, such as in the dry cleaning industry, and (2) in oligopolies with a few large service providers, such as in the airline or rental car industry. Difficulties involved in provision of services sometimes make competition-based pricing less simple than it is in goods industries.

Special Challenges in Competition-Based Pricing for Services

Small firms may charge too little and not make margins high enough to remain in business. Many mom and-pop service establishments-dry cleaning, retail, and tax accounting, among others-cannot deliver services at the low prices charged by chain operations.

Further, the heterogeneity of services across and within providers makes this approach complicated. Bank services illustrate the wide disparity in service prices. Customers buying checking accounts, money orders, or foreign currency, to name a few services, find that prices are rarely similar across providers. For example, at one point Nations Bank charged $5 for a money order when the Postal Service charged $0.75 and 7-Eleven stores charged $1.09. Compare these prices for having a check drawn on foreign currency: Bank of America, $20; Thomas Cook, $7; and Citibank, $15. And fees for cashier's checks ranged from $10 to no charge, with a nationwide average of $2.69. Banks claim that they set fees high enough to cover the costs of these services. The wide disparity in prices probably reflects the bank's difficulty in determining prices as well as their belief that financial customers do not shop around nor discern the differences (if any) among offerings from different providers. A banking expert makes the point that "It's not like buying a quart of milk.... Prices aren't standardized. Only in very standardised services (such as dry cleaning) are prices likely to be remembered and compared.

Examples of Competition-Based Pricing in Services Industries

Price signaling occurs in markets with a high concentration of sellers. In this type of market, any price offered by one company will be matched by competitors to avoid giving a low-cost seller a distinct advantage. The airline industry exemplifies price signaling in services. When any competitor drops the price of routes, others match the lowered price almost immediately.

Going-rate pricing involves charging the most prevalent price in the market. Rental car pricing is an illustration of this technique (and also an illustration of price signaling, because the rental car market is dominated by a small number of large companies). For years, the prices set by one company (Hertz) have been followed by the other companies. When Hertz instituted a new pricing plan that involved "no mileage charges, ever," other rental car companies imitated the policy. They then had to raise other factors such as base rates, size and type of car, daily or weekly rates, and drop-off charges to continue to make profits. Prices in different geographic markets, even cities, depend on the going rate in that location, and customers often pay different rates in contiguous cities in the same state. The newsletter Consumer Reports Travel Letter advises customers that the national toll-free reservation lines offer better rates than are obtained calling local rental car companies in cities, perhaps because those rates are less influenced by the going rates in a particular area.

The Global Feature in this chapter illustrates some of the practices in pricing that differ across countries.

3. Demand-Based Pricing

The two approaches to pricing just described are based on the company and its competitors rather than on customers. Neither approach takes into consideration that customers may lack reference prices, may be sensitive to non-monetary prices, and may judge quality on the basis of price. All these factors can be accounted for in a company's pricing decisions. The third major approach to pricing, demand-based pricing, involves setting prices consistent with customer perceptions of value. Prices are based on what customers will pay for the services provided.

Special Challenges in Demand-Based Pricing for Services

One of the major ways that pricing of services differs from pricing of goods in demand-based pricing is that non-monetary costs and benefits must be factored into the calculation of perceived value to the customer. When services require time, inconvenience, and psychological and search costs, the monetary price must be adjusted to compensate. And when services save time, inconvenience, and psychological and search costs, the customer is willing to pay a higher monetary price. The challenge is to determine the value to customers of each of the non-monetary aspects involved.

Another way services and goods differ with respect to this form of pricing is that information on service costs may be less available to customers, making monetary price not as salient a factor in initial service selection as it is in goods purchasing.

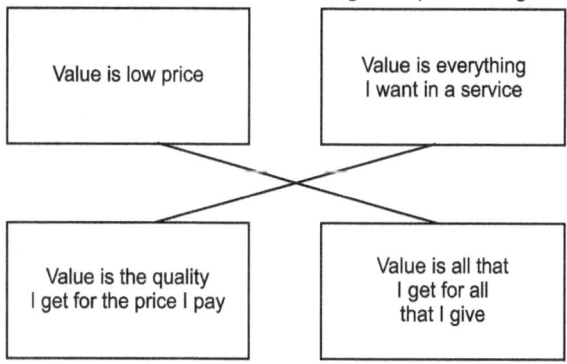

Fig. 7.2: Four Customer Definitions of Value

Source: N.C. Mohan, "Pricing Research for Decision Making," Marketing Research: A Magazine of Management and Applications 7, no. I (Winter 1995), pp. 10-19. Reprinted by permission of the American Marketing Association.

Value is Low Price: Some consumers equate value with low price, indicating that what they have to give up in terms of money is most salient in their perceptions of value, as typified in these representative comments from customers:

For dry cleaning: "Value means the lowest price."

For carpet steam cleaning: "Value is price-which one is on sale."

For a fast food restaurant: "When I can use coupons, I feel that the service is a value."

For airline travel: "Value is when airline tickets are discounted."

Value Is Whatever I Want in a Product or Service: Rather than focusing on the money given up, some consumers emphasise the benefits they receive from a service or product as the most important component of value. In this value definition, price is far less important than the quality or features that match what the consumer wants. In the telecommunications industry, for example, business customers strongly value the reliability of the systems and are willing to pay for the safety and confidentiality of the connections. Service customers describe this definition of value as follows:

For an MBA degree: "Value is the very best education I can get."

For medical services: "Value is high quality."

For a social club: "Value is what makes me look good to my friends and family."

For a rock or country music concert: "Value is the best performance."

Value Is the Quality I Get for the Price I Pay: Other consumers see value as a trade-off between the money they give up and the quality they receive.

For a hotel for vacation: "Value is price first and quality second."

For a hotel for business travel: "Value is the lowest price for a quality brand,"

For a computer services contract: "Value is the same as quality. No-value is affordable quality."

Four Meanings of Perceived Value

One of the most appropriate ways that companies price their services is basing the price on the perceived value of the service to customers. Among the questions a services marketer needs to ask are the following: What do consumers mean by value? How can we quantify perceived value in dollars so that we can set appropriate prices for our services? Is the meaning of value similar across consumers and services? How can value perceptions be influenced? To understand demand-based pricing approaches, we must fully understand what value means to customers.

This is not a simple task. When consumers discuss value, they use the term in many different ways and talk about myriad attributes or components. What constitutes value, even in a single service category; appears to be highly personal and idiosyncratic. Customers define value in four ways: (1) Value is low price. (2) Value is whatever I want in a product or service. (3) Value is the quality I get for the price I pay. (4) Value is what I get for what I give (Fig. 7.2). Let us take a look at each of these definitions more carefully.

Value Is What I Get for What I Give: Finally, some consumers consider all the benefits they receive well as all sacrifice components (money, time, effort) when describing value.

For a housekeeping service: "Value is how many rooms I can get cleaned for what the price is."

For a hairstylist: "Value is what I pay in cost and time for the look I get."

For executive education: "Value is getting a good educational experience in the shortest time possible."

The four consumer expressions of value can be captured in one overall definition consistent with the concept of utility in economics. Perceived value is the consumer's overall assessment of the utility of a service based on perceptions of what is received and what is given. Although what is received varies across consumers (some may want volume, others high quality, still others convenience), as does what is given (some are concerned only with money expended, others with time and effort), value represents a trade-off of the give and get components. Customers will make a purchase decision on the basis of perceived value, not solely to minimise the price paid. These definitions are the first step in identifying the elements that must be quantified in setting prices for services.

Incorporating Perceived Value into Service Pricing

The buyer's perception of total value prompts the willingness to pay a particular price for a service. To translate the customer's value perceptions into an appropriate price for a specific service offering, the marketer must answer a number of questions. What benefits does the service provide? How important is each of these benefits? How much is it worth to the customer to receive a particular benefit from a service? At what price will the service be economically acceptable to potential buyers? In what context is the customer purchasing the service?

The most important thing a company must do-and often a difficult thing is to estimate the value to customers of the company's services. Value may be perceived differently by consumers because of idiosyncratic tastes, knowledge about the service, buying power, and ability to pay. In this type of pricing, what the consumers value-not what they pay-forms the basis for pricing. Therefore, its effectiveness rests solely on accurately determining what the market perceives the service to be worth.

When the services are for the end consumer, most often service providers will decide that they cannot afford to give each individual exactly the bundle of attributes he or she values. They will, however, attempt to find one or more bundles that address segments of the market. On the other hand, when services are sold to businesses (or to end customers in the case of high-end services), the company can understand and deliver different bundles to each customer.

An interesting manifestation of demand-oriented pricing is shown in the Technology Spotlight.

One of the most complex and difficult tasks of services marketers is setting prices internationally. If services marketers price on the basis of perceived value and if perceived value and willingness to pay differ across countries (which they often do), then service firms may provide essentially the same service but charge different prices in different countries. Here, as in pricing domestically, the challenge is to determine the perceived value not just to different customers but to customers in different parts of the world. Pricing in Europe provides one of the most compelling examples of the pricing challenges that marketers face internationally.

Historically, Europe was considered to be a loosely aligned group of more than 12 separate countries, and a services marketer could have as many different pricing approaches as it had countries in which it offered the services. Although pricing was complex to administer, the marketer had full flexibility in pricing and could seek the profit-maximising price in. each country. Prices across countries tended to vary widely, both in services and in products: "In most markets, [there are] still enormous price differentials between countries. For identical consumer products, prices show typical deviations ranging between 30 and 150 percent-for example 115 percent for chocolate, 65 percent for tomato ketchup, and up to 155 percent for beer in Europe." The European Community created a single internal market, holding the potential to simplify marketing in the area but also creating grave concerns about pricing. The largest concern is that marketers will be required to offer all services at a single European price-the lowest price offered in any European country-which could dramatically reduce revenues and profits.

7.4 Pricing Strategies

In this section we describe the approaches to services pricing that are particularly suited to each of the four value definitions.

1. Pricing Strategies When the Customer Means "Value Is Low Price"

When monetary price is the most important determinant of value to a customer, the company focuses mainly on price. This focus does not mean that the quality level and intrinsic attributes are always irrelevant, just that monetary price dominates in importance. To establish a service price in this definition of value, the marketer must understand to what extent customers know the objective prices of services in this category, how they interpret various prices, and how much is too much of a perceived sacrifice. These factors are best understood when the service provider also knows the relative dollar size of the purchase, the frequency of past price changes, and the range of acceptable prices for the service. Some of the specific pricing approaches appropriate when customers define value as low price include discounting, odd pricing, synchro-pricing, and penetration pricing (Fig. 7.3)

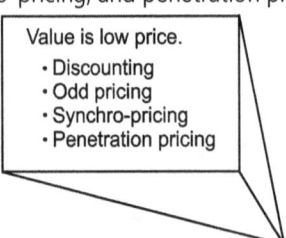

Value is low price.
- Discounting
- Odd pricing
- Synchro-pricing
- Penetration pricing

Fig. 7.3: Pricing Strategies When the Customer Defines Value as Low Price

Discounting

Service providers offer discounts or price cuts to communicate to price-sensitive buyers that they are receiving value. Colleges are now providing many forms of discounting to attract students. Lehigh University allows top students to get a fifth year of undergraduate or graduate education free, and also offers scholarships based on criteria other than financial need. The business school also cut tuition 22 percent for its master's programme and allows graduates to take two-thirds off the regular tuition price. Discount pricing has become a creative art at other educational institutions. The University of Rochester offered a $5,000 grant to all New York State residents enrolling as freshmen Miami University (in Ohio) now lists only one tuition for all students (both in-state and out-of-state). The university offers a discount to in-state students. The end result is that each group of students pays the same as before, but the perception is that in-state students get a discount.

Odd Pricing

Odd pricing is the practice of pricing services just below the exact dollar amount to make buyers perceive that they are getting a lower price. Dry cleaners charge $2.98 for a shirt rather than $3.00, health clubs have dues priced at $33.90 per month rather than $34, and haircuts are $9.50 rather than $10.00. Odd prices suggest discounting and bargains and are appealing to customers for whom value means low price.

Synchro-Pricing

Synchro-pricing is the use of price to manage demand for a service by capitalising on customer sensitivity to prices. Certain services, such as tax preparation, passenger transportation, long-distance telephone, hotels, and theatres, have demand that fluctuates over time as well as constrained supply at peak times. For companies in these and other industries, setting a price that provides a profit over time can be difficult. Pricing can, however, play a role in smoothing demand and synchronising demand and supply. Time, place, quantity, and incentive differentials have all been used effectively by service firms. Place differentials are used for services in which customers have a sensitivity to location. The front row at concerts, the 50-yard line in football, center court in tennis or basketball, ocean-side rooms in resort hotels-all these represent place differentials that are meaningful to customers and that therefore command higher prices.

Time differentials involve price variations that depend on when the service is consumed. Telephone service after 11 PM., hospital rooms on weekends, airline tickets that include a Saturday night stay, and health spas in the off season are time differentials that reflect slow periods of service. By offering lower prices for underused time periods, a service company can smooth demand and also gain-incremental revenue.

Quantity differentials are usually price decreases given for volume purchasing. This pricing structure allows a service company to predict future demand for its services. Customers who buy a booklet of coupons for a tanning salon or facial, a quantity of tokens for public bridges, or packages of advertising spots on radio or television are all responding to price incentives achieved by committing to future services. Corporate discounts for airlines, hotels, and rental cars exemplify quantity discounts in the business context; by offering lower prices, the service provider locks in future business.

Differentials as incentives are lower prices for new or existing clients in the hope of encouraging them to be regular users or more frequent users. Some professionals-lawyers, dentists, electrologists, and even some physicians offer free consultations at the front end, usually to overcome fear and uncertainty about high service prices. Other companies stimulate use by offering regular customers discounts or premiums during slow periods. Sports teams are now using differential prices as incentives to attract customers who would otherwise not be able to afford the high cost of attending sports events. For example, in 2004 the average price of an NBA ticket was $44.68, an NHL ticket was $44.22, and an NFL ticket was $52.95. The Phoenix Suns, in claiming that "You should have pricing for every pocketbook," revamped its ticket pricing by raising premium seats by 26 percent, decreasing arena seats by 31 percent, and adding 500 $10 tickets. The net result was a 6 percent increase in the average ticket price (paid for by the premium seat holders), but more attendance at the games because more fans in different segmentg could afford the seats.

Penetration Pricing

The price charged for products and services is set artificially low in order to gain market share. Once this is achieved, the price is increased. This approach was used by France Telecom and Sky TV. Penetration pricing is a strategy in which new services are introduced at low prices to stimulate trial and widespread use. The strategy is appropriate when: (1) sales volume of the service is very sensitive-'to price, even in the early stages of introduction; (2) it is possible to achieve economies in unit costs by operating at large volumes; (3) a service faces threats of strong potential competition very soon after introduction; and (4) there is no class of buyers willing to pay a higher price to obtain the service. Penetration pricing can lead to problems when companies then select a "regular" increased price. Care must be taken not to penetrate with so low a price that customers feel the regular price is outside the range of acceptable prices.

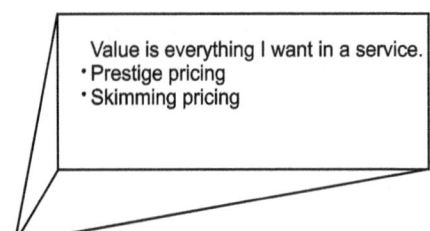

Fig. 7.4: Pricing Strategies When the Customer Defines Value as Everything Wanted in a Service

2. Pricing Strategies When the Customer Means "Value Is Everything I Want in a Service"

When the customer is concerned principally with the "get" components of a service, monetary price is not of primary concern. The more desirable intrinsic attributes a given service possesses, the more highly valued the service is likely to be and the higher the price the marketer can set. Fig. 7.4 shows appropriate pricing strategies.

3. Prestige Pricing

Prestige pricing is a special form of demand-based pricing by service marketers who offer high-quality or status services. For certain services-restaurants, health clubs, airlines, and hotels-a higher price is charged for the luxury end of the business. Some customers of service companies who use this approach; may actually value the high price because it represents prestige or a quality image. Others prefer purchasing at the high end because they are given preference in seating or accommodations and are entitled to other special benefits. In prestige pricing, demand may actually increase as price increases because the costlier service has more value in reflecting quality or prestige.

4. Skimming Pricing

Skimming, a strategy in which new services are introduced at high prices with large promotional expenditures, is an effective approach when services are major improvements over past services. In this situation, customers are more concerned about obtaining the service than about the cost of the service, allowing service providers to skim the customers most willing to pay the highest prices.

5. Pricing Strategies When the Customer Means

"Value Is the Quality I Get for the Price I Pay"

Some customers primarily consider both quality and monetary price. The task of the marketer is to understand what quality means to the customer (or segments of customers) and then to match quality level with price level. Specific strategies are shown in Fig. 7.5.

Value Pricing

The widely used term value pricing has come to mean "giving more for less." In current usage it involves assembling a bundle of services that are desirable to a wide group of customers and then pricing them lower than they would cost alone. Taco Bell pioneered value pricing with a $0.59 Value Menu.

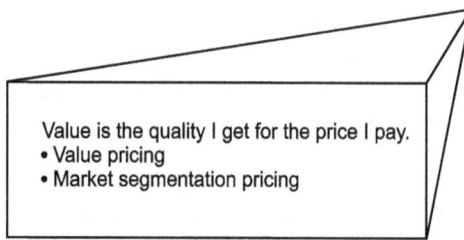

Value is the quality I get for the price I pay.
• Value pricing
• Market segmentation pricing

Fig. 7.5: Pricing Strategies when the Customer Defines Value as Quality for the Price paid

After sales at the chain rose 50 percent in two years to $2.4 billion, McDonald's and Burger King adopted the value pricing practice. The menu at Taco Bell has since been reconfigured to emphasise plain tacos and burritos (which are easier and faster for the chain to make) for less than a dollar. Southwest Airlines also offers value pricing in its airline service: a low, cost for a bundle of desirable service attributes such as frequent departures, friendly and funny employees, and on-time arrival. The airline offers consistently low fares with bare-bones service.

Market Segmentation Pricing

Market segmentation pricing, a service marketer charges different prices to groups of customers for what are perceived to be different quality levels of service, even though there may not be corresponding differences in the costs of providing the service to each of these groups. This form of pricing is based on the premise that segments show different price elasticities of demand and desire different quality levels.

Services marketers often price by client category; based on the recognition that some groups find it difficult to pay a recommended price. Health clubs located in college communities will typically offer student memberships, recognising that this segment of customers has limited ability to pay full price. In addition to the lower price, student memberships may also carry with them reduced hours of use, particularly in peak times. The same line of reasoning leads to memberships for "seniors," who are less able to pay full price but are willing to patronize the clubs during daytime hours when most full-price members are working.

Companies also use market segmentation by service version, recognizing that not all segments want the basic level of service at the lowest price. When they can identify a bundle of attributes that are desirable enough for another segment of customers, they can charge a higher price for that bundle. Companies can configure service bundles that reflect price and service points appealing to different groups in the market. Hotels, for example, offer standard rooms at a basic rate but then combine amenities and tangibles related to the room to attract customers willing to pay more for the concierge level, jacuzzis, additional beds, and sitting areas.

6. Pricing Strategies When the Customer Means "Value Is All That I Get for All That I Give"

Some customers define value as including not just the benefits they receive but also the time, money, and effort they put into a service. Fig. 7.6 illustrates the pricing strategies described in this definition of value.

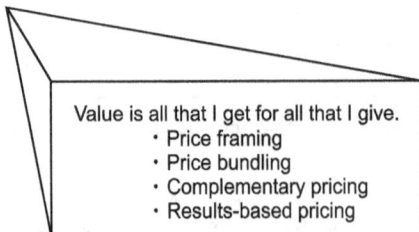

Value is all that I get for all that I give.
 • Price framing
 • Price bundling
 • Complementary pricing
 • Results-based pricing

Fig. 7.6: Pricing Strategies When the Customer Defines Value as All That Is Received for All That Is Given

Price Framing

Because many customers do not possess accurate reference prices for services, services marketers are more likely than product marketers to organise price information for customers so they know how to view it. Customers naturally look for price anchors as well as familiar services against which to judge focal services. If they accept the anchors, they view the price and service package favorably. Gerald Smith, a professor at Boston College, provided an enlightening example of the way price framing could have improved sales of the 1994 Olympic TripleCast, minute-by-minute coverage of different Olympic arenas that was a well-documented failure because customers were not willing to pay the price of $130. He suggested that if CBS had segmented the market, isolated meaningful packages of sports, and framed them in a way that was familiar to customers, the service might have been successful. He proposed a boxing package for $24.95, a skating package for $24.95, and equestrian and wrestling packages for $19.95. In each case the service could be framed in an appropriate price context. For example, boxing at $24.95 is priced somewhere between attending a boxing match and watching it on pay-per-view. Boxing aficionados would recognize that the price for the full package of matches was a value 25.

Price Bundling

Some services are consumed more effectively in conjunction with other services; other services accompany the products they support (such as extended service warranties, training, and expedited delivery). When customers find value in a package of services that are interrelated, price bundling is an appropriate strategy. Bundling, which means pricing and selling services as a group rather than individually, has benefits to both customers and service companies. Customers find that bundling simplifies their purchase and payment, and companies find that the approach stimulates demand for the firm's service line, thereby achieving cost economies for the operations as a whole while increasing net contributions. Bundling also allows the customer to pay less than when purchasing each of the services individually, which contributes to perceptions of value.

The effectiveness of price bundling depends on how well the service firm understands the bundles of value that customers or segments perceive, and on the complementarity of demand for these services. Effectiveness also depends on the right choice of services from the firm's point of view. Because the firm's objective is to increase overall sales, the services selected for bundling should be those with a relatively small sales volume without the bundling to minimise revenue loss from discounting a service that already has a high sales volume.

Approaches to bundling include mixed bundling, mixed-leader bundling, and mixed-joint bundling. In mixed bundling, the customer can purchase the services individually or as a package, but a price incentive is offered for purchasing the package. As an example, a health club customer may be able to contract for aerobics classes at $10 per month, weight machines at $15, and pool privileges at $15-or the group of three services for $27 (a price incentive of $13 per month). In mixed-leader bundling, the price of one service is discounted if the first service is purchased at full price. For example, if cable TV customers buy one premium channel at full price, they can acquire a second premium channel at a reduced monthly rate. The objective is to reduce the price of the higher-volume service to generate an increase in its volume that "pulls" an increase in demand for a lower-volume but higher-contribution margin service. In mixed joint bundling, a single price is formed for the combined set of services to increase demand for both services by packaging them together.

Complementary Pricing

Services that are highly interrelated can be leveraged by using complementary pricing. This pricing includes three related strategies-captive pricing, two-part pricing, and loss leadership. In captive pricing the firm offers a base service or product and then provides the supplies or peripheral services needed to continue using the service. In this situation the company could off load some part of the price for the basic service to the peripherals. For example, cable services often drop the price for installation to a very low level, then compensate by charging enough for the peripheral services to make up for the loss in revenue. With service firms, this strategy is often called two-part pricing because the service price is broken into a fixed fee plus variable usage fees (also found in telephone services, health clubs, and commercial services such as rentals). Loss leadership is the term typically used in retail stores when providers place a familiar service on special largely to draw the customer to the store and then reveal other levels of service available at higher prices.

Results-Based Pricing

In service industries in which outcome is very important but uncertainty is high, the most relevant aspect of value is the result of the service. In personal injury lawsuits, for example, clients value the settlement they receive at the conclusion of the service. From tax accountants, clients value cost savings. From trade schools, students most value getting a job upon graduation. From Hollywood stars, production companies value high grosses. In these and other situations, an appropriate value-based pricing strategy is to price on the basis of results or outcome of the service.

The most commonly known form of results-based pricing is a practice called contingency pricing used by lawyers. Contingency pricing is the major way that personal injury and certain consumer cases are billed; it accounts for 12 percent of commercial law billings. In this approach, lawyers do not receive fees or payment until the case is settled, when they are paid a percentage of the money that the client receives. Therefore, only an outcome in the client's favour is compensated. From the client's point of view, the pricing makes sense in part because most clients in these cases are unfamiliar with and possibly intimidated by law firms. Their biggest fears are high fees for a case that may take years to settle. By using contingency pricing, clients are ensured that they pay no fees until they receive a settlement.

In these and other instances of contingency pricing, the economic value of the service is hard to determine before the service, and providers develop a price that allows them to share the risks and rewards of delivering value to the buyer. Partial contingency pricing, now being used in commercial law cases, is a version in which the client pays a lower fee than usual but offers a bonus if the settlement exceeds a certain level. Bickel and Brewer, a commercial law firm, agreed to cap fees for legal work at $800,000 but to split with its client, Prentiss Properties, any judgment over $10 million. When the federal judge awarded Prentiss $100 million in settlement, the law firm walked away with $45 million more in payment for taking the risk.

Sealed Bid Contingency Pricing Companies wishing to gain the most value from their services purchases are increasingly turning to a form of results-based pricing that involves sealed bids guaranteeing results. Consider the challenge of a school district with energy bills (including heating oil, gas, and electricity) so high that money was diverted from its primary mission of educating students. In its most recent year, costs for energy were $775,000, and the proposed budget for the coming year was $810,000. The school board wanted a long-term solution to the problem, desiring to expend less of their budget on energy and more on direct education expenses. The EMS Company, an engineering firm providing services to control and reduce energy use in large buildings, was one of three companies submitting bids to the school district. EMS proposed a computer-controlled system that monitored energy use and operated on/off valves for all energy-using systems. The proposal specified a five-year contract with a fixed price of $254,500 per year, with the additional guarantee that the school district would save at least that amount of money each year or EMS would refund the difference. Included in the proposal was a plan to take into account energy prices, hours the buildings were in use, and degree days so as to provide a basis of calculating the actual savings occurring. After five years the school district would own the system with the option of purchasing a management operating service for an annual fee of $50,000.

Although two other firms submitted lower multiyear bids of $190,000 and $215,000 annually, neither bid provided any guarantee for energy savings. The school board was intrigued by the EMS approach, because at worst the cost of the service was zero. EMS was awarded the bid. During the first year, actual calculated savings exceeded $300,000. A cost-plus bid by EMS would have been priced at $130,000 per year. The use of contingency pricing by EMS removed the risk from the school board's decision and added profits at EMS.

Money-Back Guarantees: Vocational colleges offer one major promise: to get students jobs upon graduation. So many schools commit to this promise-often blatantly in television advertising-that prospective students have come to distrust all promises from these colleges. To give substance to its promise, Brown-MacKenzie College, a for-profit vocational college, offered a tuition-back guarantee to any graduate who, after due effort, failed to obtain a suitable position within 90 days of program completion. Although other educational institutions cannot do this, largely because the results desired do not often arrive within a 90-day period, other results-based plans are taking shape. A future-income dependent payment plan has been considered by many schools. Under such a plan, a student would receive a full scholarship and, after graduation, pay a fixed percentage of salary for a set period-for example, 5 percent of salary for 20 years. Under this plan, the more "value added" by education and the more money-oriented the student, the more the student and the institution would benefit financially.

Commission: Many services providers-including real estate agents and advertising agencies-earn their fees through commissions based on a percentage of the selling price. In these and other industries, commission is paid by the supplier rather than the buyer. Advertising agencies are paid 15 percent commission by the print and broadcast media (newspaper, radio, TV, magazines) for the amount of advertising that they place with the media, but agencies are not paid by their clients. Real estate agents are paid 6 percent of the selling price of a house.

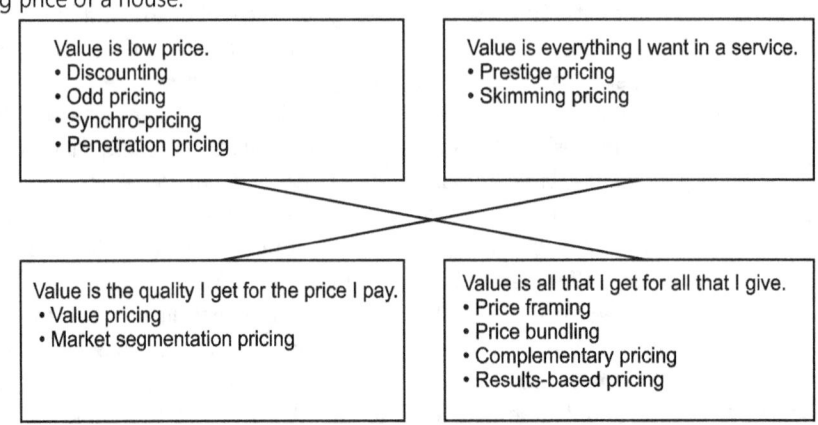

Fig. 7.7: Summary of Service Pricing Strategies for Four customer Definitions of Value

The commission approach to services pricing is compelling in that agents are compensated most when they find the highest rates and fares. It would seem that agents have an underlying motivation to avoid the lowest fares and rates for their clients.

Examples

Pricing of Training Consultancy

Training is a special form of consultancy. In training the preparation of the material for the first assignment takes considerable time, but will spread over the number of times the consultant conducts the same course. A consultant can possibly give the same lecture or input on constant basis and may be required to update the references and figures etc.

How many people should be assumed to estimate the training cost is important consideration. The cost of training can be estimated somewhat on the lines of cost of consultancy.

Assume that a full time trainer can be employed for ₹ 24,000 per month. Considering a multiplying factor of 2, the annual expense of a training will be;

₹ 24,000 × 12 × 2 = ₹ 576,000

Considering 180 days per year the daily rate will be;

(576,000 / 180 = ₹ 32,00)

If there are ten delegates in this course the organisation shall be buying this at the rate of ₹ 320 per participant per day. This figure when compared to open courses is quite low.

In case of 'in house' course, the training consultant does not have to advertise as in case of open courses. They will supply backup reading material, note pads and exercise if any. The organisations in case 'in-house' programmes benefit by getting a tailor-made programme at a little extra-cost but have to provide complete number of delegates.

The training consultant while computing the cost must consider:
1. The contents of the course to adopt requiring fulfillment of firm's needs.
2. Extra input required to adopt the course to firm's needs.
3. Cost of visits required to be undertaken.
4. Whether the existing material can be used with little upgradation or it is totally new assignment.

The consultant should also judge the going rate for similar programmes before making offer.

If the amount of additional work involved in adopting the course to the needs of the client can be compared with the advantage of having a readymade course of delegates, and priced accordingly.

If only a little adoption of an existing course is required, the price can be set at a substantial percentage say 50 percent of delegates day cost of open course. For example, if the open course is ₹ 2,000 per delegate per day, it could be set as ₹ 1000 per delegate day and for ten delegates the course could be offered for ₹ 10,000 per day. In this way, the firm gains in having the course at less cost compared to sending the delegates in the open course. If the course is to be designed specially for the client the consultant may offer the course at the cost of open course. In such case consultant is to design a tailor made course and may be required to pay visits to client or course discussions.

The above method is only for guidelines and training organisations should select figures as per their organisation norms.

General Hotel Pricing Strategy

Large hotels do lucrative business with firms which hold conferences, training sessions and business meets. At popular conference centres during peak periods demand always exceeds supply and hotelier almost are having seller market. As the year moves towards off peak period-the hotels are no more having conferences, training sessions and supply exceeds demand. In such situations, room inventories are changed and rechanged to suit the dynamic marketing situations. The hoteliers at this stage devise prices to cultivate secondary markets in order to maintain the projected revenues. Thus, pricing becomes a key tool with the more price sensitive customers. The price sensitive customer are in a better position to negotiate because they are able to play one hotel against another. In this situation the problems before the hoteliers are –
(a) What lowest rates to be offered?
(b) Preventing the customer from going to competitor.

Like any other business, hotel business costs can also be divided into two categories:

1. Fixed costs that have to be paid irrespective of any amount of business.

2. Variable cost which varies directly with the number of clients.

The fixed costs are very high in case of hotel industry compared to variable cost and typically variable cost varies between 10-25% of room cost.

Marketers have two views on contribution towards payment of fixed overheads:

1. Any revenue that exceeds the variable cost contributes something towards fixed overhead.

2. Every product should contribute towards the fixed cost.

In manufacturing industry, the products which do not contribute towards fixed cost are normally dropped from the product line. Thus, the second view is relevant only to a non-service business environment.

In hotel industry, the variable cost of room is relevant to pricing decision. Any revenue in excess of this is productive, otherwise it is going to perish for ever.

So hoteliers concern should be more on devising long term strategies for more revenue and long term profits.

7.5 Demand Variations and Capacity Constraints

The fundamental issue underlying supply and demand management in services is the lack of inventory capability. Unlike manufacturing firms, service firms cannot build up inventories during periods of slow demand to use later when demand increases. This lack of inventory capability is due to the perishability of services and their simultaneous production and consumption. An airline seat that is not sold on a given flight cannot be resold the following day. The productive capacity of that seat has perished. Similarly, an hour of a lawyer's billable time cannot be saved from one day to the next. Services also cannot be transported from one place to another or transferred from person to person. Thus the Phoenix Ritz-Carlton's services cannot be moved to an alternative location in the summer months say, to the Pacific Coast where summers are ideal for tourists and demand for hotel rooms is high.

The lack of inventory capability combined with fluctuating demand leads to a variety of potential outcomes, as illustrated in Fig. 7.8. The horizontal lines in Fig. 7.8 indicate service capacity, and the curved line indicates customer demand for the service. In many services, capacity is fixed; thus capacity can be designated by a flat horizontal line' over a certain time period. Demand for service frequently fluctuates, however, as indicated by the curved line. The topmost horizontal line in Fig. 7.8 represents maximum capacity. For example, in our opening vignette, the horizontal line would represent the Phoenix Ritz-Carlton's 281 rooms, or it could represent the approximately 70,000 seats in a large university football stadium. The rooms and the seats remain constant, but demand for them fluctuates. The band between the second and third horizontal lines represents optimum capacity-the best use of the capacity from the perspective of both customers and the company (the difference between optimal and maximum capacity utilisation is discussed later in the chapter). The areas in the middle of Fig. 7.8 are labeled to represent four basic scenarios that can result from different combinations of capacity and demand:

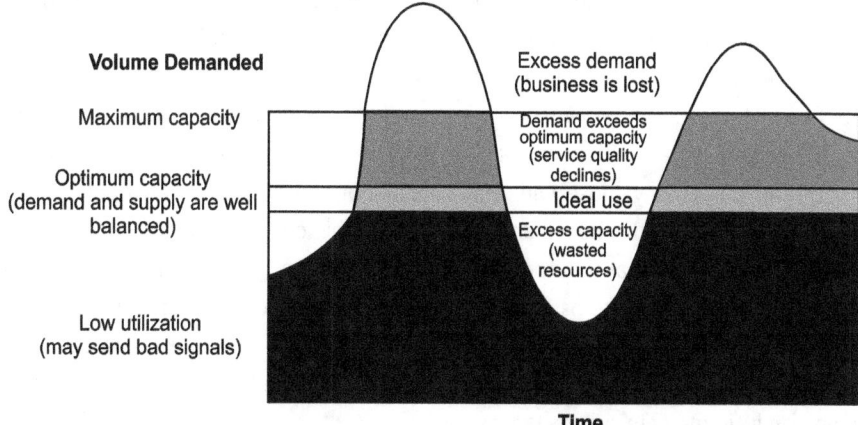

Fig. 7.8: Variations in Demand Relative to Capacity

Source: Reprinted from C. Lovelock, "Getting the Most Out of Your Productive Capacity," in Product Plus (Boston: McGraw Hill, 1994), chap. 16, p. 241 © 1994 by The McGraw-Hill Companies, Inc. Reprinted by permission of The McGraw-Hill Companies.

1. **Excess demand:** The level of demand exceeds maximum capacity. In this situation some customers will be turned away, resulting in lost business opportunities. For the customers who do receive the service, its quality may not match what was promised because of crowding or overtaxing of staff and facilities.

2. **Demand exceeds optimum capacity:** No one is being turned away, but the quality of service may still suffer because of overuse, crowding, or staff being pushed beyond their abilities to deliver consistent quality.

3. **Demand and supply are balanced at the level of optimum capacity:** Staff and facilities are occupied at an ideal level. No one is overworked, facilities can be maintained, and customers are receiving quality service without undesirable delays.

4. **Excess capacity:** Demand is below optimum capacity. Productive resources in the form of labour, equipment, and facilities are underutilised, resulting in lost productivity and lower profits. Customers may receive excellent quality on an individual level because they have the full use of the facilities, no waiting, and complete attention from the staff. If, however, service quality depends on the presence of other customers, customers may be disappointed or may worry that they have chosen an inferior service provider.

Not all firms will be challenged equally in terms of managing supply and demand. The seriousness of the problem will depend on the extent of demand fluctuations over time, and the extent to which supply is constrained (Table 7.1). Some types of organisations will experience wide fluctuations in demand (telecommunications, hospitals, transportation, restaurants), whereas others will have narrower fluctuations (insurance, laundry, banking). For some, peak demand can usually be met even when demand fluctuates (electricity, natural gas), but for others peak demand may frequently exceed capacity (hospital emergency rooms, restaurants, hotels). Those firms with wide variations in demand (cells 1 and 4 in Table 7.1), and particularly those with wide fluctuations in demand that regularly exceed capacity (cell 4), will find the issues and strategies in this chapter particularly important to their success. Those firms that find themselves in cell 3 need a "one-time-fix" to expand their capacity to match regular patterns of excessive demand. The example industries in Table 7.1 are provided to illustrate where most firms in those industries would likely be classified. In reality, an individual firm from any industry could find itself in any of the four cells, depending on its immediate circumstances.

To identify effective strategies for managing supply and demand fluctuations, an organisation needs a clear understanding of the constraints on its capacity and the underlying demand patterns.

Table 7.1: Demand versus supply

Extent to which supply is constrained	Extent of Demand Fluctuations Over Time	
	Wide 1	Narrow 2
Peak demand can usually be met without a major delay	Electricity Natural gas Hospital maternity unit Police and fire emergencies	Insurance Legal services Banking Laundry and dry cleaning
Peak demand regularly exceeds capacity	Accounting and tax preparation Passenger transportation Hotels Restaurants Hospital emergency rooms	Services similar to those in 2 that have insufficient capacity for their base level of business

Source: C. H. Lovelock, "Classifying Services to Gain Strategic Marketing Insights;' Journal of Marketing 47, (Summer 1983): 17 Reprinted by permission from the American Marketing Association

7.5.1 Capacity Constraints

Later in the chapter, some creative ways are presented to expand and contract capacity in the short and long term, but for our discussion now, you can assume that service capacity is fixed. Depending on the type of service, critical fixed-capacity factors can be time, labour, equipment, facilities, or (in many cases) a combination of these.

Time, Labour, Equipment, Facilities

For some service businesses, the primary constraint on service production is time. For example, a lawyer, a consultant, a hairdresser, a plumber, and a psychological counselor all primarily sell their time. If their time is not used productively, profits are lost. If there is excess demand, time cannot be created to satisfy it. From the point of view of the individual service provider, time is the constraint.

From the point of view of a firm that employs a large number of service providers, labour or staffing levels can be the primary capacity constraint. A law firm, a university department, a consulting firm, a tax accounting firm, and a repair and maintenance contractor may all face the reality that at certain times demand for their organisations' services cannot be met because the staff is already operating at peak capacity. However, it does not always make sense (nor may it be possible in a competitive labour market) to hire additional service providers if low demand is a reality at other times.

In other cases, equipment may be the critical constraint. For trucking or air-freight delivery services, the trucks or airplanes needed to service demand may be the capacity limitation. During the Christmas holidays, UPS, FedEx, and other, delivery service providers face this issue. Health clubs also deal with this limitation, particularly at certain times of the day (before work, during lunch hours, after work) and in certain months of the year. For network service providers, bandwidth, servers, and switches represent their perishable capacity.

Finally, many firms face restrictions brought about by their limited facilities. Hotels have only a certain number of rooms to sell, airlines are limited by the number of seats on the aircraft, educational institutions are constrained by the number of rooms and the number of seats in each classroom, and restaurant capacity is restricted to the number of tables and seats available.

Many examples illustrate the most common capacity constraint for each type of service. In reality, any of the service organisations listed can be operating under multiple constraints. For example, a law firm may be operating under constrained labour capacity (too few attorneys) and facilities constraints (not enough office space) at the same time.

Table 7.2: Constraints on Capacity

Nature of the Constraint	Type of Service
Time	Legal
	Consulting
	Accounting
	Medical
Labour	Law firm
	Accounting firm
	Consulting firm
	Health clinic
Equipment	Delivery services
	Telecommunications
	Network services
	Utilities
	Health club
Facilities	Hotels
	Restaurants
	Hospitals
	Airlines
	Schools
	Theaters
	Churches

The examples illustrate the most common capacity constraint for each type of service. In reality, any of the service organisations listed can be operating under multiple constraints. For example, a law firm may be operating under constrained labour capacity (too few attorneys) and facilities constraints (not enough office space) at the same time.

Understanding the primary capacity constraint, or the combination of factors that restricts capacity, is a first step in designing strategies to deal with supply and demand issues (Table 7.2).

Optimal versus maximum Use of Capacity

To fully understand capacity issues, it is important to know the difference between optimal and maximum use of capacity. As suggested in Fig. 7.8, optimum and maximum capacity may not be the same. Using capacity at an optimum level means that resources are fully employed but not overused and that customers are receiving quality service in a timely manner. Maximum capacity, on the other hand, represents the absolute limit of service availability. In the case of a football game, optimum and maximum capacity may be the same. The entertainment value of the game is enhanced for customers when every single seat is filled, and obviously the profitability for the team is greatest under these circumstances. On the other hand, in a university classroom it is usually not desirable for students or faculty to have every seat filled. In this case, optimal use of capacity is less than the maximum. In some cases, maximum use of capacity may result in excessive waiting by customers, as in a popular restaurant. From the perspective of customer satisfaction, optimum use of the restaurant's capacity will again be less than maximum use.

In the case of equipment or facilities constraints, the maximum capacity at any given time is obvious. There are only a certain number of weight machines in the health club, a certain number of seats in the airplane, and a limited amount of space in a cargo carrier. In the case of a bottling plant, when maximum capacity on the assembly line is exceeded, bottles begin to break and the system shuts down. Thus it is relatively easy to observe the effects of exceeding maximum equipment capacity.

When the limitation is people's time or labour, maximum capacity is harder to specify because people are in a sense more flexible than facilities and equipments. When an individual service provider's maximum capacity has been exceeded, the result is likely to cause decreased service quality, customer dissatisfaction, and employee burnout and turnover, but these outcomes may not be immediately observable even to the employee herself. It is often easy for a consulting firm to take on one more assignment, taxing its employees beyond their maximum capacity, or for an HMO clinic to schedule a few more appointments in a day, stretching its staff and physicians beyond their maximum capacity. Given the potential costs in terms of reduced quality and customer and employee dissatisfaction, it is critical for the firm to understand optimum and maximum human capacity limits.

7.5.2 Demand Patterns

To manage fluctuating demand in a service business, it is necessary to have a clear understanding of the demand patterns, why they vary, and the market segments that comprise demand at different points in time. A number of questions need to be answered regarding the predictability and underlying causes of demand.

The Charting of Demand Patterns

First, the organisation needs to chart the level of demand over relevant time periods. Organisations that have good computerised customer information systems can chart this information very accurately. Others may need to chart demand patterns more informally. Daily, weekly, and monthly demand levels should be followed, and if seasonality is a suspected problem, graphing should be done for data from at least the past year. In some services, such as restaurants or health care, hourly fluctuations within a day may also be relevant. Sometimes demand patterns are intuitively obvious; in other cases patterns may not reveal themselves until the data are charted.

Predictable Cycles

In looking at the graphic representation of demand levels; is there a predictable cycle daily (variations occur by hours), weekly (variations occur by day), monthly (variations occur by day or week), and/or yearly (variations occur according to months or seasons)? In some cases, predictable patterns may occur at all periods. For example, in the restaurant industry, especially in seasonal tourist locations, demand can vary predictably by month, by week, by day, and by hour.

If a predictable cycle is detected, what are its underlying causes? The Ritz-Carlton in Phoenix knows that demand cycles are based on seasonal weather patterns and that weekly variations are based on the workweek (business travelers do not stay at the hotel over the weekend). Tax accountants can predict demand based on when taxes are due, quarterly and annually. Services catering to children and families respond to variations in school hours and vacations. Retail and telecommunications services have peak periods at certain holidays and times of the week and day. When predictable patterns exist, generally one or more causes can be identified.

Random Demand Fluctuations

Sometimes the patterns of demand appear to be random-there is no apparent predictable cycle. Yet even in this case, causes can often be identified. For example, day-to-day changes in the weather may affect use of recreational, shopping, or entertainment facilities. Although the weather cannot be predicted far in advance, it may be possible to anticipate demand a day or two ahead. Health-related events also cannot be predicted. Accidents, heart attacks, and births all increase demand for hospital services, but the level of demand cannot generally be determined in advance. Natural disasters such as floods, fires, and hurricanes can dramatically increase the need for. such services as insurance, telecommunications, and health care. Acts of war and terrorism such as that experienced in the United States on September 11, 2001, generate instantaneous need for services that cannot be predicted.

AT&T was faced with a sudden increase in demand for services to the military during the Gulf War. During this period, 500,000 US troops were deployed to the Middle East, many without advance warning. Before their deployment these men and women had little time to attend to personal business, and all of them left behind concerned family and friends. With mail delivery between the United States and the Middle East taking more than six weeks, troops needed a quick way to communicate with their families and to handle personal business. Communications with home were determined by the military to be essential to troop morale. AT&T's ingenuity, responsiveness, and capacities were challenged to meet this unanticipated communication need. During and after the Gulf War crisis more than 2.5 million calls were placed over temporary public phone installations, and AT&T sent more than 1.2 million free faxes to family and friends of service men and women.'

Our Global Feature illustrates how one company with seemingly random and chaotic demand for its services was able to change its business to serve customers. The feature is also a good example of organisational learning across cultures.

Demand Patterns by Market Segment

An organisation that has detailed records on customer transactions may be able to disaggregate demand by market segment, revealing patterns within patterns. Or the analysis may reveal that demand from one segment is predictable whereas demand from another segment is relatively random. For example, for a bank, the visits from its commercial accounts may occur daily at a predictable time, whereas personal account holders may visit the bank at seemingly random intervals. Health clinics often notice that walk-in or "care needed today" patients tend to concentrate their arrivals on Monday, with fewer needing immediate attention on other days of the week. Knowing that this pattern exists, some clinics schedule more future appointments (which they can control for later days of the week, leaving more of Monday available for same-day appointments and walk-ins.

7.5.3 Strategies for Matching Capacity and Demand

When an organisation has a clear grasp of its capacity constraints and an understanding of demand patterns, it is in a good position to develop strategies for matching supply and demand. There are two general approaches for accomplishing this match. The first is to smooth the demand fluctuations themselves by shifting demand to match existing supply. This approach implies that the peaks and valleys of the demand curve (Fig. 7.9) will be flattened to match as closely as possible the horizontal optimum capacity line. The second general strategy is to adjust capacity to match fluctuations in demand. This implies moving the horizontal capacity lines shown in Fig. 7.9 to match the ups and downs of the demand curve. Each of these two basic strategies is described next with specific examples.

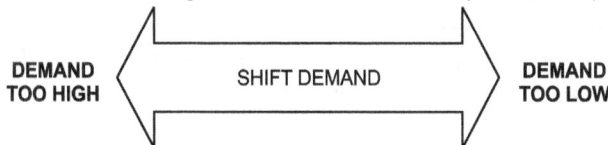

| DEMAND TOO HIGH | SHIFT DEMAND | DEMAND TOO LOW |

- Use signage to communicate busy days and times.
- Offer incentives to customers for usage during nonpeak times.
- Take care of loyal or "regular" customers first.
- Advertise peak usage times and benefits of nonpeak use.
- Charge full price for the service-no discounts.

- Use sales and advertising to increase business from current market segments.
- Modify the service offering to appeal to new market segments.
- Offer discounts or price reductions.
- Modify hours of operation.
- Bring the service to the customer.

Fig. 7.9: Strategies for Shifting Demand to Match Capacity

Shifting Demand to Match Capacity

With this strategy an organisation seeks to shift customers away from periods:n which demand exceeds capacity, perhaps by convincing them to use the service during periods of slow demand. This change may be possible for some customers but not for others. For example, many business travelers are not able to shift their needs for airline, car rental, and hotel services; pleasure travelers, on the other hand, can often shift the timing of their trips. Customers who cannot shift and cannot be accommodated will represent lost business for the firm.

During periods of slow demand, the organisation seeks to attract more and/or different customers to utilise its productive capacity. A variety of approaches, detailed in the following sections, can be used to shift or increase demand to match capacity. Frequently a firm uses a combination of approaches. Ideas for how to shift demand during both slow and peak periods are shown in Fig. 7.9.

Vary the Service Offering

One approach is to change the nature of the service offering, depending on the season of the year, day of the week, or time of day. For example, Whistler Mountain, a ski resort in Vancouver, Canada, offers its facilities for executive development and training programs during the summer when snow skiing is not possible. A hospital in the Los Angeles area rents use of its facilities to film production crews who need realistic hospital settings for movies or television shows. Accounting firms focus on tax preparation late in the year and until April 15, when federal taxes are due in the United States. During other times of the year they can focus on audits and general tax consulting activities. Airlines even change the configuration of their plane seating to match the demand from different market segments. Some planes may have no first-class section at all. On routes with a large demand for first-class seating, a significant proportion of seats may be placed in first class. Our opening vignette featured ways in which downtown hotels have changed their offerings to appeal to the family market segment on weekends. In all these examples, the service offering and associated benefits are changed to smooth customer demand for the organisation's resources.

Care should be exercised in implementing strategies to change the service offering, because such changes may easily imply and require alterations in other marketing mix variables such as promotion, pricing, and staffing-to match the new offering. Unless these additional mix variables are altered effectively to support the offering, the strategy may not work. Even when done well, the downside of such changes can be a confusion in the organisation's image from the customers perspective, or a loss of strategic focus for the organisation and its employees.

Communicate with Customers

Another approach for shifting demand is to communicate with customers, letting them know the times of peak demand so they can choose to use the service at alternative times and avoid crowding or delays. For example, signs in banks and post offices that let customers know their busiest hours and busiest days of the week can serve as a warning, allowing customers to shift their demand to another time if possible. Forewarning customers about busy times and possible waits can have added benefits. Many customer service phone lines provide a similar warning by informing waiting customers of approximately how long it will be until they are served. Those who do not want to wait may choose to call back later when the lines are less busy or to visit the company's website for faster service. Research in a bank context found that customers who were forewarned about the bank's busiest hours were more satisfied even when they had to wait than were customers who were not forewarned.

In addition to signage that communicates peak demand times to customers, advertising and other forms of promotion can emphasise different service benefits during peak and slow periods. Advertising and sales messages can also remind customers about peak demand times.

Modify Timing and Location of Service Delivery

Some firms adjust their hours and days of service delivery to more directly reflect customer demand. Historically, U.S. banks were open only during "bankers' hours" from 10 A.M. to 3 PM. every weekday. Obviously these hours did not match the times when most people preferred to do their personal banking. Now U.S. banks open early, stay open until 6 P .m. many days, and are open on Saturdays, better reflecting customer demand patterns. Online banking has also shifted demand from branches to "anytime, anywhere" websites. Theatres accommodate customer schedules by offering matinees on weekends and holidays when people are free during the day for entertainment. Movie theaters' are sometimes rented during weekdays by business groups-an example of varying the service offering during a period of low demand.

Differentiate on Price

A common response during slow demand is to discount the price of the service. This strategy relies on basic economics of supply and demand. To be effective, however, a price differentiation strategy depends on solid understanding of customer price sensitivity and demand curves. For example, business travelers are far less price sensitive than are families traveling for pleasure. For the Ritz-Carlton in Phoenix (our opening vignette), lowering prices during the slow summer months is not likely to increase bookings from business travelers dramatically. However, the lower summer prices attract considerable numbers of families and local guests who want an opportunity to experience a luxury hotel but are not able to afford the rooms during peak season.

The maximum capacity of any hotel, airline, restaurant, or other service establishment could be reached if the price were low enough. But the goal is always, to ensure the highest level of capacity utilization without sacrificing profits. We explore this complex relationship among price, market segments, capacity utilisation and profitability later in the chapter in the section on yield management.

Heavy use of price differentiation to smooth demand can be a risky strategy. Overreliance on price can result in price wars in an industry irp which eventually all competitors suffer. Price wars are well known in the airline industry, and total industry profits often suffer as a result of airlines simultaneously trying to attract customers through price discounting. Another risk of relying on price is that customers grow accustomed to the lower price and expect to get the same deal the next time they use the service. If communications with customers are unclear, customers may not understand the reasons for the discounts and will expect to pay the same during peak demand periods. Overuse or exclusive use of price as a strategy for smoothing demand is also risky because of the potential impact on the organisation's image, the potential for attracting undesired market segments, and the possibility that higher paying customers will feel they have been treated unfairly.

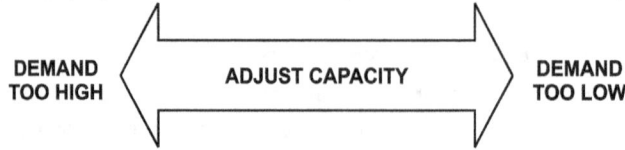

DEMAND TOO HIGH	DEMAND TOO LOW
• Stretch time, labour, facilities, and equipment.	• Perform maintenance, renovations.
• Cross-train employees.	• Schedule vacations.
• Hire part-time employees.	• Schedule employee training.
• Request overtime work from employees.	• Lay off employees.
• Rent or share facilities.	
• Rent or share equipment.	
• Subcontract or outsource activities.	

Fig. 7.10: Strategies for Adjusting Capacity to Match Demand

Adjusting Capacity to Meet Demand

A second strategic approach to matching supply and demand focuses on adjusting capacity. The fundamental idea here is to adjust, stretch, and align capacity to match customer demand (rather than working on shifting demand to match capacity, as just described). During periods of peak demand the organisation seeks to stretch or expand its capacity as much as possible. During periods of slow demand it tries to shrink capacity so as not to waste resources. General strategies for adjusting the four primary service resources (time, people, equipment, and facilities) are discussed throughout the rest of this section. In Fig. 7.10, we summarise specific ideas for adjusting capacity during periods of peak and slow demand. Often, a number of different strategies are used simultaneously.

Stretch Existing Capacity

The existing capacity of service resources can often be expanded temporarily to match demand. In such cases no new resources are added; rather the people, facilities, and equipment are asked to work harder and longer to meet demand.

Stretch Time

It may be possible to extend the hours of service temporarily to accommodate demand. A health clinic might stay open longer during flu season, retailers are open longer hours during the holiday shopping season, and accountants have extended appointment hours (evenings and Saturdays) before tax deadlines.

Stretch Labour

In many service organisations, employees are asked to work longer and harder during periods of peak demand. For example, consulting organisations face extensive peaks and valleys with respect to demand for their services. During peak demand, associates are asked to take on additional projects and work longer hours. And frontline service personnel in banks, tourist attractions, restaurants, and telecommunications companies are asked to serve more customers per hour during busy times than during hours or days when demand is low.

Stretch Facilities

Theaters, restaurants, meeting facilities, and classrooms can sometimes be expanded temporarily by the addition of tables, chairs, or other equipment needed by customers. Or, as in the case of a commuter train, a car that holds a fixed number of people seated comfortably can "expand" by accommodating standing passengers.

Stretch Equipment

Computers, power lines, and maintenance equipment can often be stretched beyond what would be considered the maximum capacity for short periods to accommodate peak demand.

In using these types of "stretch" strategies, the organisation needs to recognise the wear and tear on resources and the potential for inferior quality of service that may go with the use. These strategies should thus be used for relatively short periods in order to allow for later maintenance of the facilities and equipment and refreshment of the people who are asked to exceed their usual capacity. Sometimes it is difficult to know in advance, particularly in the case of human resources, when capacity has been stretched too far.

Align Capacity with Demand Fluctuations

This basic strategy is sometimes known as a "chase demand" strategy. By adjusting service resources creatively, organisations can in effect chase the demand curves to match capacity with customer demand patterns. Time, labour, facilities, and equipment are again the focus, this time with an eye toward adjusting the basic mix and use of these resources. Specific actions might include the following.

Use Part-Time Employees

In this situation the organisation's labour resource is being aligned with demand. Retailers hire part-time employees during the holiday rush, tax accountants engage temporary help during tax season, tourist resorts bring in extra workers during peak season. Restaurants often ask employees to work split shifts (work the lunch shift, leave for a few hours, and come back for the dinner rush) during peak mealtime hours.

Outsourcing

Firms that find they have a temporary peak in demand for a service that they cannot perform themselves may choose to outsource the entire service. For example, in recent years, many firms have found they do not have the capacity to fulfill their own needs for technology support, Web design, and software-related services. Rather than try to hire and train additional employees, these companies look to firms that specialise in outsourcing these types of functions as a temporary (or sometimes long-term) solution.

Rent or Share Facilities or Equipment

For some organisations it is best to rent additional equipment or facilities during periods of peak demand. For example, express mail delivery services rent or lease trucks during the peak holiday delivery season. It would not make sense to buy trucks that would sit idle during the rest of the year.

To determine an effective pricing strategy, a firm has to have a good understanding of its costs, the value created for customers and competitor pricing. Defining costs tends to be more difficult in a service business than in a manufacturing operation. Without a good understanding of costs, managers cannot be sure that the prices set are, in fact sufficient to recover all costs. A pricing strategy must address the central issue of what price to charge for selling a given unit of service at a particular time. Because services often combine multiple elements, pricing strategies need to be highly creative. Creating a more flexible approach to productive capacity allows a firm to adopt strategy to match capacity to demand. Decisions on place and time are closely associated with balancing demand and capacity.

Questions for Discussion

1. Why is capacity management particularly significant for service firms?
2. Out of cost-based, competition based and demand-based approaches which one is most appropriate to customers?
3. How will you price the following services?
   (a) Education
   (b) Training
   (c) Hotel Rooms
4. Discuss the pricing strategies that link to the value.
5. Write a short note on:
   (a) Customer perceived value
   (b) Skimming and Penetration pricing
   (c) Market segmentation pricing

■■■

$\mathcal{C}hapter$ **8**...

People

Contents ...

8.1 Introduction

Service is all about people. People buy and use services and people deliver the service. An essential ingredient to any service provision is the use of appropriate staff and people. Recruiting the right staff and training them appropriately in the delivery of their service is essential if the organisation wants to obtain a form of competitive advantage. Consumers make judgements and deliver perceptions of the services based on the employees they interact with. Staff should have the appropriate interpersonal skills, aptitude and service knowledge to provide the service that consumers are paying for.

Quality movement that has swept the manufacturing sector over the last decade is beginning to take shape in the service sector worldwide (Business Week 1991; Crosby 1991, Bitner, Booms and Mohr 1999). According to some, the shift to a quality focus is essential to the competitive survival of service business, just as it has become essential in manufacturing (Heskett et al. 1994; Schlesinger and Heskett 1991, Bitner et.al, 1999).

Service quality researchers have suggested that "the proof of service [quality] is in its flawless performance" (Berry and Parasuraman 1991, p.15), a concept akin to the notion of "zero defects" in manufacturing. Others have noted that "breakthrough" service managers pursue the goal of 100% defect-free service (Heskett, Sasser and Hart 1990, Bitner 1999). Customers consider that the most immediate evidence of service occurs in the service encounter or the 'moment of truth 'when the customer interacts with the firm. Thus, 'zero defects' in the service is the most expected goal to achieve a 100% flawless performance in service encounters. Here, flawless performance is not means to imply rigid standardisation, but rather 100% satisfying performance from the customers' point of view. The cost of not achieving the flawless performance is the 'cost of quality', which includes the costs associated with redoing the service, or compensation for the poor service, lost customer, negative word of mouth.

8.2 The Key Role of Service Employees in a Service Business

In an era of rapid growth of service firms, both researchers and practitioners have come to acknowledge that employee performance plays a vital role for the success of a service brand. Thus, the task of getting employees to build and strengthen an organisation's brand image—that is, getting them to act as "brand champions"—is a major challenge for service firms in many industries.

The role played by service employees in creating satisfied customers and in building customer relationships cannot be denied. According to Leonard Berry, companies that represent sustained service success all recognise the critical importance of their employees.

People i.e. frontline employees and those supporting them from behind the scenes are essential to the success of any service organisation. The significance of people in the marketing of services is evident in the people element of the services marketing mix. They are the human actors who play a part in service delivery and thus influence the buyer's perceptions; namely the firm's personnel, the customer and other customers in the service environment. In services marketing it is important to understand that the focus here is on customer-contact service employees because:

- They are the service.
- They are the organisation in the customer's eyes.
- They are the brand.
- They are marketers.

In many cases, in a service, there is just the employee and nothing else i.e. employee is the service, e.g. haircutting, physical trainers, legal services etc. This means that the service being offered by the business is the employee. Thus, investing in the employee is same as investing in the manufacture of a product.

A customer-contact service employee may reflect the image of the service organisation even if he or she is not directly providing the required service. If a person enters a hospital, every employee that he encounters from the receptionist to the clerk might influence his opinion about that organisation. Thus, employees sometimes do become the organisation in customer's eyes.

Employees also become the brand for a service. A very good example can be of a university which is well reputed amongst students. The quality of most universities is judged by the calibre of the teachers that are teaching there. When a student interacts with a professor, he has positive emotions about the university only when he feels that the teacher is knowledgeable and understanding and has complete control over his subject.

Because contact employees represent the organisation and can directly influence customer satisfaction, they perform the role of marketers. They physically embody the service and are walking billboards from a promotional point of view. If we are on the road and we see a person sitting on a motorcycle, going to deliver a free delivery or to deliver letters or documents, you can tell from their appearance, clothing or even kind of vehicle that which organisation they belong to. So, even when the service employees are just doing their duty, they are acting as marketers for their organisation.

While consumers of physical products seldom see the factory or meet the people who produce them, consumers of services do both. Service employees are a vital, tangible criterion by which an intangible like a service is evaluated. These employees vary to the extent in which they have contact with the customer and are visible to him or her. A characteristic phenomenon is that there always seems to be a back office and a front office in services. In fact many organisations have their own terminology for these positions, for example, front stage/back stage, front-of-house/back-of-house. Cowell (1987) has used the dimensions of contact and visibility to classify service personnel as shown in Table 8.1.

Table 8.1: Personnel involved in service product performance and delivery

	Contact with client	Non-contact with client
Visible to client	Waitress	Cook in steak house
	Service engineer	Computer operator
Non-visible to client	Telephone operator	Maintenance worker
	Airline pilot	Accountant

Source: Cowell (1987, p. 204)

The extent to which service employees and customers are part of the service process differs from service to service. This customer contact, defined as the customer's physical presence in the system, varies between being high contact and low contact. Figure 8.1 provides an example of different services classified according to the extent of customer contact.

High contact	Pure services
	Health centres
	Restaurant
	Public transport
	Education
	Personal services
Low contact	Mixed services
	Banking
	Public transport
	Real estate
	Funeral services
	Post office
	Public service

Fig. 8.1: Classification of services by extent of customer contact

Source: Adapted from Chase (1978, p. 138)

From the above discussion it is obvious that employees play an important role in services marketing because of the very reason that employees are involved in the process of delivery of any service, e.g. a waiter in a restaurant is actually the conductor of all the processes related to the customers. So it is of great importance that he gives the right image to the customer otherwise the customer might never return.

Service Culture

The role of the employee in service delivery cannot be discussed without looking at the bigger picture. The culture of an organisation heavily influences the behaviour of employees. Culture refers to an organisation's values, beliefs and behaviours. In general, it is concerned with beliefs and values on the basis of which people interpret experiences and behaviour, individually and in groups. Culture has also been defined as "the way we do things around here".

Most experts suggest that a customer oriented, service oriented organisation will have at its heart a service culture which can be defined as "a culture where an appreciation for good service exists, and where giving good service to internal as well as ultimate, external customers is considered a natural way of life and one of the most important norms by everyone."

Providing the necessary management leadership is crucial to developing a customer service culture, irrespective of the number of staff employed by the business. It is important to ensure that any business has the right service culture that allows good customer service practice to be successfully implemented and maintained. Good service can only occur where the management culture brings together a service environment that integrates the staff with the processes, systems and policies that are focused on servicing the customer.

No two organisations operate in the same manner, have the same focus, or provide management that accomplishes the same results. Among other things, a culture includes values, beliefs, norms, rituals, and practices of a group or organisation. Any policy, procedure, action or inaction on the part of an organisation, and its employees contribute to the service culture. Most importantly, each employee plays a key role in communicating the culture to its customers. This may include such things as personal appearance, the way employees interact with customers and service provider's knowledge, skill and attitude level. Culture also encompasses an organisation's products and services, and the physical appearance of the organisation's facility, equipment, or any other aspect of the organisation with which the customer comes into contact.

Service culture comprises many facets with each impacting customers and helping to determine the success or failure of customer service initiatives. Too often, organisations over-promise and under-deliver because their cultural and internal systems (infrastructure) do not have the ability to support customer service initiatives. For example, assume that the management of an organisation has their marketing department develop a slick piece of literature describing all the benefits of a new product or service provided by a new corporate partner organisation. They then establish a special 800 number for responses, but fail to hire additional staff or adequately train current employees to handle the customer calls. The project is likely doomed to fail.

8.3 The Services Marketing Triangle

Some models and frame works are useful for dealing with the questions that arise in the minds of service marketer for services marketing and management decisions, at both the strategic and implementation levels. Services marketing triangle / pyramid and service marketing mix are relevant and need to be indexed in the minds of service professionals. They provide frames which help in planning and delivering better service to customers to increase satisfaction and loyalty.

The Services Marketing Triangle

The services marketing triangle has three groups that work together to develop, promote and deliver services in tandem. These providers/customers are on the points of the triangle; the company, the provider, and the customers. Between these three points on the triangle, there are three types of marketing activities carried out for a service: external, internal, and interactive marketing. All these activities revolve around making and keeping promises to customers. All these marketing activities are essential for building and maintaining relationships with customers which leads to satisfaction, loyalty and enhanced profitability for the company.

Fig. 8.2: The Services Marketing Triangle

External Marketing

With its external marketing efforts, a company promises to its customers, regarding what they can expect and how it will be delivered. Marketing activities such as advertising, sales promotions, and pricing facilitate external marketing. For services the promise to customers is communicated also through the service employees, the layout, the design and decor of the facility and the service process itself. Service guarantees and two-way communication are additional ways of communicating service promises. All these communication options must be consistent and realistic promises are set to have a solid foundation for customer relationship.

Internal Marketing

Internal marketing, takes place through the enabling of Promises. In order for service providers and systems to deliver on the promises made, they must have the skills, abilities, tools, and motivation to deliver which must be enabled. The people should be recruited, trained, provided with tools and supporting internal systems, and rewarded for good service. Internal marketing is based on the assumption that employee satisfaction and customer satisfaction are directly related.

Marketing usually is externally focused, with most of the activities concentrating on reaching the customers in the market place. No firm can be successful without the involvement and support of its most valuable resources 'its employees.' It is the importance of people within the marketing of services that has created the need for internal marketing. The internal marketing is defined as meeting the needs of the employees so that they can meet the needs of their customers. It has been found that customer attitude, intentions and perceptions are affected by what employees experience in their firm. The employee has to handle the employee-customer relationship by 'Mirroring' in which the employees feel is the way your customers will feel, who in turn, will feel the way your customers do.

As per Berry, 'We can think of internal marketing as viewing employees as internal customers, viewing jobs as internal products and then endeavouring to offer internal products that satisfy the needs and wants of these internal customers while addressing the objectives of the firm'. All internal customers must be convinced about the quality of the service being provided and be happy in their work. Every individual should recognise that they have customers to serve. The main thrust in this concept is that it is not just the customer contact employee who need to be concerned about satisfying customer but all the service employees as well in order that the ultimate customer receives a quality service, every individual employee and every department within the organisation must receive and provide a quality service. In fact each functional department should be treated as the customer of another functional department Internal Customers must be convinced about the quality of the service being provided.

For becoming effective employees it is imperative to understand and approve of the mission of the firm to ensure everyone is working towards the common goals in alignment. In order to achieve this, the services offered by the firm need to be promoted to internal as well as external customers.

Internal marketing is applied to ensure a corporate culture that instills customer focused values in all employees. To deliver services to the expectations of the customers, the importance of attracting, motivating, training and retaining customer-conscious employees, at all levels must be recognised.

When employees have clarity with the norms and values of a firm, they are less inclined to leave and furthermore, customers are likely to be more satisfied with the service. Satisfied employees are also able to communicate the service values and norms better than newcomers and give better performance due to repetition over a period of time. Employee satisfaction in internal markets is thus a prerequisite to customer satisfaction for external markets.

Two aspects of internal marketing

1. Every employee/department within a firm has roles both as internal customers and internal suppliers. To ensure high quality external marketing, every individual/ department within a service firm must provide and receive excellent service.
2. Employee must work together in a way that is aligned with the firm's vision, mission and goals. This is very important within, when there are high levels of interaction between the service provider and customer.

In practice, internal marketing deals with communications, developing responsiveness, responsibility and unity of purpose. The fundamental aims of Internal Marketing are to develop internal and external customer awareness and remove functional barriers to enhance organisational effectiveness. The idea is to ensure that all members of staff provide the best possible contribution to the marketing activities of the company and successfully complete all interactions with customers in a way that adds value to the service encounter.

An increasing number of companies have recognised the need and have started implementation of these programmes in recent years. In fact, some firms have started to view internal marketing as a strategic tool to help retain customers through achieving high quality service delivery and increased customer satisfaction. In internal marketing firms perform two basic management functions:

1. The process of motivating people to buy into corporate goals.
2. Managing the information that employees need to enable them to perform effectively.

Thus internal marketing is a basket with a range of internal activities, used in the management of attitude and communications, including training, empowerment, recognition, team building, and management support with information sharing.

Using traditional marketing tools for employees

The techniques of market research, segmentation, targeting and promotion is relevant and applicable to Internal Marketing.

1. **Market Research** helps to understand needs of employees and identify the gaps in internal communication so that the firm can take corrective action.

2. **Advertising, sales promotion, personal selling** are available to influence the behaviour and attitude of current and potential customers. Each form of the promotion can help the firm achieve slightly different promotion objective e.g. sales promotion techniques are short term incentives aimed at encouraging the employees to increase sales for the quarter. These schemes might include trips to the Far East or cash awards. A special recognition may be given to an employee who on all working days in a month has attended satisfactorily 200 calls in the call center. This definitely will motivate not only the employee but egg on other employees as well for the next one. The best way to achieve employee motivation is to use advertising programmes to influence the behaviour of employees on how to greet and receive external customers. Employees are treated as customers and provided with job as their product to satisfy their needs. The people who buy goods and services in the role of the consumer and the people who buy jobs in the role of the employee are the same people. In case of employees, they exchange human resources for jobs that provide among other things economic resources.

3. **Segmentation:** The service firms can design attractive service package for group of employees with certain similarities based on the employees of same age, gender, ambition, previous experience, performance achievement and management can design job specification for them appropriately. Internal marketing has led to concepts such as 'flexitime', 'fast track' flower pot.'

4. **Targeting:** The right employees should also be targeted for appointment, followed by training and matching the right employee to the right job with job enrichment and enlargement possibilities.

Importance of Internal Marketing

1. Internal marketing can reduce conflict between the functional areas of business.
2. Internal marketing helps in building customer focused firm.
3. The mission and goals are clearly communicated.
4. It can facilitate a spirit of innovation within the firm.
5. Internal marketing creates a climate of commitment and result orientation at the management level, at employees level and enables a conducive environment for cooperation and productivity.
6. It can help a firm to have a competitive advantage by adopting differentiation strategy.

Criteria's for better performance from employees

1. Employees with customer contact have dear performance standards and their role within the firm spelt out.
2. Employees must have high degree of empathy whether it pertains to customers or other employees.
3. Employees must be empowered by management to do whatever it takes to satisfy the customer.
4. Employees must be imparted special training in customer care.

Interactive Marketing

Keeping promises is the second type of marketing activity captured by the services marketing triangle and is the most critical from the customer's point of view. Service promises are most often kept or broken by the employees of the firm or by service providers, most often in real time.

In interactive marketing occurs the moment of truth, when the customer interacts with the firm and the service is produced and consumed. Interestingly, promises are kept or broken and the reliability or service is tested every time the customer interacts with the firm.

In interactive marketing occurs the moment of truth, when the customer interacts with the firm and the service is produced and consumed. Interestingly, promises are kept or broken and the reliability of service is tested every time the customer interacts with the firm.

Interactive marketing is the conceptualisation and implementation of a marketing policy that is based on direct interactive contact with the customer. In interactive marketing, the idea is that all individuals within the firm successfully complete all interactions that adds value to service encounter. With the advent of new technologies, the service delivery systems are changing at a fast pace and consumer is now an active participant from the product development stage, to disposition of the product and interacting with the service providers, in the service delivery process.

The information technology has revolutionised the business environment and has changed economies, organisation social structure and business structure. The customer is being offered the goods and services at a click of a mouse. In order to succeed and stay successful, marketers continually need to look at opportunities in the market and cope with the speed of change. The change in the business environment is forcing firms to adapt and draw up new plans and reorient. The forces acting have made marketers interactive. Now, marketing is interaction between buyer and seller and business is the interaction between company and market. The employees, who are customer contact employees have to be trained to interact effectively with the customer as this will not only help them to achieve a break through but will also determine the success of company at operational and strategic levels. These employees have to keep an eye on the quality of the offering and listen to the customer. It is service and its quality which retains the customer. Regular interaction with the customer can be of help in customising the offering to gain better control.

4C'S OF CUSTOMER SERVICE MIX

Service firms are using 4C's of customer service mix to deliver superior customer service: convenience, connectedness, choice and creativity.

Convenience: The consumer needs are speedily accessed by using technology, by analysing data to enable the service provider to meet the needs in the shortest possible time with minimal resource. Technology facilitates convenience for customer to access the firm's homepage on Internet and get all data and delivery with a click of the mouse.

Connectedness: The interactive technology enables firms to connect to their current customers and prospective customers. Thus connectedness allows company to detect and respond quickly the changing between buyer and seller. Interactive technology helps the company to develop new products by facilitating consumer research with accuracy, by tracking present trends in consumer lifestyle, purchasing and expectations. Connectedness increases communication of internal customers with internal suppliers and better-networked employees respond quickly to customers.

Choice: Interactive technology has facilitated consumers to choose the best from the range based on price, size, benefits based on economics within budget.

Creativity: New technology had led us into a new dimension of customer as the creator or co-creator of products in each stage of product development by consistently meeting their need. Producer provides just-in-time products at desired level of quality and guaranteed customer satisfaction.

Aligning the Sides of the Triangle

In a triangle, all three sides are essential to complete the whole to have synergy. For services all three marketing activities, represented by the sides of the triangle, are critical to success; without one of the sides in place or weak, the triangle, or the total marketing effort, cannot be optimally supported. Each side represents significant challenges, and we will discuss, approaches and strategies for dealing with all three. This is core for any service marketer to remember, internalise and build upon to make successful career.

SERVICES MARKETING PYRAMID

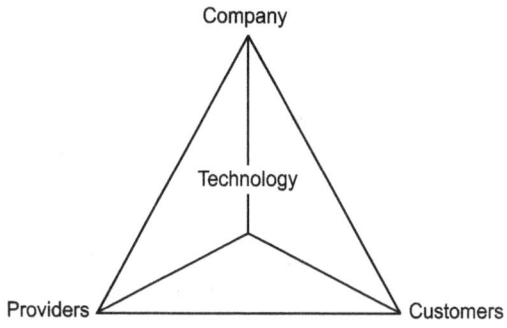

Fig. 8.3: Services Marketing Pyramid

Since technology impacts all dimensions of service and service delivery, the service marketing triangle has now been expanded to explicitly include technology, converting the triangle into a pyramid. In the pyramid concept, interactive marketing can be the result of customers, service providers, and technology or some combination of the three interacting in real time to produce the service. It suggests that management has the possibility to facilitate not only the delivery of service through people but through technology as well. Customers will sometimes, interact only with technology and therefore will need to acquire skills and abilities and also be motivated to receive services in this manner. This is initially going to be more successful in Indian urban markets with the educated segment. Customer satisfaction with technology delivered services will lead to minimisation of error with better response time and for some services round the clock.

8.4 Service Profit Chain

When service companies put employees and customers first, a radical shift occurs in the way they manage and measure success.

Top-level executives of outstanding service organisations spend little time setting profit goals or focusing on market share, the management mantra of the 1970s and 1980s. Instead, they understand that in the new economics of service, frontline workers and customers need to be the centre of management concern. Successful service managers pay attention to the factors that drive profitability in this new service paradigm: investment in people, technology that supports frontline workers, revamped recruiting and training practices, and compensation linked to performance for employees at every level.

The new economics of service requires innovative measurement techniques. These techniques calibrate the impact of employee satisfaction, loyalty, and productivity on the value of products and services delivered so that managers can build customer satisfaction and loyalty and assess the corresponding impact on profitability and growth. In fact, the lifetime value of a loyal customer can be astronomical, especially when referrals are added to the economics of customer retention and repeat purchases of related products.

The service-profit chain, developed from analyses of successful service organisations, puts "hard" values on "soft" measures. It helps managers target new investments to develop service and satisfaction levels for maximum competitive impact, widening the gap between service leaders and their merely good competitors.

The service-profit chain establishes relationships between profitability, customer loyalty, and employee satisfaction, loyalty, and productivity. The links in the chain (which should be regarded as propositions) are as follows: Profit and growth are stimulated primarily by customer loyalty. Loyalty is a direct result of customer satisfaction. Satisfaction is largely influenced by the value of services provided to customers. Value is created by satisfied, loyal, and productive employees. Employee satisfaction, in turn, results primarily from high-quality support services and policies that enable employees to deliver results to customers.

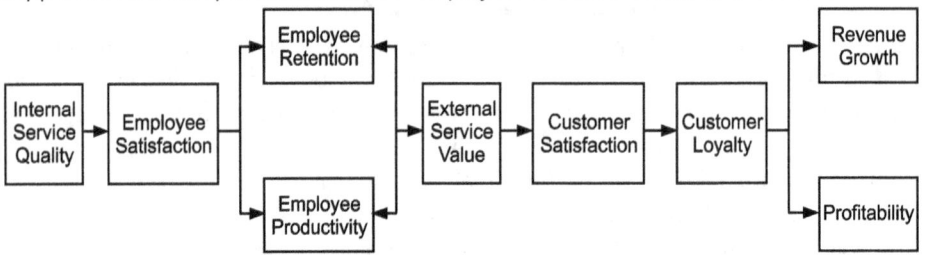

Fig. 8.4: The Service Profit Chain

The service-profit chain is also defined by a special kind of leadership. CEOs of exemplary service companies emphasise the importance of each employee and customer. For these CEOs, the focus on customers and employees is no empty slogan tailored to an annual management meeting. For example, Herbert Kelleher, CEO of Southwest Airlines, can be found aboard airplanes, on tarmacs, and in terminals, interacting with employees and customers. Kelleher believes that hiring employees that have the right attitude is so important that the hiring process takes on a "patina of spirituality." In addition, he believes that "anyone who looks at things solely in terms of factors that can easily be quantified is missing the heart of business, which is people."

The service-profit chain is a powerful phenomenon that stresses the importance of people – both employees and customers – and how linking them can leverage corporate performance. The service-profit chain is an equation that establishes the relationship between corporate policies, employee satisfaction, value creation, customer loyalty, and profitability.

8.5 Concept of Service Encounter- Moment of Truth

What is an encounter?

The concept of an encounter means coming into contact with someone or something. Such contact may occur by chance or unexpectedly, e.g. running into an old friend. That will invariably be an amicable encounter. Equally more routine encounters, say with a car mechanic or a hotel receptionist, may be particularly pleasant. On the other hand, encounters in general with a work colleague, an organisation or simply a 'friend' may be much less enjoyable. Additionally, an encounter can be with an inanimate object in the form of a sign, vending machine, website, car wash. That also can be pleasing or frustrating. Clearly providers of services seek to make any encounter with a customer pleasurable. To achieve this, service organisations will resort to using a variety of tools/techniques. Although there is a growing tendency for encounters to be with 'things' most services still retain, in part or in total, face-to-face contact with the customer.

Whether at arm's length or face-to-face, interaction between customer and organisation lies at the heart of service delivery. The interaction may take many forms, from a brief encounter with a directions sign to a protracted encounter with a service employee. Whatever the nature and type of contact, each represents a moment of truth for the customer. This section will focus on customers engaging with organisations through the medium of service personnel.

In particular, a service encounter is a type of contact where behaviour, attitudes, emotions and body language are visible from both sides (service provider and customer). That, in itself, represents a challenge for service organisations to manage.

Service Encounter as Theatre

For addressing or managing that challenge, some have drawn on the writings of Erving Goffman, particularly his book, The Presentation of Self in Everyday Life and portrayed the service encounter as equivalent to a performance in the theatre. In both cases, service encounter and theatre, the aim quite simply is to create a favourable impression before an audience. On the surface, the service encounter bears all the hallmarks of a theatrical production:

- **Front stage:** The setting comprising scenery, props, atmosphere. More specifically, décor, lighting, use of space, seating comfort, furnishings, equipment, noise level. (the physical evidence)
- **Front line:** Service employees in the role of actors dressed accordingly and with the help of a script deploy the necessary skills and attributes to impress an audience.
- **Audience:** Customers with expectations for and perceptions of the performance.
- **Process:** The manner in which the service is delivered and the actions that shape the customers' experience (the performance).

The main problems with the theatre as a framework for discussing and understanding the service encounter is that the customer (in the audience) does not interact or engage directly with those providing the performance. It is essentially a passive encounter with customer response coming at the end of the performance, coupled sometimes with laughter or applause in between. Furthermore, there is little likelihood of other members of the audience affecting the enjoyment or otherwise of the service. Such conditions are not normally characteristic of service encounters. So in considering the following elements of a theatrical nature it is important to bear in mind the impact of customer involvement. Two particular tools/techniques that emanate from a theatre perspective are however deployed by organisations in the service encounter. They are scripts and emotional labour and each is inextricably bound up with the other.

Scripts

Just as in the theatre, scripts are widely in evidence in service encounters. A script is regarded as 'a predetermined, stereotyped sequence of actions that defines a well known situation'. People experience hundreds of scripts as part of everyday life, e.g. travelling by air, visiting a dentist, eating in a restaurant, attending a tutorial, telephoning a call centre. In these and many other service situations knowledge of the script helps us understand and become involved in the sequence of events as well as how we and others are expected to behave. Basically, we are acquiring knowledge of what is supposed to happen or the rules of engagement. One of the best-known examples and one to which most people can relate is the restaurant script, developed by Schank and Abelson (1977). As with other scripts, it has standard roles to be played, standard props or objects, ordinary conditions for entering upon the activity, a standard sequence of scenes or actions and some normal results from performing the activity successfully. It appears that the script is a highly structured sequence of actions and events and in many cases that will be so. However, any script will be subject to deviations or violations.

Service encounter or the moment of truth is thus defined as the period of time that a customer interacts with a service (Shostack, 1985). The definition of a service encounter is broad and includes a customer's interaction with customer-contact employees, machines, automated systems, physical facilities, and any other service provider visible elements. A service encounter is a period of time during which customer interact directly with a service. It is also called as "Moment of Truth". On the Web, customers engage in service encounters with businesses by visiting their Web site, navigating through it, searching for product and service information, communicating with customer service representatives, and perhaps purchasing a product and/or service. Researchers (e.g., Czepiel, 1990; Gronroos, 1990; Mohr & Bitner, 1995; Collier & Meyer, 1998) believe that the quality of the interaction between customers and service providers during the service encounter is important because it is at this level where customers judge the services provided to them. They also agree that a service encounter is composed of a service outcome (i.e., what the customer receives during the exchange) and the process of service delivery (i.e., the way through which the outcome is delivered to the customer). They maintain that customer satisfaction with service encounters, also known as transaction satisfaction, is a combination of the customer satisfaction with the service outcome and the customer satisfaction with the process of service delivery.

Moreover, customers with multiple encounters with a service provider will develop an overall perception of service quality and, hence, an overall satisfaction or dissatisfaction with the service provider.

"Service encounters are critical moments of truth in which customers often develop indelible impressions of a firm... From the customer's point of view, these encounters are the service". (Bitner, Brown & Meuter, 2000).

"In most services, quality occurs during service delivery, usually in an interaction between the customer and contact personnel of the service firm." (Zeithaml, Berry, & Pararsuraman, 1988).

Encounters can take place face-to-face in a "service setting," over the phone, through the mail, or over the Internet.

Why Service Encounters Matter ?

Every encounter is an opportunity for the firm to satisfy the customer, to reinforce the value of its offerings, and to sell the customer on the benefits of a long-term relationship Service encounters immediately impact customer satisfaction and also shape longer-term factors like intention to return, likelihood of communicating positively about the service, and customer loyalty.

Customers need to have as many as twelve positive experiences with a service provider in order to overcome the negative effects of one bad experience. The expense of acquiring customers and their potential lifetime value means that losing a customer because of a negative encounter can have staggering costs.

Every customer-facing business should identify the points where it interacts with customers. In businesses with complex services (hospitals, airlines, hotels...) there may be dozens of these touch points or service encounters. The service provider needs to distinguish between ordinary "humdrum" transactions that don't have the potential for creating an emotional bond with the customer and those that do... but "many companies make the mistake of overinvesting in the former and thus don't differentiate themselves on the latter.

Moments of Truth

From the customer's point of view, the most vivid impression of service occurs in the **service encounter** or "**Moment Of Truth**," when the customer interacts with the service firm. This is the foundation to "Satisfaction of Service Quality" – it is where the promises are kept or broken. This concept was put forth by Richard Norman, taking the metaphor from Bull Fighting. Most services are results of social acts, which take place in direct contact between the customer and the service provider. At this stage the Customer realises the perceived service quality.

Encounter Cascade

Every Moment of Truth is Important – according to Scandinavian Airlines, each one of their 10 million customers come in contact with 5 employees. Thus the airlines say there 50 million moments of truth – each one is managed well and "They prove they are the BEST".

However, some encounters are more critical. The encounter cascade refers to a series of encounters right from the time a customer comes to take the service. The encounter cascade can be important as any encounter can be critical, as it determines customer satisfaction and loyalty. If it's the first interaction of the customer then the initial interaction will be the first impression. So, these interactions have to be given importance, as they are critical and influences customer's perception of the organisation.

Example:

A customer calling for the repair service may switch to some other company if he is put on hold for a long time or even treated rudely. Even if the technical quality of that firm is superior, the firm may not get a chance to prove themselves in front of the customer. When the customer has had many interactions with firm, each encounter will be important as it will create a combined image of that firm. Many positive experiences will give an image of High Quality and many negative experiences will represent a bad image. Combination of positive and negative interactions will leave the customer confused about the Quality.

It is suggested that not all encounters are equally important in building long-term relations. For every organisation, certain encounters can act as a key to customer satisfaction. **For example:** for most hotels, it is the early encounters that are important. In a hospital context, a study of patients revealed that encounters with the nursing staff were more important in predicting customer satisfaction. As it is rightly said "one bad apple can ruin the whole basket of apples." The same applies in this too; one negative encounter can drive the customer away, no matter how many encounters had taken place in the past. So a firm has to give a lot of importance to such encounters. "A customer who has been using a bank for nearly 15 years is quite happy with the service. He has a huge deposit and many accounts. One fine morning, when he comes out of the bank the watch man asks Rs. 10 for parking charges of his car. He goes inside the bank and informs the clerk at the counter, who directs him to the officer. The officer directs him to the Manager, who says he is helpless as this is a new policy of the bank. The customer who was so happy with the bank services decides to close all his accounts – "Some encounters can be very Critical".

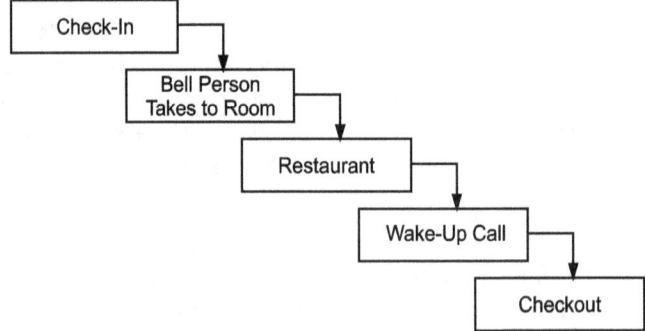

Fig. 8.5: A service encounter cascade for a hotel visit

Among the service encounters a hotel customer experiences are checking in, being taken to the room, eating a restaurant meal etc. as shown in Fig. 8.5. It is in these encounters that the customer receives an overall view of the organisations service quality and encounter contributes to customer satisfaction and willingness to do business with the organisation again. As for the company, each encounter represents an opportunity to prove its potential as a quality service provider and to increase customer loyalty.

Some services have few service encounters and others have many. Mistakes or problems that occur in the early levels of the service cascade can e critical because failure at one point results in greater risk of dissatisfaction in the long run. The hotels learned this through their extensive customer survey to determine what service element contributes to customer loyalty. They found that 4 out of 5 factors came into play in the first 10 minutes of the guest's stay.

Types of Encounters

A service encounter occurs every time a customer interacts with the service organisation. There are three general types of encounters - *remote encounters, phone encounters, and face – to – face encounters.* A customer may experience any of these types of encounters or a combination of all three in his or her relations with a service firm.

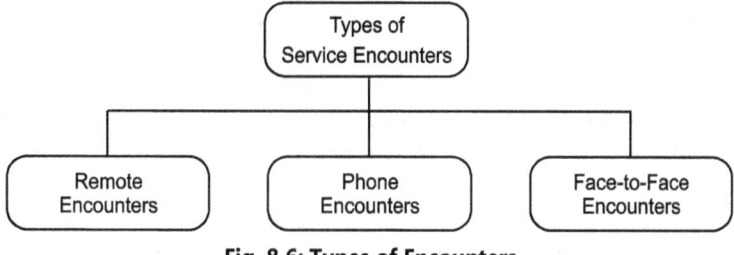

Fig. 8.6: Types of Encounters

Remote Encounter

An encounter that can occur without any direct human contact is called as Remote Encounters. Such as, when a customer interacts with a bank through the ATM system, or with Ticketron through an automated ticketing machine, or with a mail-order service through automated dial-in ordering. Remote encounters also occur when the firm sends its billing statements or communicates others types of information to customers by mail. Although there is no direct human contact in these remote encounters, each represents an opportunity for a firm to reinforce or establish perceptions in the customer. In remote encounter the tangible evidence of the service and the quality of the technical process and system become the primary bases for judging quality.

Example

Services are being delivered through technology, particularly with the advent of Internet applications. Retail purchases, airline ticketing, repair and maintenance troubleshooting, package and shipment tracking are just a few examples of services available via the Internet. All of these types of service encounters can be considered remote encounters.

Phone Encounters

In many organisations, the most frequent type of encounter between a customer and the firm occurs over the telephone is called as phone encounter. Almost all firms (whether goods manufacturers or service businesses) rely on phone encounters in the form of customer-service, general inquiry, or order-taking functions. The judgment of quality in phone encounters is different from remote encounters because there is greater potential variability in the interaction. Tone of voice, employee knowledge, and effectiveness/efficiency inhandling customer issues become important criteria for judging quality in these encounters.

Face-to –Face Encounters

A third type of encounter is the one that occurs between an employee and a customer in direct contact is called as Face-to-Face Encounter. In a hotel, face–to–face encounters occurs between customers and maintenance personnel, receptionist, bellboy, food and beverage servers and others. Determining and understanding service equality issues in face–to–face context is the most complex of all. Both verbal and non-verbal behaviours are important determinants of quality, as are tangible cues such as employee dress and other symbols of service (equipments, informational brochures, physical settings). In face–to–face encounters the customer also play an important role in creating quality service for herself through her own behaviour during the interaction. At Disney theme parks, face-to-face encounters occur between customer and ticket-takers, maintenance personnel, actors in Disney character costumes, ride personnel, food and beverage servers, and others. For a company such as, IBM, in a business-to-business setting direct encounters occur between the business customers and salespeople, delivery personnel, maintenance representatives, and professional consultants. Of all determining and understanding service quality issues in face-to-face context is the most complex. Both verbal and non-verbal behaviours are important determinants of quality, as are tangible cues such as employee dress and other symbols of service (e.g., equipment, informational brochures, and physical settings). In face-to-face encounters the customer also plays a role in creating quality service for herself through her own behaviour during the interaction.

Contact Employee Viewpoints

Frontline personnel are a critical source of information about customers. There are basically two ways that customer knowledge obtained by contact employees is to improve services: firstly, such knowledge is used by the contact employee themselves to facilitate their interactions with customers and secondly, it is used by the firm for making decisions. Employees often modify their behaviour from moment to moment on the basis of the feedback they receive while serving customers. Schneider (1980) argues that people who choose to work in service occupations generally have a strong desire to give good service. To the extent that this is true, contact personnel can be expected to look frequently for cues that tell them how their service is received by the customers. The more accurate their perceptions are, the more likely their behavioural adjustments are to improve customer satisfaction.

Second, because contact personnel have frequent contact with customers, they serve a boundary spanning role in the firm. As a result, they often have better understanding of customer needs and problems than others in the firm. Researchers have theorised and found some evidence that open communication between the frontline personnel and managers is important for achieving service quality (Parasuraman, Berry and Zeithaml 1990; Zeithaml, Berry and Pararuraman 1988, Bitner et.al, 1999). Schneider and Bowen (1984) argued that the firms should use the information which they gathered from their contact employees in their strategic planning, especially in new service development and in service modifications.

According to the Bitner, Booms and Mohr (1999), accurate employee understanding of customers enables both the employee and firm to adjust appropriately to customer needs. However, Schneider and Bowen (1985) and Schneider, Parkington and Buxton (1980) found high correlations between employee and customer attitudes about overall service quality in a banking sector. Their results are contradicted, however, in a study by Brown and Swartz (1989). Similarly, another study of 1300 customers and 900 customer service professionals conducted by Development Dimensions International found differences in perceptions between the two groups (Service Marketing Newsletter 1989). Customer service professionals in that study consistently rated the importance of particular service skills and competencies. In the same way, Langeard and Colleagues (1981) found that field managers at two banks tended to overestimate (compared with customer ratings) the importance of six board service delivery dimensions. Other studies have found differences when comparing customer and employee evaluations of business situations using scenarios and role playing in product failure contexts (Folks and Kotsos 1986), a complaint context (Resnik and Harmon 1983) and the context of retailer responses to customer problems (Dornoff and Dwyer 1981). The Critical Incident Technique (CIT) has been used extensively in this context in recent years to explore service research issues and has been instrumental in advancing our understanding of these issues.

The concept of CIT usually employed in service research to (a) help current and future researchers employing the CIT method to examine their methodological decisions closely and (b) suggest guidelines for the proper application and reporting of the procedures involved when using this method. Although the CIT method appeared in the marketing literature as early as 1975 (Swan and Rao), the major catalyst for use of the CIT method in service research appears to have been a Journal of Marketing study conducted by Bitmer, Booms, Tetreault(1990) that investigated sources of satisfaction and dissatisfaction in service encounters. Service researchers have found CIT to be a valuable tool, as the analysis approach suggested by the CIT method often results in useful information that is mere rigorously defined than many other qualitative approaches. It allows researchers to focus on a very specific phenomenon because it forces them to define the "specific aim" of their study and helps identify important thematic details, with vivid examples to support their findings. Bitmer, Booms, Tetreault's (1990) study focusing on service encounters provides an example of the value of the CIT method to service research. Their analysis of 700 critical service encounters in three industries, examined from the perspective of the customer, led to the identification of three types of employee behaviours (ultimately labeled recovery, adaptability, spontaneity) as sources of satisfaction and dissatisfaction in service encounters. Prior to their research, much of what scholars understood about such evaluations was limited to global assessments of satisfaction or abstract concepts (e.g., service quality). On the basis of the knowledge gained from the 1990 study Gremler and Bitner (1992) extended the generalisability of the 1990 study by investigating the service encounters across broad range of service industries. In a recent study, Bitner and colleagues used the CIT method to examine self-service encounters where there is no employee involved in service delivery (Meuter et al. 2000). The findings from this study suggest a different set of factors are sources of satisfaction and dissatisfaction when service is delivered through technology-based means. As these studies suggest, the CIT method is flexible enough to allow service encounters to be extensively studied in a variety of ways. Bitner's research on service encounters has focused primarily on customers' cognitive response and/or assessments of service encounters; van Dolen et al. (2001) have extended service encounter research by focusing on understanding affective consumers responses in service encounters by examining the emotional content in narratives of critical incidents. Keaveney's (1995) study on service switching also illustrated the contribution that the use of the CIT method has made to service research.

Therefore, it can be deduced from the above discussion that the heart of a service is the encounter between the server and the customer. It is here where emotions meet economics in real time and where most people judge the quality of service. As currently conceived, service science treats customer satisfaction with an encounter predominantly as a function of engineering measures of throughput and output quality. Thus if a service is performed efficiently and process output variability is low, it is assumed that the service process has been optimised.

Recovery-Employee Response to Service Delivery System Failures

In the case of service delivery, if there is any failure in the service delivery system and an employee is required to respond in some way to customer complaints and disappointment. The content or the form of the employee's response is what causes the customer to remember the events either favourably or unfavourably. One of the root causes of customer dissatisfaction is the employee response to service delivery system failure (Bitner, Booms and Mohr, 1999). According to some service providers the failure of the service delivery system is the second most important reason for customer dissatisfaction. In explaining the reason for slow service they shared few external reasons. The service delivery system fails firstly because of the slow speed of the service. Secondly, if the service is not available, the specific reason is not known by the employees, it depends on the management. Sometimes, they blame each other. It can be concluded that employee response to service delivery system failure is the second reason for customer dissatisfaction and the employees should be in 'recovery' mood to handle the customer encounters.

Adaptability-Employee Response to Customer Needs and Requests

Satisfaction or dissatisfaction in a service encounter depends on how adaptable the service delivery system is when the customer has special needs and requests that place demands on the process. In these cases, customers judge service encounter in terms of flexibility of the employees and the system. Customers request for customization of the service to meet a need. The third important reason for customer dissatisfaction is employee response to customer needs and requests, which has a similarity with the study finds of Bitner, Booms and Mohr, (1999). The employees feel that they should consider the special needs of the customer to satisfy them. But it is really difficult to pay customer attention to each individual customer.

Spontaneity-Unprompted and Unsolicited Employee Action

Even when there is no system failure or no special requests or needs, customers can still remember service encounters as being very satisfying or dissatisfying. Satisfying incidents in this group represents surprising events for the customers (special attention, being treated royally, receiving something nice even though not requested) whereas dissatisfying incidents in this group represents negative and unexpected employee behaviours (e.g. rudeness, stealing, discrimination, ignoring the customer etc.). Unprompted or unsolicited employee behaviour means unexpected employee behaviour. They consider that if the employee does not act according to the cultural norms or in adverse conditions then the customers are dissatisfied. According to the present study, unprompted and unsolicited employee action is the fourth reason for customer dissatisfaction.

Managing the Service Encounter

Being an effective service manager demands more than just the direct management of service encounters. The below given section shall cover some different approaches to managing services in an indirect way.

Role Theory

Role theory is a _learned_ set of behaviours that guides or directs how an individual operates in a given setting. Roles are passed down from employee to employee through on-the-job training. Thus, by understanding the frameworks of roles, managers can exert indirect control over the service encounter. Customers' satisfaction derives from how well both the consumers and service providers have performed their roles relative to expectations. This is called _role congruence._

Most roles in organisations are paired, some examples from different industry sectors are:

- host and guest ¾ hospitality.
- master and servant ¾ personal service.
- mentor and student ¾ education.
- buyer and seller ¾ retailing.

Script Theory

Script theory is an extension of role theory. In role theory, employees are linked to actors on a stage, so with script theory, we think of them as using scripts.

Script theory is concerned with the use of key words and phrases which both participants recognise, and in effect can be used by employees to guide the customer through a transaction. Many organisations prepare scripts for emergency situations such as bomb threats and handling customer complaints because during service interruptions, panic or stress can interfere with the ability of an employee to think clearly. The script then becomes a device for coping with problems.

A basic difference between role and script theory is that role theory is based on the commonality of behaviour across individuals with the focus on only the interpersonal service encounter. Script theory however, is based on the individual differences arising from social and cultural experience and relates to the total service experience.

Below is an example of a simple script for telephone use in a company:

1. The telephone is to be answered within three rings by the nearest person. But do not leave a customer you are attending in order to answer the phone

2. Company phones are not to be used for personal business. Incoming calls for employees will not be permitted except in emergencies

3. Employees answering the telephone should say 'Good (morning/afternoon/ evening) (name of organisation) (your location) (your name) speaking, how may I help you?'

4. Always thank the caller. Say 'Thank you for calling' before hanging up.

8.6 Training and Development of Employees

All customer facing personnel need to be trained and developed to maintain a high quality of personal service. Training should begin as soon as the individual starts working for an organisation during an induction. The induction will involve the person in the organisation's culture for the first time, as well as briefing him or her on day-to-day policies and procedures. At this very early stage the training needs of the individual are identified. A training and development plan is constructed for the individual which sets out personal goals that can be linked into future appraisals. In practice most training is either 'on-the-job' or 'off-the-job.' On-the-job training involves training whilst the job is being performed e.g. training of bar staff. Off-the-job training sees learning taking place at a college, training centre or conference facility. Attention needs to be paid to Continuing Professional Development (CPD) where employees see their professional learning as a lifelong process of training and development.

Human Resource Strategies

Human resources decisions and strategies primary goal is to motivate and enable employees to deliver customer-oriented promises successfully. The strategies presented here are organised around four basic themes. To build a customer-oriented, service-minded workforce, an organisation must:

1. Hire the right people
2. Develop people to deliver service quality.
3. Provide the needed support systems.
4. Retain the best people.

1. Hire the right people

One of the best ways to close gap 3 is to start with the right service delivery people from the beginning. This implies that considerable attention should be focused on hiring and recruiting service personnel.

(a) **Compete for the best people:** To get the best people, an organisation needs to identify them and compete with other organisations to hire them. The firm act as marketers in their pursuit of the best employees, just as they use their marketing expertise to compete for customers. Thinking of recruiting as a marketing activity results in addressing issues of market (employee) segmentation, product (job) design, and promotion of job availability in ways that attract potential long-term employees.

(b) **Hire for service competencies and service inclination:** Once potential have been identified, organisations need to be conscientious in interviewing and screening to truly identify the best people from the pool of candidates. It has been suggested that service employees need two complementary capacities: they need both service competencies and service inclination. Service competencies are the skills and knowledge necessary to do the job. Achieving particular degrees and certifications validates competencies, such as attaining a doctor of law degree and passing the relevant state bar examinations for lawyers. Service competencies may not be degree related, but may instead relate to basic intelligence or physical requirements.

(c) **Be the preferred employer:** One way to attract the best people is to be known as the preferred employer in a particular industry or in a particular location. Other strategies that support a goal of being the preferred employer include providing extensive training, career and advancement opportunities, excellent internal support and attractive incentives and offering quality goods and services that employees a proud to be associated with.

2. Develop people to deliver service quality

To grow and maintain a workforce that is customer oriented and focused on delivering quality, an organisation must develop its employees to deliver service quality. That is, once it has hired the right employees, the organisation must train and work with these individuals to ensure service performance.

(a) **Train for technical and interactive skills:** To provide quality service, employees need ongoing training in the necessary technical skills and knowledge and in process or interactive skills. Examples of technical skills and knowledge are working with accounting systems in hotels, cash machine procedures in a retail store, underwriting procedures in an insurance company, and any operational rules the company has for running its business. Most service organisations are quite conscious of and relatively effective at training employees in technical skills. Companies are increasing their use of information technology to train employees in the technical skills and knowledge needed on the job. Service employees also need training in interactive skills that allow them to provide courteous, caring, responsive, and empathetic service.

(b) **Empower employees:** Empowerment means giving employees the desire, skills, tools, and authority to serve the customer. While the key to empowerment is giving employees authority to make decisions on the customer's behalf, authority alone is not enough. Employees need the knowledge and tools to be able to make these decisions and they need incentives that encourage them to make the right decisions. Organisations are well suited to empowerment strategies to ones in which (1) the business strategy is one of differentiation and customization, (2) customers are long-term relationship customers, (3) technology is non-routine or complex,

(4) the business environment is unpredictable, and (5) managers and employees have high growth and social needs and strong interpersonal skills.

(c) **Promote teamwork:** The nature of many service jobs suggests that customer satisfaction will be enhanced when employees work as teams. Because service jobs are frequently frustrating, demanding and challenging, a teamwork environment will help to alleviate some of the stresses and strains. Employees who supported and that they have a team backing them up will be better able to maintain enthusiasm and provide quality service. By promoting teamwork an organisation can enhance the employee's abilities to deliver excellent service while the camaraderie and support enhance their inclination to be excellent service providers.

3. Provide need support systems

To be efficient and effective in their jobs, service workers require internal support systems that are aligned with their need to be customer focused. Without customer-focused internal support and customer-oriented systems, it is nearly impossible for employees to deliver quality service no matter how much they want to. In examining customer service outcomes researchers found that internal support from supervisors, teammates, and other departments as well as evaluations of technology used on the job were all strongly related to employee satisfaction and ability to serve customers.

(a) **Measure internal service quality:** One way to encourage supportive internal service relationships is to measure and reward internal service. By first acknowledging that everyone in the organisation has a customer and then measuring customer perceptions of internal service quality, an organisation can begin to develop an internal quality culture. Internal customer service audits and internal service guarantees are two strategies used to implement a culture of internal service quality. Through the audit, internal organisations identify their customers, determine their needs, measure how well they are doing, and make improvements.

(b) **Provide supportive technology and equipment:** When employees don't have the right equipment, or their equipment fails, they can be easily frustrated in their desire to deliver quality service. To do their jobs effectively and efficiently, service employees need the right equipment and technology, having the right technology and equipment can extend into strategies regarding workplace and workstation design.

(c) **Develop service-oriented internal processes:** To best support service personnel in their delivery of quality service on the front line, an organisation's internal processes should be designed with customer value and customer satisfaction in mind. In other words, internal procedures must support quality service performance. In many companies internal processes are driven by bureaucratic rules, tradition, cost efficiencies, or the needs of internal employees. Providing service and customer oriented internal processes can therefore imply a need for total redesign of systems. This kind of wholesale redesign of systems and processes has become known as "process reengineering."

4. Retain the best people

An organisation that hires the right people, trains and develops them to deliver service quality, and provides the needed support must also work to retain the best ones. Employee turnover, especially when the best service employees are the ones leaving, can be very detrimental to customer satisfaction, employee morale, and overall service quality. Some firms spend lot of time attracting employees but then tend to take them for granted, causing these good employees to search for job alternatives.

(a) **Include employees in the company vision:** For employees to remain motivated and interested in sticking with the organisation and supporting its goals, they need to share an understanding of the organisation's vision. People who deliver service day in and day out need to understand how their work fits into the big picture of the organisation and its goals.

(b) **Treat employees as customers:** If employees feel valued and their needs are taken care of, they are more likely to stay with the organisation. Many companies have adopted the idea that employees are also customers of the organisation, and thus basic marketing strategies can be directed at them. The products that the organisation has to offer its employees are a job and quality of work life. To determine whether the job and work life needs of employees are being met, organisations conduct periodic internal marketing research to assess employee satisfaction and needs.

(c) **Measure and reward strong service performers:** If a company wants the strongest service performers to stay with the organisation, it must reward and promote them. Often the reward systems in organisations are not set up to reward service excellence. Reward systems may value productivity, sales or some other dimension that can potentially work against good service. Reward systems need to be linked to the organisation's vision and to outcomes that are truly important.

If a firm has good people, investments in training can yield outstanding results. Good service providers show a high commitment to training, in words, money, and action. As Benjamin Schneider and David Bowen put it, "The combination of attracting a diverse and competent applicant pool, utilizing effective techniques for hiring the most appropriate people from that pool, and then training them would be gangbusters in any market." According to *Lovelock, Wirtz and Chatterjee*, service employees need to learn:

- **The organisational culture, purpose, and strategy.** A company should start strong with new hires, and focus on getting emotional commitment to the firm's core strategy. Promoting core values such as commitment to service excellence, responsiveness, team spirit, mutual respect, honesty, and integrity are also essential ingredients. Managers should be taught to teach, and focus on "what," "why; and "how" rather than on the specifics of the job.

- **Interpersonal and technical skills.** Interpersonal skills tend to be generic across-service jobs, and include visual communications skills such as making eye contact, attentive listening, body language, and even facial expressions. Technical skills encompass all the required knowledge related to processes (e.g., how to handle a merchandised return), machines (e.g., how to operate the terminal, or cash machine), and rules and regulations related to customer service processes. Both technical and interpersonal skills are necessary, but neither alone is sufficient for optimal job performance.

- **Product/service knowledge.** Knowledgeable staff is a key aspect of service quality. They must be able to explain product features effectively and also position the product correctly.

There is no doubt that training has to result in tangible changes in behaviour. If staff personnel do not apply what they have learned, the investment in their training is wasted. Learning is not only about becoming smarter, it is also about changing behaviours and improving decision making. To achieve this, practice and reinforcement are needed. Supervisors can play a crucial role by following up regularly on learning objectives, for instance, meeting with staff to reinforce key lessons from recent complaints and compliments.

Training and learning professionalises the front line, moving these individuals away from the common (self)-image of being in low-end jobs that have no significance. Well-trained employees are and feel like professionals. A waiter who knows about food, cooking, wines, dining etiquette, and how to interact effectively with customers (even complaining ones) feels professional, has higher self-esteem, and is respected by his customers. Training is therefore extremely effective in reducing person/role stress.

8.7 Motivation and Empowerment of Employees

Most exceptional service firms have great stories of employees who recovered failed service transactions, or walked, the extra mile to make a customer's day, or avoid some kind of disaster for that client. To allow this to happen, employees have to be empowered. Employee self-direction has become increasingly important, especially in service firms, because front-line staff frequently operates on their own, face-to-face with their customers, and it tends to be difficult for managers to monitor their behaviour closely. Research has also linked high empowerment to higher customer satisfaction.

For many services, providing employees with greater discretion (and training in how to use their judgment) enables them to provide superior service on the spot. Empowerment looks to front-line staff to find solutions to service problems, and to make appropriate decisions about customising service delivery.

Importance of Empowering People in Services

An organisation that emphasises customer service needs people at the frontline to do the service, to use discretions be concerned about the customer, to take initiative to provide satisfaction through exceptional service. The person at the front must fell empowered to do in the circumstances. Empowering cannot be done through a formal delegation of authority. A person with authority may not exercise that authority, if he does not feel empowered.

The importance of empowering the people in services is as follows:

1. An empowered employee focuses on results. He is not inhabitant by formalities of position, authority or function.
2. He does not consider himself bound by rules and procedure.
3. He believes that the organisation expects him to be aware of the ends to be achieved and to act in furtherance thereof. He "sees" constraints but not does not feel prevented thereby, from what is to be done, instead he tries to overcome the constraints.
4. He believes that the organisation will not find fault with him for having one something new and nusual. On the contrary, he believes that the organisation will applaud him for having done something that had to be done.

5. He believes that he is expected to take the initiative and ensure that the customer needs are met and thereby maintain and enhance the reputation of the organisation.

6. He feels that he is dedicating to satisfy the customer to upgrade organisation reputation.

7. An empowered employee may be willing to challenge company policies at meetings with sensors.

Researchers claim that the empowerment approach is more likely to yield motivated employees and satisfied customers than the "production-line" alternative, in which management designs a relatively standardised system and expects workers to execute tasks within, narrow guidelines. However, David Bowen and Edward Lawler suggest that different situations may require different solutions, declaring that "both the empowerment and production-line approaches have their advantages ... and ... each fits certain situations. The key is to choose the management approach that best meets the needs of both employees and customers." According to *Lovelock, Wirtz and Chatterjee*, it is not necessary that all employees are eager to be empowered. Many employees do not seek personal growth within their jobs and may even prefer to work to specific directions rather than to use their own initiative. In their book "Services Marketing-People, Technology and Strategy", *Lovelock, Wirtz and Chatterjee* say that research has shown that a strategy of empowerment is most likely to be appropriate when most of the following factors are present within the organisation and its environment:

*   The firm's business strategy is based on competitive differentiation, and on offering personalised, customised service.

*   The approach to customers is based on extended relationships rather than on short-term transactions.

*   The organisation uses technologies that are complex and non-routine in nature.

*   The business environment is unpredictable and surprises are to be expected.

*   Existing managers are comfortable letting employees work independently for the benefit of both the organisation and its customers.

*   Employees have a strong need to grow and deepen their skills in the work environment, are interested in working with others, and have good interpersonal and group process skills.

Empowerment is based on the involvement (or commitment) model, which assumes that employees can make good decisions, and produce good ideas for operating the service business, if they are properly socialised, trained, and informed. This model also assumes that employees can be internally motivated to perform effectively and that they are capable of self-control and self-direction.

Schneider and Bowen emphasise that "empowerment isn't just 'setting the frontline free' or 'throwing away the policy manuals.' It requires systematically redistributing four key ingredients throughout the organisation; from the top downwards." The four features are:

- Power to make decisions that influence work procedures and organisational direction (e.g., through quality circles and self-managing teams)
- Information about organisational performance (e.g., operating results and measures of competitive performance)
- Rewards based on organisational performance, such as bonuses, profit sharing, and stock options.
- Knowledge that enables employees to understand and contribute to organisational performance (e.g., problem-solving skills).
- In-the control model, the four features are concentrated at the top of the organisation, whereas in the involvement model these features are pushed down through the organisation.

Levels of Employee Involvement

The empowerment approach reflects increasing levels of employee involvement as additional knowledge, information, power, and rewards are pushed down to the front line. Empowerment can take place at several levels:

- Suggestion involvement empowers employees to make recommendations through formalised programmes.
- Job involvement. Jobs are redesigned to let employees to use a wider array of skills. In complex service organisations such as airlines and hospitals, in which individual employees cannot offer all facets of a service, job involvement is often accomplished through the use of teams. To cope with the added demands accompanying this form of empowerment, employees require training, and supervisors need to be reoriented from directing the group to facilitating its performance in supportive ways.
- High involvement gives even the lowest-level employees a sense of involvement in the company's overall performance. Information is shared. Employees develop skills in teamwork, problem solving, and business operations, and they participate in work-unit management decisions. There is profit sharing, often in the form of bonuses.

Build High-Performance Service Delivery Teams

Many services require people to work in teams, often across functions, in order to offer seamless customer service processes. Traditionally, many firms were organised by functional structures, under which, for example, one department is in charge of consulting and selling (e.g., selling a cell phone with a subscription contract), another is in charge of customer service (e.g., activation of value-added services, changes of subscription plans), and still a third is in charge of billing. This structure prevents internal service teams from viewing end customers as their own, and this structure can also mean poorer teamwork across functions, slower service, and more errors between functions.

The Power of Teamwork in Services

Jon Katzenbach and Douglas Smith define a team as "a small number of people wit complementary skills who are committed to a common purpose, set of performance goals; and approach for which they hold themselves mutually accountable." Teams, training, and empowerment go hand in hand. Teams facilitate communication among team members and the sharing of knowledge. By operating like a small independent unit, service teams take on more responsibility and require less super vision than more traditional, functionally organised customer service units Also, teams often set higher performance targets for themselves than supervisors would.

Team ability and motivation are crucial for effective delivery of many types of services, especially those involving individuals who are each playing specialist roles. Health care services depend heavily on effective teamwork.

Motivate and Energise People

Once a firm has hired the right people, trained them well, empowered them, and organised them into service delivery teams, how can it ensure that they will deliver service excellence? Staff performance is a function of ability and motivation. Effective hiring, training, empowerment, and teams give a company capable people; reward systems, meantime, are the key to motivation. Service staff must get the message that providing quality service holds the key for them to be rewarded. Motivating and rewarding strong service performers are some of the most effective ways of retaining them. Staff pick up quickly whether those who get promoted are the truly outstanding service providers, and whether those who get fired are those who haven't delivered at the customer level.

A manager in the service industries such as the hotel, resort, restaurant, or other travel business, is judged not only by the good meal, the restful night's sleep, or the weekend of fun that the guests enjoyed.

A manager is judged also by the friendliness of his staff, their alertness, their attitude, how they look, and the way they do their job.

Some ways of motivating and empowering employees:

1. Seeking and using employee's own ideas.
2. Keeping employees informed.
3. Expressing personal interest in employees.
4. Instilling pride in work well done.
5. Providing effective supervision.

Seeking and Using Employee's Ideas

To feel very much a part of the service business and to be given an incentive, each employee must understand that he is free to contribute ideas. Management must encourage employee ideas and provide the necessary mechanism for obtaining them. Suggestion boxes and idea-discussion employee meetings are a couple of possibilities. The manager can encourage employees to think about problems of the business. Some excellent ideas for their solution may be forthcoming. As manager, carefully consider all ideas, and if adopted, commend or reward the giver. If not adopted, a word of explanation and appreciation should always be given.

Keeping Employees Informed

Successful service industry managers build good attitudes in their employees by keeping them well informed of affairs of the business. Important methods of informing employees include personal communication, use of a bulletin board, regular employee newsletter or newspaper, individual written notices and meetings.

For example: meetings are one of the best forms of management-employee communi-cation. They should be kept short and purposeful. There are two types of meetings, the regular stop meeting and the problem or opportunity meeting.

Staff meetings are usually held for supervisors and department heads. However, all employees should be invited to a staff meeting, probably once a month or perhaps once each quarter. Topics could include coming events, business trends, notable achievements, and employee recognition.

The problem or opportunity meeting is called when someone has a problem or an idea worthy of consideration and assistance by others in the organisation. After the first meeting, the manager usually sets a period of time for considering the problem or idea. The parties get back together for a follow-up meeting to resolve the matter, having had time to think it over and reach some conclusions. This form of communication and mutual effort contributes importantly to the organisation's spirit of teamwork.

These procedures make each person feel important to the success of the business. The employee recognises his value and sees how his efforts help create success.

Holding regular meetings for the employees is one of the best means of motivating your staff and building self-esteem. The manager can write up the minutes of the meeting and distribute these to all concerned on the same day the meeting was held. This practice summarizes the most important points and makes them readily available for future referral and use.

Expressing Personal Interest

Another way to create motivation is the personal conference held in private with each employee.

For example: managers or supervisors should find time at least once each year to sit down in private with each employee. In a friendly manner, discuss both business and personal matters. Such talks smooth out problems and difficulties which may be blocking the motivation of the employee. The talks are also helpful to you, the supervisor or manager, as you may receive information which would come to you in no other way.

Instilling Pride in Work

One definite advantage of employment in the service industries is that much of it is still of a "craft" nature. Craft work with the hands produces a complete finished product that can be admired (with accompanying satisfactions.)

Management should show public satisfaction with accomplishment by occasionally complimenting and expressing appreciation to the employee for work well done.

Furthermore, increased automation in manufacturing will force a growing number of persons to look for jobs, as the labour supply exceeds the demand. Many will find their way into the service industries.

A job in tourism is often seen as a privilege, since most jobs in this industry have a measure of glamour and excitement. Managers can build pride, and this should be done to keep good workers and attract new ones. Employee status can be elevated by following the suggestions in this bulletin. Respect and pride for all employees is the foundation for increasing status.

Pride in work well done also builds morale. Morale can be defined as an emotional attachment to the business itself. It is the end product of skilled management and is reflected in each individual and in the general tone of all employees toward their employer and towards each guest. When employee satisfactions and needs are being met, excellent morale is the certain result. Morale thus becomes an important indicator of the quality of employee management and should be carefully watched and measured as an integral part of the total management process. Any weaknesses which may appear should promptly receive attention and correction by the manager.

Providing Effective Supervision

The supervisor is the basic managerial element in the business organisation. He forms the essential link between the general manager and the workers. The entire organisation is dependent on him. He must follow the fundamentals of good management - Planning, Organising, Motivating, and Controlling. Actually, his functions in the latter two are more important than the former, but nevertheless, he does operate within all of the management procedures.

Usually, the supervisor is responsible for the training needed within his department. He owes each person under him the opportunity for training and self improvement and should be entitled to similar opportunities himself.

The worker must have good and effective supervision to perform to the best of his ability. Poor supervision brings about the opposite results. According to an authoritative source, one-third of all employee job changes can be attributed to poor supervision. Thus, quality of supervision will largely determine the level of employee performance.

Work Incentives

To effectively motivate, a definite system of incentives or rewards is necessary. Such a system requires a combination of several groups of incentives, the most important of which are:

1. Recognition-both monetary and non-monetary.
2. Social prestige.
3. Achievement.
4. Self-esteem

Recognition-Monetary

The first thought concerning recognition is usually money. Good pay is vital. However, there are others of major importance-steady work, comfortable working conditions, good working companions, good supervision, the actual nature of the job itself, and opportunities for advancement. Good pay is essential to employee satisfaction and must be carefully considered in all personnel matters. The employee should not feel that he is underpaid. Pay is the best and most tangible form of recognition of the employee's worth to the company.

Besides actual pay increases, other forms of monetary recognition commonly used are a bonus plan, profit-sharing and extra pay for reducing costs (cost reduction programmes).

Bonus Plan

When considering a bonus plan, first think about its objectives:

- To produce extra efforts from participants.
- To favourably direct their efforts.
- To provide extra compensation according to the financial success of the company and department. To raise morale and enthusiasm of all the staff.
- To increase the profitability of the company.

Any extra reward system should have the following characteristics:

- Clearly understood and meaningful to all.
- Judged to be equitable.
- Be results-oriented and reflect employee performance. High producers should get the big bonus and low producers a low bonus or none.
- Be closely linked in time to the performance upon which the bonus is based. A quarterly or semi-annual period is suggested, but annual is often used.
- Evaluation should be as objective as possible.

Good communication is an essential element in the bonus plan. When formulating the plan, seek free exchange of ideas. The manager must be willing to listen to employees and make constructive changes in the plan when needed.

Suggestions concerning a bonus system

- All employees should be eligible.
- If employed in a profit-making department, the bonus should be directly related to the profit of that department. If not in such a department, the bonus formula is determined by the supervisor.
- Overhead expenses, over which the employee has no control, should be considered separately when determining departmental profit. Appropriate statements of revenues and expenses chargeable to the department must be prepared according to an accounting method clearly understood and recognized as fair by all.
- All persons involved in the bonus should be able to periodically measure themselves during the year. (A financial report of some type should be made available.)

Some suggested rules

- Must be an employee for 1 year before being eligible for a bonus.
- Performance should be objectively rated by supervisor as being unsatisfactory, satisfactory, or superior, etc. If unsatisfactory, he would not be eligible for a bonus and the supervisor would explain why to the employee. If satisfactory, the employee would receive the regular bonus, as determined by formula. If superior, he might receive more, perhaps twice as much.

To determine a bonus for managers and supervisors, use a variation of the bonus plan. A group of major factors needed for success in a given department is outlined-cleanliness, training ability, service, volume, profit, quality, or cost factors. Assign a point value to these, such as "0" for unsatisfactory "1" for satisfactory and "2" for superior. At the end of each 6 months, the general manager objectively rates the supervisor on each of the agreed upon factors. For example, if five factors were being evaluated, a score of "10" would be the best possible. This total is equated to a percentage for the bonus, such as 20 percent of the base salary. If total point score were "9" the bonus would be 15 percent, etc. Annual salary increases could also be equated to average bonus percentage for the year.

The supervisor or department head might also be awarded a bonus based upon increases in total sales volume. His extra reward could be a percentage of any sales gain plus a percentage of the profit, providing that gross profit amounted to a certain percentage of gross sales. These percentages would be agreed upon by the manager and his supervisors or department heads through mutual discussion and consideration. Thus, subordinates and the manager work out the details of the bonus plan together.

Another possible arrangement is a sliding scale of bonus payments in which increments in sales and profits yield step increases in the percentages of bonus paid.

Profit Sharing

There are several important considerations in formulating a profit sharing plan.

- The employee must be with the company for 1 year before being eligible to participate.
- The amount received by each participant should be related as closely as possible to performance. Some may receive more and others less. (See applicable concepts and principles under Bonus Plan.)

Under the cash plan, profits to be distributed are paid in cash currently-usually quarterly, semi-annually, or annually. Total profit to be distributed to the employees is usually an amount fixed by a formula. For example, one company's employees receive $33^{1/3}$ percent of net profits before taxes, but not over 15 percent of the payroll.

Under the deferred plan, a trust fund is set up to provide employees with future benefits. The fund is created by contributions from participating employees and from the company, according to a formula. The deferred plan provides retirement, death, supplemental unemployment, health insurance, and disability payments. Also, some plans provide for loan and withdrawal privileges which make possible immediate financial assistance in time of unusual need.

These plans have a certain advantages: (1) profit sharing tends to become a unifying force drawing management and employees together, (2) such plans are definitely work incentives, since every employee can see that the profitability of the business and his own personal welfare are necessarily related, and (3) each worker has an incentive to be more creative and think of ways to increase sales and reduce or eliminate expenses.

An alternative to profit sharing which might be more understandable and appealing to certain groups of employees is cost reduction. Every employee knows that when he breaks a dish, for example, there is a cost to the company. If he knew that he would share in the amount saved by the company by being more careful and efficient, he would have much more interest in helping reduce costs.

Here's how the program works. A certain base period for comparing subsequent periods, is established. All expenses in future periods are compared with the base period. Any savings in costs are shared with the employees, usually a certain percentage. The formula used by a steel corporation is a payment of 37.5 percent of the savings to the employees. In the service industries, expenses have to be adjusted to the volume of business and inflationary cost increases which occurred during the periods being compared. The relationships can be readily figured and savings determined.

Recognition-Non-monetary

Non-monetary recognition can be tangible or intangible. Examples of tangible recognition: pins or plaques for length of service or special accomplishments; announcing a promotion with a story and employee's picture in the local newspaper, or advertisement in the local newspaper featuring pictures of key personnel, highlighting their training, experience, and outstanding services.

Intangible means of recognition are less formal. A kind word of praise: "Joe, the gardens and lawn look just great. We've really got a good grounds' man" builds good will and is recognised by both parties as respect and recognition. Or, take employees out to lunch at regular intervals, arrange a party for them, such as at Christmas, or send each one a card on his birthday, or when sick.

Social Prestige

Present-day management theory says it is no longer sufficient to satisfy only subsistence needs. Such a policy is too limited to motivate employees enough for today's competitive business conditions. Superior employee performance will be obtained only when his social and self-esteem needs are supplied on the job. "More money" often becomes an insistent demand when management is concerned only with satisfying minimum cost-of-living needs. When the "whole person" is involved within an enterprise, the employee is often content with less money than he might make elsewhere, simply because he enjoys his work and experiences self-esteem and accomplishment through his work.

Prestige is built in the relationships between people. Employees, like everyone else, feel a strong need to belong and feel accepted. These are important factors in good employee management. The intelligent and efficient manager carefully considers them when he formulates policy governing work incentives for his business family.

Let's consider the social and relaxation needs of your staff. Suppose you encourage a 10-minute rest break for the housekeepers. If you provide an attractive room where they can sit down and enjoy a few minutes of each other's company and a little refreshment, important social needs have been fulfilled. Employees become better acquainted and develop friendships. Such a management policy encourages employee cooperation and provides incentive to work toward the best interests of all of the employees and the business.

Or, encourage social events or special dinners for: achieving some goal, an employee's retirement, a special event in the life of the business such as the anniversary of the founding date, or similar occasion. You might plan recreation programmes,-bowling and softball leagues, swimming, golf, or other group-oriented sport.

Achievement

Ambition falls off when employees do not have enough to do. The only way to solve this problem is to establish reasonable work production standards for each job. Study and evaluation of standards and worker production should result in a reasonable level of output for each position. Living up to these standards brings a sense of achievement.

Better Placement

Workers will be more productive and interested if they feel they are in the right job, best suited for the occupation in which they are employed, and being used to the fullest capacity. Periodic checks of employee's production and talks with his supervisor will establish his level of performance. Appropriate adjustments in his job assignment help to keep his work up to his capabilities and are of long-term benefit to both worker and employer.

Better Environment

Some places of business look fine from the outside, and to the customer, but much less attractive behind doors in the work areas. This is detrimental to morale. Also, there are indirect, bad effects on habits and sanitation standards. Working areas should be made light, airy, comfortable, orderly, quiet, and clean. Actual tests have proven that morale and productivity are much higher when employees work in pleasant and clean areas than when the work environment is unattractive and depressing.

Self-Achievement, Advancement, Growth

Self-achievement (also called self-fulfilment or self-actualisation) tops all other considerations as an additional incentive especially for the more ambitious and resourceful employee.

Simply stated, a person knows he can climb the business ladder as far as his ability can take him.

This incentive is especially powerful for younger members of an organisation. To motivate and keep the services of the most intelligent and capable of your younger employees, you must offer opportunity for advancement. Openings for positions of greater authority and responsibility occur from time to time, and each business can offer its own particular inducements.

Self-Esteem

This group of needs differs from others in that it is concerned with the employee's view of himself. Examples are the opportunity for recognition, status in the community, respect, distinction, attention, importance, and appreciation. These are the most difficult needs to provide.

Recognition of achievement as previously described, is a good example of improving an employee's view of himself. Pins, plaques or recognition in the newspaper are excellent ways to denote worth to the company. Self-improvement, hence self-esteem, can be improved by sending your people to special schools or short courses, or paying for home study courses or similar improvement programs.

Enhancing self-esteem improves feelings of self-confidence, strength, worth, and usefulness to the business organisation. Denying this need leads to a feeling of inferiority which brings about discouragement.

These are practical employee management suggestions which will bring about more productive and better satisfied employees. The team approach and provisions for high quality supervision are essential elements in motivation. Use of specific incentives (rewards) in monetary and non-monetary forms constitute tangible results for the employee. Employee who are recognised for their worth to the company and rewarded accordingly will multiply this value in guest satisfaction and profits.

Implementing these suggestions in no way implies lack of leadership. In fact, such procedures actually increase leadership ability. Each employee is invited to assist management and is expected to participate in plans and discussions. Thus, management and employees have similar responsibility in maintaining good leadership. By following these recommendations, the manager can build a better management team and strengthen his position as a leader.

Questions for Discussion

1. What is the services marketing triangle?
2. Explain the concept of a service encounter.
3. Explain: managing of people in service encounter.
4. Explain the concept of services profit chain.
5. Explain the role of human resources and internal marketing in dealing with service encounters.
6. Explain training, development, motivation and empowerment of employees.
7. Explain the concept of service personnel in a service business.
8. State the key role of service employees in a service business.

■■■

Chapter **9**...

Physical Evidence

Contents ...

9.1 Introduction

As services are intangible, customers are searching for evidence of service in every interaction they have with an organisation. The three major categories of evidence as experienced by the customer: people, process, and physical evidence together represent the service and provide the evidence that tangibilises the offering. The new mix elements essentially are evidence of service in each moment of truth.

All of these evidence elements or a subset of them are present in every service encounter a customer has with a service firm and are critically important in managing service encounter quality and creating customer satisfaction.

When a guest enters the hotel for a stay the first encounter of the guest is the door attendant and frequently with receptionists at the reception. The quality of that encounter will be judged by how the registration *process* works (How long is to wait? Is the registration system computerised and accurate?) The actions and attitudes of the *people* (Is the receptionist courteous, helpful, knowledgeable? Does she handle the enquiries fairly and efficiently?) and the *physical evidence* of the service (is the awaiting area clean and comfortable). The three types of evidence may be differentially important depending on the type of service encounter (remote, phone, face – to – face). All these types will operate in face – to- face service encounters as in the one just described.

9.2 Nature of Physical Evidence

Physical evidence is the material part of a service. Strictly speaking there are no physical attributes to a service, thus a customer tends to depend on material cues. There are many examples of physical evidence, including some of the following:

- Packaging.
- Internet/web pages.

- Paperwork (such as invoices, tickets and despatch notes).
- Brochures.
- Furnishings.
- Signage (such as those on aircraft and vehicles).
- Uniforms.
- Business cards.
- The building itself (such as prestigious offices or scenic headquarters).
- Mailboxes and many others . . . . . .

Physical environment can be said to be the environment in which the service is delivered and where the firm and customer interact and any tangible components that facilitate performance or communication of service.

It includes all tangible representations of the service-such as brochures, letter head, equipment etc. in some cases the physical facilities where service is offered is important e.g., in a hotel the parking lot, surroundings are important. In other services such as telecommunication the physical facilities may be irrelevant. In this case other tangibles like billing statements become important. Physical evidence includes:

(A) Physical facilities (essentials and peripherals)

(B) Physical setting (appearance of premises)

(C) Social setting (appearance of staff)

The decision on the physical evidence will differ in terms of customer-employee interaction. At one end is self-service of customer without any interaction with employee (ATM) where physical facilities must be to attract customer and user friendly.

At the other end employees perform without any interaction (mail order business). Here physical evidence is designed to promote operational efficiency. Between the two extremes is a situation where both customer and employee interact. In this case physical evidence must be planned to facilitate the activities of both. (E.g., Banks, Airlines). Certain service environments are simple requiring very little space or equipment (ATM, Vending machine). They are called lean environment. Others like hospitals, hotels are elaborate environment where proper planning is needed.

(a) **Physical facilities:** The potential customers form impression about the service organisation on the basis of physical evidence like building, furniture etc.
   - **Essential Evidence:** They are dominant features like building area, parking space, signboards.
   - **Peripheral Evidence:** They are less dominant like admission card, medical reports, etc.

(b) **Physical Setting:** Physical setting consists of the service environment
   - Ambient factors (light, colour, temperature)
   - Space (spatial layout and functionality- i.e., ability of equipment and furniture to accomplish interactions)
   - Decor and artefacts.

(c) **Social setting:** Employee uniform, appearance etc. of the service scape can influence customer expectation, satisfaction and other behaviour. In shopping mall soft music is played/crossroads had hired separate parking space.

The marketers tangibilise of services to create a service evidence. All three elements of the augmented service mix i.e. people physical evidence and process are considered while managing the evidence of service. The figure below shows modified frame work of "tourism offering" where in the sub elements of main elements play a significant role in tangibilising the services and create a service evidence.

According to Boom and Bitner the elements of physical evidence are as given in the table 9.1.

Table 9.1: Elements of Physical Evidence

(Organisation Physical facilities service scape)	Other tangibles
Facility Exterior	Business cards
Exterior design	Stationary
Signage	Billing statements
Parking	Reports
Landscape	Employee dress
Surrounding environment	Uniforms
Facility Interior	Brochures
Interior design	
Equipment	
Signage	
Layout	
Airquality / Temperature	

The above table includes:

- Organisation physical facility elements.
- Other forms of tangible communication.

However the customers have own view about the service with regard to organisation's physical facilities and other forms of tangible communication. The table 9.2 highlights the organisation's physical facilities and also the other forms of tangible communication.

It will be observed from this table that some services e.g. Airlines, Themeparks, communicate dominantly through physical evidence and other e.g. Insurance, speed post through limited physical evidence.

Table 9.2: Physical Evidence: Customer Point of View

Service	Physical evidence Organisation physical facilities (Service Scape)	Other tangibles

Airlines	Airline lounges
	Terminal Exteriors
	Air plane exterior
	Air plane interiors
	   • Décor
	   • Seats
	   • Ambience
	   • Music
		Tickets
		Embarkation cards
		Uniformed employees
		Food

Theme Park	Gate area Parking area Signage Layout Rides Lighting	Brochures Tickets Customed characters
Insurance	–	Policy document Brochures Periodic statements Demand notes etc.
Speed post	–	Vehicles Uniforms Computers Packaging

It will be observed from the above table that marketers must create evidence of services from the point of view of the customers to enable them to build trust.

9.3 Importance of Physical Evidence in Services

Customers heavily depend on tangible cues because services are intangible. These tangible cues or physical evidence as it is called are required by customers to evaluate the service before purchasing it and to assess their satisfaction with the service during and after consumption.

Physical evidence, according to Zeithaml, Bitner, Gremler and Pandit, is particularly important for communicating about credence services and also for services such as hotels, hospitals and theme parks that are dominated by experience attributes.

Physical Evidence communicates with customers and plays a vital role in creating the service experience, in satisfying customers and in enhancing customers' perceptions of quality. It can play a major role in determining service quality expectations and perceptions.

As a rule, services lack tangibility. They thus require evidence to prove that they exist and in the same form as is being claimed. A good on the other hand hardly requires evidence, since it is in itself evidence.

A piece of physical evidence is 'a physical object accompanying a service that cannot be categorised as true product elements' (Shostack, 1977, 1987). As an example, for an educational institution, its brochure, buildings, class rooms and faculty form the evidence of a service that the institution proclaims to provide. Similarly for a bank, its computers, personnel, ATMs, premises, ledgers form some of the pieces of evidence that will be sought by its customers to appreciate the nature of service to be expected from the bank. Physical or Service evidence, according to Shostack (1977), 'plays a critical role in verifying either the existence or the completion of a service'.

In practice, however, service evidence plays a bigger role in the evaluation of services by customers (Zeithaml, 1981). Since buying of services entails a high degree of uncertainty and anxiety, service evidence, plays a 'risk reduction' role as well in service buying. Thus, a patient at a hospital undergoes higher anxiety about the service, sometimes for his very survival. However, the sight of a well-equipped hospital and the availability of trained and competent staff reduces the risk to a large extent. Service evidence plays yet another role. It is to differentiate a particular service and a service provider from their competitors. Continuing with the example of a hospital taken earlier, having an MRI facility in a hospital differentiates it from another hospital, even though both may have a similar reputation for their staff competence. Thus, a service provider can impact the customer evaluation process through the clever utilisation of a single piece of evidence or through the whole configuration. The configuration of evidence is all that matters in a service organisation. The configuration includes two types of evidence (Shotstack, 1977); the essential evidence and the peripheral evidence. Essential evidence serves only for the sight of service buyers and cannot be taken away after the use of the service. Thus, a computer in a bank or MRI in a hospital or a teacher in a management institute is essential evidence of these service providers. The essential evidence is 'so dominant in its impact on the service purchase and use that it must be considered virtually an element in its own right.

Peripheral evidence, unlike essential evidence, can be given away or taken away by service customers. Thus, an in-flight magazine in an airline or the course material in an academic institution and the passbook in a bank are peripheral evidence of these service providers. Peripheral evidence plays an emotional role in consumer evaluation of a service before, during and after purchase (Zeithaml, 1981). It can influence the mood of the service encounter and experience. It is quite unfortunate that in the era of computerization, the Indian Railways lost wonderful peripheral evidence that they had for years for Rajdhani passengers. The travel ticket was distinctly recognizable from other travel tickets. Therefore, Rajdhani passengers proudly put it in their front pockets for every one to see. Of course, with computerized homogeneity, it now does not matter, as all tickets look alike. But the credit card companies did not repeat the mistake. They leveraged on permitting the pictures chosen by the customers on their Credit cards. This is an excellent indication of the potential that peripheral evidence holds for marketing services.

Service marketers are expected constantly to search, identify, innovate and sustain various configurations of service evidence, for it is these configurations that will provide 'clues and confirmations (or contradictions) that the service user seeks and needs to formulate a specific reality for the service' (Shostack 1977).

However, many service entrepreneurs and executives mistake the making of evidence configurations as 'mere marketing gimmicks, packaging and visual ornaments'. They tend to overlook that service evidence goes much deeper. It is a careful strategy to influence the perceptions of customers and services employees alike. It is a serious exercise in strategy formulation for service marketers and can impact the very survival and competitiveness of the service firm.

9.4 Tangibilising through Physical Evidence

Among the four characteristics; intangibility, inseparability, variability, and perishability; which differentiate products from services, there is argument that the single most important characteristic is intangibility. Moreover, it has been said that intangibility is the key to determining whether or not an offering is a service or product (Zeithaml and Bitner, 1996). Indeed, the broad definition of services implies intangibility as a key determinant of whether an offering is a service or not (Oberoi and Hales, 1990; Zeithaml and Bitner, 1996). This intangibility characteristic has a profound effect on the marketing of services (Lovelock, 1991; Rushton and Carson, 1989). This characteristic OF intangibility, has been found in many literatures to be the most likely reason for the other three characteristics; inseparability, variability, and perishability.

However, some scholars have argued that the intangible-tangible dimension is difficult for consumers to understand, and that the importance of intangibility might have been overemphasised (Bowen, 1990; Wyckham et al., 1975). They proposed that the service provider's offer is their "productive capacity", rather than the tangible or intangible nature of the offer. In other instances, some scholars claim that it is nearly impossible to say that a certain business offering is pure product or pure service. The use of products/services bundle is proved to be more usable than the traditional approach of categorising products and services and their tangibility/intangibility. The products/services bundle refers to the inseparable offering of many goods and services (Gronroos, 1977; Levitt, 1980, 1981). This fact, which has been recognised in the classification scheme of others, suggests that the conceptualisation of "the bundle" may not be separable in the consumer's evaluation of service quality. This results in a product and service continuum (As discussed in the

4th Chapter), where highly tangible goods are placed at one end of one continuum, and highly intangible services are placed at the opposite end, and the goods service bundle is located somewhere in between the two.

Despite contradictory opinions regarding the uses of tangibility and intangibility to differentiate services, the attempts to make services more tangible proves to produce fruitful results in the marketing of services.

Why Tangibilise?

Services are intangible by nature. You can't see, touch, smell, or taste them before you buy them. This intangibility often makes services difficult to depict in clear and meaningful ways. Many companies' inability to depict their services tangibly leads to the following symptoms and conditions:

1. **Difficult to conceptualise:** Clients and prospects have difficulty picturing, in their mind's eye, the services process and outcomes.
2. **Difficult to evaluate:** The difficulty in conceptualising leads to difficulty in evaluating the service.
3. **Uncertainty and perceived risk:** Without a clear evaluation framework, the client level of uncertainty and perceived risk rises. Added uncertainty and risk is anathema to selling services, especially in new client generation where trust has yet to be established.
4. **Difficult to promote the offering:** Difficulty in conceptualising also leads to difficulty in creating focused marketing communications (from the firm's perspective) and difficulty selling the services internally to colleagues (from the client's perspective).
5. **Difficult to control service quality:** The less tangible the process and expected outcomes of a particular service, the more difficult it is to measure the service quality. And, as we all know, what can't be measured can't be managed or controlled.
6. **Difficult to set prices:** The less we know about the actual service delivery process, the less we understand the cost-basis of providing the service. The less tangible the delivery outputs and expected business outcomes, the less we can establish the business value of the service. Thus, it's difficult to set price on either a cost-plus basis (#1) and/or a value basis.

Physical evidence plays an important role in communicating promises and creating customer expectations. Unplanned, contradictory, and mismatched physical evidence can contribute to dissatisfaction. It is thus essential to tangibilise the service through physical evidence in a proper manner. The below given section suggests some general guidelines for an effective physical evidence strategy.

1. **Recognising the Strategic Impact of Physical Evidence:** Physical evidence can play a major role in shaping service quality expectations and perceptions. For many organisations, just acknowledging the impact of physical evidence is a key first step.

They can then take advantage of the potential of physical evidence and plan strategically. For the evidence strategy to be successful it should be linked clearly to the organisation's overall goals and vision. Thus, planners must know what those goals are and then determine how the evidence strategy can support them. It is important to thus define the basic service concept, identify the target markets (both internal and external), and know the company's general vision of its future. Because many evidence decisions are relatively permanent and costly (particularly servicescape decisions), they must be planned and executed purposely.

2. **Mapping the Physical Evidence of Service:** Mapping the service is the next step. Everyone should be able to see the service process and the existing elements of physical evidence. An efficient way to depict service or physical evidence is through the service map, or blueprint. While service maps clearly have manifold purposes, they can be predominantly useful in visually capturing physical evidence opportunities. People, process, and physical evidence can be seen in the service map. From the map one can read the actions involved in service delivery, the intricacy of the process, the points of human interaction that provide evidence opportunities, and the tangible representations which exist at each step.

3. **Assessing and Identifying Physical Evidence Opportunities:** One question to ask is: Are there missed opportunities to present service evidence? The service map of an insurance or utility service may demonstrate that little if any evidence of service is ever provided to the customer. A plan might then be developed to provide additional evidence of service to illustrate to customers precisely what they are paying for. Or it may be revealed that the evidence provided is sending messages that don't serve to augment the firm's image or goals. Another set of questions to deal with concerns whether the current physical evidence of service suits the needs and preferences of the target market.

4. **Updating and Modernising the Evidence:** Some facets of the physical evidence need regular or periodic updating and modernising. Time takes a toll on the evidence and this may necessitate change and modernisation. This should cover all aspects of the physical evidence as over time different colours, style and designs may communicate different messages.

It is essential for companies to think and plan strategically about tangibilising through physical evidence because of the importance of physical evidence and its powerful influence on both customers and employees. If physical evidence is researched, planned and implemented effectively key problems which can lead to service quality shortcomings can be avoided. An effective physical evidence strategy can play a critical role in communicating to customers and guiding them to understand the company's offerings.

9.5 Servicescapes

Servicescapes, are not only an important component of a customer's impression formation, but also an important source of evidence in the overall evaluation of the servicescape itself and the service organisation in general. Bitner (1992) asserted that human behaviour is influenced by the physical setting and the organisation's physical setting influences customer and employee behaviours. Customers seek evidence of the ultimate quality of the intangible service by observing the tangible elements (physical surroundings), called servicescape (Berry & Parasuraman, 1991). Service products are unique because they are generally produced and consumed simultaneously (Bitner, 1992). Service products are a combination of intangible and tangible components, such as a meal at a restaurant provided with services by wait staff. The actual service provided by the wait staff is intangible (Namasivayam & Lin, 2008). However, the service environment where the service is provided consists of both tangible and intangible elements (Namasivayam & Lin, 2008). Bitner (1992) defined servicescape as the built environment, which has artificial physical surroundings as opposed to the natural or social environment.

Namasivayam and Lin (2008) described servicescape as the physical environment of an organisation encompassing several different elements, such as overall layout, design, and décor of a store. The servicescape also includes aspects of atmospherics, such as temperature, lighting, colours, music, and scent (Bitner, 1992; Namasivayam & Lin, 2008). The servicescape is important, since it influences not only consumers' cognitive, emotional, and physiological states but also their behaviours (Bitner, 1992; Namasivayam & Lin, 2008). Therefore, it is important for service organisations, including hospitality entities, to manipulate the servicescape effectively to enhance customer satisfaction and increase repeat business (Namasivayam & Lin, 2008).

Servicescapes are an important tangible component of the service product that provide cues to customers and create an immediate perceptual image in customers' minds (Kotler, 1973). Levitt (1981) notes that when customers evaluate intangible products (e.g., services), they always depend to some extent on both appearance and external impression; servicescapes, in this context, encompass the appearance and impression of the service organisation's overall products and services.

All physical elements in venues of service providers such as lighting, signage, textures, materials, upholstery, colour, music, fragrances, and temperature of the environment contribute to creating the servicescape (Namasivayam & Lin, 2008). Bitner (1992) viewed the servicescape as the packaging of services and categorised it into three components—ambient conditions, spatial/function, and signs, symbols and artifacts. Ambient conditions involve sensory elements, such as temperature, colour, lights, noise, music, scent, and so on (Bitner, 1992), which affect customers' perceptions of the service environment (Nguyen, 2004). Spatial layout embraces layout, equipment, furnishings, and so on (Bitner, 1992), which reflects physical and spatial environments where the service occurs. Signs, symbols, and artifacts relate to signage, personal artifacts, style of décor, and so on (Bitner, 1992), which contribute to creating an appropriate atmosphere and direct customers to service experiences during their service encounter (Nguyen, 2006).

The servicescape also affects the overall image of a service organisation. In terms of marketing strategies, corporate image is important because it is associated with customers' perceptions of the products/services offered (Zeithaml & Bitner, 2000), and, in turn, corporate image can influence customer satisfaction and ultimately customer loyalty (Andreassen & Lindestad, 1998). Moreover, a company's image contributes to value addition and increases customer satisfaction during the consumption of products/services (Kandampully & Suhartanto, 2000).

Also, a company's image evokes service experiences and memories after the consumption of products/services (MacInnis & Prices, 1987). A study in the hotel services showed that corporate image and customer satisfaction are positively related to customer loyalty (Kandampully & Suhartanto, 2000).

It has not been long since servicescape has been recognised as an important factor affecting the process of managing corporate image (Bitner, 1990; Nguyen, 2006). Servicescape is crucial in service organisations because a customer usually encounters servicescape prior to his/her interactions with a service provider (Namasivayam & Mattila, 2007). In their study, Namasivayam and Mattila investigated whether servicescape has an important effect on customers' mood states. They empirically examined the joint effects of servicescape and the interaction with a service provider on customer satisfaction.

Role of Servicescape in Marketing of Services

The concept of a servicescape was developed by Booms and Bitner to emphasise the impact of the physical environment in which a service process takes place. Booms and Bitner defined a servicescape as "the environment in which the service is assembled and in which the seller and customer interact, combined with tangible commodities that facilitate performance or communication of the service" (Booms and Bitner, 1981, p. 36).

For e.g. Mango Masala, the hangout restaurant in the city centre Ajmer uses fluorescent colours, wrought iron furniture, collages on the walls and a mock aeroplane suspended from the ceiling to excite its guests and suggests that it is the 'happening place' of the city. Depending on the nature of desired and designed encounter a servicescape can be of the three possible types.

A Self Service Servicescape

The service is designed around a customer helping self with the service. The role of service employees is limited. Customer performs most of the activities, either on their own or with a little help from the provider. Examples are ATMs, cinema halls, gymnasium and self service restaurants etc. The service provider must plan the facility exclusively with the customer in mind. The facility design can attempt to position it for the desired market segment, by making the facility pleasing and appropriate to use for them. A gym layout and design and design (choice of equipment) conveys the segment of population that is targeted – slimming enthusiasts, body shapers, sportspersons, business executives and housewives or the youth.

An Interpersonal Servicescape

When a service encounter requires a close interaction between the customer and provider the servicescape must be facilitate this interaction. An interpersonal servicescape is appropriate. Hotels, hospitals, schools and banks are examples of this type of servicescapes, they must be designed to attract, satisfy and facilitate the activities of both conducive to the interaction between the two.

A Remote Servicescape

There are service settings where there is little or no customer involvement in the servicescape. Telecommunications, insurance and call centres etc., are examples of remote encounters. These use remote servicescapes. They are back office. The place has to be designed to keep employees' motivation and morale high. The servicescape should premeditate ergonomically to facilitate teamwork, supervision and operational efficiency.

Furthermore, every type of servicescape can be detailed and lean. Lean servicescape will have simple processes, simple layout little equipment, little geographic (physical) spread and few simple interactions. STD-PCO, an ATM, a dry cleaner and filling station are examples of lean servicescapes. For these, the designing is simple and uncomplicated, and more so if they are self service or remote servicescape with either customers or providers on the scene a five star resort or theme park or an airport etc. are examples of elaborate servicescapes with complex and dynamic interactions between customer-employees, customers-customers, customers-equipments, equipments-employees, and employees-employees. While customer presence requires elements of comfort and convenience to be built in, the providers seek productivity, operational conveniences and amenities.

Table 9.3: Typology of Servicescape

Servicescape usage	Elaborate	Lean
Self-service (customer only)	Sports complex Cinema hall	ATM Internet services Express mail drop-off
Interpersonal services (both customer and employeee)	Hotel Restaurants Hospital Bank Airline School	Dry cleaner Video library Hair salon
Remote service (employee only)	Telephone company Insurance company Utility Many professional services	Call centres Automated voice-messaging-based services

Roles of Servicescape

A servicescape is not a passive setting it plays an important role in service transactions. An evaluation of the roles they have in service encounters will reveal how important it is to design an appropriate servicescape. A servicescape plays four important roles.

Package

Servicescapes 'package' the service offer and communicate an image to the customers of what they are going to get. It is the corporeal manifestation of the service idea for interest groups to form a shared appreciation. They are predetermined to render an intended image to the service concept and evoke a particular sensory and emotional reaction that sets the stage for a germane experience that augments the efficacy of the offer. Appropriate servicescaping is a sure shot way to create an image that the service provider is seeking to put up. It also helps moderate customer expectation and reinforces his experience and reminiscences. Servicescape is an outward appearance of organisation and thus can be critical in forming initial impressions or setting up customer expectation.

Facilitator

Another important job of servicescape is to act as a facilitator in assisting both the customers and service employees to make most of the opportunity it should make the service consumption comfortable convenient for the customer. For employees it should be pleasant to conduct activities. This setting is designed can enhanced or inhibits the efficient flow of activities in the service setting making it easier or harder for customer and employee to accomplish their goals.

Socializer

Design of servicescapes aids in socialization of both the customers and employees, conveying expected roles, behaviour and relationship. Compare the servicescape of a public bank with that of a private bank. In a public bank a large part of the floor is marked as restricted, leaving little space in the form of an arrow aisle along the outer walls of the hall for customers. The message is clear –customer must not enter the restricted area, that is where the most important job of the bank, internal operations, is conducted and by entering that area, customers will be interfering with that task. Whereas private banks approach customers with conviviability. The air conditioned lounge with comfortable seats and a cold water dispenser as you pass through a spotlessly clean glass door, makes customers feel welcome. They are allowed more space to move and occupying a seat across from executives desks suggest that customer are indeed central to all activity. The service with public bank also suggests that customers have a formal –official relationship with public bankers, whereas servicescapes in private banks encourage casual –affable interactions.

Differentiator

With the layouts a customer can make out what kind of bank it is. A dominance of green at IDBI bank differentiates it with red of HDBC bank. Candle lit tables with smooth classical music and tables with clothes and pre-laid cutlery differentiates a restaurant from other with flour cent colours and pattern on the walls, blasting music, crowded with young boys and girls and motorcycles at the makeshift parking in front. Clearly the design of the servicescape differentiates one provider from its competitors, and hints at eth segment the services are targeted at. Companies adapt servicescape to reposition the services or identify new customer segments.

Although it is useful from a strategic point of view to think about the multiple roles of the servicescape and how they interact making actual decision about servicescape design requires an understanding of why the effects occur and how to manage them. The roles played by servicescape in a particular situation will aid in identifying opportunities and deciding just who needs to be consulted in making facility design decisions.

As explained earlier in the chapter servicescapes include various cues. These are discussed in the section below.

Visual cues

The various visual cues within a servicescape include the following: colour, lighting, space and function, personal artifacts and plants, and layout and design (Bitner, 1992).

Colour

Colour is one of the obvious visual cues in a servicescape. According to Eiseman (1998), colour is a strong visual component of a physical setting, particularly in an interior setting. Research has shown that different colours stimulate varying personal moods and emotions. In evaluating a servicescape, this visual sensory input includes forming a mental picture through cognitive processing prior to affecting individuals' personal moods and emotions. Many researchers assume, contrary to this model, that environmental cues within a servicescape directly stimulate people's emotional response without being cognitively processed first.

For example, Bellizzi and Hite (1992) found that consumers react more favorably to a blue environment in retail settings, and that warm-coloured backgrounds seem to be more capable of eliciting attention and attracting people to approach a store.

Boyatzis and Varghese (1994) found that children often related positive emotions with light colours and negative emotions with dark colours.

Space and function

The furnishings in a servicescape link the space with its occupants and convey the personality of the servicescape through form, line, colour, texture, and scale. The furniture placement may convey a sense of enclosure, define spatial movement, function as walls, and communicate visible or invisible boundaries. Recognisable changes in ceiling heights affect spatial perception more than a similar change in room width or length. High ceilings convey feelings of spaciousness, whereas low ceilings are associated with coziness and intimacy (Ching, 1996). All of these elements help individuals form a mental picture prior to affective response and judgments toward a specific servicescape.

Lighting

The type of lighting in an environment directly influences an individual's perception of the definition and quality of the space, influencing his or her awareness of physical, emotional, psychological, and spiritual aspects of the space (Kurtichand Eakin, 1993). Light influences the perceptions of form, colour, texture, and enclosure (Ching, 1996). Environmental psychology has assessed the relationship between light intensity and task productivity, revealing that people's perceptions of light influence their perceptions of the environment. Researchers have found that participants perceived tasks more positively and reported decreased boredom in a room with windows, in contrast to a room without windows (Kim, 1998; Stone and Irvine, 1994).

Gifford (1988) researched the influence of lighting level and room decor on interpersonal communication, comfort, and arousal. Results indicated that general communication was more likely to occur in bright environments, whereas more intimate conversation occurred in softer light. Steffy (1990) suggested that environments in which the lighting is designed to harmonise with furniture and accessories are perceived as more pleasant than environments in which lighting does not harmonise with other elements of the room.

Auditory cues

Music

In a servicescape, guests take note of music and noise as auditory components of their evaluations. Studies on music and consumer behaviour have demonstrated that music can be used as an effective tool to minimise the negative consequences of waiting in any service operation (Hui et al., 1997). Music can also be a positive auditory cue stimulating specific consumer behaviours and emotions, as many research studies have discovered.

Perhaps music itself has a direct impact on an individual's physiological, arousal response. However, when evaluating a servicescape, researchers should perhaps combine music with other environmental cues, because as discussed above, when one evaluates a servicescape, one tends to view an environment holistically prior to making specific judgements. A piece of music that does not fit the surroundings will not contribute positively to customers' evaluations.

Olfactory Cues

Since studies have confirmed that scents can be a powerful tool in increasing sales, they have gained much more attention in the retail business. Scents can influence a consumer's desire to make a purchase; for instance, they can increase a bakery's sales by as much as 300% (Hirsch, 1991).

Hvastja and Zanuttinit (1991, p. 245) found that an olfactory cue can "heighten the awareness; it alerts the organism to existence of agents in the air, to check their quality for guidance of behaviour on the basis of previous encounters, to avoid or approach certain substances". Ambient odours may also simply influence a consumer's mood (Bone and Ellen, 1999). Mood and affect shifts are the most frequently suggested mediators of olfactory effects on individual's perception and behaviours (Bone and Ellen, 1999).

Similar to music, scent should be evaluated with other environmental cues when examining the impact of a servicescape on customer behaviour. Individuals do not assess a specific servicescape based on only one environmental stimulus. All distinct pieces unite to form a holistic picture. In this case, it is through various environmental cues that individuals receive input through their sensory systems to form a mental picture, which then stimulates an emotional response. Finally, based on the emotional response, individuals then again process cognitively by evaluating the servicescape.

Emotional Response

Mehrabian and Russell (1974, p. 55) note, "A person's feeling at any time can be characterised by the three dimensions in our framework (e.g., pleasure, arousal, dominance)". Pleasure is a feeling state that is similar to liking, but also correlates with arousal. Arousal is also conceptualised as a feeling state varying along a single dimension ranging from sleep to frantic excitement (Mehrabian and Russell, 1974). Dominance is a feeling state that is based on the extent to which he has control over his act or not in variety of ways in a servicescape (Mehrabian and Russell, 1974).

A servicescape that is considered flexible is associated with feeling of dominance for the individual (Mehrabian and Russell, 1974). On the other hand, a servicescape that is rated as more intense, more ordered, and more powerful is associated with submissive feeling for the individual (Mehrabian and Russell, 1974).

Cognition precedes emotion or vice versa?

How do consumers evaluate a servicescape? Do customers think first or feel first when they first enter a servicescape? Over the years, an immense literature has developed on emotion and cognition. Researchers have argued from both stances— either cognition precedes emotion (Lazarus, 1999) or emotion precedes cognition (Pham et al., 2001). However, this question still remains unanswered. Lazarus (1999, p. 127) argues that "cognitive activity causally precedes an emotion in the flow of psychological events, and subsequent cognitive activity is also later affected by that emotion". The causal cognitive activity continues into the emotional response itself as an integral feature". As mentioned earlier, individuals form a holistic mental image based on elements in the servicescapes, which influences emotional/affective responses. According to Lazarus, this leads to cognitive appraisal and interpretation of the affective response. Finally, individuals respond behaviourally (e.g., approach or avoidance behaviour) (Mehrabian and Russell, 1974).

Many prior studies of the effects of servicescapes have ignored the cognitive processes, and have examined the effects of environmental stimuli directly on individuals' emotional responses and behaviours. When consumers walk into a servicescape, there are numerous environmental cues that they sense and visualise. Hence, unconsciously, consumers are in fact gathering and retrieving all the cues together to create a mental picture in their minds. This stage of the cognitive processing is important because consumers are also believed to form specific expectations of a product/servicescape prior to actual purchase (Oliver, 1980, 1981).

Human sensory perception is understood as immediate, basic, and direct experiences of stimulus attributes such as warm, loud, blue, and the like caused by the appropriate stimulation of a sensory organ (Schiffman, 2001). It is these inputs of visual, audio, and olfactory sensations, also known as the sense modality variable (Mehrabian and Russell, 1974), that individuals recruit to form a cognitive schema, or image of a servicescape. Hence, these sense modality variables should be considered compulsory moderators of our subsequent moods, emotions, and behaviours.

Behavioural responses

A wealth of literature exists on the effects of environmental cues on behaviours. However, much of the research in the area of environmental psychology is focused on retail stores, e.g., supermarkets (e.g., Hirsch, 1991; Donovan and Rossiter, 1982; Bellizzi and Hite, 1992; Bellizzi et al., 1983; Spangenberg et al., 1996; Areni and Kim, 1993; Yalchand Spangenberg, 1990, 2000). This research also only considers consumers' immediate emotional responses to environmental cues, without taking into account the moderating or mediating effect of variables (e.g., individuals' cognitive style, personalities). Many studies also fail to consider people's subconscious processes of perceptual organisation prior to measuring their emotional response and behaviour. Individuals are more likely to retrieve sensory reactions prior to emotional responses (Lazarus, 1999). An individual's evaluation of a servicescape arises from the individual, the environment, and the ongoing contact between the two. These evaluations may vary with biology, personality, socio-cultural experience, goals, expectations, and internal and external factors (Walshet al., 2000). Evaluation may include any of the environment's many attributes, and may involve varying amounts of feeling or mental activity. It may also happen from the content or meaning of the form, and this requires more mental activity in order to recognise the content, place it into a mental framework, and then evaluate it.

Service providers need to define their market positioning, segmentation, and target market by creating a servicescape that will meet the target customers' needs, wants, and expectations. In the framework of services marketing, uniformity between brand insight and the design of the physical environment is critical. Designers need to create a servicescape that fits the rationale of customers' consumption experience and the functionality of both private and public areas of a specific service environment.

Various service environments provide guests with different functions. For example, a hotel guestroom and a hotel lobby each has its own purpose. A hotel guestroom is considered a private environment, while a hotel lobby is considered a public space. Because these two locations play different roles in the mind of hotel guests, understanding consumers' evaluating processes and the different purpose of private and public space will allow service providers to make better decisions in creating a pleasant servicescape for specific service settings.

Private Space

According to Rutes et al. (2001), a private setting such as a hotel guestroom has a greater influence on guests' overall hotel experience than a public setting. Hotels aim to adopt a "home-like style" (Siguaw and Enz, 1999) in order to provide a harmonious and comfortable environment where guests can feel like they are at home. Siguaw and Enz also noted that the best hotel design organisations emphasise the importance of creating a residential feel. Ultimately, guestroom surroundings are a place where a guest will want to relax and rest. Therefore, service providers should understand the function or purpose of the environment from a consumer's perspective in order to adopt the right color combinations, music, and decor to create a pleasant servicescape.

Public Space

A public space such as a hotel lobby or a restaurant typically creates the first and most lasting impression in customers. It is also a main source of information for the subsequent evaluation of the entire service organisation. Rutes et al. (2001) suggest that the overall layout and design of a hotel lobby must provide guest circulation from the entrance to the front desk to elevators in a logical and convenient fashion. Rutes et al. also emphasised the success of good design by balancing the visual impact and functionality of the space.

A servicescape is made up of many elements. These elements include specific environmental cues. When an individual perceives these specific cues through his or her sensory system, that person is essentially creating a cognitive schema and forming a specific mental image. For example, when service providers make decisions about the overall layout and design of a service environment, the purposive visual targets should be taken into account and put together so as to form a perceptual figure that stands out from the background.

Servicescapes play a significant role in many service organisations (e.g., hotels, restaurants, and hospitals). They give a first impression, before customers have a chance to interact with service employees. Consequently, these servicescapes are an important element that customers will use to guide their beliefs, attitude, and expectations of a service provider. Customers interact with the physical facility continuously, an experience that outweighs their interactions with service employees.

Questions for Discussion

1. What is physical evidence? Explain the importance of physical evidence in marketing services.

2. State the nature of physical evidence.

3. Explain the maintenance of physical evidence.

4. Explain the term servicescapes.

5. Explain with examples the physical evidence of services in banking, health and insurance sectors.

6. Explain: Tangibilising through physical evidence.

7. Explain the role of servicescapes in services marketing.

Chapter **10**...

Process

Contents ...

10.1 Introduction

Process is another element of the extended marketing mix, or 7P's. There are a number of perceptions of the concept of process within the business and marketing literature. Some see processes as a means to achieve an outcome, for example - to achieve a 30% market share a company implements a marketing planning process.

For the purposes of the marketing mix, process is an element of service that sees the customer experiencing an organisation's offering. It's best viewed as something that customers participate in at different points in time.

Services are process and experience based and in many cases dependent on human, interpersonal delivery systems, suggesting a need to focus on process, delivery, and experience, innovation.

The service process is an element of the augmented marketing mix and a vital point of the value chain. The adoption of processes which add value to the service offering without incurring major cost disadvantages are beneficial to the customers and the organisation.

General meaning that we understand from word process in service marketing is that they are means of transaction, supplying information and providing services in a way which is acceptable to the consumer and effective to the organisation. For introducing Process the marketer needs to understand exactly the needs and wants of customer and pattern of behaviour.

The processes by which services are created and delivered to the customer is a major factor within the service marketing mix as services customer will often perceive the service and the way it is been delivered as a part of service itself. All work activity is Process. Processes involve the procedure, tasks, schedules, mechanisms, activities and routines by which product or service is delivered to the customer.

10.2 Services as Processes and a System

According to Lovelock, Wirtz and Chatterjee, processes are the architecture of services. Processes they say describe the method and sequence in which service operating systems work, specifying how they link together to create the value proposal that has been promised to customers. According to them customers themselves are an integral part of the system in high-contact services and the process becomes their experience.

One of the most characteristic features of services is their process nature. Unlike physical goods, services are dynamic, unfolding over a period of time through a progression or constellation of events and steps. The service process can be viewed as a chain or constellation of activities that allow the service to function efficiently. For example, a professional consulting service is represented by events occurring between business partners, beginning with learning about each other, developing a service agreement, a series of meetings, project deadlines, and deliverables. This service could take place over a small time frame or it could take place over several years. To function successfully for the client, the entire sequence of consulting activities should be coordinated and managed as a whole, over time, with stress on including the resources and steps that produce value for the customer. An analysis of the client's consumption and co-creation process, interactions with the provider firm, and the underlying support systems is essential to managing this chain of service activities. While many of the essential activities that support the consulting service are invisible to the client, understanding that fact and how these activities link to the client is essential to ensuring the value proposition.

Understanding how customers evaluate the service process, and how those judgements evolve, is also important. Some research suggests that it is the summing up of all the steps, or service encounters, within a service process that is evaluated by the customer and not just individual interactions with service providers. Other research examines the distinct events (i.e., service encounters) associated with a service process that are evaluated along unique attribute dimensions. Still others propose that the character of the process itself may play a greater role than the actual outcome in determining overall evaluations. Developing a deeper understanding of the way customers experience and evaluate service processes is but one of many challenges faced by firms that undertake the design, delivery, and documentation of a service offering. Service blueprinting is a flexible approach that helps managers with the challenges of service process design and analysis. It is a powerful technique that can be used to depict a service at multiple levels of analysis. That is, service blueprinting can facilitate the detailed refinement of a single step in the customer process as well as the creation of a comprehensive, visual overview of an entire service process.

One of the characteristics of service we all know is Inseparability, it is process through which consumers interact with the service provider e.g. in tourism, they include the booking system for transportation and accommodation, the use of plastic money(credit cards) for payments, design of queuing system at visitor attractions. They are designed to assist interaction between staff and customers at the critical point of contact. Market is Paramount in this regard.

While designing a process the process designer has to maintain a balance between functionality and security, aesthetic and ease of use by the customer. This is not always possible and at times there can be difficulties. This ease in operation gives competitive advantages to a marketer in many aspects e.g. positioning service. But in order to educate people about functionality and use of new system a special publicity campaign is required because at this point it has to be considered that people are much used to with old technology. Those organisations which use this concept are using promotional techniques to advise customers about the processes to expect when consuming the service. E.g. tourism organisations run direct marketing campaigns where potential customers can send for a holiday Planner, video explaining how to obtain the best from a holiday trip.

In service marketing since customers are often involved in the production of services, marketers need to understand the nature of the service process and the stages in this process that are exposed to customers. It is important for the service marketer to understand each of the moments of truth involved in the service process because the service brand will be developed only when each of them have been managed in an honest and sincere manner. The process is a special method of operation wherein several steps or activities are performed in a defined sequential manner. Consider for example, the case of the customer wants to travel from one destination to another, then it important to know the steps that this customer would go through several steps, e.g. starting from reservation, ticketing, baggage screening, checking in, waiting at the airport lounge, announcements, entering in air craft, in-flight services, food services and finally checking out from the airport terminal. At each stage the customer come in contact with the air line staff and its various equipment and technology. Every time that the customer comes in contact with the organisation a moment of truth is created. This creation of moment of truth helps to create stable relationship between service provider and user. Stable relationship is a distinctive factor in case of most of the services. It is obvious that people and objects are two major inputs processed in the service industry. E.g. burger is an object in case of McDonalds. In another case like in the software industry, malfunctioning of computer is an object that requires service support. When it comes to the service industry the service utiliser is said to be a Guest not a customer which is typical in case of product which is a physical object.

The company needs to research the requirements of its customers and set its processes accordingly so that the required service is delivered. Since requirements of customers vary widely, processes cannot be standardised. But if a process is allowed too much flexibility, the efficiency of the facility goes down. Therefore, customer requirements should not be allowed to vary widely. Through targeting smaller segments of customers, variation in their requirements can be controlled. The processes are very important because in some services they are visible to customers. Some time effectiveness of a process can be compromised in the effort to make it look good to the customer, e.g. some patients feel good when they are extensively examined by the doctor though it may not be necessary. Some processes in personal grooming and hair care salons are not really required but service professionals have to carry them out because customers have come to expect them. E.g. class room lectures may come out ineffective and boring by student's point of view but students will feel that they have not been taught at all if such lectures are not held. The idea is that customers have to be educated about the need or irrelevance of certain processes. A process should be employed only when it is required to provide a service and not because customers have come to expect it.

Process is the principle by which service delivery process can be designed implemented and monitored are really not much different from those mentioned relative to the field of manufacturing, computing and so on. There are certain specific characteristics of service process design and implementation which should be considered are as follows

Customer Participation in the Process

The level of environment or participation of the customer in the service process varies e.g. surveying to customer (guest) is different in case of butler service and different in a self service restaurant.

Location of Service Delivery

Should the process be carried out in the service only at provider's premises or at the consumer's home? For some services, this seems simple decision-plumbing or car painting work should be carried out only at customers home while dry-cleaning or dance performance will be carried out at a specialist's outlet or venue.

High /low Services

The level of contact between customer and the service provider's personnel this can range form nil to very high, for example, use of ATM or vending machine or ticket booking machines (low contact), very high contact as in medical or professional services where the client or organisation's personnel for varying period of time.

Degree of standardisation in service delivered is in very standard format, e.g. McDonald's fast food experience or some customisation is created, e.g. professional services like Doctor, advocate where each clients needs are identified and served accordingly. The extent to which services can be customised or altered form the standard to meet the needs of different customers or users may be termed as divergence.

Complexity of Services

A number of activities and steps towards the service delivery measure this. To ensure tourists had a memorable and enjoyable trip will include many steps like travel arrangement, hotel operations management, high level of customer contact and service so on. Less intricate process like bank cashier accepting deposit and updates bank pass-book or routine car service will include less activities. Through these examples one can understand divergence.

The immediacy of production of services can be used to advantage in the tailoring of the services product to meet customer needs, For example, one holiday tour company may offer low cost trips of fixed duration to specific location for the economy customer. Another company may offer to meet specific customer requirements of time of travel, accommo-dation requirements, entertainments needs and other personal specifications. The appropriate process will depend on the market segment which has been selected, positioning decision, and the needs of the customer.

Decision making in process are also of relevance. Some service providers give their service delivers the autonomy to make decisions. E.g. the billing of legal service is largely within the hands of the principal working in case. A law firm will charge out rates for an individual within the firm but these will vary according to the real and perceived complexity of the case where value based billing is used. It is therefore discretion of a principal working on the case as to the appropriate fee level to be billed. Other service providers have little room for flexibility in pricing decisions. A waiter will bill a customer for food at a published price. If the customer (Guest) is dissatisfied then he or she will often have to refer a manager or supervisor.

Blueprinting Evolution and Components

Service blueprinting is a process analysis methodology proposed by Shostack (Shostack, 1982, 1984). It is a visual portrayal of a service plan. Shostack's methodical procedure draws upon time/motions method engineering, PERT/project programming and computer system and software design. The proposed blueprint allows for a quantitative description of critical service elements, such as time, logical sequences of actions and processes, also specifying both actions/events that happen in the time and place of the interaction (front office) and actions/events that are out of the line of visibility for the users, but are fundamental for the service. (Zeithaml, Bitner et al. 2006) define service blueprinting as a tool for simultaneously depicting the service process, the points of customer contact, and the evidence of the service from the customer's point of view. With this description, the authors emphasise the different systemic layers overlapping in a service, from the layer of customer interaction and physical evidence to the layer of internal interaction within the service production process. Layers of interaction in service blueprint (source Zeithaml, Bitner et al 2006)

Service blueprinting involves the description of all the activities for designing and managing services, including schedule, project plans, detailed representations (such as Use cases) and design plans, or service platforms. Blueprinting is often supported by methodologies that elicit functional elements of services, as well as their qualitative/implicit characteristics, including TQM techniques, such as Quality Function Deployment (Ramaswamy, 1996), Just in Time, and capacity planning (Hollins, 2006), or IDEF0 (N. Morelli, 2006)Service blueprinting was initially introduced as a process control technique for services that offered several advantages: it was more precise than verbal definitions; it could help solve problems preemptively; and it was able to identify failure points in a service operation. Just as firms have evolved to become more customer-focused, so has service blueprinting. One early adaptation was the clarification of service blueprinting as a process for plotting the customer process against organisational structure.

Service blueprinting was further developed to distinguish between onstage and backstage activities. These key components still form the basis of the technique and its most important feature, that of illuminating the customer's role in the service process. In addition, it provides an overview so that employees and internal units can relate what they do to the entire, integrated service system. Blueprints also help to reinforce a customer-orientation among employees as well as clarify interfaces across departmental lines.

Service blueprinting shares similarities with other process modeling approaches in that it

1. Is a visual notation for depicting business processes via symbols that represent actors and activities,

2. Can be used to represent high-level overviews of conceptual processes or details of particular support or sub-processes, and

3. Will accommodate links to parallel and sub-process documents and diagrams via other more internally-focused process modeling tools and languages such as BPMN (Business Process Modeling Notation) and UML (Unified Modeling Language). However, service blueprinting is not as complex or as formal as some business process modeling tools such as UML. Service blueprints are relatively simple and their

graphical representations are easy for all stakeholders involved – customers, managers, front-line employees – to learn, use, and even modify to meet a particular innovation's requirements.

Components of Service Blueprints

There are five components of a typical service blueprint:

- Customer Actions,
- Onstage/Visible Contact Employee Actions,
- Backstage/Invisible Contact Employee Actions,
- Support Processes, and
- Physical Evidence.

"Customer actions" include all of the steps that customers take as part of the service delivery process. Customer actions are depicted chronologically across the top of the blueprint. What makes blueprinting different from other flowcharting approaches is that the actions of the customer are central to the creation of the blueprint, and as such they are typically laid out first so that all other activities can be seen as supporting the value proposition offered to or co-created with the customer.

The next critical component is the "onstage/visible contact employee actions," separated from the customer by the line of interaction. Those actions of frontline contact employees that occur as part of a face-to-face encounter are depicted as onstage contact employee actions. Every time the line of interaction is crossed via a link from the customer to a contact employee (or company self-service technology, etc.), a moment of truth has occurred.

The next significant component of the blueprint is the "backstage/invisible contact employee actions," separated from the onstage actions by the very important line of visibility. Everything that appears above the line of visibility is seen by the customer, while everything below it is invisible. Below the line of visibility, all of the other contact employee actions are described, both those that involve non-visible interaction with customers (e.g., telephone calls) as well as any other activities that contact employees do in order to prepare to serve customers or that are part of their role responsibilities.

The fourth critical component of the blueprint is "support processes" separated from contact employees by the internal line of interaction. These are all of the activities carried out by individuals and units within the company who are not contact employees but that need to happen in order for the service to be delivered. Vertical lines from the support area connecting with other areas of the blueprint show the inter-functional connections and support that are essential to delivering the service to the final customer.

Finally, for each customer action, and every moment of truth, the physical evidence that customers come in contact with is described at the very top of the blueprint. These are all the tangibles that customers are exposed to that can influence their quality perceptions. This has already been discussed in Chapter 9.

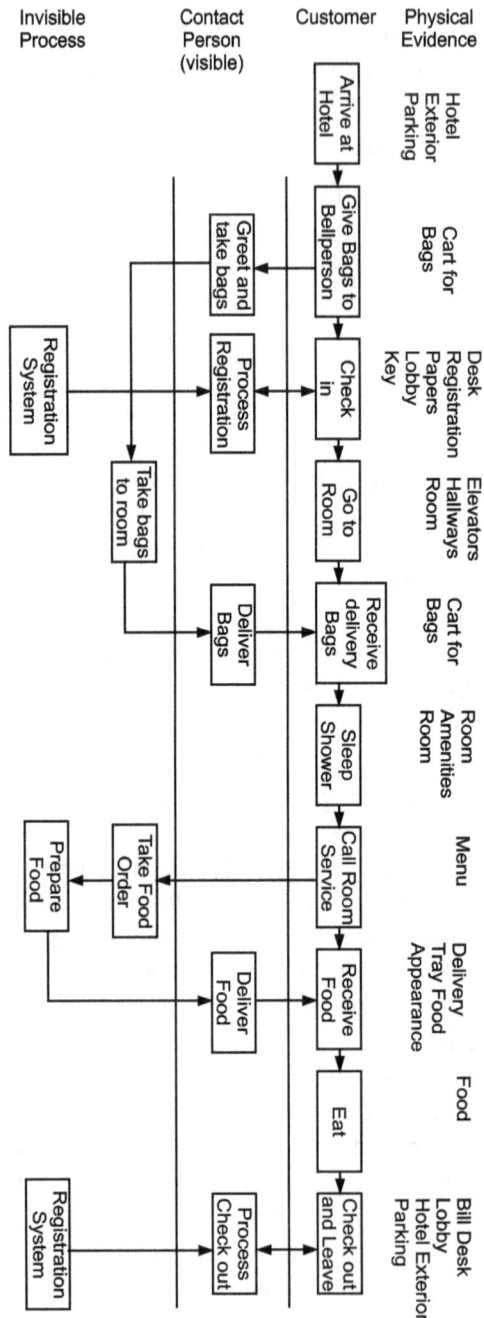

Fig. 10.1: An example of a Service Blueprint

Source: Services Marketing, Rampal, Gupta.

Building a Blueprint

When building a blueprint, the first step is to clearly articulate the service process or sub-process to be blueprinted. Because companies often modify service processes to fit the needs and wants of different target customers (e.g., check in process for an airline frequent flyer or first class passenger versus other passengers), it is important to specify which segment of customers is the focus of the blueprint.

Once this has been decided, the actions of customers should be delineated first because this component serves as the foundation for all other elements of the blueprint. At times, this can be more challenging than anticipated. Questions such as "When does the service start and stop from the customer's point of view?" tend to generate considerable discussion. After that has been established, the contact employee actions, both onstage and backstage, can be delineated, followed by support processes. At this point, links can be added that connect the customer to contact employee activities and to needed support functions. Physical evidence is typically the last component added to the blueprint. Blueprints are ideally developed by cross-functional teams, possibly even involving customers.

Process Mapping

Process mapping is a description of how an organisation works—for example, what happens to a client when they come for treatment, where they wait, who they see first, and so on. After process mapping, one will have an exact picture of the way the organisation delivers its services. This makes it easier to see what works well and what doesn't, so one can think about how to improve things that aren't working well.

A process map also gives one a starting point (a baseline), against which one can measure the effects of the changes being made. It also provides a very useful tool for orienting new staff.

Process mapping will:

- Provide a picture of what is being done.
- Highlight where things aren't working well.
- Show everyone how things happen.
- Helps to assess the flow of activity
- Helps to work out how resources (money and staff) are used
- Helps to work out how many services one can deliver, and how well the organisation can deliver them
- Provide the baseline data for improving service and measuring how well changes work.

The three types of processes that are mapped are as follows:

- **Organisational processes**

  These are the processes of governance and management, and are mapped between and within organisations in 'entity relationship' diagrams. Mapping the links between an organisation and other service providers is known as 'service mapping'.

- **Core business processes**

  These are the core business processes of the service model in general.

- **Support processes**

  These are processes that support the main things the organisation does, and the supporting system in general.

  After activities and flows have been set out across these main areas, each of the processes can be mapped on levels.

The Service Process Matrix

The Service Process Matrix is a classification matrix of service industry firms based on the characteristics of the individual firm's service processes. The matrix was derived by Roger Schmenner and first appeared in 1986. Although considerably different, the Service Process Matrix can be seen somewhat as a service industry version of Wheelwright and Hayes' Product-Process Matrix. The Service Process Matrix can be useful when investigating the strategic changes in service operations. In addition, there are unique managerial challenges associated with each quadrant of the matrix. By paying close attention to the challenges associated with their related classification, service firms may improve their performance.

The classification characteristics include the degree of labour intensity and a jointly measured degree of customer interaction and customisation. Labour intensity can be defined as the ratio of labour cost to plant and equipment. A firm whose product, or in this case service, requires a high content of time and effort with comparatively little plant and equipment cost would be said to be labour intense. Customer interaction represents the degree to which the customer can intervene in the service process. For example, a high degree of interaction would imply that the customer can demand more or less of some aspects of the service. Customisation refers to the need and ability to alter the service in order to satisfy the individual customer's particular preferences.

The vertical axis on the matrix, is a continuum with high degree of labour intensity on one end (bottom) and low degree of labour intensity on the other end (top). The horizontal axis is a continuum with high degree of customer interaction and customisation on one ends (right) and low degree of customer interaction and customisation on the other end (left). This results in a matrix with four quadrants, each with a unique combination of degrees of labour intensity, customer interaction and customisation.

The upper left quadrant contains firms with a low degree of labour intensity and a low degree of interaction and customisation. This quadrant is labeled "Service Factory." Low labour intensity and little or no customer interaction or customisation makes this quadrant similar to the lower right area of the Product-Process Matrix where repetitive assembly and continuous flow processes are located. This allows service firms in this quadrant to operate in a fashion similar to factories, hence the title "Service Factory." These firms can take advantage of economies of scale and may employ less expensive unskilled workers as do most factories. Firms classified as service factories include truck lines, hotels/motels, and airlines.

The upper right quadrant contains firms with a low degree of labour intensity but a high degree of interaction and customisation. The upper right quadrant is labeled "Service Shop." Hospitals, auto repair shops and many restaurants are found in this quadrant.

The lower left quadrant contains firms with a high degree of labour intensity but a low degree of interaction and customisation. This quadrant is labeled "Mass Service." Mass service providers include retail/wholesale firms and schools.

Finally, the lower right quadrant contains firms with a high degree of labour intensity and a high degree of interaction and customisation. The lower right quadrant is labeled "Professional Service." This quadrant is similar to the upper left section of the Product-Process Matrix where job shops and batch processes are found. Doctors, lawyers, accountants, architects, and investment bankers are typical service providers that tend to be labour intense and have a high degree of customer interaction and customisation.

In 1994, Dotchin and Oakland proposed that in addition to the four categories: service factory, service shop, mass service and professional service, a fifth category should be added: personal service. They justify the inclusion by describing personal services as those directed at people, thereby high contact, as opposed to professional services which are directed to things, thereby, achieved with little contact time.

Movement within the Matrix

On Wheelwright and Hayes' Product-Process Matrix processes appear on a diagonal running from the upper left corner to the lower right corner. Firms that position themselves directly on the diagonal are seen to be the most efficient. Similarly, a notional diagonal can be said to run from the upper left corner to the lower right corner of the Service Process Matrix. Schmenner states that many of the segmentation steps taken by service firms have been toward the diagonal. The attraction seems to be better control. From the perspective of the matrix, need for control would be greater for service shops, which lie completely above the diagonal, and mass services, which lie below the diagonal. The need for control is not as great for service factories and professional services, as evidenced by the fact that the diagonal transverses each of those quadrants.

Schmenner also states that most services that have changed their positions within the matrix over time have tended to move up the diagonal. This, of course, implies a decrease in the degree of interaction and customisation and a decrease in labour intensity. Those firms most affected by a move up the diagonal would be found in the professional services where labour intensity and interaction/ customisation was high. Obviously, any move up the diagonal, be it with professional services, mass service, or service shops, would be a movement toward the service factory.

The legal field, a Professional Service, is a prime example of "up the diagonal" movement. Most have surely noticed the increase of television advertising on the part of some in the legal profession. Other than personal injury, the most prolific amount of advertising seems to come from lawyers seeking cases involving bankruptcy and uncontested divorces. Obviously, these are the cases that require the least amount of customisation. By handling this case "in bulk" the attorney also lowers the labour intensity by handling multiple cases in one trip to the court house and enjoys economies of scale just like a factory, a Service Factory.

The traditional restaurant had a considerable degree of customisation, customer interaction putting it into the Service Shop category. The fast food industry has taken restaurants into the Service Factory area through the dramatic elimination of customisation and lowering of labour intensity. However, the degree of standardisation may vary.

Managerial Challenges

There are a number of proposed challenges for management that are inherent in a firm's position within the Service Process Matrix. For firms with low labour intensity, plant and equipment choices are extremely important, implying the need to closer monitor technological advances. Since capacity is somewhat inflexible, scheduling service delivery is more important so demand must be managed. For firms with high labour intensity, workforce issues such as hiring, training, employee development and control, employee welfare and workforce scheduling are critical. Firms with low customer interaction and customisation face more marketing challenges than other firms.

The need to "warm up" the service dictates special attention to physical surroundings. For these firms standard procedures are safe to use. In addition, the classic managerial pyramid with many layers and a rigid relationship between layers is appropriate. Firms with high degrees of interaction and customisation must manage higher costs resulting from lack of economies of scale. In addition, higher skilled labour costs more and demands more attention, benefits, quality of work life and benefits. The managerial hierarchy tends to be flatter and less rigid.

10.3 Strategies for Managing Inconsistency

Inconsistency also known as hetrogeneity is the characteristic of services that makes them less standardised and uniform than goods.

By their very nature, several services are highly uneven in their quality. For example, it is very complicated for the hairdresser to dress hair exactly the same every time and for marketing consultants to make sales forecasts for their clients that are always accurate.

Also most of the services being labour intensive - people are involved in delivering them. This factor makes them prone to high variability. But what service firm can do is endeavour to make their performance as efficient and consistent as possible.

Strategies for Dealing with Inconsistency

For standardisation of services generally two methods are used which are explained below.

1. Industrialise services
2. Establish set rules and procedure

Industrialise Services

For standardisation of service, organisations generally do industrialisation of services delivery which lowers inefficiency and excessive variability through:

*   Hard technologies
*   Soft technologies
*   Hybrid technologies

Hard Technologies

Hard technology means substituting machinery for people. Hard technologies can not be applied to services which are highly labour oriented and those which require personal skills and contact. For example, medical, legal, accountancy and hairstyling services. But services where it is possible to substitute machines for people it has been possible to standardise services to an appreciable extent.

For example,

*   You be in Tokyo or Moscow or New Delhi if you order a Big Mac you know what are you going to get. This has been achieved by McDonald's by industrialising their service delivery.
*   Banks have reduced the inconsistency of teller services by providing automatic teller machines.
*   Airport X-ray surveillance equipment has replaced manual searching for baggage.
*   Automatic car washes have replaced manual washing drying and waxing ensuring consistent quality.

Soft Technologies

Soft technology is a way to industrialise services by substituting pre-planned systems (such as prepackaged vacation tours) for individual services.

For example,

Many travel firms sell pre-packaged vacations tours. This standardised transportation, accommodation, food and sight seeing.

Hybrid Technologies

Hybrid technology is a technique for industrialising services that mix both hard and soft technologies.

For example,

- Computerised truck routing.
- Specialised low priced repair services.
- Establish set rules and procedures routine.

The use of pre-planned systems with specific set of rules and routines can be used to - manage human performance effectively in service delivery. Though perfect standardisation is not possible but reliability to a reasonable extent is achieved.

For example: Limited menu restaurants like Pizza hut and TGI Friday ensure high uniformity from one visit to the next because they have standardised preparation procedures.

10.4 Customer Role in Services

Service processes require the participation of the customer. Without the customer, service processes cannot take place. The fact that the service provider is dependent on customer participation causes difficulties in managing service processes efficiently and effectively because customer's contributions can only be influenced by the provider up to a certain extent.

Customers as Productive Resources

Service customers can be referred to as "partial employees" of the organisation human resources who add to the organisation's productive capability. Some management experts have recommended that the organisation's boundaries be extended to consider the customer as part of the service system. In other words, if customers give effort, time, or other resources to the service production process, they should be considered as part of the organisation.

Services customers themselves have critical roles to play in creating service outcomes and eventually enhancing or detracting from their own satisfaction and the worth received. This is true whether the customer is an end consumer (for example, consumers of health care, education, personal care, or legal services) or a business (for example, organisations purchasing maintenance, insurance, computer consulting or training services). In all of these examples, customers themselves take part at some level in creating the service and ensuring their own satisfaction.

Experts believe that services can be delivered most proficiently if customers are actually viewed as partial employees and their co-production roles are intended to maximize their contributions to the service creation process. The logic behind this view is that organisational productivity can be increased if customers learn to perform service-related activities they currently are not doing or are educated to perform more effectively the tasks they are already doing.

Customers can engage in a variety of roles.

1. The customer as productive resource;
2. The customer as contributor to quality, satisfaction and value; and
3. The customer as competitor to the service organisation.

These roles are not mutually exclusive, meaning an individual's co-productive behaviours in a specific situation may apply to more than one of the three roles. Elements of each role may be at play in a given service transaction. A description of these roles and their implications follows.

For over a decade, researchers have advocated that organisations view service customers as "partial" employees (e.g. Bowen, 1986; Mills and Morris, 1986; Mills, Chase and Margulies, 1983). This perception expands the boundaries of the service organisation to incorporate service recipients as temporary members or participants. It recognises that customers contribute inputs, much like employees, which impact the organisation's productivity both via the quantity and quality of those inputs and the resulting quality of output generated (Mills et al., 1983). For example, in contributing information and effort in the diagnoses of their ailments, patients of a healthcare organisation are part of the service production process. If they provide accurate information in a timely fashion, physicians will be more efficient and accurate in their diagnoses. Thus, the quality of the information patients provide can ultimately affect the quality of the outcome. Furthermore, in most cases, if patients follow their physician's advice, they will be less likely to return for follow-up treatment, further increasing the healthcare organisation's productivity.

Customer participation in service production raises a number of issues for organisations. Because customers can influence both the quality and quantity of production, some experts believe that the delivery system should be isolated as much as possible from customer inputs in order to reduce the uncertainty customers can bring into the production process. This view reasons that the less direct contact there is between the customer and the service production system, the greater the potential for the system to operate at peak efficiency (e.g. Chase, 1978). The introduction of ATM machines and automated customer service telephone lines in the banking industry are both examples of ways to reduce direct customer contact in that industry, resulting in greater efficiencies and reduced costs.

Other experts believe that services can be delivered most efficiently if customers truly are viewed as partial employees and their participative roles are designed to maximise their contributions to the service creation process. The logic in this case is that organisational productivity can be increased if customers learn to perform service-related activities more effectively (e.g. Mills et al., 1983). The extreme case would be full self-service where the customer produces the service for him or herself with very little intervention or support from the organisation's employees. This case is similar to Bateson's (1983) "full participator" group uncovered in his empirical study of the self-service customer.

Customers as contributors to quality, satisfaction and value

Another role that customers can play in services delivery is that of contributor to their own satisfaction and the ultimate quality of the services they receive. Customers may not care that they have increased the productivity of the organisation through their participation, but they probably do care a great deal about whether their needs are fulfilled. Effective customer participation can increase the likelihood that needs are met and that the benefits the customer is seeking are actually attained. This is particularly apparent for services such as health care, education, personal fitness, weight loss, and others where the service outcome is highly dependent on customer participation. In these cases, the customer is an integral part of the service and unless he/she performs his/her role effectively, the desired service outcome is not possible. The same is true for an organisational customer purchasing management consulting services. Unless the organisation uses or implements the advice it has purchased, it cannot expect to get the full value of the service. Recognising this, many management consultants now get involved in teaching customers to use the information they provide.

In addition to contributing to their own satisfaction by improving the quality of service delivered to them, some customers simply enjoy participating in service delivery. These customers find the act of participating to be intrinsically attractive (Bateson, 1983, 1985; Dabholkar, 1996). They enjoy using the computer to obtain airline tickets, or they may like to do all of their banking via ATMs and automated phone systems, to interact with service providers through the Internet, or to pump their own gasoline. In some cases, there is a price discount advantage for self-service, but other times, customers may be motivated by convenience, a sense of greater control over the service outcome, timing of delivery, or simple enjoyment of the task (Dabholkar, 1996).

Because service customers must participate in service delivery, they frequently blame themselves (at least partially) when things go wrong. If customers believe they are partially (or totally) to blame for the failure, they will be less dissatisfied with the service provider than when they believe the provider is responsible and could have avoided the problem (Bitner, 1990; Folkes, 1988; Hubbert, 1995).

Customers as Competitors

A final role played by service customers is that of potential competitor. In many situations, customers (whether individuals or companies) have the choice of purchasing services in the marketplace or producing the service themselves, either fully or in part. Customers in a sense are competitors of the companies that supply the service. The decision whether to produce services for themselves (internal exchange) versus have someone provide the service for them (external exchange) is a common decision for consumers (Lusch, Brown and Brunswick, 1992). For example, a car owner who needs maintenance on his car can choose to do all his own maintenance (assuming he has the skills), to have someone else do all the maintenance tasks, or to do some tasks himself (e.g. changing oil) while reserving more complex tasks for a car maintenance shop. At one extreme, the car owner does all of his own maintenance, while at the other he pays to have someone do everything for him. Parallel examples can be imagined for child care, landscaping, home maintenance, and other services needed by households. Bateson's (1983) "full participator", if he/she possesses the motivation and the needed skills, can be regarded as a prime candidate to engage in internal exchange and produce the service without the aid of a service provider. Similar internal versus external exchange decisions are made by organisations. Firms frequently choose to outsource service activities such as payroll, data processing, research, accounting, maintenance and facilities management. They find that it is advantageous to focus on their core businesses and leave these essential support services to others with greater expertise.

10.5 Customers as Co-producers

Customer experiences are the basis for competitive differentiation, value creation and brand identity. While some companies create emotion-driven customer experiences that leave an impact on customers, some create experiences in which customers are active co-producers. In other words, customers are the co-creators of the value that results from the experience.

These kinds of experiences are called "co-production experiences." For example, a hotel provides the physical resources for a good night's sleep. The guest provides the "labour" to activate those resources to make the experience come alive.

Both the company and customer add toward achieving a desirable and valuable goal. When well designed, such experiences are the foundation for increased levels of customer satisfaction, trust, loyalty, and lifetime value.

In an age of online banking, self-checkout, and other self-service business transactions, companies are asking customers to do more work. In some ways, customers are the substitute employees of many companies. Like employees, customers who are more efficient and effective with goods and services generate greater value for both themselves and the company. Competitive advantage, therefore, depends on companies' designing co-production experiences that improve customer performance.

Customer inputs can have an effect on the organisation's productivity through both the quality of what they add and the resulting quality and quantity of output generated. In a business-to-business services context, the contributions of the customer can augment on the whole the productivity of the company in both quality and quantity of service. In a very different context, some airlines depend on customers to carry out significant service roles for themselves, consequently increasing the overall productivity of the airline. Passengers are asked to take their own bags when transferring to other airlines, get their own food, and seat themselves.

Customer participation in service production raises a number of issues for organisations. Because customers can influence both the quality and quantity of production, some experts consider the delivery system should be isolated as much as possible from customer inputs in order to decrease the uncertainty they can bring into the production process. This view sees customers as a major source of uncertainity the timing of their demands and the uncontrollability of their attitudes and actions. The logical conclusion is that any service activities that do not require customer contact or involvement should be performed away from customers. The less direct contact there is between the customer and the service production system, the greater the potential for the system to operate at peak efficiency.

Four Principles

To design great co-production experiences for hotels, airlines, auto insurance, computer networking gear, or in any other B2C or B2B industry, one must integrate into the experience four key design principles: vision, access, incentive, and expertise.

These principles can be seen by further analysing the hotel experience described earlier:

- **Vision** defines the goals, expectations, plans, and feedback associated with an experience. Clearly communicating the expectations for both the hotel staff and the customers sets the desired conditions for the experience. Customers have a role in delivering the "Quiet Floor" experience and thus must be told what their role and goals are.

- **Access** describes the physical environment in which the experience occurs. The hotel room environment has tools and interfaces the support customer performance: eyeshades, earplugs, drape clip, nightlight, and CD player, as well as the enhanced pillows, sheets, and mattress. Nuances such as the audio programme and aroma (the lavender spray) help stimulate all the senses.

- **Incentive** reflects how the company motivates the customer to perform. Rewards are a key tactic. Offering a guaranteed wake-up call is the incentive for motivating customers to try all the resources that the hotel offers. After all, what's the point of wearing eyeshades and earplugs if you don't wake up in time for your meeting or flight?

- **Expertise** specifies the knowledge and skill that customers must have to perform well. Educational content on the CD package and the relaxation exercises on the CD build customer expertise. These resources provide ideas for eating right, relaxing, and generally getting one's body ready for a good night's sleep.

Customers' participation in service co-production processes has been increasing with the speedy development of self-service technologies and business models that rely on self-service as the main service delivery channel. However, little is known about how the level of participation of customers in service delivery processes influences the competition among service providers.

Levels of customer participation

The level of customer participation required in a service experience differs across services. In some cases, all that is required is the customer's physical presence (low level of participation), with the employees of the firm doing all of the service production work, as in the case of a movie. Movie-goers must be present to receive the entertainment service, but little else is required once they are seated. In a business-to-business context, examples of services that require little participation are less common. One example is that of providing plant and flower interior landscaping services. Once the service has been ordered, little is required from the organisation other than to open its doors or provide access to the service provider to move plants in and out.

In other cases, consumer inputs are required to aid the service organisation in creating the service (moderate level of participation). Inputs can include information, effort or physical possessions. All three of these inputs are required for a CA to prepare a client's tax return effectively: information in the form of tax history, marital status and number of dependents; effort from the client in putting the information together in a useful fashion; and physical possessions such as receipts, past tax returns, etc. Similar types of information, effort and possessions are required when the customer is an organisation seeking to outsource services such as payroll, customer database management, or tax accounting.

In some situations, customers can actually be involved in co-creating the service (high level of participation). For such services, customers have essential production roles that, if not fulfilled, will affect the nature of the service outcome. All forms of education, training and health maintenance fit this profile. Unless the customer does something (e.g. studies, exercises, eats the right foods), the service provider cannot effectively deliver the service outcome. Similarly, an organisation seeking training services for its employees will need to help define the nature of the training, identify the right employees for the training, provide incentives for them to learn and facilitate their use of the training on the job. If the organisation does not do this, it and the employees involved will not receive the full benefits of the service.

The effectiveness of customer involvement at all of the levels will impact organisational productivity and ultimately quality and customer satisfaction.

10.6 Self-Service Technologies

Today's fast-paced world is becoming increasingly characterised by technology-facilitated transactions. Growing numbers of customers work together with technology to create service outcomes instead of interacting with a service firm employee. Self-service technologies (SSTs) are technological interfaces that facilitate customers to create a service independent of direct service employee involvement.

Examples of SSTs include automated teller machines (ATMs), automated hotel checkout, banking by telephone, and services over the Internet, and online brokerage services.

Self-service technologies (SSTs) are services created wholly by the customer without any direct involvement or interaction with the firm's employees. SSTs stand for the ultimate form of customer participation along a continuum from services that are produced entirely by the company to those that are produced fully by the customer.

Although extensive academic research has explored the characteristics and dynamics of interpersonal interactions between service providers and customers (Bettencourt and Gwinner 1996; Bitner, Booms, and Tetreault 1990; Clemmer and Schneider 1996; Fischer, Gainer, and Bristor 1997; Goodwin 1996; Goodwin and Gremler 1996; Hartline and Ferrell 1996; Rafaeli 1993), much less research has investigated customer interactions with technological interfaces (Bitner, Brown, and Meuter 2000; Dabholkar 1996).

Advances in technology, particularly the Internet, have allowed the introduction of a wide variety of self-service technologies. These technologies have proliferated as companies see the possible cost savings and efficiencies that can be achieved, potential sales growth, improved customer satisfaction, and competitive advantage. A partial list of some of the self-service technologies available to consumers includes

- ATMs.
- Pay at the PUMP.
- Airline check-in.
- Hotel check-in and checkout.
- Automated car rental.
- Automated filing of legal claims.
- Automated betting machines.
- Electronic blood pressure machines.
- Various vending services.
- Tax preparation software.
- Internet banking.
- Vehicle registration online.
- Online auctions.
- Home and car buying online.
- Automated investment transactions.
- Insurance online.
- Package tracking.
- Internet shopping.
- Internet information search.
- Interactive voice response phone systems.
- Distance education.

It is progressively more obvious that these technological innovations and advances will continue to be a vital component of customer–firm interactions. These technology based interactions are expected to become a key decisive factor for long-term business success. Parasuraman (1996) lists the growing importance of self-service as a fundamental shift in the nature of services. Although many academic researchers have acknowledged a need for greater understanding in this area (Dabholkar 1994, 1996; Fisk, Brown, and Bitner 1993; Meuter and Bitner 1998; Schneider and Bowen 1995), little is known about how interactions with these technological options affect customer evaluations and behaviour.

Recently, academic researchers have recognized the critical importance of technology in the delivery of services (Bitner, Brown, and Meuter 2000; Dabholkar 1994, 1996; Parasuraman 1996; Quinn 1996). Some suggest that the traditional marketplace interaction is being replaced by a marketspace transaction (Rayport and Sviokla 1994, 1995). The marketspace is defined as "a virtual sphere where products and services are present as digital information and can be delivered through information based channels" (Rayport and Sviokla 1995, p. 14). The foundation of customer–company interactions has significantly changed in this new marketspace environment.

Self-service technologies are a characteristic example of marketspace transactions in which no interpersonal contact is required between buyer and seller. Several studies have investigated issues involving SSTs, mainly focusing on the development of user profiles (Bateson 1985; Darian 1987; Eastlick 1996; Greco and Fields 1991; Langeard et al. 1981; Zeithaml and Gilly 1987).

Some of the SSTs listed above-ATMs, pay-at-the-pump gas. Internet information search-have been very successful, embraced by customers for the benefits they offer in terms of convenience, accessibility, and ease of use. Benefits to companies, including cost savings and revenue growth, can also result for those SSTs that do well. Others airline ticket kiosks, online hotel bookings, have been less swiftly embraced by customers.

Failure can result when customers see no special benefit in the new technology or when they do not have the capability to use it or know what they are supposed to do. Qften, adopting a new SST requires customers to alter their traditional behaviours considerably, and many are reluctant to make those changes. Research looking at customer adoption of SSTs found that "customer readiness" was a key factor in determining whether customers would even try a new self-service option." Customer readiness results from a grouping of personal motivation (What is in it for me?), ability (Do I have the ability to use this SST?), and role clarity (Do I understand what I am supposed to do?) Other times customers see no value in using the technology when compared to the alternative interpersonal form of delivery; or the SSTs may be so inadequately designed that customers may prefer not to use them.

From a strategic perspective, research suggests that as companies move into SSTs as a form of delivery, these questions are important to ask:

- What is our strategy? What do we hope to achieve through the SST (cost savings, revenue growth, and competitive advantage)?
- What are the benefits to customers of producing the service on their own through the SST? Do they new and understand these benefits'?
- How can customers be motivated to try the SST? Do they understand their role? Do they have the capability to perform this role?
- How "technology ready" are our customers? Are some segments of customers more ready to use the technology than others"?
- How can customers be involved in the design of the service technology system and processes so that they will be more likely to adopt and use the SST?
- What forms of customer education will be needed to encourage adoption? Will other incentives be needed?
- How will inevitable SST failures be handled to retain customer confidence?

Uses of SSTs

Companies provide SSTs for a variety of purposes. First, many forms of customer service are now provided through technology. Questions regarding accounts, bill paying, frequently asked questions, and delivery tracking are just a few examples of customer service that are now provided through SSTs.

A second extremely rapidly growing arena for SSTs is direct transactions. The technology enables customers to order, buy, and exchange resources with companies without any direct interaction with their employees. Examples of outstanding SST transactions are Charles Schwab's online trading service, Amazon.com, and the SABRE Group's Travelocity, an Internet-based travel ticketing service. Recent studies cite rapid growth in Internet-based transactions for both consumer and business-to-business sales (Hof 1999).

The third use of SSTs is the broad category called self-help, which refers to technologies that enable customers to learn, receive information, train themselves, and provide their own services. Examples include health information Websites, tax preparation CDs and software, self-help videos, and telephone-based information lines. In a business-to-business context, GE Medical Systems provides video and satellite-television–based "just-in-time training" on its equipment for hospital and clinic customers, which enables customers to train themselves at their convenience.

10.7 Customer Service in Services Marketing

Consider this scenario

You have been staying at a five star resort on holidays at a destination you had to fly eight hours to reach followed by an hour in a taxi. Your check-in experience was delightful. A welcoming band, a glass of sparkling wine, personal service you did not have to wait for and you were shown to your room by a smiling, informed and informative attendant who did not expect a tip for their services.

The room was delightful with a balcony overlooking the sea. The amenities at the resort were truly first class. They included a championship golf course, spa, gym, indoor and outdoor swimming pools, tennis courts, four restaurants, a child minding service and a wide range of activities and tour options. You were paying top dollar but the facilities were worth it.

There were a few glitches though; probably no-one's fault. Your first night at your choice of restaurant, you were turned away as they were full. Apparently, you should have been told at check-in to book early as that restaurant was always popular. Your second night when you had booked early, you were put into a small alcove off the kitchen, almost as if you were an afterthought. You had trouble getting the waiter's attention from your position and went without drinks for most of the night. The food was good though.

Golf was much more expensive than you thought, but you were really surprised how much they charged for the hire of the clubs and shoes. What is more, it rained very heavily from the fourth hole and by the ninth you were soaked. You asked if you could stop playing and get a refund as the course was almost unplayable and you did not come all this way to get a drenching. You were informed that under club rules the course was not unplayable, so you could not get a refund.

Aside from these irritations and the cancellation of a tour you had wanted to go on because there were insufficient numbers the stay was enjoyable with many highlights, such as the really friendly and helpful spa staff who made your time so relaxing you wanted to go again and again.

1. Did you get good customer service?
2. Would you come back to this resort?
3. Was it value for money when you considered the travel and cost?

Only you will know because customer service is judged by customers. It depends on what they value and perceive and their mood.

One of the effective strategies to differentiate a service from those of the competitors is superior customer service. It is the key to market penetration, repeat purchases and growth. A company's long term success has deep roots in competitive excellence in providing service to the customers and establishing lasting relationship with them. It involves treating customers as the first priority in the business.

Many sales professionals neglect customer service and thus fail to acquire the repeat business that is so important to success. Often they serve their potential customers faster and with a higher level of empathy and enthusiasm than they serve their existing clients. Others may offer service depending on their clients' celebrity status. Both the approaches are a prescription for marketing disaster.

Superior customer service must define a company's overall mission. It should adapt its mission to that of the customer. The goal of the company should be to build its business for repeat business. In essence, it is finding out the customers' needs, and ensuring that the company is actively working to fulfil these needs on a daily basis to secure the clientele. Increasing competition is forcing businesses to pay much more attention to satisfying customers, by providing strong customer service.

According to Jamier L. Scot (2002), "Customer service is a series of activities designed to enhance the level of customer satisfaction – that is, the feeling that a product or service has met the customer expectation."

Customer service is normally an integral part of a company's customer value proposition. In their book Rules to Break and Laws to Follow, Don Peppers and Martha Rogers, Ph.D. write that "customers have memories. They will remember you, whether you remember them or not." Further, "customer trust can be destroyed at once by a major service problem, or it can be undermined one day at a time, with a thousand small demonstrations of incompetence."

From the point of view of an overall sales process engineering effort, customer service plays an important role in an organisation's ability to generate income and revenue. From that perspective, customer service should be included as part of an overall approach to systematic improvement.

Customer service may be provided by a person, viz., a sales person or a company representative or by automated means called self-service. Examples of self service are Internet sites. The experience a customer has of a product also affects the total service experience, but this is more of a product feature than what is included in the definition of customer service.

The importance of customer service varies by product, industry and customer. It may be provided by a person, viz., a sales person or a company representative or by automated means called self-service. The experience a customer has of a product also affects the total service experience, but this is more of a product feature than what is included in the definition of customer service.

There here is no common agreement as to what Customer service is and what might it cover. This expression has been used in diverse ways like:

- The activities occupied in ensuring that a product or service is delivered to the customer on time and in accurate quantities.
- The interpersonal working relationship between the employees and the supplier and a customer.

- Provision of after sales repair and maintenance facilities.
- The department of an organisation which handles complaints.
- The order taking department of an organisation.

Several approaches were used to define customer service. Lalonde and Zinszer defined customer service as 'those activities that occur at the inter-face between the customer and the corporation which enhance or facilitate the sale and use of the corporation's products or services.' They divided customer service into a temporal sequence.: Pre-transaction elements, transaction elements and post transaction elements.

Pre-transaction elements

These elements set up an atmosphere for good customer service, and include:
- Written customer service policy - is the policy communicated internally or externally, is it understood, is it quantified where possible?
- Accessibility - are we easy to contact/do business with?
- Organisation structure - is there a customer service management structure in place? Does its personnel have appropriate authority and responsibility?
- System flexibility - can the system be adapted to meet particular customer needs? Can the system continue to function in the face of unexpected problems, e.g. strikes, adverse weather conditions.

Transaction elements

These elements are those that directly result in the delivery of the product to the customer, for example:
- Order cycle time - what is the total elapsed time from initiation of the order by the customer until delivery to the customer?
- Stock availability - what percentage of demand for each item can be met from stock?
- Order status information - how long does it take to respond to a customer query with the required information? Is the customer informed of problems or do customers contact the company to hear of problems?

The transaction elements of customer service are the most observable because of the direct impact they have on sales.

Post-transaction elements

These elements represent the array of service needed to support the product in the field:
- Availability of spares - what are the in-stock levels of service parts?
- Call-out time - how long does it take for the engineer to arrive? What is the 'first call fix rate?
- Product tracing - are we able to recall potentially dangerous products from the marketplace?
- Customer complaints - how promptly are complaints and returns dealt with? Do we measure customer satisfaction with our response?

Though the temporal sequence relates to product environment but most of its constituents are applicable to the service sector and specifically to industrial and after sale service.

Customer service is a very difficult area and it is practically not possible to reach an agreement on its meaning. But in order to understand the possible meaning of it - the organisation can be divided into activities in two parts i.e., primary and secondary activities. These activities are explained as under by taking an example of a hotel, transport operator and a restaurant.

Primary activity of

Hotel	:	Providing rooms on rent.
Transporter operator	:	Provide transport for carrying goods.
Restaurant	:	Cook and sell meals.

Secondary activity of:

Hotel	:	After sales service, complaints handling, terms of payment.
Transporter operator	:	Provision of information to customer.
Restaurant	:	Physical distribution.

It can be seen from the above that primary activities are the fundamentals and minimum to "enter the market and secondary activities form the basis of customer service.

Source: Lalonde, 8./. and Zinszer, P.H., Customer service: Meaning and Measurement, National Council of ' physical Distribution Management, 1976.

The customer is exposed to several products and services everyday. It becomes difficult for him to distinguish amongst the core products /services under the primary activities. The service firms are moving into the field of customer service to stay competitive and are differentiating themselves on the basis of customer service. The customers expect them to be treated in a certain way and they are opting for those firms which meet their expectations. Therefore service marketers must understand their customer and address their needs.

Why is customer service important?

Because of what customers do if they perceive they have received poor customer service:

- 80% of people who do not receive good service do not complain
- 73% complain when things go badly wrong
- A person who does complain tells nine people
- 12-16% leave without registering a complaint after receiving poor service
- 10-30% of customers leave after one complaint
- >80% leave if they have experienced three or more mistakes
- 5% increase in retention increases profits by 25-125%

Acquiring new customers can cost five times more than satisfying and retaining current customers

What are the elements of customer service?

Information/advice

When customers become aware of a need to buy, they seek information and advice. Giving good information and advice is our first opportunity to deliver customer service and encourage a customer to continue their buying journey with us.

Price

Getting a price that seems fair is important to customers. Getting a price that fits their budget is also important. Pushing customers to buy more than they can afford destroys customer loyalty and is not good customer service.

Achieving a perceived price reduction is important to some customers. Understanding against what bench mark the price reduction must be perceived, e.g. list price, competitor price, first offered price, allows to build into pricing strategy opportunities for customers to receive this perceived element of customer service. An example is a price guarantee.

Quality

Quality is measured in various ways.

Performance

- Did the service perform the way the advertising said it would?
- Did the service perform the way I expected it would?

Conformance to standards

Does the product or service conform to a known standard? E.g. ISO Standards,

Government Standards

Service features

Are the features of this service what I thought they would be?

- Reliability;
- Does this service operate the way it is supposed to all the time?
- Does this sevice have a life time which matches my expectation?

Personal approach

A customer's perception of service depends on their mood and, in order, these three categories of personal approach;

- **Concern:** When interacting with a customer concern must be shown for the customer rather than policy or meal break or other such internal issue.
- **Congeniality:** Matching the environment of surroundings and staff appearance and posture helps customers perceive that service is good.
- **Civility:** Using rude language and aggressive body language are obvious destroyers of the perception of service. However, so are over friendly terms, slang and over officious terms.

- **Convenience:** Travelling a long way, having to fill out forms in triplicate, being passed through several hands or just being put on hold for five minutes are all perceived as elements of poor customer service. The converse is true.
- **Follow up:** Experiencing buyer's remorse can make the best service appear to be poor service. Following up buyers by means of a telephone call, an email, a web survey or using loyalty schemes ensures either the customer's belief that they have made a good purchase or that one will able to rectify a fault immediately.

Meeting the Service Challenge

In service industry service is key success and this success is a result of how well a customer feels his or her requirements are being met. Recently competition has increased considerably in the service sector. The customer has extensive options to choose if he is not being treated the way he wants to be treated. Losing a customer costs a lot to the company. To make sure that a customer is retained - companies have to do extremely well in customer service. Over a period, studies have shown that the market share captured by offering exclusive product feature has declined while the share captured by customer service continues to increase.

The reason for the above trend is straightforward. The service firms that provide unique offerings find that competition soon copy their approach. As a result these offerings are expected by the customers and become generic e.g. as soon as the frequent flier programme was introduced by one airline it was immediately copied by the others.

In such conditions, the only way to do extremely well is by providing customer service that it is customised to meet specific demands of its customers. This is the key to success. For service organisations, it is not enough to get a customer's business, getting the customer to come back again and again for repeat business is the key to profitable enterprise. It means, companies must meet the quality challenges and work towards providing best services at attractive - prices. The best run firms are meeting the challenge in a number of ways. One way is by creating a right philosophy to guide the service providers.

Creating the Right Service Philosophy

Service quality begins with the employees. Every person who works for a service organisation must understand the values, beliefs, and overriding objectives of the organisation. In this way, everyone is working from a similar set of values. Normally this is done is by creating mission statements or guiding philosophies and then disseminating these to all concerned, so that everyone understands what is expected of them.

Several well-run service firms follow the pattern of carefully and simply spelling out what they expect their employees to do in order to deliver quality service. As an example at the Sheraton Hotels, there is a four-step guest satisfaction system:

- Every time you see a guest, smile and offer and appropriate hospitality comment.
- Speak to every guest in a friendly, enthusiastic, and courteous tone and manner.

- Answer guest questions and requests quickly and efficiently, or take personal responsibility to get the answer.
- Anticipate guest needs and resolve guest problems.

The Cost of Poor Service

The other important issue in meeting the service quality challenge is to find an answer to the following question,

How much does it cost our firm when we fail to provide good service?

Researchers have found that the cost of losing a customer can be tremendously high while the profits linked with keeping the customer can be particularly rewarding. Table 10.1 gives a characteristic worksheet for determining how much it costs a hospitality organisation every time it loses a customer.

Table 10.1: Calculating the Cost of Poor Service

	Item	Cost to the organisation
Lost Revenue	1. Amount that the average customer spends in one year	
	2. Number of customers lost each year	____
	3. Revenue from lost customers(#1 x #2)	____
	4. Lost revenue from potential customers who are dissuaded from doing business with the organization because of the poor experience of others (#3 x 10)	
	5. Time spent redoing things that were done incorrectly the first time	____
Other Costs	6. Time spent apologising to customers	____
	7. Telephone and mailing costs associated with apologising and/or explaining things to customers	____
	8. Cost of liability insurance	____
	9. Legal costs	____
	10. Cost of collections from customers who refuse to pay	____
	Total costs (#3 through #10)	____

It has been revealed by research that each dissatisfied customer who has received a bad service is likely to talk to ten others about his or her negative experience. The fourth entry under Lost Revenue measures how much money is lost because dissatisfied customers talk to others about their bad experience and the latter in turn, do not do business with the organisations. Therefore, a dissatisfied customer often costs the organisation much more than the revenue that the individual would have spent there in the future. The customer has an impact on the others as well.

Building blocks for superior customer service:

Customer service involves a programme of activities, comprising of building blocks that support the overall goal of retaining customers for life. These building blocks can be identified with two distinct yet very connected groups: internal customers, or the employees, and external customers. A successful customer service strategy involves building a service culture that targets both groups.

Customer service Programme for Employees: The employees of a company are in the front line in the entire programme of customer service activities. They need to be prepared and motivated to play an active role in it. The measures needed are:

Have a company mission statement that includes a statement about the customers. The mission statement lays out the vision and core values of the business, especially as they relate to the customers. The mission statement and the values should be communicated to the employees effectively, so that they are aware of what is expected of them. The top management should make sure that the employees understand the importance of superior customer service. This should be reinforced at team meetings to focus on company goals. Customer service should be number one on the agenda.

1. A customer service plan has no value unless it is communicated effectively to the employees. The management should spend time with the employees and clearly communicate to them how the company expects them to treat customers. All measurement data and other results should be shared with all employees. The employees may also have ideas and concerns. These need to be understood. The method for communication should be chosen carefully.

2. Leadership in providing superior customer service is essential. This includes how the management treats both the employees and customers. An enthusiastic and positive approach motivates the employees better than lengthy notes and lectures. The management should be honest with them and earn their trust. Employees observe the behaviour of the managers and are quick to see inconsistencies between what is said and what is done by them. They will also not generally give more than what the managers give.

3. Giving positive feedback and recognising employee achievement in customer service is a good motivating factor. Where appropriate, good results should bring the employee added responsibilities and increased compensation.

4. Build long term relationships with employees. Long term employees are one of the most valuable assets a business has. They are trained and knowledgeable about the products and services offered. They know the customers and have developed meaningful relationships with them. A high employee retention rate means the business avoids "quitting" costs associated with employee turnover, including the cost of advertising, interviewing, training and lost productivity. A high employee turnover may result in high customer turnover.

5. Training employees in customer service. The hiring practices should be focused on having new employees who fit into the organisation culture and have a positive attitude. The next step is to train them in the skills they need. Formal training is the most cost-effective method of instructing the employees about the business of the company, its customer service program, the company's expectations from the employees and their responsibilities. There are four types of skills employees will need, viz. technical skills, interpersonal skills, product or service knowledge and customer knowledge. Active support and involvement by the supervisor is critical in reinforcing these messages.

Customer Service Programme for External Customers

1. Providing good quality product/service, building reliability and credibility into it, represented in the brand image, and which meets customer expectations.

2. Personal attention. Customers expect that the company knows who they are and what their needs are. Customers expect you to find what they want and show that you care about.

3. Communicating with the customers in a quality manner. Apart from the actual words, the body language of the employee or sales representative, who interacts with the customer, should be given adequate attention.

4. A good feedback system. A customer feedback system empowers the customers by including them in the company's service programme. This indicates an open, trusting relationship with the customers, and allowing them to give the company their input about their needs and the level of satisfaction they derived would help build relationships. A company Website that gives an e-mail address for customer comments would be very useful. A feedback system will result in positive and negative assessments. The negative feedback should be used as opportunities for improvement in service.

5. Providing quality support services to customers. It involves keeping the promises made by the company. This includes warranties and guarantees, parts and repairs service, training in the use of the product and the handling of refunds and complaints. It helps in building trust and customer loyalty. It acknowledges that the responsibility of the company goes beyond actual sale of the product.

6. Finding deeper solutions. Almost every customer support problem has two solutions. The superficial or the immediate solution aimed to just to solve the customer's problem. But there could be a deeper solution, or a way to prevent this particular problem from ever happening again. Achieving this would resolve many customer service issues successfully. This would not only add to the confidence level of the company representatives, but also result in better acceptance of the product in the market.

Characteristics of firms excelling in customer service

Market leaders or firms which excel in product and service quality have the following characteristics:

1. **Vision:** They believe that the quality of customer service is crucial for gaining a competitive advantage and achieving corporate growth. For them, customer service is a never-ending focus for the entire organisation.

2. **High standards:** They set very high standards for customer service. It is not good service, but highest standards in service that can differentiate the best firm from the rest. Such companies would focus on zero defect consistently and try to improve reliability continuously.

3. **Leadership:** The leaders of the most successful companies communicate their vision to all stakeholders and lead from the front, motivating the entire organisation to excel and focus on improved customer service.

4. **Integrity:** Such companies strive to build trust, as the foundation for a sound customer-provider relationship is trust, fairness, integrity and consistency.

5. **Concern for customers:** For such companies, customers come first. Their opinions and feedback are valued. They are willing to listen to the customers and learn from them. Thus, they involve the customers in the growth of the company.

6. **Use of technology:** Technology can make operations more efficient and thus reduce costs for the provider. But successful companies would also look at technology as a tool for providing better customer service and reducing response time. Especially, the use of information technology greatly facilitates real time data collection, analysis and finding solutions to customers' problems. Customer care call centres, on-line booking of air and train tickets, on-line banking, telemedicine etc., are examples where customers have benefited because of technology.

7. **Organisational structure and Team building:** Companies that focus on customer service generally have flat organisations, with little or no hierarchical structures. This makes the organisation more flexible. They are also more decentarlised and hence the employees are able to take more risks and are able to respond to customer needs and expectations quickly. The individual employees are given more freedom and hence their entrepreneurial skills are developed. Such organisations are able to develop highly motivated teams.

8. **Training of Employees:** The training strategies adopted by such companies are more suited to a shared value of a high level of customer satisfaction. These companies earmark sufficient funds for training in all aspects of customer relationship.

The Three 'S's of Customer Service

Globalisation has virtually redefined every function of an organisation and intense competition in almost all product/service areas has made it imperative for companies to rethink each and every role it performs. One thing competition has done to industries is compression of deadlines. The job descriptions are getting enlarged and companies are under constant pressure to look beyond the obvious and become innovative in finding solutions, not only in product development, manufacturing and marketing, but also n providing high quality customer service. Managers have to find ways to improve performance both individually and collectively.

The three 'S's of customer service are:

Service: Customer service is a broader function than it is usually understood to be, and is not limited to the client-facing teams. It encompasses various aspects of both internal and external customer related service. There is no gainsaying that customer service should be of a very high quality to sustain competitive advantage. At the same time, the internal clients, viz., the various departments and peer teams that ultimately add up to the final product also need equal consideration, as they play a pivotal role in tuning out an acceptable product and also support the front line representatives. In fact, a weak chain of internal support system can snowball into a major market failure. Internal service actually drives the effectiveness of external customer service.

Speed: Along with the quality of the product or the service, the overall speed and the agility of the organisation is another factor that distinguishes between a customer oriented business from one that is not. This indicates an ability to respond to the changing client expectations, flexibility to change the project plan if required as well as the capability to think quicker. Generally, to prioritise on the activities in order to achieve speed, the 80/20 rule is used, according to which 80 percent of the reward comes from 20 percent of the effort. Hence, the firm has to identify those 20 percent activities which are crucial in delivering speedy customer service. Again, for effective time management, one can adopt the Time Jar model. This requires assuming an empty jar, which represents time. First rocks are put into it, indicating the hard rocks of priority activities, which cannot be avoided. Then pebbles, indicating enjoyable activities are added to it. Fill the remaining space with sand, which represent things which have to be done. Finally water is poured into it. This indicates things that clutter up and get in everywhere. This model helps in classifying activities according to how important they are, so that there is a balance. It helps people organise their activities, so that they respond to situations speedily.

Synchronisation: Organisations need to develop team work, so that their activities, individually and collectively, is in synch with the speed of the organisation as well as the changing expectations of the customers. In these days of computers, Blackberries etc., the feeling of being in 'synch' has attained a whole new dimension. From the personal effectiveness perspective, this concept is about analysing the list of daily tasks and preparing an action plan. It shows tasks a team member has to perform by himself, and those that should be delegated, and keeping track of them. Globalisation requires companies to manage a number of tasks across multiple time zones and languages, and yet be effective.

Questions for Discussion

1. Explain the role of customers in services marketing.
2. State the various types and strategies for managing inconsistencies.
3. Explain: service as a process and as a system.
4. State the different process aspects of services.
5. State the various managerial challenges for service processes.
6. State the scope of customer service in services marketing.
7. Explain the concept of self service technologies.

■■■

Chapter **11**...

Customer Satisfaction and Service Quality

Contents ...

11.1 Introduction

In today's fast-paced and increasingly competitive market, the bottom line of a firm's marketing strategies and tactics is to make profits and contribute to the growth of the company. Customer satisfaction, quality and retention are global issues that affect all organisations, be it large or small, profit or non-profit, global or local. Many companies are interested in studying, evaluating and implementing marketing strategies that aim at improving customer retention and maximising share of customers in view of the beneficial effects on the financial performance for the firm.

Quality and customer satisfaction have long been recognised as playing a crucial role for success and survival in today's competitive market. Not surprisingly, considerable research has been conducted on these two concepts. Notably, the quality and satisfaction concepts have been linked to customer behavioural intentions like purchase and loyalty intention, willingness to spread positive word of mouth, referral, and complaint intention by many researchers (Olsen, 2002; Kang, Nobuyuki and Herbert, 2004; Söderlund and Öhman, 2005).

The most commonly found studies were related to the 'antecedents, moderating, mediating and behavioural consequences' relationships among these variables – customer satisfaction, service quality, perceived value and behavioural intentions. However, there have been mixed results produced.

11.2 Customer Satisfaction and Service Quality

Customer satisfaction, a business term, is a measure of how products and services supplied by a company meet or surpass customer expectation. It is seen as a key performance indicator within business and is part of the four perspectives of a Balanced Scorecard.

In a competitive marketplace where businesses compete for customers, customer satisfaction is seen as a key differentiator and increasingly has become a key element of business strategy.

There is a substantial body of empirical literature that establishes the benefits of customer satisfaction for firms.

Organisations are increasingly interested in retaining existing customers while targeting non-customers. Measuring customer satisfaction provides an indication of how successful the organisation is at providing products and/or services to the marketplace.

Customer satisfaction is an ambiguous and abstract concept and the actual manifestation of the state of satisfaction will vary from person to person and product/service to product/service. The state of satisfaction depends on a number of both psychological and physical variables which correlate with satisfaction behaviours such as return and recommend rate. The level of satisfaction can also vary depending on other options the customer may have, which would make him/her compare the company's products or services.

Defining Customer Satisfaction

Because the concept of customer satisfaction is new to many companies, it's important to be clear on exactly what's meant by the term.

Customer satisfaction is the state of mind that customers have about a company when their expectations have been met or exceeded over the lifetime of the product or service. The achievement of customer satisfaction leads to company loyalty and product repurchase. There are some important implications of this definition:

- Because customer satisfaction is a subjective, non-quantitative state, measurement won't be exact and will require sampling and statistical analysis.
- Customer satisfaction measurement must be undertaken with an understanding of the gap between customer expectations and attribute performance perceptions.
- There should be some connection between customer satisfaction measurement and bottom-line results.

"Satisfaction" itself can refer to a number of different facts of the relationship with a customer. For example, it can refer to any or all of the following:

- Satisfaction with the quality of a particular product or service
- Satisfaction with an ongoing business relationship
- Satisfaction with the price-performance ratio of a product or service
- Satisfaction because a product/service met or exceeded the customer's expectations

Because the variables contributing to customer satisfaction are basically at the psychological level, care should be taken in the effort of quantitative measurement, although a large quantity of research in this area has recently been developed. Work done by Bart Allen and Brodeur between 1990 and 1998 has defined ten 'Quality Values' which influence satisfaction. This was, further expanded by Berry in 2002 and called it the ten domains of satisfaction. These ten domains of satisfaction include:

- Quality,
- Value,
- Timeliness,
- Efficiency,
- Ease of Access,
- Environment,
- Inter-departmental Teamwork,
- Front line Service Behaviours,
- Commitment to the Customer and
- Innovation.

These factors are considered crucial in defining customer satisfaction and hence, this model highlights the need for continuous improvement on these parameters. It calls for organisational change measurement. These parameters are most often utilised to develop the architecture for satisfaction measurement as an integrated model.

Many researchers (Oliver, 1981; Brady and Robertson, 2001; Lovelock, Patterson and Walker, 2001) conceptualise customer satisfaction as an individual's feeling of pleasure or disappointment resulting from comparing a product's perceived performance (or outcome) in relation to his or her expectations. Generally, there are two general conceptualisations of satisfaction, namely, transaction-specific satisfaction and cumulative satisfaction (Boulding et al., 1993; Jones and Suh, 2000; Yi and La, 2004). Transaction-specific satisfaction is a customer's evaluation of his or her experience and reactions to a particular service encounter (Cronin and Taylor, 1992; Boshoff and Gray, 2004), and cumulative satisfaction refers to the customer's overall evaluation of the consumption experience to date (Johnson, Anderson and Fornell, 1995).

Intentions are subjective judgements about how a person will behave in the future and usually serves as dependent variables in many service research and satisfaction models (Boulding et al., 1993; Soderlund and Ohman, 2003).

The usual measures of customer satisfaction involve a survey with a set of statements using a Likert Technique or scale. The customer is asked to evaluate each statement regarding the level of satisfaction with the product or service along various attributes, and their perception and expectation of the organisation's performance.

Methodologies

1. American Customer Satisfaction Index (ACSI) is a scientific standard of customer satisfaction. It is produced by the National Quality Research Center (NQRC) at the University of Michigan in Ann Arbor, Michigan.

   Academic research has shown that the national ACSI score is a strong predictor of Gross Domestic Product (GDP) growth, and an even stronger predictor of Personal Consumption Expenditure (PCE) growth. On the microeconomic level, ACSI data is used as predictor of stock market performance, both for market indices and for individually traded companies. Increasing ACSI scores has been shown to predict loyalty, word-of-mouth recommendations, and purchase behaviour. The ACSI measures customer satisfaction annually for more than 200 companies in 43 industries and 10 economic sectors. In addition to quarterly reports, the ACSI methodology can be applied to private sector companies and government agencies in order to improve loyalty and purchase intent.

2. The Kano Model is a theory of product development and customer satisfaction developed in the 1980s by Professor Noriaki Kano that classifies customer preferences into five categories:

   - Attractive,
   - One-Dimensional,
   - Must-Be,
   - Indifferent,
   - Reverse.

   The Kano model offers some insight into the product attributes which are perceived to be important to customers. Kano also produced a methodology for mapping consumer responses to questionnaires onto his model.

3. SERVQUAL or RATER is a service-quality framework that has been incorporated into customer-satisfaction surveys, such as the revised Norwegian Customer Satisfaction Barometer, to indicate the gap between customer expectations and experience.

4. J.D. Power and Associates provides another measure of customer satisfaction, known for its top-box approach and automotive industry rankings. Their marketing research consists primarily of consumer surveys and is publicly known for the value of its product awards.

5. Other consulting firms such as A.T. Kearney offer customer satisfaction survey models. The Kearney Customer Satisfaction Audit Process incorporates the Stages of Excellence framework and which helps define a company's status against eight critically identified dimensions.

6. For Business to Business (B2B) surveys there is the InfoQuest box. This has been used internationally since 1989. The box is targeted at "the most important" customers and avoids the need for a blanket survey.

7. The International Customer Service Institute (TICSI) has released The International Customer Service Standard (TICSS). TICSS enables organisations to focus their attention on delivering excellence in the management of customer service, whilst at the same time providing recognition of success through a third Party registration scheme. TICSS draws the attention of organisation to delivering increased customer satisfaction by providing a Service Quality Model. The TICSS Service Quality Model uses the 5 Ps, viz., Policy, Processes, People, Premises, Product/Services, as well as performance measurement. The implementation of a customer service standard should lead to higher levels of customer satisfaction, which in turn leads to customer retention and customer loyalty.

8. In India, a number of consulting companies undertake marketing research for consumer products and durables, as well as services like banking, insurance etc.

11.3 Monitoring and Measuring Customer Satisfaction

Measuring customer satisfaction is a relatively new concept to many companies that have been focused exclusively on income statements and balance sheets. Companies now recognise that the new global economy has changed things forever. Increased competition, crowded markets with little product differentiation and years of continual sales growth followed by two decades of flattened sales curves have indicated to today's sharp competitors that their focus must change.

Most service companies have research programmes designed to measure service quality and/or customer satisfaction. Such programmes are designed to allow management to manage service provision and relationship building initiatives. They provide essential information to guide efforts to reduce variability in service quality and to provide customers with the service that will help ensure their continued patronage. While there is little direct evidence as to the link between service quality and better company performance, company-level data suggests a link between higher quality, higher market share and improved profitability (Buzzell and Gale 1987; Buzzell et al. 1975; Rust and Zahorik 1993).

Competitors that are prospering in the new global economy recognise that measuring customer satisfaction is the key. Only by doing so can they hold on to the customers they have and understand how to better attract new customers. The competitors who will be successful to recognise that customer satisfaction is a critical strategic weapon that can bring increased market share and increased profits.

The problem companies face, however, is exactly how to do all of this and do it well. They need to understand how to quantify, measure and track customer satisfaction. Without a clear and accurate sense of what needs to be measured and how to collect, analyse and use the data as a strategic weapon to drive the business, no firm can be effective in this new business climate. Plans constructed using customer satisfaction research results can be designed to target customers and processes that are most able to extend profits.

Too many companies rely on outdated and unreliable measures of customer satisfaction. They watch sales volume. They listen to sales reps describing their customers' states of mind. They track and count the frequency of complaints. And they watch ageing accounts receivable reports, recognising that unhappy customers pay as late as possible if at all. While these approaches are not completely without value, they are no substitute for a valid, well-designed customer satisfaction surveying programme.

It's no surprise to find that market leaders differ from the rest of the industry, in that they're designed to hear the voice of the customer and achieve customer satisfaction. In these companies:

- Marketing and sales employees are primarily responsible for designing (with customer input) customer satisfaction surveying programmes, questionnaires and focus groups.
- Top management and marketing divisions champion the programmes.
- Corporate evaluations include not only their own customer satisfaction ratings but also those of their competitors.
- Satisfaction results are made available to all employees.
- Customers are informed about changes brought about as the direct result of listening to their needs.
- Internal and external quality measures are often tied together.
- Customer satisfaction is incorporated into the strategic focus of the company via the mission statement.
- Stakeholder compensation is tied directly to the customer satisfaction surveying programme.
- A concentrated effort is made to relate the customer satisfaction measurement results to internal process metrics.

To be successful, companies need a customer satisfaction surveying system that meets the following criteria:

- The system must be relatively easy to design and understand.
- It must be credible enough that employee performance and compensation can be attached to the final results.
- It must generate actionable reports for management.

Clearly defining and understanding customer satisfaction can help any company identify opportunities for product and service innovation and serve as the basis for performance appraisal and reward systems. It can also serve as the basis for a customer satisfaction surveying programme that can ensure that quality improvement efforts are properly focused on issues that are most important to the customer.

Customer Satisfaction Measurement Facts

- A 5-percent increase in loyalty can increase profits by 25%-85%.
- A very satisfied customer is nearly six times more likely to be loyal and to repurchase and/or recommend your product than is a customer who is just satisfied.
- Only 4 percent of dissatisfied customers will complain.
- The average customer with a problem eventually tells nine other people.
- Satisfied customers tell five other people about their good treatment.

11.3.1 Objectives of a Customer Satisfaction Surveying Programme

In addition to a clear statement defining customer satisfaction, any successful surveying programme must have a clear set of objectives that, once met, will lead to improved performance. The most basic objectives that should be met by any surveying programme include the following:

- Understanding the expectations and requirements of all your customers.
- Determining how well your company and its competitors are satisfying these expectations and requirements.
- Developing service and/or product standards based on your findings.
- Examining trends over time in order to take action on a timely basis.
- Establishing priorities and standards to judge how well you've met these goals.

Before an appropriate customer satisfaction surveying programme can be designed, the following basic questions must be clearly answered:

- How will the information we gather be used?
- How will this information allow us to take action inside the organisation?
- How should we use this information to keep our customers and find new ones?

Careful consideration must be given to what the organisation hopes to accomplish, how the results will be disseminated to various parts of the organisation and how the information will be used. There is no point asking customers about a particular service or product if it won't or can't be changed regardless of the feedback.

Conducting a customer satisfaction surveying programme is a burden on the organisation and its customers in terms of time and resources. There is no point in engaging in this work unless it has been thoughtfully designed so that only relevant and important information is gathered. This information must allow the organisation to take direct action. Nothing is more frustrating than having information that indicates a problem exists but fails to isolate the specific cause. Having the purchasing department of a manufacturing firm rate the sales and service it received on its last order on a scale of 1 (terrible) to 7 (magnificent) would yield little about how to improve sales and service to the manufacturer.

The lesson is twofold. First, general questions are often not that helpful in customer satisfaction measurement, at least not without many other more specific questions attached. Second, the design of an excellent customer satisfaction surveying programme is more difficult than it might first appear. It requires more than just writing a few questions, designing a questionnaire, calling or mailing some customers, and then tallying the results.

11.3.2 Understanding Differing Customer Attitudes

The most basic objective of a customer satisfaction surveying programme is to generate valid and consistent customer feedback (i.e., to receive the voice of the customer, which can then be used to initiate strategies that will retain customers and thus protect the most valuable corporate asset--loyal customers).

As it's determined what needs to be measured and how the data relate to loyalty and repurchase, it becomes important to examine the mind-set of customers the instant they are required to make a pre-purchase (or repurchase) decision or a recommendation decision. Surveying these decisions leads to measures of customer loyalty. In general, the customer's pre-purchase mind-set will fall into one of three categories-rejection (will avoid purchasing if at all possible), acceptance (satisfied, but will shop for a better deal), and/or preference (delighted and may even purchase at a higher price).

This highly subjective system that customers themselves apply to their decisions is based primarily on input from two sources:

- The customers' own experiences-each time they experience a product or service, deciding whether that experience is great, neutral or terrible. These are known as "moments of truth."

- The experiences of other customers-each time they hear something about a company, whether it's great, neutral or terrible. This is known as "word-of-mouth."

There is obviously a strong connection between these two inputs. An exceptional experience leads to strong word-of-mouth recommendations. Strong recommend-dations influence the experience of the customer, and many successful companies have capitalised on that link.

How does a customer satisfaction surveying manager make the connection between the survey response and the customer's attitude or mind-set regarding loyalty? Research conducted by both corporate and academic researchers shows a relationship between survey measurements and the degree of preference or rejection that a customer might have accumulated. When the customer is asked a customer satisfaction question, the customer's degree of loyalty mind-set (or attitude) will be an accumulation of all past experiences and exposures that can be indicated as a score from 1 (very dissatisfied) to 5 (very satisfied). It can also be captured with other response formats with an odd number of choices (e.g., 1 to 3 or 1 to 7) to allow for a neutral response.

Obviously, the goal of every company should be to develop customers with a preference attitude (i.e., we all want the coveted preferred vendor status such that the customer, when given a choice, will choose our company), but it takes continuous customer experience management, which means customer satisfaction measurement, to get there-and even more effort to stay there.

Customer satisfaction involves determining the degree to which a company's products or services meet the requirements of the end user. Companies that are certified ISO 9001:2000 must now demonstrate how they measure customer satisfaction, and how they are improving in this area. Firms planning to become ISO certified will need to begin developing these capabilities.

Customer Satisfaction and Customer Inputs are specifically referred to and required by clauses of the ISO 9001-2000 standard. The Management responsibility section 5.2 cites relevant clauses for compliance; 7.2.1 and 8.2.1.

Clause 7.2.1 requires an ISO certified organisation to communicate with customers on feedback, including customer complaints.

Clause 8.2.1 deals with measures of Quality System effectiveness and cites customer input as one measure that will be tracked.

Additionally, ISO clause 8.5.1 states that the organisation shall continually improve the effectiveness of their Quality Management System. From these clauses, there is little doubt that customer satisfaction is a central part of any effective Quality Management System.

What are the benefits of determining customer satisfaction?

The need to determine customer satisfaction will vary somewhat by the competitive circumstances of a given industry. In intense consumer-focused activities, measuring customer satisfaction is critical. But every company in every industry can benefit by examining the needs of their customers. Some of the areas where improvement may be expected include:

1. Better determination of customer uses and needs.
2. Identification of problems with customer services.
3. A sharper focus on areas having the greatest need for improvement.
4. Gaining insight for new products and/or service offerings.

Consumer behaviour as a distinct discipline dates only from the mid 1960s. Interest in understanding and tracking specific consumer problems grew dramatically in the late 1970s under the broad label of consumer satisfaction/dissatisfaction (CS/D) research. Its growth coincided with a growing interest on the part of government regulators and consumer advocates in making policy formulation more rational and systematic. The earliest comprehensive CS/D studies were, in fact, motivated by the policy planning needs of a public regulatory agency, the Federal Trade Commission (Technical Advisory Research Program 1979), and a private non-profit sector organisation, Ralph Nader's Centre for Study of Responsive Law. Most CS/D research from 1975 to 1985 was conducted within product and goods industries. Only after 1980 were initial concepts and models developed to measure consumer satisfaction/dissatisfaction within service industries.

Since 1985, two different patterns have emerged. First, there has been a considerable drop in CS/D research from a public policy perspective. At the same time, however, there has been substantial growth in interest in the topic of consumer satisfaction research in the private sector. This has been driven primarily by the growth of the service sector of the economy where managers have realised that tracking satisfaction is crucial to success when intangibles such as personal attention and atmospheres are the "product". A number of private sector satisfaction tracking services have emerged. Many of these services have made extensive use of earlier methodological developments in social policy research.

Most of the early studies were based on survey data. An alternative approach was complaints data, data on the extent to which consumers voluntarily speak up about their dissatisfactions. Such data have the advantage of not requiring field surveys; however, they are typically biased in two important ways.

First, some types of problems in some types of industries are more likely to be voiced than others, and some problems are less serious than others and/or less costly than others. Monopolies, such as some transit systems, are often relatively "immune" to complaining except from a small elite. Finally, not all consumers complain. These problems have led researchers in recent years to fall back on the more costly, but more objective, survey research methods.

Initial survey research studies on CS/D sought to calibrate the amount and types of dissatisfaction in the marketplace as a basis for policy planning. This body of research was largely descriptive. Wide variation was found across purchase categories. These studies differ widely in the basic measure of dissatisfaction they used. Some focused on more or less objective measures of "problems", others on subjective feelings of "dissatisfaction." Some counted any negative experience whatsoever, some only "serious" dissatisfactions, and some only the most recent problem. Also, there was the issue of opportunity for problems. Definitional problems persist today.

Customer satisfaction research literature traditionally agrees that service quality is a measure of how well the service level delivered matches customer expectations. Delivering quality service means conforming to customer expectations on a consistent basis. However, clearly, the fact that expectations are confirmed is not always sufficient for satisfaction.

Regardless of what eventual quantitative analytical approaches are used, the process must begin with acquiring a list of service attributes from the customers, through an exhaustive "listening to the voice of the customer" process. This qualitative research is usually conducted through a series of focus groups. Customers are requested to describe the ideal service or product in all of its feature details. Then customers are asked to list their basic service or product requirements, starting with primary requirements and continuing through the secondary and tertiary components of each of these requirements. The moderator proceeds until the group has exhausted all the possible attributes of service quality they would consider.

This process is repeated at multiple geographic and customer segment sites and the results are combined and itemised into a full and complete attribute listing. The wording of the attributes is refined for clarity and linkage with expected results. For example, "frequent service so that wait times are short". (Or if further quantification is desirable: "frequent service so that wait times do not exceed 15 minutes".) This process usually results in a listing of 40 to 55 defined attributes of transit service that can be rated by customers.

11.3.3 Quantitative Analytical Techniques

Overview

In a typical quantitative customer satisfaction study, respondents evaluate overall satisfaction, then rate each individual service attribute that customers have defined. A key question for researchers is which attributes are the drivers of overall satisfaction (since not all attributes have equal impact)? When there are 40 to 50 attributes that can impact customer satisfaction, and transit agency resources are limited, how can it be determined which limited number of attributes should be targeted for problem occurrence reduction, in order to produce the greatest possible increase in overall customer satisfaction with transit service?

Researchers have suggested many procedures for dealing with this problem. Several are considered by Green and Tull (1975) and reviewed in The Maritz Marketing Research Report (1993). Work continues in this area; no true "answer" for all applications has emerged. However, derived importance measures are usually preferred over stated importance measures.

Stated importance measures ask respondents to explicitly state their perception of the importance of each attribute, usually using a 10-point scale. The results of this method can be straightforwardly interpreted; however, results can be few, if any, statistical differences among attributes, so the aim of the method — to prioritise attributes — is thwarted. This makes quadrant analysis unreliable since differentiations among attributes by their mean importance or mean satisfaction ratings may not be statistically significant, at least without very large sample sizes. The statistical significance challenge is compounded when the results of a new tracking survey are compared with benchmark results. Additionally, the approach does not take into account, or provide a reliable means, for measuring the relative impact of service attributes on overall satisfaction.

Derived importance methods rely on the statistical association between individual ratings (predictors) and an overall satisfaction rating. The importance of an attribute is statistically determined from this relationship. These measures can be generally described as follows:

1. **Bivariate (Pearson) Correlation**

This measure separately tests the strength of the relationship of each independent variable (attribute) with the dependent variable (overall satisfaction). It has the advantages of familiarity and relative simplicity. However, joint effects with other attributes go undiscovered, and often many attributes are similarly correlated with overall satisfaction.

2. **Multiple Regression Analysis**

This approach allows the inclusion of additional independent variables (attributes) when testing the relationship with the dependent variable (overall satisfaction). However, an important consideration is that it is common in customer satisfaction research for attributes to be correlated — sometimes highly — with each other. This multi-colinearity makes it difficult to measure the separate effects of the individual attributes on overall satisfaction using the multiple regression approach.

3. **Factor Analysis**

Factor analysis is a statistical technique that is used for many purposes including:

- revealing patterns of inter-correlationships among variables, and
- reducing a large number of variables to a smaller number of statistically independent variables (dimensions) that are each linearly related to the original variables.

4. **Combining Factor Analysis and Multiple Regression Analysis**

When multi-colinearity is encountered in multiple regression modelling, factor analysis can be used to first transform the independent variables to a smaller set of dimensions or artificial variables that are uncorrelated among themselves. Then multiple regression modelling is performed to predict the relative impact of the newly constructed dimensions on the dependent variable (overall satisfaction).

To date, factor analysis combined with multiple regression analysis has been the most prevalent analytical technique applied in customer satisfaction research within the transit industry.

11.3.4 Uses of Quadrant Analysis

Quadrant analyses of customer satisfaction measures are often used to provide an underlying understanding of ratings. Thus, for example, "strengths" are shown in one quadrant of the graphs as those attributes that are above the median in customer importance and also above the median in customer satisfaction. (Sometimes, as in a Gap Analysis, importances are derived by a bivariate correlation of attribute satisfaction with overall satisfaction). Likewise, the "weaknesses" or "opportunity" quadrant contains those attributes above the median in importance, but below the median in satisfaction. Those attributes below the median in importance, but above the median in satisfaction can be labeled the "maintenance of effort" quadrant; while the last "non-critical" quadrant contains those attributes low in importance on which satisfaction is also judged to be low.

The disadvantages of this approach are that the divisions by quadrant are somewhat arbitrary and the magnitude of the differences between attribute ratings is not usually taken into account. This approach, while giving a general overview of the relationship between attribute importance and satisfaction ratings, does not provide a stable quantitative measure of the impact of attributes on overall customer satisfaction. There are no established numbers for each attribute that provide the benchmarks against which future similarly collected customer satisfaction attribute measures can be tested — for statistically significant changes in customer perception.

11.3.5 Regional and Industry Response Bias

Customer measurements are often contaminated by a culture-induced scale bias that may invalidate cross-national or regional comparisons. The bias reveals itself as a tendency for some customers to give consistently higher or lower ratings of performance (even when actual performance levels are identical and expectations are controlled).

"While methods exist for estimating scale bias, all require that additional information be obtained from customers. Some of these methods are rather elaborate and tedious (e.g., conjoint-based) and/or are difficult to explain to customers (e.g., magnitude estimation). A (proprietary) technique developed by Symmetrics (Crosby, 1994; Crosby, 1992) makes it possible to reliably estimate the magnitude of the scale bias by asking customers additional questions that are a part of the International Scale Bias Index (ISBI). The index is formed averaging the ratings of composite items. The items are statements of performance categorised into six life domains: suppliers, sports, arts, education, science, and services. Differences between regions/countries in their mean index scores are mainly reflective of culture induced scale bias, i.e., a generalised tendency to be a harder or easier grader of performance. The index scores can be used to make adjustments in the customer measurements from each region/country in order to facilitate "apples-to-apples" comparisons."

11.3.6 Customer Loyalty and Establishing Customer Satisfaction Indices

Most major conceptual and measurement models of customer satisfaction explicitly include elements related to customer value and customer loyalty. Satisfaction is a necessary, but not a sufficient condition of customer loyalty (D. Randall Brandt, 1996). Customer loyalty is not repeat users or transit dependent riders. Many repeat customers may be choosing transit because of necessity, convenience, or habit. For these customers, if an alternative becomes available, they may quickly switch to that service or mode. Instead, customer loyalty is reflected by a combination of attitudes and behaviours. It usually is driven by customer satisfaction, yet also involves a commitment on the part of the customer to make a sustained investment in an ongoing relationship with transit service. Attitudes and behaviours that go with customer loyalty include:

- An intention to use the service again.
- A willingness (often an eagerness) to recommend the service to friends, associates, and other persons.
- Commitment to, and even identification with, service.
- Disinterest in and/or a general resistance to alternative means of transportation, when these are available.

One measure of customer loyalty is the Secure Customer Index (D. Randall Brandt, 1996). A secure customer is one who says that he or she is:

- Very satisfied with the service.
- Definitely will continue to use the service in the future.
- Definitely would recommend the service to others.

Secure Customer Index

Responses to the three items — overall satisfaction, likelihood to continue using the service, and likelihood to recommend — can be combined to create multiple classifications or segments based on the degree of customer security. For example:

- Secure Customers = % very satisfied/definitely would repeat/definitely would recommend.
- Favourable Customers = % giving at least "second best" response on all three measures of satisfaction and loyalty.
- Vulnerable Customers = % somewhat satisfied/might or might not repeat/might or might not recommend.
- At Risk Customers = % somewhat satisfied or dissatisfied/probably or definitely would not repeat/probably or definitely would not recommend.

The capacity to establish linkages between customer satisfaction, customer loyalty and business results should be part of the architecture of any organisation's customer satisfaction measurement process.

11.3.7 Linking Customer Satisfaction to Performance Measures

The process of linking goals to performance through measuring Customer Satisfaction (CS) is exploratory and preliminary for even the most forward-thinking companies. First, companies must formalise and quantify the relationship between CS and firm or agency performance. By determining how CS improves performance or what specific CS components correlate with different improvements, corporations can focus on only the most effective endeavours, allowing them to become more efficient in implementation.

Most firms are not focused on satisfying customers, even though research now correlates CS with improved performance. A firm's CS implementation process must reflect the needs of individual customer segments, and the overall programme must be flexible enough to allow each business unit to develop measures and processes that fit its management needs.

Properly implemented and managed, the performance measures process ensures that customer input drives an organisation's efforts to improve and innovate, and that the impact of these efforts can be assessed. The key question is how does the "voice of the customer" data compare with the "voice of the process" data? Customer expectations must be translated to, and linked with, performance measures for the organisation.

11.4 Order Fulfillment and Customer Satisfaction

Managing orders and ensuring that products are despatched to customers in a timely and reliable manner is of course important for any business, whether online or offline. This is generally referred to as fulfilment.

In order to attain and retain customer satisfaction, generate repeat business and build up a strong online reputation, one will need to have efficient order management and fulfilment systems in place.

Increase customer satisfaction by using an order fulfilment solution that improves order capture and enhances delivery confidence. Search inventory, planned production, capacity and material availability to determine the fastest way to service a customer request.

11.5 Service Guarantee

Service guarantee is an assurance of the quality of or length of use to be expected from product/service offered for sale, often with a promise of reimbursement. It is a marketing tool and defines, cultivates and maintains quality throughout the firm. Initially, very few firms gave guarantee but with passage of time more, service guarantees are being offered by more and more firms. An effective guarantee can affect profitability as it builds customer awareness and loyalty by positive word of mouth and through reduction in costs as service improvements are made and service recovery expenses are reduced. The guarantee can reduce costs of employee turnover by creating a positive service culture for the firm. Service guarantees are not appropriate for every firm and certainly not in every service situation. Hence they need to be planned and executed with finesse.

11.5.1 Benefits of Service Guarantees

The benefits to the firm of an effective service guarantee areas follows:

1. Guarantees reduce risk of customers and increase positive evaluation of the service prior to purchase by consumers.

2. To develop a meaningful guarantee, the firm must have a customer focus. Hence they must know what customers expect and value as well as clearly understand what satisfaction means for its customers.

3. A guarantee sets specific standards for the firm. The firm communicates to its employees what are their deliverables and the employees align their behaviours around customer strategies. In case of Dominos Pizza for home delivery, all the employees in the organisation know that they have to deliver the Pizza in 30 minutes otherwise it is free for the customer.

4. It provides an incentive for customers to complain and since more customers give feedback to the company because of guarantee being violated, the quality of feedback is more accurate. The guarantee communicates to customers that they have the right to complain.

5. A feedback information system between customers and service operation decisions can be strengthened through the guarantee.

6. A guarantee generates a sense of pride among employees and enhances employee morale and loyalty. Through feedback from the guarantee, improvements can be made in the service that benefit customers and indirectly the employees.

7. When a guarantee is invoked there is an instant opportunity to recover as the customer comes in contact. So one can satisfy the customer and earn loyalty.

11.5.2 Types of Service Guarantees

Satisfaction versus Service Attribute Guarantees

Modi Xerox guarantees it will completely satisfy its customers in terms of contract performance. Due to the size and customised nature of its contracts with customers, Modi Xerox enters into unconditional guarantees with specific customers so that both parties are clear at the outset on what exactly constitutes satisfaction for that customer.

Some firms offer guarantees of particular aspects of the service that are important to customers. Federal Express guarantees package delivery by a certain time.

McDonald's advertised a guarantee that stated 'Hot Food; Fast, Friendly Delivery; Double-Check Drive-Thru Accuracy We'll make it right, or your next meal is on us.'

Hence, the companies have guaranteed elements of the service that they know are important to customers.

11.5.3 Characteristics of Effective Guarantees

As per Christopher Hart, the following characteristics make guarantees effective:

1. **Unconditional:** The guarantee should make its promise and have no strings attached.

2. **Meaningful:** It should guarantee elements of the service that are important to the customer. The compensation should cover fully the customer's dissatisfaction.

3. **Easy to Understand and Communicate**

   For customers - they need to understand what to expect.

   For employees-they need to understand what to do.

4. **Easy to invoke and collect**

The guarantee clause in auto sector pertaining to warranty of parts as well as service in two wheelers leave a lot to be desired as companies have so many restrictive clauses in fine print in the contract that neither customers nor employees are certain what is being guaranteed. And when the customer goes to invoke the guarantee, they don't have a good experience. The formalities are too many and companies use documentation shortfalls as escape routes. Hence, a customer instead of invoking the guarantee just switch by saying 'It is not worth wasting their resources and time'.

11.5.4 Issues of Guarantee a Firm should consider

1. The customer inputs must be considered to decide on content and type of guarantees.

2. Culture must be appropriate and it must be top down approach with the top management committed to a guarantee.

3. The guarantee design must be a team effort.

4. Service quality is truly uncontrollable. However, a couple of examples may illustrate situations where this is the case. It would not be a good practice for a training organisation to guarantee that all participants would pass a particular certification exam on completion of the training course if passing depends too much on the participants own effort. The company could, however, guarantee satisfaction with the training or particular aspects of the training process.

5. The quality standards must be high catering to service expectations of their customers.

6. The existing service quality of the firm is poor. Before instituting a guarantee, the firm should fix any significant quality problems as certainly it will draw attention to the failures and the quality, the costs of implementing the guarantee could easily outweigh any benefits. These costs include actually monetary payouts to customers for poor service as well as costs associated with customer goodwill.

7. The customer risk must be minimal.

8. Offerings of a guarantee must be superior to competitors.

9. The type of guarantee - an unconditional guarantee or a specific-outcome one should be decided as per applicability.

10. Service standards must be measurable.

11. The elements of specific guarantee must be spelt out clearly.

12. The guarantee must be affordable to the firm.

13. The guarantee must be easy to invoke and payout be quick but as there is opportunity to recover the customer if one devise means to satisfy the customer and earn loyalty.

14. The guarantee doesn't match the firm's image. If the firm already has a reputation for very high quality and in fact implicitly guarantees its service, then a formal guarantee is most likely unnecessary.

15. Cost of the guarantee outweighs the benefits.

16. Customers perceive little risk in service.

Guarantees are usually most effective when customers are uncertain about the company and/or the quality of its services.

The guarantee can allay uncertainties and help to reduce risk. If customers perceive little risk, if the service is relatively inexpensive with lots of potential alternative providers, and quality is relatively invariable, then a guarantee will likely produce little effectiveness for the company, other than perhaps some promotional value.

This offer must have an effective service recovery strategy for retaining customers and increasing positive word of mouth. Another major benefit of an effective service recovery strategy is the information it provides that can be useful for service improvement. The potential downsides of poor service recovery are -negative word of mouth, lost customers and declining business when quality issues are not addressed. Some customers respond to service failures and some complain while others do not. Customers expect to be treated fairly when they complain-not in terms of the actual outcome or compensation they receive, but also in terms of the procedures that are used and how their limitations are treated.

Strategies that work for service recovery

1. Doing it right the first time.
2. Welcoming and encouraging complaints.
3. Acting quickly.
4. Treating customers fairly.
5. Learning from recovery experiences.
6. Learning from lost customers.

Service guarantees is a tool used by many firms as a foundation for service recovery and are a must for a receive firm.

11.6 Handling Customer Complaints

Management finds out about customer dissatisfaction through two mechanisms: Voice and Exit. "Voice" represents complaints ... the voice of the customer. "Exit" occurs when the customer stops buying or using the services. All of us have exited at one time or another, for example, if you've changed your doctor, telephone carrier, or plumber due to poor service.

Service providers employ all sorts of strategies to avoid customer turnover. Smart organisations know that it is not enough to have the lowest price or the best technology – there always seems to be a competitor who can do it better or cheaper. There are no guarantees, but one of the best customer retention strategies is to provide superior customer service. And that means listening to one's customers.

How well does an organisation listen and respond to complaints from its customers? All organisations aim to be customer focused ... claim to be customer focused ... but need to become MORE CUSTOMER FOCUSED.

Although listening and responding is necessary, it's not good enough. Too often, a response is reactionary and one can easily find yourself reacting over and over again to the same complaint (sometimes this is called "firefighting"). The organisation needs to listen and PROACT. That means listening to the voice of the customer and making process improvements based on that feedback so that the same complaints don't recur.

A complaint is any measure of dissatisfaction with the product or service, even if it's unfair, untrue, or painful to hear! Complaints may be about:

- Service Content, Delivery or Quality
- Personnel
- Requests
- Communication Response Time
- Documentation
- Billing
- Follow Up

To increase the visibility of complaints, the organisation should:

- **Listen to the Customer:** Complaints don't always identify themselves. Someone who is requesting the same information for the 5th time isn't asking for information anymore ... it's a complaint!
- **Solicit Complaints:** Everyone in the organisation should collect and report complaints. All this input should funnel to one place where your objective is to build a valid database of complaints. Most of us are accustomed to environments in which receiving customer complaints is considered negative – an interruption to doing business. But in the Customer Complaint Resolution Process, the more complaints one logs, the better! This is one of the biggest cultural issues for organisations to overcome.

- **Record Complaints:** Create complaint categories that make sense for your organisation. For example, data that tells you that you had 123 complaints about adoptions last month tells you nothing. The 123 complaints need to be broken down into categories so that you can get to a root cause analysis.

If you only respond to complaints without correcting the root cause, you're spinning your wheels and you'll find yourself fighting fires instead of putting them out for good. You can identify root cause if you collect, categorise, and analyse complaints. As a result, process improvements will be complaint-driven and thus should be high-priority. This is a customer complaint resolution process that anyone can implement:

- **Focus on the Customer:** If you can't immediately solve the problem, respond to the customer and identify an "owner" who will be responsible for final resolution. Complete the communication loop with the customer. If you've referred the complaint to others, make sure there's closure. If you've left the customer hanging without a response, you've become part of the problem.

- **Focus on the Complaint:** Collect all complaints from all external customers and categorise them in a way that allows you to analyse data to see trends, patterns, concentrations, tendencies, etc.

- **Focus on Process Improvement:** Use the database of complaints to define processes that are important from the customer's perspective and to improve the most critical ones. Based on analysis of the database, make appropriate investments to prevent issues that result in customer complaints. Look for permanent improvements to response time, cycle time, internal processes related to the complaints, and complaint frequency.

Customer satisfaction levels can actually increase based on how companies handle customer complaints. A problem or issue does not define the staff or the company. How it is handled does define the staff or company.

Customer complaints often stem from the customer not feeling understood. They feel they are being treated like a non-entity, and not like a real person with real frustrations when issues arise.

Feelings of alienation set in when customers don't feel listened to. When the statements "It's our policy to..." or "It's not our policy to do that." comes into play, any relationship that has been built with that customer will be damaged.

11.7 Customer Service Satisfaction

With customers we initiate sales as an initial transaction, which results in revenue generation and we get cash flow. The health of the firm depends over a period of time on the quantum of cash flow. Therefore customers are the foundation of the business based on sales done with them over a period of time. Sales volume require repeat business, which we get from only satisfied customers. Satisfied customers are the firms' best source, which enable the firm to create strong bonds. The business is to continue smooth operation with excellent financial health.

'Customer satisfaction is customer's perception that a supplier has met or exceeded their expectations.' The keyword to understand this definition is perception. Customer satisfaction is in customer's mind and may or may not conform to the reality of the situation. It is a fact that people form attitudes but change them only slowly. The firm must realise that the customers value things like reliability, courtesy, responsiveness and flexibility. In sales of service firms, we have to consider what is being sold and how it is being sold. Hence the firm, which wants to be successful consistently, must service their customers effectively and efficiently.

11.7.1 Scope of Customer Service

1. The activities involved in ensuring that a product or service is delivered to the customer at the right time, at the right place and in right quantity.
2. The working relationship between the staff, the supplier and the customer.
3. Provision of after sales service with repair facilities.
4. The people of the firm, who handle complaints.
5. The sales and process for handling orders and customers.

The customer service as defined by Lalonde and Zinszer is 'those activities that occur at the interface between the customer and the firm, which enhance or facilitate the sale and use of the firm's products or services.

They divided customer service into Pre-transaction elements, transaction elements and post transaction elements.

Pre-transaction elements help to establish a framework for excellent customer service.
1. A written service policy is communicated internally and externally and ensured that it is understood by all and quantified wherever possible.
2. Organisation structure geared to service customers as per norms. The employees have recovery authority and responsibility to meet the commitments they are making.
3. Accessibility to the employees easy and hence business can de done as and when required.
4. System flexibility to adapt to meet customer needs despite unexpected uncontrolled problems which are rare but occur like a whirlwind.

Transaction elements help in the delivery of the product to the customer and they are visible:

1. Minimal cycle time so that the elapsed time from initiation of the order by the customer to delivery, is minimised.
2. Stock availability to ensure no stock out.
3. Online order status information so that response to a customer query in minimum time.

Post-transaction elements ensure the array of service needed to support the product in the field:

1. Availability of spares/service personnel to ensure that repairs are done in minimum time after receipt of complaint.
2. Customer complaint system ensures that complaints are dealt with immediately. Continuous monitoring of customer satisfaction and taking corrective action if required.
3. Response time to attend to complaints as well as first call fix accuracy to ensure higher customer satisfaction.

'Customer satisfaction measurement is a measure of how a firms' total product performs in relation to a set of customer expectations'.

We need to know what is total product and who should define the total product. Total product encompasses anything and everything contributing to how customers perceive it.

In addition to core product, organisation's image and customers satisfaction will be influenced by a wide range of additional factors.

To understand this consider the total product of a restaurant. The restaurant's core product is the food, the main factor contributing to the success to the business. So, if the food is disappointing, forget it! Customer satisfaction and repeat business will be low and the restaurant will soon develop a poor reputation even with people who have never dined there. On the other hand, if the food is delicious, that benefit alone may secure enough repeat business and favourable word of mouth to ensure the success of the business, regardless of the other aspects or the restaurant's total product.

However, a few businesses will be at either extreme of this spectrum. More typically, customers' overall level of satisfaction and the consequent success of the business will be based on many additional factors the quality of the food will not always be the most important one. Diners will certainly be influenced by the decor and the ambience of the restaurant, by the friendliness of the waiter or waitress and by the efficiency and quality of the service. Perhaps the chef will add value by talking to diners about the dishes offered. How they are presented and described on the menu, the quality of the menu's print and graphic design may play a part. For some diners, the atmosphere and image the restaurant creates will be the deciding factor - they will choose the restaurant because it is the place to go: The total product is very diverse and one must cover all its components.

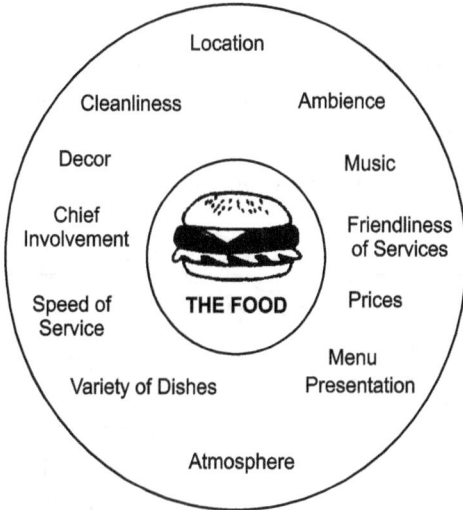

Fig. 11.1

Define the total product by a combination of your staff and customers inputs. The customer is exposed to several products and services everyday. It becomes difficult for him to distinguish amongst the core products or services. The service firms in the field of customer service, to stay competitive, are differentiating themselves on the basis of customer service. The customers expect them to be treated in a certain way and they are opting for those firms, which meet their expectations.

Excellent service is needed to ensure customer satisfaction. The aim of the firm is to make profit with efficient service with value for money to the customer. It is possible to have very satisfied customer who are not profitable and to invest in high quality service, which does not affect the customer buying behavior. It is also possible to over invest in quality to such an extent that the customer finds the service unattractive. It is therefore important to find out which factors of service influence most the customer's propensity to buy and to be ahead of nearest rivals of these factors in terms of service offer to have an edge in market place.

11.7.2 Factors Influencing Customer Satisfaction

As per M.M. Lele and J.D.Sheth,four factors influence the customer satisfaction namely Product, Sales Activity, After Sales Service, and Culture.

1. **Product:** The providers have to take into account the customers' needs and design, process and in built quality of the product.

2. **Sales Activity:** The positive messages the firm sends out in its advertising and promotion programmes and how it chooses and monitors its sales force and intermediaries and the image that it projects to the customer.

3. **After-Sales Service:** Guarantees, service, feedback, complaints handling, and responsiveness to a customer to ensure satisfaction.

4. **Culture:** Values and beliefs of the firm as well as the tangible and intangible systems it uses to instill these values into employee behaviour at all levels.

Marketers must make a distinction between one's core product offering and one's value-added services to have a competitive edge.

Table 11.1

Level	Type of Service	Description	Example
I	Core	Basic service product	Food in a restaurant.
II	Expected	Basic product and minimum conditions that are a must to be met	When the customer enter the restaurant, they expect in addition to comfort, lovely decor, prompt seating, on display menu card and a smiling waiter.
III	Augmented	Basic product and minimum conditions that are a must and something different which enables differentiation.	Two restaurants are offering vegetarian food with excellent reputation of customer service, but one may be differentiating itself from the other by 'adding values' to the core product in terms of responsiveness by serving food within ten minutes.
IV	Potential	Contains potentially feasible and useful benefits that results in holding and attracting the customer.	A customer orders food in a restaurant based on selections made on menu but is offered a desert within the same price. This offer exceeds the expectation which enables marketers to win customer loyalty.

In customer satisfaction studies, the customers are judging them on value added component of offering while customers assume that the core offering will necessarily be of high quality. Hence if core is poor, it will result in customer dissatisfaction but if core is good it does not lead to customer satisfaction. With competitors there is very little variability in the core product offerings like in airlines. They usually do arrive safely, food served is hot, the covers and the seats are decent and clean, the ambience is nice and comfortable. In some cases, consumers find the core of some services hard to judge like strategic management consultancy. What varies more and is easier to evaluate are the supplemental services like interpersonal skills, which differ greatly from pilot to pilot, hostess-to-hostess, chef-to-chef, cleaners to cleaners and consultant to consultant as all these things are easy to judge.

The customer care continuum is used to design customer care programmes. These programmes are focused on training the staff more about their attitude than skills. It helps in formulating a systematic strategy, which needs continual adjustment in the light of changes in the market place and changes in customer requirement. Continuous updating and training of the service staff accomplishes the mission of the organisation.

The marketers can design customer care programmes to deliver customer satisfaction by using the supplemental services as a part of the marketing strategy.

Marketers must determine what customers want and then give it to them. This can be done in several ways. First get buyer preferences and then use this information to customise the service delivery.

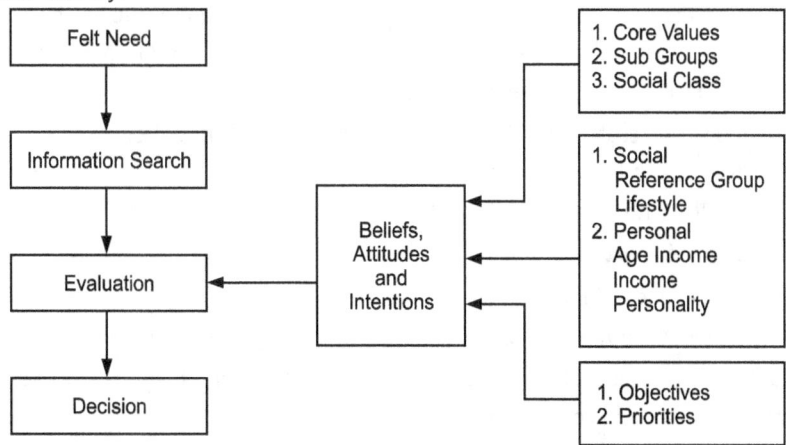

Fig. 11.2

Need Recognition

It could be basic need like food, clothing or shelter or the more sophisticated needs associated with job satisfaction and social status i.e. psychogenic needs.

The consumer must first become aware of the existence of a need. This is also called **problem recognition**. Once the consumer has perceived this felt need, he or she will be motivated towards its satisfaction. A need can be aroused through internal or external stimuli

- hunger pangs may originate purely internally if a long time has elapsed since eating, or they may be triggered by external stimuli of aroma when walking past a baker's shop early in the morning.

After a person is aware of a need, it gets converted into drive because he or she feels driven to satisfy it. Firms must therefore understand what it is that drives a consumer to choose their particular product or service rather than that of their competitors. Motor cycle purchase may satisfy a need for transportation, a need for status or a need for excitement. Firms use promotional and selling techniques to position their product or service in the market in such a way that it will appeal to potential customers.

Information search

Once aware of a need or problem, an individual will set about solving it. Sometimes a problem is solved immediately; hunger is felt and a biscuit may be eaten. Sometimes the problem is more complex and the individual has to seek out information to help him or her solve it.

Internal Search from Memory

There is a major implication in this for customer satisfaction measurement. An individual's memory is often not a particularly reliable guide to what actually happened and subjective perceptions of events occur and it usually does not conform to reality. We often remember those things we choose to remember. In particular, we tend to remember bad, as opposed to good experiences, more vividly and for longer.

But the individual customer will be quite happy with all this, his or her perception of events is reality and has to become reality for any supplier, trying to sell goods or services to that individual. Often, however, the information search will be more lengthy.

Sources of External Search:

1. Personal sources of information; a friend the neighbour next door, or a relative who has experience of this kind of purchase and could give me good advice.

2. Public sources like yellow pages, buyers guides, consumer magazine. These sources will provide a good comparison of alternative products.

3. Commercial sources of information like advertising in the local press, call centres etc.

It will depend upon the requirement and urgency which necessarily puts a time limit on the information search stage. In some high involvement products the buyer may spend a considerable time at the information search stage. They will not be actively seeking information the whole time but they will be in a state of heightened attention. In other words, they will be alert to any information concerning that felt need whether it arises in advertisements, articles or casual conversation.

Evaluation

By this time a number of alternative ways of meeting a felt need will have become evident. These alternatives must now be evaluated and this involves determining how well each option meets the felt need. This process may be very objective, with the advantages and disadvantages of each option weighed against other alternatives, some people might even compile a list to help in their evaluation. However objective the individual intends to be, subjective factors always influence the evaluation process to a greater or lesser extent.

Three sets of subjective factors have an influence at the evaluation stage: beliefs, attitudes and intentions.

Beliefs: Beliefs are deeply entrenched views, often based on the core values of an individuals country, subgroup (for example, ethnic group) and social class. Beliefs are sometimes hard to articulate; they nevertheless form the foundation for decision making behaviour. Beliefs are also, of course, social, political and religious. An individual might believe that 'branded' products are of a higher quality than 'own label products.

Attitudes: An individual's underlying beliefs help to form attitudes about specific events, places, products, and services. These attitudes are liable to change more frequently than beliefs, being strongly influenced by family, social reference groups, lifestyle, age and income.

An individual's attitude towards a particular brand of tea might be influenced by an individual's spending power and the persons with whom the individual in socializing.

Therefore, the individual might hold the attitude that, for example, Green label tea provides better value for money than cheaper own label alternatives.

Intentions: Individuals also have objectives, priorities and aspirations that they are striving to attain, and these will often be reflected in their purchasing decision, especially for variable purchases such as cars or clothing. Thus, one factor in an individual's choice of Green label tea might be wanting visitors to know their gradation of choice.

All three components of the customer's evaluation process is necessary to understand customers' satisfaction. Thus, customer satisfaction is not a simple relationship between provider and customer. An individual's evaluation of a product or service will al most always be affected by others.

Decisions: After having weighed up the alternatives, a decision is made. Even this decision may still be little more than an 'intention to purchase'. Unless the buyer is in the shop handing over cash for the item, the purchase decision is usually a stage which precedes the purchase by some time. High Involvement Product (HIP) being considered, the decision in principle to buy and the choice of one of the alternative could precede the actual purchase by a period of time like a few months.

An additional factor at this stage is the level of risk the consumer will associate with purchase. The risk level is higher for HIP where the buyer's product knowledge is poor and consequently difficulty arises in evaluating alternatives. Conspicuous purchases, which may affect the buyer's credibility in the eyes of others, also tend to be associated with a high level of risk. Some individuals of course are more prone to uncertainty than others, but virtually everyone will be uncertain about some purchases in their lives.

Outcomes

Of those decision makers who do carry out their intention to purchase, some will be totally satisfied with the product and others less. So whatever the outcome, the buyer is likely to remember this level of satisfaction and, for all but the most minor purchases, memory is likely to be influential in subsequent similar decision making situations.

In this situation it is wise for companies to do all they can to reinforce consumers' confidence in their choice. Some advertisements for inherently high-risk purchases such as cars is aimed at recent purchasers by showing satisfied buyers with their new car. Supportive communications can also be sent through the post or reassuring telephone calls made. It is in these situations that post-transaction customer satisfaction measurement is most useful. The possibility of cognitive dissonance should always be borne in mind by those carrying out the measurement; it is particularly important to ensure swift action to resolve any customer dissatisfaction, however small. An implication here is that post-transaction customer surveys should not be anonymous.

11.7.3 Satisfaction versus Service Quality

Satisfaction is a broader concept while service quality assessment focuses specifically on dimensions of service. Hence perceived service quality is a component of customer satisfaction.

Customer perception of quality and customer satisfaction service quality is an evaluation, that reflects the customer's perception of five dimensions of service: reliability, responsiveness, assurance, empathy and tangibles. Customer satisfaction is influenced by perceptions of service quality, product quality and price, as well as situational and personal factors.

For example, a swimming pool is judged on attributes such as cleanliness; whether the filtration plant is in working order or not, how responsive the instructors are to customer needs, how skilled the trainers are, and whether the facility is well-maintained. Customer satisfaction with the swimming pool is a wider concept that will be influenced by perceptions of service quality but that will also include perceptions of product quality like diving boards, floats; price of membership, personal factors such as the moods of the consumer and even uncontrollable situational factors such as weather conditions and experiences on the poolside while relaxing. and in line a with other customers.

Internal and External Customer Perceptions

The dimensions of service and the ways in which customers evaluate service are similar whether, the customer is internal or external to the firm. When we refer to customer perceptions and how customers evaluate services, we can assume that both internal and external customers are included and the definitions, scope, strategies, and approaches can apply to either group.

Since satisfaction is different to different people, the researchers have given various definitions of customer satisfaction as detailed below:

1. Customer satisfaction is customer's perception that a supplier has met or exceeded their expectations.

2. A complex process involving prior attitude towards a product or service or a consumption experience resulting in positive or negative disconfirmation of expectancies followed by feelings of satisfaction or dissatisfaction which change post consumption attitude and subsequently influences future purchase behaviour.

3. A subjective evaluation of the various experiences and outcomes associated with acquiring and consuming a product relative to a set of subjectively determined expectations.

4. Satisfaction is a consumer's fulfillment response. It is a judgment that a product or service feature or the product or service itself, provides a pleasurable level of consumption related fulfillment.

Hence due to complexity, there are difficulties involved in implementing and subsequently measuring customer's satisfaction. Modified disconfirmation model by authors of consumer satisfaction has drawn attention and interest to understand the concept of customer satisfaction more closely. Consumer satisfaction results from a subjective comparison of expected and perceived attribute level. This model highlights that where perceived performance meets or exceeds expectations the customer is satisfied or even perhaps delighted; where performance falls short of expectations the customer is dissatisfied. In other words before any measurement occurs, marketers must be aware of a number of issues and some of them are given below.

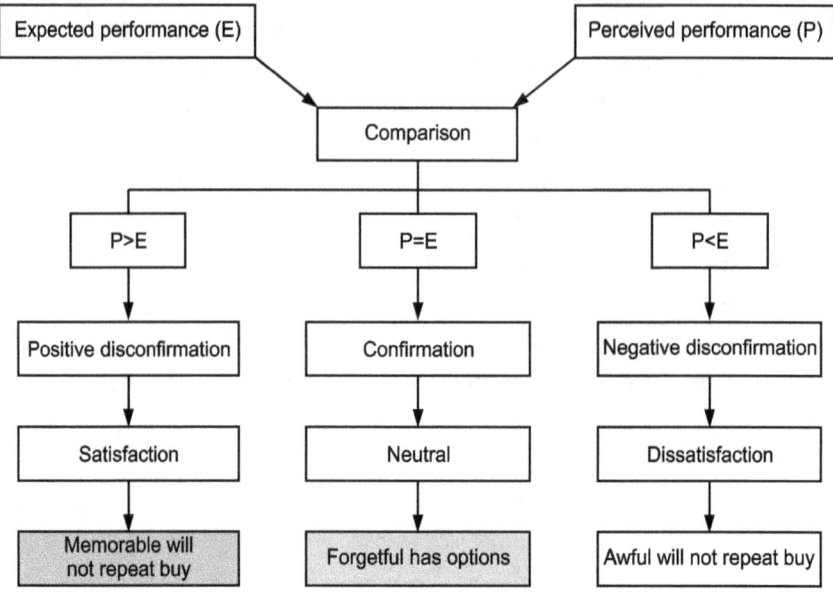

Fig. 11.3

Issues in Expectations

1. **Knowledge and Experience:** Customer expectation vary with knowledge and experience. A prospects expectation is different than a customer and a customer expectation is different than that of a client with the same service provider. A prospects expectation would be unclear, impractical, unrealistic and could easily undergo a change.

2. **Level of expectation varies** from individual to individual

3. Customer satisfaction will vary according to the outcome of service performance. Even if customer expected with medium level of satisfaction are exceeded, the customers with high level of satisfaction may not be satisfied.

4. Performance, significantly below expectations, as consumers may be expecting too much.

5. Exceeding expectations. The customers get service better than the expected. Namely delighting the customer. However the firm will have to do things so that the expected experience continues to amaze the customer in future as well.

6. Components of expectations. There are three aspects of expectations.

   (a) Anticipated performance level.

   (b) Probability estimate of the likelihood of the level that it is occurring.

   (c) An evaluation of the anticipated attribute level.

11.7.4 Customer Loyalty

Customers' purchase decisions are affected by many subjective factors, which are not necessarily rational or economic choice. One of these factors is the customer's loyalty to an existing supplier or a last used supplier for occasional purchases. Loyalty is relevant and meaningful to customer satisfaction measurement. There are many degrees of customer loyalty and they are depicted as a ladder, a pyramid or a continuum. The pyramid approach shown below graphically represents a typical spread of customers through the various loyalty levels.

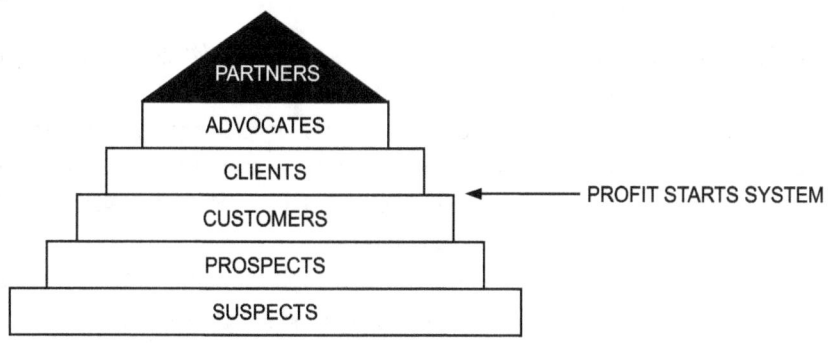

Fig. 11.4

Six Loyalty levels:

1. **Suspects:** All the buyers of the product/service category in the marketplace. Suspects are either unaware of your firm's product or service or have no inclination to purchase it.

2. **Prospects:** They are potential customers who have some attraction towards your firm but have not yet taken the step of doing business with you.

3. **Customers:** Typically a one-off purchaser of your product while a few may buy again who have no feelings of loyalty towards your firm.

4. **Clients:** Repeat customers who have positive feelings of loyalty towards your firm but whose support is passive rather than active, apart from making purchases.

5. **Advocates:** Advocates are clients who actively support your firm by recommending it to others.

6. **Partners:** A partnership is the strongest form of customer-supplier relationship which is sustained because both parties see it as mutually beneficial.

Loyalty, then, involves more than just making a purchase or even repeat purchases. It represents a positive level of commitment by the customer to the supplier and it is the degree of positive commitment which distinguishes truly loyal customers. The degree of customer loyalty can be used in customer satisfaction measurement to segment the customer base and identify those customer groupings that are most at risk of defection. These customer loyalty segments may well have different needs and priorities; certainly, they will have different perceptions of your firm's performance. Therefore, you may define distinct priorities for improvements for different segments.

Satisfaction with past transactions is not the only determinant of customer loyalty. It is also affected by other factors such as the supplier's image, the relative performance or perceived attraction of competitors and the level of customer inertia in the marketplace. All of these factors would be covered by a market survey.

Loyalty levels may also differ between High Involvement Product(HIP) purchases. There is usually a stronger bond of loyalty to a good supplier in HIP purchases which tend to have a lengthier decision making process, more customer-supplier contact, and where the consequences of making a poor decision are perceived to be serious by the customer. There is, therefore, a high risk factor in changing suppliers. Inertia is likely to be a more prominent reason for repeat purchase in LIP decisions and this can make customers more vulnerable to competitors who can break down the inertia barriers through appropriate communications.

Customer satisfaction measurement study must, then, identify what matters most so that appropriate priorities for improvements can be set and to defend the more vulnerable segments of your customer base. A market survey should identify the benefits, which will appeal most strongly to your competitors' feast loyal customer segments. It is unwise to target competitors' partners or advocates, but their 'customers' could be very vulnerable provided your marketing communications focus on the right benefits. These will be product or service attributes important to the segment and where your competitors' performance is perceived to be relatively poor namely those areas of priorities for improvement for competitor.

Increase in retention rate enhances customer life time value

Customer satisfaction leads to increased customer loyalty which is measured by customer retention rate. With the firm's improved retention rate, the average life of a customer increases and the firm is able to increase its average retention it enhances actually the average customer lifetime value.

Lifetime value of a customer is computing from firm's point of view of their lifetime revenue and profitability contribution to a firm. The firm starts with assuming the building of long-term relationships with their customers over time and computing the financial value.

$$\text{Lifetime Value} = \text{Average transaction value} \times \text{Frequency of purchase} \times \text{Customer life expectancy}$$

One customer buys on an average four dosa per week at Vaishali hotel over a ten year period which would be worth ₹ 40, 000 (₹ 4 × 20 × 50 × 10) to the hotel, leaving aside inflation. Financials do reflect total sales revenue but lead to increased profitability for which seven reasons are given below:

1. Costs of acquiring new customers can be substantial.
2. Loyal customers tend to spend more.
3. Regular customers tend to place frequent orders and usually cost less to serve.
4. Satisfied customers introduce new customers through word of mouth.
5. Satisfied customers are willing to pay premium prices to a supplier they know and trust.
6. Retaining customers makes market entry difficult for new entrants.
7. Data mining on loyal customers allows the firm to communicate regularly with them and enables them to encourage to buy more through special offers.

11.8 Defections, Failures and Recovery

One of the world's accomplished investors, Warren Buffett said in a speech in 1991 at the Emory Business School in Atlanta, Georgia, "*I've often felt there might be more to be gained by studying business failures than business successes. In my business, we try to study where people go astray and why things don't work. We try to avoid mistakes. If my job was to pick a group of ten stocks in the Dow-Jones average that would outperform the average itself, I would probably not start by picking the ten best. Instead, I would try to pick the 10 or 15 worst performers and take them out of the sample and work with the residual. It's an inversion process. Albert Einstein said, 'Invert, always invert, in mathematics and physics,' and it's a very good idea in business, too. Start out with failure and then engineer its removal.*"

It is reported that on average, the CEOs of U.S. corporations lose half their customers every five years. This fact shocks most people. It shocks the CEOs themselves, most of whom have little insight into the causes of the customer exodus, let alone the cures, because they do not measure customer defections, make little effort to prevent them, and fail to use defections as a guide to improvements. Yet customer defection is one of the most illuminating measures in business.

- It is the clearest possible sign that customers see a deteriorating stream of value from the company.
- A climbing defection rate is a sure predictor of a diminishing flow of cash from customers to the company, even if the company replaces the lost customers, because new customers cost money to acquire and because older customers tend to produce greater cash flow and profits than newer ones.

In general, the longer a customer stays with a company, the more that customer is worth. Long-term customers buy more, take less of a company's time, are less sensitive to price, and bring in new customers. Best of all, they have no acquisition or start-up cost. Good long-standing customers are worth so much that in some industries, reducing customer defections by as little as five points from, say, 15% to 10% per year, can double profits. CEOs would prefer to have loyal customers. But without doing the arithmetic that shows just how much a loyal customer is worth over the whole course of the customer life cycle, and without calculating the net present value of the company's present customer base, most CEOs gauge company performance on the basis of cash flow and profit.

By searching for the root causes of customer departures, companies with the desire and capacity to learn, can identify business practices that need fixing and, sometimes, can win the customer back and reestablish the relationship on firmer ground.

The following are the reasons why companies do not give ample attention to customer defection:

- Many companies are not really alarmed by customer defections or they are alarmed too late, because they do not understand the intimate, causal relationship between customer loyalty on the one hand and cash flow and profits on the other.
- It is unpleasant to study failure too closely, and in some companies trying to analyse failure can even be hazardous to careers.
- Customer defection is often hard to define.
- Sometimes defining the customer itself is hard, especially the kind of customer it is worth retaining.
- It is extremely hard to uncover the real root causes of a customer defection and get the appropriate lessons.
- Getting the right people in the organisation to learn those lessons and then commit to acting on them is a challenge.
- It is difficult to conceptualise and set up the mechanisms that turn the analysis of customer defections into an ongoing strategic system, closely supervised by top managers and quickly responsive to changing circumstances.

Loyalty and Profits

What keeps customers loyal is the value they receive. One of the reasons so many businesses fail is that too much of their measurement, analysis, and learning revolves around profit and too little around value creation. They become aware of problems only when profits start to fall, and in struggling to fix short-term profits, they concentrate on a perceived symptom and miss the underlying breakdown in the value-creation process. They see customer issues as subsidiary to profits and delegate them to the marketing department for routine responses.

Years of continuing defection can mean that former customers, convinced by personal experience that the company offers inferior value, will eventually outnumber the company's loyal advocates and dominate the collective voice of the marketplace. When that moment arrives, no amount of advertising, public relations, or ingenious marketing will help in developing strategies with respect to pricing and new-customer acquisitions. This will hurt the company's reputation.

Although some executives do realise that profits are really a downstream benefit of delivering superior value to customers, and that customer loyalty is therefore the best indicator of strategic success or failure, they lack the necessary tools for focusing their organisational learning towards this most basic building block of profitable growth. They undertake standard market research and customer-satisfaction surveys, but such tools are not adequate to measure customer defections. The information a company needs to understand customer defections and design possible remedies is available with the customers, even as the trouble starts unfolding. They are always the first to know when a company's value proposition is failing in the face of competition.

Defining Defection

Some customer defections are easier to spot than others. Customers who close their accounts and shift all their business to another supplier are clearly defecting. But there would be customers who shift some of their purchases to another supplier, and also those who actually buy more, but their purchases from the company represent a smaller share of their total expenditures, or represent a smaller share of the wallet.

Need for Failure Analysis

A company can encourage adaptive change by promoting employee learning, and the most useful and instructive learning grows when the employees and the entire organisation develops the capability to recognise failures and learn from them. The first step in this is overcoming their preoccupation with success. Of course, success has lessons to teach. Academicians, consultants, and executives are constantly looking for approaches that have led to big profits in one situation so they can apply them in others. Yet this quest for best practices has created much less value than expected for the following reasons:

- When a system is working well, its success rests on a long chain of subtle interactions and it is not easy to determine which links in the chain are most important.

- Even if the critical links in success stories are identifiable, their relative importance would-shift as the business environment would be different. It would not be possible to reproduce all the relationships or the external environment in which they operate.

- Psychologically and culturally, it is difficult and sometimes threatening to look at failure too closely. Ambitious managers want to link their careers to successes. Failures are usually examined for the purpose of assigning blame rather than detecting and eradicating the systemic causes of poor performance.

Hence, it is necessary to study failures and learn from them. In technical issues, failure analysis is critical. Similarly, in business, companies can build stronger strategies by analysing the critical problem areas. For failure analysis, companies should consider the following steps:

- The employees should be trained to differentiate between complete defectors and those customers who had closed business or partial defectors. They should know that even customers who buy some equipment, some consumables, or some service from other suppliers, (fractional defections) also have meaning especially in a highly competitive environment.

- Careful analysis of the billing records to identify the lost customers and potential defectors.

- Interviewing the lost customers and a large number of the partial defectors, to look for the root causes of each defection, especially when customers had migrated to competitors.

- Redefining defection to include those who were showing tendency to defect, or where the company had lost a part of the customer's orders. This will help the company define who the core customers are, so as to serve them better.

The company thus gets an opportunity to listen to the complaints and take corrective action. It could be by way of redesigning the product, bringing out a low-end product to meet the requirements of a price-sensitive customer or redesigning the customer-service protocol to make sure that issues raised by the customers are prioritised and immediate attention is given to equipment faults, delivery problems etc. Tracking and responding to customer defections can become central to the way a company does business.

There is always a strong temptation to rationalise customer complaints. This is nothing but a failure of failure analysis. The sales personnel may argue that those were not good customers to begin with. They may blame the customer's technical staff for not sophisticated enough to use the company's products. They may even claim that the customers have been extremely demanding and hence, servicing their complaints involved a lot of expenditure.

Service Recovery

What ever any service firm will do for its customer, there is bound to be complaints that they have not got what they had in mind or that their expectations or the promises made by the firm have not been met. It is necessary to listen to these complaints and convert them into positive experiences for the customer, so that the customer feels that the firm has done something for him which he has not anticipated. The reason why people complain is because they have received the service below the zone of tolerance. The reasons could be many but one has to go into the depth to understand them.

Managing Conflicts and Establishing Relationships

Problems arising out of conflicts are God sent opportunities which must be tackled by a service provider.

1. Each and every customer relationship is valuable so one must listen carefully. Every customer is valuable so trivial issues must be resolved immediately. A real estate agent had a customer to whom he sold a flat at the outskirts of the city. Since the customer was a senior citizen, he complained about the lack of transportation as he had to visit hospital on weekly basis.

2. Responding to the situation is the first rule of business. The real estate agent responded by arranging spontaneously a tie up with a rickshaw driver.

3. Finding the root cause is the second rule of business to prevent failure again. The agent further discussed the issue with the builder and they decided that a dedicated bus service would be provided based on frequency for school going children, office goers, shoppers and aged people based on need assessment from one time fund of the society that was being formed.

4. One incident is a bell weather, signaling you that all your customer relationships are at risk. For e.g. a stock broker was charging in Pune 1.25% as brokerage for sales of shares as compared to information that brokers in Mumbai were charging as low as 0.25%. One morning one customer walked in and announced that he had found a tie up with a broker in Mumbai at 0.5%.Yet the Pune broker did not pay attention and it was a matter of months that most of the customers quit who had been doing business for over a decade.

5. The employees need to be trained specifically to handle these complaints with the golden rule of Under promise and over deliver. Human resource strategies for closing Gap 3. Between service quality specifications and service delivery, is to hire the right employees from the beginning and train them to deliver service quality. Give them all the support systems and process to enable the customer get effectively what they want and then retain the best people, so that the customers' benefit the most.

The Technical Assistant-Research Programme (TARP) model of complaint handling

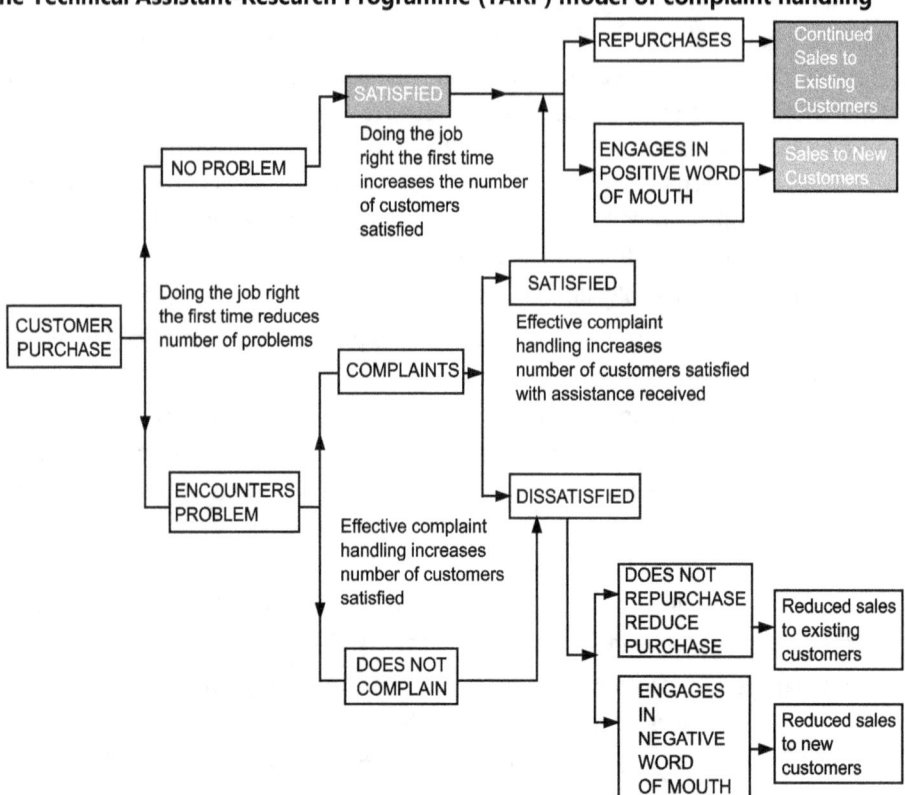

Fig. 11.5

(Adapted from Adamson, C., Complaint handling:benefits and best practise'.)

Recovery Service System

Keeping and developing relationship with existing customers is a key to business strategy. Yet problems and complaints occur during the life time of customer relationship.

Identifying Service Failures

The major barrier to effective service recovery is the firm learning about failure as less than ten percent of dissatisfied customers choose to complain following a service failure. Instead, most silently switch service providers or try to get even with the firm by making negative comments to others. Customers are reluctant to complain because they fear that it may result in lower service quality when the need for service arises again.

Setting Clearly defined Service Standards and communicate it by service guarantees. By promising free delivery if a customer does not receive a pizza in half an hour, Domino's makes it clear that the customer will get the pizza free.

A restaurant after determining that customers want lunch service within ten minutes, even placed alarm clocks on tables, so that customers are fully aware of its compliance to standards. Customers who wait for a table more than ten minutes beyond the reservation time are offered free drinks.

Service standards can enable recovery to take place without the customer having to lodge a complaint.

Communicating the importance of service recovery to the employees is by making them responsible for service failures and accountable for resolving the problems.

1. Employees are important listening posts for discovering customer concerns and facilitating recovery.

2. Communicating the importance of service recovery companies even use physical symbols to communicate the importance of service recovery.

Hotel Oberoi has the policy that 'do everything you possibly can to never lose a guest'. By communicating the value of service recovery in a firm, the firm creates an atmosphere conducive to identifying failures and achieving effective recovery.

Make Customers' Complain: Many firms tell customers how to lodge a complaint and what to expect from the process by using technological support. The use of toll-free telephone, call centres to handle customer contacts, including complaints, is a growing trend. The call centers offer several advantages over written complaints in providing customers with convenient, low-cost access which helps in service recovery. Oral communication is better suited to conveying compassion and empathy to irate customers than written communication, has been established by research. In addition, customers may feel more comfortable complaining over the phone than face-to-face. Call centres are widely used where there is a small or minor tangible component to the service like cellular operators and when customers are present and have the option of complaining directly to a service provider. The complaints are quickly diagnosed and problems solved, enhancing customer perceptions of responsiveness and lowering the cost of complaint.

Some firms are now using Internet web sites to facilitate service recovery with Cisco's policy – 'You don't have to touch customers personally to make them feel good about your service. The standard queries are answered a key word search of questions and answers for customers. Any new problems are added instantaneously to the database after solution has been found. The troubleshooting engine that takes the users through problem identification and resolution process solves complex problems. The firm's online service-recovery programme has resulted in higher customer satisfaction score with enhanced loyalty and profitability.

Resolving Customer Problems

Researchers have found that most complaints are lodged when customers experience what they perceive to be a serious problem and when voiced, they expect complaints to be attended to promptly and with fairness. Customers form perceptions of fairness by assessing three aspects of service recovery: Procedural, treatment during interaction and outcome.

Procedural fairness refers to the policies, rules, and timeliness of the complaint process. Treatment during interaction is the interpersonal treatment received during the complaint process. Outcome fairness deals with the results, customers receive from complaints.

Being Fair with Customers: Critical need for firms to devote far more attention to service recovery especially where customers believed that they had been treated unfairly and overall were dissatisfied with the way their complaint was handled.

Providing Fair Outcomes: When services fail to deliver the promise, customers expect compensation. The types of compensation are refunds, credits, correction of charges, repairs, and replacements, either alone or in combination. Apologies contribute to customers' compensation for being inconvenienced or treated rudely. Most customers surveyed, judged the outcomes they received to be unfair. The driving force behind unfair assessments was the failure of the firms to compensate adequately for the harm done or to recognise the costs incurred by customers in getting their complaint resolved. The most negative reactions were in response to complaints that were never resolved. Hence, firms need to understand the outcomes better that customers expect from a service failure and to give compensation packages that acknowledge costs of the failure to the customer as per their expectations.

Providing Fair Process: Fair procedures begin with the firm assuming responsibility for the failure and the complaint must be handled quickly by the first person who is contacted taking the responsibility. A flexible system to customise is to take into account and obtain input from the customer on what the final outcome should be. Surveys reveal that less than half the customers found the recovery procedures they experienced to be fair and even when the procedures were rated as fair, it was mostly because process was clear to the customer and the problem, was dealt with quickly and hassle free.

Process customers' who judged procedures to be unfair were those who were frustrated by a prolonged inconvenient process that required them to repeat their complaint to several firm representatives who seemed unconcerned about the situation.

Providing Fair Interactions: Fair interpersonal behaviour involves dealing with politeness, concern, honesty; providing and explanation for the failure; and making a genuine effort to resolve the problem showing utmost care.

Customers often enter the complaint process in an angry mood; so considerable skill is required to defuse the anger and address the problem. Moreover, employees often lack the empowerment to take care of the problem. The situation is frustrating for both, but more so for the customer who expects immediate action.

Research show that the fairness dimensions strongly affect customers' evaluations of service recovery, together contributing to eighty five percent of the variation in satisfaction with complaint handling.

Strategies for Successful Recovery:

The four practices that dramatically improve service recovery effectiveness are hiring, training and empowerment, establishing service recovery guidelines and standards, providing effective responses system determining.

Hiring, Training and Empowerment: Research indicates that successful service recovery is highly influenced by the effectiveness of the front-line employee who receives the complaint. This is not surprising since 80 percent of the complaints were initiated with front-line workers. Hence the design of a recovery system must focus on the initial contact and on developing policies that enable employees to resolve the complaint efficiently.

Developing hiring criteria and training programmes that take into account employees' service-recovery role directly affects customers' fairness evaluations.

KSB Pumps includes recovery skills in the training of employees at its Customer Training Centre, where the primary responsibility is service recovery. Among the training topics covered are company policies, warranties, pricing, delivery schedule, listening skills, defusing anger, and interpersonal skills.

Providing employees with the empowerment to service failures strongly affects all three fairness dimensions.

1. Employees' attitudes improve and their efforts increase when they are given the power to resolve problems.
2. The speed and convenience of the process are enhanced when employees can act immediately rather than having to seek out a manager or another department to respond to the problem.
3. Outcome fairness improves if employees have the flexibility to provide the empowerment complements the use of service guarantees.

While empowerment contributes to service recovery in several ways, if used inappropriately it can lead to problems. Companies can overcome the difficulties by setting boundaries.

2. Establishing Guidelines and Standards

Developing guidelines for service recovery that focus on achieving fairness and customer satisfaction represent a direct approach to improving performance. The 'AAA' action plan for service recovery which scores highly on all three fairness dimensions.

1. Acknowledge mistakes when they occur without placing blame or making excuses sincerely.
2. Apologise for the mistake, even if you are not at fault.
3. Make amends for the mistake by taking corrective action, and following up to ensure the problem has been resolved.

Effective Responses System

In addition to removing barriers to the customers decision to complain, call centres contribute to all three fairness dimensions. They operate twenty four hours a day, 365 days a year and the timely customer and product information at the GE call centre make for convenient access and fast resolution, enhancing procedural fairness. GE follows up with a letter of apology to all callers, which contributes to procedural outcome and treatment during interaction fairness. Customers receive a goodwill certificate, free home repair, and/or compensation for food spoilage, depending on the nature of the failure. These gestures further contribute to customer perceptions of fairness outcomes.

Data Mining

Using databases in conjunction with call centres and websites helps firms achieve fairness goals. The firm uses customer-knowledge databases as the key source for immediate problem solving. The databases capture historic trends of clients and complaints. This is analysed and they develop appropriate treatment protocols and plans; a win-win outcome for its customers and firm.

KSB Pumps limited maintains databases on customer purchases and service incidents that help guide recovery decisions. Customers become particularly upset when products fail just a few days after a warranty expires. So it should include warranty information in the customer database that the service staff can adjust compensation accordingly to waiver of the cost of the repair call or only material cost.

Classifying Service Failures

The practical guideline on service recovery is to do whatever is necessary to take care of guests and build measure and follow up on how to handle it better next time. Most firms fail to document and categorise complaints adequately, making learning difficult. There are four explanations for this failure.

(a) Employees showed little interest in listening to the customer to get to the core problem. They treated the complaint as an isolated case needing a solution but not requiring a report to management.

(b) Many employees waste their energies by avoiding responsibility for the problem and instead blame the customer for the failure.

(c) Numerous complaints were never resolved and telephonic messages, complaints to more than one employee and written letters resulted in no action.

(d) In the firms' there was no integrated system to collect, collate, distribute, make individuals accountable and responsible who take ownership and monitor to ensure that complaints had been handled satisfactorily. Data mining is to categorise customers who complain with the nature and frequency of complaints and resolution of complaints in norms of the firm.

1. Having complaint forms which are internal documents used to record service failures by employees and not customers including documentation of service guarantees have been invoked. The purpose of the complaint form is to facilitate firms' learning and ensure that the complaint is brought to a fair conclusion by having a team for handling complaints. This team will ensure that any deviation to the norm is discussed and the process is modified to ensure that issue is not repeated. The customer is called up to ensure that they are happy with the service and have no issues or feelings with them due to the problem. The financial implications are compiled, discussed and suitable strategy is drawn.

2. Customers often lodge complaints with the first employee they can find. Hence, firms have to ensure that complaints delivered in this way are communicated back into the system by the employee. Hence the firm must involve front-line employees in the management of quality and customer satisfaction and reward them rather than punish them for reporting the complaint. Thus an empowerment culture has to be instilled in the firm.

3. Classify the customer who has complained as it has two benefits.

    An effective service recovery effort can generate high levels of satisfaction and enhanced business from customer. Also a customer who complains frequently or is never satisfied with recovery efforts maybe the wrong customer. These customers may be seeking benefits beyond the firms' terms and may require more resources to serve which may result into loss. Hence to manage this problem, maintain a database of customers who have invoked its guarantee and map the customer who has violated their trust and politely the next time give the option that currently there is no capacity.

Effective System Service

(a) Customers log in complaints only about problems that they find important to them but do not report when a service fails. So firms wishing to improve service quality need to compile this information. The data compilation must be relevant, credible and timely information must be disseminated to everyone involved in decisions on investments in service quality.

(b) Service Quality Information System by Berry and Parasuraman is a comprehensive approach to service improvement planning and resource allocation. The system inputs compiled are from multiple sources like customer, employee, mystery shopping, focus groups, competitor survey, and service performance data from operations. Information from call centres and customer databases is also valuable. GE monitors the lifetime performance of every appliance sold as well as the quality of every customer interaction. The company integrates the data collected into its product and service design decisions. Mediclaim agents retrieve data of policy lapse and call on the customer to determine the cause of non renewal. This is an excellent way to assess the situation and also to win the customer back to ensure business sustenance.

Online data availability of the data compiled by software is made available to those responsible for implementing service improvements. KSB Pumps via e-mail distributes complaint information gathered at its customer service centre directly to the dealerships responsible for setting the dispute and simultaneously conveys the same information to engineering and marketing department, which integrate the complaint data with additional research information to make changes if required. Firms which have to determine investment priorities in service improvement must rank the impact of various options like increasing the speed of customer care with expanding authorised service centers on customer satisfaction, repurchase intention, process cost, and market share. The goal is to identify those process improvements that will have the greatest impact on profitability. Investment decisions should also be driven by customer profitability assessments.

Enhances Profit

The relationship between service recovery and firm profitability can be clearly seen from the service-profit chain. The profit chain concept argues that profit results from customer satisfaction with the service system, customer satisfaction is generated by satisfied, loyal and productive employees. The impact of service recovery can be traced through improvements in the service system and through the direct effect on satisfaction of resolving a customer complaint. Resolving problems effectively and efficiently has a strong impact on customer satisfaction and loyalty

Customer scoring high on satisfaction measures tend to be both loyal and advocates for the firm. Since recovery is closely tied to satisfaction, the revenue and profitability impact of service recovery can be dramatic. Data analysis on the ROI in complaint-handling units like retailing, banking, and automotive service indicate that service- recovery investments provide substantial returns, ranging from 25 percent to 100 percent.

Most negative reactions to poor recovery are expressed by customers previously loyal to the company. Loyal customers expect problems to be dealt with effectively and were disappointed when they were not, making service recovery key to maintaining the loyalty of these customers satisfaction. Sustaining satisfaction over many encounters builds credibility with customers, strengthening loyalty and profitability increases.

Another important profitability question for companies to consider is how service recovery, affects the employees involved. In examining the customer descriptions of service recovery, we found two interesting themes related to employees. First, customers who found the service recovery, handled fairly, commented that the employee was concerned about the problem eager to help, and happy that the complaint was resolved to the customer's satisfaction. Second, when customers indicated that they found the complaint handled unfairly, employees were frequently observed to be rude and defensive, indifferent to providing assistance, and increasingly angry as the dispute progressed. These findings suggest that individual service-recovery incidents affect the satisfaction of not only the customer but also the employees involved. Our research further suggests that employees faced with a large number of complaints to handle and no effective way to deal with them are likely to be very dissatisfied. Therefore, developing effective recovery programs and improving the service system should enhance service quality and increase employee satisfaction and loyalty, contributing to customer value and ultimately to improved profitability.

Customer loyalty which pushes up profitability in service industries has led firms to shift this focus away from aggressive strategies aimed at seeking new customers towards defensive strategies aimed at satisfying and keeping current customers in their fold. Service recovery is the backbone of customer satisfaction strategy. In the lifetime of customer relationships, conflicts are bound to occur but managing conflicts effectively is vital in maintaining customer loyalty and trust. Hence firms need to develop a comprehensive service recovery system that encourages dissatisfied customers to voice their complaints and that provides a fair process and outcome which is monitored and on line for easy retrieval.

Consequences of complaints

People complain because the service they have received is below their zone of tolerance. There are many reasons for this. In hospitals, complaints that are registered by disgruntled customers include unclean rooms, not operational climate controls, inadequate housekeeping and lack of prompt attendance by the nurse. If these complaints are not resolved to the satisfaction of the patient, there can be serious consequences. In particular, the individual is likely to tell others and this is likely to result in falling business for the hospital, it has been observed that customers who have had problems that have been satisfactorily resolved, quickly tend to be loyal customers. Moreover, five out of six people who complain will continue business with the firm even if the problem is not resolved to their satisfaction. To handle efficiently and effectively the complaints of individual customers collect, aggregate and analyse complaint data to pinpoint and correct the root causes of customer problems and correct it.

A disappointed customer does not simply go-away. It has been found that the impact of word of mouth on a customer's repurchase decision is twice as important as corporate advertising and a customer unhappy will do enough damage to the firm.

Find what unhappy customers want:

1. Customers want what they were promised.
2. Customers want personal attention.
3. Customers want an apology in case of service failure with humility.
4. Customers want they should not be made to feel that they are the cause of the problem though in many cases they are responsible for creating the problem.

For service recovery what we need is to make a planned service recovery an effective practice for more business.

Handling dissatisfied customers

Service firms need to establish a consistently evolve process to ensure effective handling of dissatisfied customers. The process must meet customer expectations.

(a) **Apologise:** Apologise for the inconvenience the customer is experiencing. Apology rendered in first person is a powerful tool as against verbal acknowledgement given on behalf of the firm.

(b) **Listen:** A good listener allows customers to vent their feelings, frustration, anger and yet show concern by believing the customers and reporting the incident or error in the system.

(c) **Give a quick solution:** Customers want the error to be corrected and expect service provider to be skilled and empowered to set it right. Offer a logical explanation and demonstrate sensitivity and concern which the customer will approach. A value added atonement will keep the customer with you. Follow up and ensure that implemented service recovery was satisfactory.

(d) **Keep Your Promises:** Customers should not be misled and given the actual picture about the extent and time frame for resolving the problem.

The internal systems must be stringent and monitored online. Service employees should be able to communicate inside their firms to ensure that the solutions they have started are actually executed to perfection.

The Customer ISN'T Always Right !

Given the many benefits of long-term customer relationships, it would seem that a firm would not want to refuse or terminate a relationship with any customer. The assumption that all customers are good customers is also very compatible with the belief that the customer is always right; an almost a golden rule of business. Yet any service provider knows that this statement isn't true, and in some cases it may be preferable for the firm and the customer to discontinue their relationship. A firm cannot target its services to all customers; some segments will be more appropriate than others. It would not be beneficial either for the firm or the customer to establish a relationship with a customer whose needs the company cannot meet. A business school offering a one day programme for MBA would not encourage a full-time working person to apply for its programme, knowing fully well that the student's needs will not be met.

11.9 Service Quality

The intangibility of many services means that it can be very difficult for service quality to be measured and assessed. Inseparability of the service itself from the service provider highlights the role of people in the service transactions, and their influence on quality levels. The heterogeneous nature of service means that a service is never exactly repeated and will always be variable to some extent. The perishable nature of services can lead to customer dissatisfaction if demand cannot be met, for example if a hotel room or air ticket is not available when customer demands.

11.9.1 Perspectives of Service Quality

The word 'quality' means different things to people. Quality in service is quite an illusive concept and thus measuring it is a challenging task. Quality in services is basically a customer – oriented phenomenon. The dimension deals with the image of the manufacturer of the product or the provide of the service. In products or services bought mainly on the trust in the brand name or the company name, this is a very important dimension. Baby products fall into this category and hence even in the advertisement of these type of products trust of generations of users is highlighted.

David Garvin identifies five perspectives on quality, they are:

1. **Transcend Approach:** The transcendent view of quality is synonymous with innate excellence is a mark of uncompromising standards and high achievement for example, Rolls Royce car, Rolex watch. This viewpoint is often applied to the performing and visual art. It argues that people learn to recognise quality only through the experience gained from repeated exposure. From a practical standpoint, however suggesting that managers or customer will know quality when they see it is not very helpful. This approach inherits a danger that it confuses quality with grade. Customer usually confuse quality with grade as whenever one speaks of high quality products, he/she often mean high grade or even perhaps, just expensive. Customers usually presume expensive products means high quality or high grade. The grade and quality of a service or product are quite different. Grade refers to product standards and is reflected in the specifications of the product and quality refers to the extent to which a product or service is and does what it claims to be and do. One can have products or services of a lower grade that meet the standards laid down.

2. **The Product-based approach:** It sees quality as a precise and measurable variable. Differences in quality, it argues, reflect differences in the amount of an ingredient or

attribute possessed by the product. Quality reflects the quantity of ingredients or attributes a product or service contains. As attributes are considered costly to produce, the higher quality goods will be more expensive. Because this view is totally objective, it fails to account for differences in the tastes, needs and preferences of individual customers or even entire market segments. For example, a service delivered with proactive peripherals will be expensive. A watch designed to run without the need for servicing for life time with a guarantee to give time correct to within five seconds will be expensive.

3. **User-based approach:** This definition starts with the premise that quality lies in the eyes of the beholder. According to this approach the goods that best satisfy customer preferences are believed to be of high quality. These definitions equate quality with maximum satisfaction. This subjective, demand-oriented perspective recognises that different customer have different wants and needs. For example, a consumer may enjoy a particular brand because of its unusual taste or features yet may still regard some other brand as being of higher quality.

4. **The manufacturing-based approach:** It is supply based and is concerned primarily with engineering and manufacturing practices. Quality is operations driven in case of services. It focuses on conformance to internally developed specifications, which are often driven by productivity and cost-containment goals.

5. **The Value-based approach:** This defines quality in terms of value and price. By considering the trade-off between performance and price, quality comes to be defined as "affordable excellence". A customer may buy a product with lower specifications if the price is low.

Garvin suggests that these alternatives views of quality help to explain the conflicts that sometimes arise between managers in different functional departments.

Dimensions of Service Quality

So far organisational dimensions and general approach to quality has been emphasised. However, to develop, design, produce and deliver a product or service one must look into the dimensions of quality. Garvin proposed eight dimensions of quality for products. These dimensions might be useful as a framework for analysis and strategic planning for product quality.

1. **Performance:** On the core products primary operating characteristics. For example, sound and picture clarity in a television, handling, comfort, acceleration in a car and cleaning and shining abilities of a detergent. Performance differences are not necessarily due to quality differences. For example 200 watt and 100 watt bulbs will perform differently as they belong to two different performance classes.

2. **Features:** Secondary characteristics augment the basic functions (e.g., supplementary service elements or surround/ peripheral services leading to pro-activity. for example, remote facility in a TV).

3. **Reliability:** Probability of product breaking down and this applies to consumer durables in particular, such as, refrigerators, washing machines and to industrial machinery, such as, lathe machines, printing press.

4. **Conformance:** The degree to which a products design and operating characteristics match pre-established standards. For example, ISI mark or ISO mark on products certifies conformance to standards.

5. **Durability:** How much use does one get from a product before it breaks down and has to be either repaired or replaced? How long a product continue to be useful?

6. **Serviceability:** The speed and competence of repair and courtesy received.

7. **Aesthetics:** How the product looks, feels, sounds, tastes, smells? Appeal of a product to five senses.

8. **Perceived:** Image, reputation, brand name etc. Consumers do not always possess complete information about the attributes of the product or even understand the information that they do have. They use indirect measure like image, reputation, brand name etc., when comparing products.

11.9.2 Determinants of Services Quality

In services, it is the consumer who defines quality. Therefore, human side of service is key to deliver quality. No doubt many of the determinants for quality of products can be applied to the service but the human side of service is missing to a considerable extent in case of services. Parasuram A, Zeithaml V. A and Berry L.L, a group of researchers in marketing proposed quality dimensions of their own. Originally their study consisted of ten dimensions which are given below in the following table 11.2.

Table 11.2: Determinants of Service Quality

Determinant	Core Features	Examples
Reliability	Consistency of performance and dependendability, getting it right first time keeping promises	• Airlines ensuring that the baggage arrives on same flight as passenger at same destination • Waiters bringing the ordered dishes to the right table • Opening the store at accurate time
Responsiveness	Willingness and readiness of employees to provide service Timeliness of service	• Responding to a customer enquiry • Transport operations keeping to timetable • Is the electrician willing to give me a specific time when he will show up to do the repair

contd. ...

Competence	Existence of required skills and knowledge especially in contact personnel	• Tourist information staff knowing exactly where places are located and best to arrive there.
Access	Ease of contact	• Hotel groups answering the telephone within 3 or 4 rings • Tourist information centres being located near flows of visitors and open seven days a week • Short waiting times
Courtesy	Respect and consideration, friendliness	• Visitor attraction staff helping families to enjoy their day without being over familiar
Communication	Informing customers in language they can understand, explanation of service offered	• Coach driver assuring passengers that the party will reach the ferry in good time
Credibility	Trustworthiness, believability and honesty	• Travel agent offering advice about long haul travel
Security	Freedom from danger, risk or doubt	• A hotel providing safes for expensive items
Understanding the customer	Making the effort to understand customer's needs	• Hotel reception staff making guess feel welcome on arrival
Tangibles	Physical evidence, facilities and appearance	• Entrance to a country park being designed to encourage exploration on foot rather than by car

Later on these ten dimensions were pooled into five dimensions as given below:

Reliability : Ability to perform the promised service dependably and a accurately.

Assurance : Knowledge and accuracy of employees and their ability to convey trust and confidence.

Tangibles : Appearance of physical facilities, equipments, personnel and communication materials (physical evidence of facilities).

Empathy : Caring, individualised attention the firm provides its customers.

Responsiveness : Willingness to help customer and provide prompt service.

In providing quality service, the above five dimensions of services warrant consideration. These dimensions are explained below:

1. Reliability: As already is the ability to perform the promised service dependably and a accurately, normally this may be turned as "No excuses" service delivery. Reliability means that:

- Organisation does what it is supposed to do
- It does it right
- It does it right the first time

2. Assurance: It relates to knowledge and accuracy of employees and their ability to convey trust and confidence. This inspires trust and confidence. This dimension is of great significance for services where a customer perceives high risk and is not sure of the outcome. The type of services where a customer perceives high risk includes legal services, medical services, brokerage and stock services. Most of the services are procured through a channel member who acts as a link between the service provider and the customer. The knowledge, genuineness, honesty and ability to perform the service by the link member or front office staff generate trust in the mind of the customer.

The service organisations empower their customer contact people and train them in skills to build trust and loyalty between employee and the customers. Many services organisations are assigning their staff to individual customers to build relationship by getting to know them personally and all service encounters are personally looked into by this assigned staff member.

3. Tangibles: They are appearance of physical facilities, equipments, personnel and communication materials. The customers evaluate the quality of services on above tangible features. The marketers of services emphasise on tangiblising the intangibles. The service organisations try to enhance their image, provide continuity and through tangibles signal quality to the customers. Most organisations combine tangibles and other dimensions to create a service quality strategy. For example, some hair dressers provide fast, efficient service, comfortable, clean, waiting area thus combining responsiveness and tangibility in service delivery.

4. Empathy: It is the ability to provide caring individualised attention the firm provides its customer. Empathy means treating the customers as individuals, i.e., it calls for customised services. For organisations, each customer is unique and they provide personalised services to their customers. To be empathetic, organisations make effort to know their customer fully and make the customers feel important to the organisations.

5. Responsiveness: It is willingness to help the customer and provide prompt service. The focus, under this quality determinant is our attentiveness and promptness in dealing with the customer queries i.e., requests, problems, complaints and questions of the customer. The customers relate responsiveness to length of time, they had to wait for assistance, queuing time, time taken to answer the queries and handling the problems. The successful service organisations set speed o service standards for service delivery from customer's point of view rather than organisation point of view. This quality determinant emphasises on the training of service provider to respond up to customers expectations.

These five dimensions of quality can be used in analysing and responding to the needs of all customers. For example, a hotel customer needs following basic things.

Clean rooms: They want clean, well laid down interiors to ensure hygiene and comfort. The toilet papers and room spray in the hotel shows the concern of the management about the cleanliness and hygiene.

Security: Customers want room to be safe and secure. When they go out for day's work or turn in for the evening they should not be concerned one some will break in. The hotel providing facility of lockers to keep the valuables in safe custody ensures security for their customers.

Treated like a guest: The customer should not be allowed to feel as if he is an intruder who has dropped by at the last minute.

Keeping promises: If the customer checks in at the informed time, he expects the room nicely made up and ready for check-in.

The table 11.3 shows how the four demands of the customers match up with five dimensions of service quality.

Table 11.3: Customer and Service Dimension Match

Expectations	Service Dimensions				
	Reliability	**Tangibles**	**Respon-siveness**	**Assurance**	**Empathy**
Clean room	Yes	Yes			
Security	Yes	Yes			
Treated like a guest			Yes	Yes	Yes
Keeping promises			Yes	Yes	Yes

Application of Service Quality Determinants

For the purpose of design and control of quality determinants consider the examples given in table 11.4. Some of these determinants are easily measurable than others. For example the reliability in terms of time is easily measurable compared to assurance. The challenge before the designers and quality engineers is one of developing specifications and standards that are understood and desired by the consumers. The marketers should be able to compare what consumer expects with what they perceive is delivered.

Table 11.4: How the Customers Apply Quality Determinant

Dimensions	Car Repair	Air Journey	Architectural Services	Information Processing
Reliability	Mean time failures, problem fixed right first time and delivered as promised	Keeping the flights to published schedules	Delivery of house plans as promised and within the budget	Availability of information when desired
Responsiveness	No waiting easy to access and willing less to respond requests	Prompt and speedy handling of ticketing, check in and baggage	Adapts to changes in plans and modifies budgets. Responds to queries/questions	No official hazards, quick response to requests for data, handling problems promptly
Assurance	Knowledge of the mechanics to rectify the fault/problem	Trusted name, competent and experienced staff. High performance levels	University degree, field experience, reputation and goodwill	Trained and experienced employees
Empathy	Accessibility and understanding of the customer problem and preferences called customer by name and knowing he history of the care	Understanding and anticipating problems and needs of the customers	Understanding clients and housing requirements adapting the requirements in housing plans	Understanding of functional departmental needs and needs of the individual, in the departments knowing individuals personally
Tangibles	Unified employees comfortable waiting area, good laid out work shop with modern equipment for repairs	Physical facilities like waiting lounges, check-in counters, baggage areas, uniformed employees and aircraft itself.	Office, office décor, construction reports, billing statements employee uniforms, drawing boards and computer facilities	Internal reports, data analysis statements, information processing equipments, informed employees.

11.10 Concept and Importance of Quality in Services

Service quality is a concept that has aroused considerable interest and debate in the research literature because of the difficulties in both defining and measuring it with no overall consensus emerging on either. Customer satisfaction and service quality are often treated together as functions of customer's perceptions and expectations and research has shown that high service quality contribute significantly to profitability. Service quality is required to be first measured in order to improve the quality in a service organisation. In services marketing, the single most researched area is service quality. In the service quality during the last decade the focus has been on quality, total quality management and customer satisfaction in business. PZB (Parasuram, Ziethaml and Berry) have pioneered research in service quality in marketing and a measurement instrument SERVQUAL was developed for assessing it.

The concept of quality is subjective and difficult to define. Certain aspects of quality can be identified. However, ultimately the judgement rests with the customer. Quality does not happen by accident, concrete plan is needed for the achievement of the quality. Today, quality no longer is the technical issue, it is the business issue and in order that the company programme to success, the top management must be involved and committed to its success. Quality has several dimensions and it is a continuous process and there are costs associated with poor quality.

Service Quality

As per Lewis and Booms, 'Service Quality is a measure of how well the service level delivered matches comer expectations. Delivering service quality means conforming to customer expectations on a consistent basis'.

David Collier has defined service quality as: 'Excellent service quality is consistently meeting or exceeding customer expectations and service delivery system performance criteria during all service encounters. Excellent service quality is achieved by the consistent delivery to the customer of a clearly defined consumer and/or employee benefit package, and the process and service encounters which are set for many Internal and external standards of performance!

Service quality is where ten dimensions are taken care of:

1. Excellent means of achieving performance standards 100% of the time.
2. Customer is the individual/department/firm that receives, pays for, uses or experiences the output of the service delivery system.
3. Service is any primary or peripheral activity that does not directly produce a physical product and it is the transaction between customer and seller without any goods.

4. A consumer or employee benefit package is a defined set of tangible and intangible attributes which the customer or employee recognise, pay for, use or experience.

5. Quality is the distinctive tangible/intangible properties of a consumer benefit package that is perceived by the customer as better than a competitor's package.

6. Consistent means conforming to standards of performance every time.

7. Delivery means getting the right consumer benefit package through process quality to the customer at the right time and at the right place.

8. Internal standards of performance focus on internal operations and numerical measurement is possible.

9. External standards of performance focus on external operations and the marketing criteria that the customer expects and perceives while experiencing the consumer benefit package. Here, the measurement is judgmental based on human perception.

10. Service Encounter is one or more moments of truth. A moment of truth is an episode in which a customer comes into contact with any aspect of the firm, however remote, and thereby has an opportunity to form an impression.

Customer Perceptions

In the perceived service box in the gaps model, perceptions are considered relative to expectations. Expectations are dynamic so evaluations may also shift overtime or vary from person to person and even from culture to culture. Hence quality service which may satisfy customers today may not be the same tomorrow. Quality and satisfaction is based on customer perception of service and not by some predetermined objective criteria of what service is or should be. Customers perceive services in terms of the quality of the service and how satisfied they are overall with their experiences. Firms pan compete more effectively by distinguishing themselves with respect to service quality and enhanced customer satisfaction.

In the case of pure services, service quality will be the dominant element in customers' evaluations. In cases where customer service or services are offered in combination with a physical product, service quality may also be very critical in determining customer satisfaction. Studies across the globe have highlighted these relationships.

It is very important to understand the role of process and its impact on the technical outcome quality. Customer judge the quality of services on their perceptions of the technical outcome provided as well as how that outcome was delivered in reality. In case of a plumber, client will judge the quality of the outcome by how the tap leakage was resolved and also the quality of the process. Process quality would include plumber's timeliness, responsiveness in returning the call, empathy for the client as the customer mentioned that it was the incoming tap to the bungalow that was leaking profusely and he was without water for the last eight hours, as well as courtesy and listening skills. If the service has a specific outcome like in case of the repairs, the customer can judge the effectiveness of the service on the basis of that outcome. However, many services offered by professionals such as teachers, engineers, accountants, and doctors are highly complex, and a clear outcome is not always possible. In these situations, the technical quality of the service competence of the service provider or effectiveness of the outcome is not easy for the customer to judge.

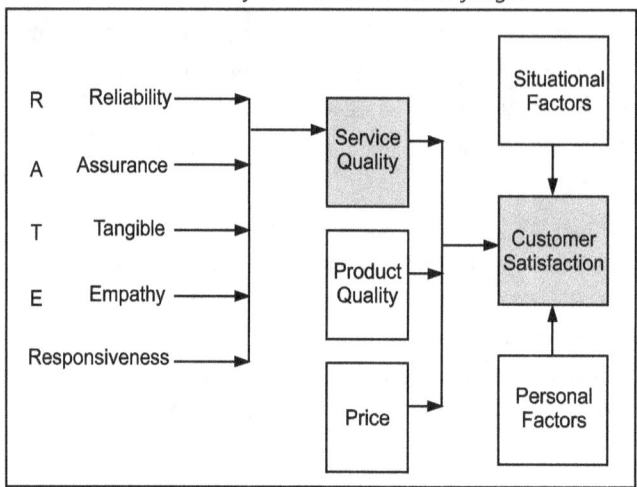

Fig. 11.6

In case of professors, in management institutions, the students are there to learn what they do not know. Even without knowing the subject they are studying, they make judgments about their professors only after the first few lectures. The tangibles that accompany the service like presentation slides, the smile or grim look, the degree of confidence communicated verbally and through body language, the content coverage and ability to answer queries of the students are used to rate the professor. Therefore, the professor can alter some of the students' impressions by making an impact on these cues.

The existence of both process and outcome quality can explain why a pediatrician with excellent skills and certification can fail to compete effectively with another pediatrician like Dr. Anand Pandit who can deliver superior interpersonal quality like ability to empathise, listen, maintain timely appointments and courtesy.

When customers cannot accurately evaluate the technical quality of a service, they form impressions of the service including its technical quality from situational and personal factors, using their own cues, that may not be apparent to the provider.

Service Quality Dimensions

Customers perceive quality as a multi-dimensional concept as they have many factors in their perception. The factors could be performance, features, reliability, conformance, durability, serviceability, aesthetics, prestige, functionality, ease of use etc. based on application.

In the case of pure services, service quality will be the dominant element in customers' evaluations. In cases where customer service or services are offered in combination with a physical product, service quality may also be very critical in determining customer satisfaction. Studies across the globe have highlighted these relationships.

Consumers have five dimensions in their assessments of service quality,

1. **Reliability:** Ability to perform the promised service dependably and accurately.
2. **Assurance:** Employees' knowledge and courtesy and their ability to inspire trust and confidence.
3. **Tangibles:** Appearance of services capes like physical facilities, equipment, personnel and written materials.
4. **Empathy:** Caring, individualised attention given to customers.
5. **Responsiveness:** Willingness to help customers and provide prompt service.

1. Reliability:

It is one of the most important determinant of perceptions of service quality among customers. Reliability is the ability to perform the promised service dependably repeatedly and accurately. In a broad sense, reliability means that the company delivers on its promises which could be related to pricing, delivery, billing accuracy, warranty, service provision and timely problem resolution. Customers want to do business with companies that keep their promises, particularly their promises about the core service attributes.

All firms need to be aware of customer expectations of reliability. Firms that do not provide the core service that customers think they are buying fail their customers and they will have high dissatisfaction.

Federal Express effectively communicates and delivers on the reliability dimension. The reliability message of FedEx for service is: 'Absolutely, positively has to get there.'

1. The firm will perform the service right the first time itself.
2. Error free records of utility bills.
3. The firm will provide service at the right time.
4. Promises to do a thing by a specified time it complies to it.
5. Customer complaints or problems the firm shows immediate concern in solving it. e.g. Opening the consultants office on time.

2. Assurance:

1. Requisite skills and knowledge in contact personnel. Software engineers having requisite skills to develop the software.
2. Employees are friendly and courteous, e.g. A warm welcome with a soothing drink by hotel during check in.

3. The behaviour of the employee will impress the customers about the reliability of service and instill confidence. e.g. A newspaper boy gives you a wake up call at 6 am everyday.

4. Customers feel safe and confident when transacting with the employees e.g. A facility to lock your valuables in a hotel.

3. Tangibles:

1. More modern equipment in operating condition.

2. Physical facilities visually appealing.

3. Brouchers, letterheads, tools and material must be visually attractive matching with the firm's image.

4. Employees neatness and dress sense must match with the natural setting.

4. Empathy:

1. Pay attention to each customer individually.

2. Call centres responding within three rings.

3. Extended hours of service to cater to customer's requirement.

4. The firm will have customer's interest first.

5. The firm will understand specific needs of each customer. The attendant of the train informing that you will reach port in time, while welcoming the customer at the airport understanding any additional requirement during stay at the hotel.

5. Responsiveness:

1. Employees will attend to customers first.

2. Employees will tell exact time of service delivery.

3. Employees will always be willing to help customers.

4. Employees will give prompt service to customers.

11.11 Service Quality Models

Servqual

A consumer's perception of quality levels has long been a focus for marketing literature research. For example, the consumer's judgement concerning an entity's overall level of excellence or superiority has been used as a measurement of perceived quality. Objective measures of quality, measured by elements such as the "conformance to requirements" or "freedom from deficiencies" have been defined as the basis for quality assessment. However, these objective measures are difficult to translate into methods for assessing service (as opposed to product) quality. This difficulty led to the development of ServQual, intended to assess user perceptions of quality in a service environment.

To measure customer satisfaction with different aspect of service quality, Valarie Zeithaml and her colleagues developed a survey research instrument called SERVQUAL. It is base on the premise that customers can evaluate a firm's service quality by comparing their perceptions of its service with their own expectations. SERVQUAL is seen as a generic measurement tool that can be applied across a broad spectrum of service industries.

SERVQUAL was originally measured on 10 aspects of service quality: reliability, responsiveness, competence, access, courtesy, communication, credibility, security, understanding or knowing the customer and tangibles. It measures the gap between customer expectations and experience.

By the early nineties the authors had refined the model to the useful acronym RATER:
- Reliability
- Assurance
- Tangibles
- Empathy, and
- Responsiveness

SERVQUAL has its detractors and is considered overly complex, subjective and statistically unreliable. The simplified RATER model however is a simple and useful model for qualitatively exploring and assessing customers' service experiences and has been used widely by service delivery organisations. It is an efficient model in helping an organisation shape up their efforts in bridging the gap between perceived and expected service.

The SERVQUAL for typical service having 22 items is given in the table 11.5.

Table 11.5

Dimension	Question
Reliability	1. When XYZ company promise to do something by a certain time, the promise is always kept. 2. When customers complain or have problems, XYZ company will show great concern or solving them 3. XYZ company will perform the service right the first time 4. XYZ company will provide the services at the time agreed on. 5. XYZ company will assist on error free records (The recorders of XYZ company will never be incorrect).
Assurance	6. The behaviour of employee of XYZ company will impress customers will reliability of service and instill confidence 7. Customers will feel safe and confident when transacting with employees of XYZ company 8. Employees of XYZ company will always be friendly and courteous 9. Employees of XYZ company possess knowledge to answer question of customers

contd. ...

Tangibles	10. XYZ company will have modern looking equipment.
	11. The physical facilities at XYZ company will be visually appealing
	12. Employees of XYZ company will be dressed and neat appearing
	13. Materials and tools associated with the service will be visually appealing
Empathy	14. XYZ company will pay attention to each customer individually.
	15. XYZ company will have opening hours convenient to all their customers.
	16. XYZ company will have employees who give personal attention to each customer.
	17. XYZ company will have customers best interest at heart.
	18. The employees of XYZ company will understand the specific needs of their customers.
Responsiveness	19. Employees of XYZ company will tell customers exact time of service delivery
	20. Employees of XYZ company will give prompt service to customers
	21. Employees of XYZ company will always be willing to help customer
	22. Employees of XYZ company will never be busy to help customers immediately

According to PZB, the instrument has been designed to be applicable across a broad spectrum of services. As such it provides a basic skeleton through its expectations/ perceptions format encompassing statements for each of the five service quality dimensions. The skeleton, where necessary, can be adapted or supplemented to fit the characteristics or specific research needs of a particular organisation. SERVQUAL is most valuable when it is used periodically to track service quality trends.

Appropriate SERVQUAL can be used for variety of purposes like:

- Determine the average gap score between customers perceptions and expectations for the each service attribute.
- Assess the organisation's service quality along each of the five dimensions of SERVQUAL.
- Compute organisation's overall weighted SERVQUAL score, which not only accounts for service quality gap for each dimensions individually but also the relative importance of the dimension.
- Track customer's expectations and perceptions (an individual service attribute and /or on the SERVQUAL dimensions) over time.
- Compare organisations SERVQUAL score against those of the competitors.

- Identify and examine customer segments that significantly differ in their assessments of company's service performance.
- Assess internal service quality (i.e., the quality of service rendered by one department or division of a company to others within same company)

Several comments regarding SERVQUAL have been received from time to time. There have been arguments and counter arguments about the realistic application of the criteria to measure the service quality. Based on the criticism and comments the instrument has been refined.

Although SERVQUAL has been widely used by service companies, doubts have been expressed with regard to both its conceptual foundation and methodology limitations. To evaluate the stability of the five underlying dimensions when applied a variety of different service industries, Mela, Boshoff and Nel analysed data sets from banks, insurance brokers, vehicle repair shops, electrical repair shops and life insurance firms.

The findings suggest that in reality SERVQUAL differences scores measure only two factors: intrinsic service quality and extrinsic service quality. In another study Lam and Woo found that the SERVQUAL was not stable over time, as revealed by insignificant correlations between test scores and retest scores. Although scores on items in the expectations battery remained fairly stable over time the performance items were subject to instability even in a one-week test-retest interval.

Showing Customer Feedback Survey from 'GO High' Airways

Your opinion on Today's 'Go High' Flight

Name (Surname first): Mr./Mrs./Ms.: _____

Your flight

Flight Number _____ from _____ to _____

Date _____ Seat No._____Class of Travel: Premiere/Economy

		Excellent	Good	Average	Poor
Frequent Flyer Programme	Are you a member of our "Frequent Flyer" programme? If yes, how do you rate the programme				
Accessi-bility	**Accessibility of our telephone numbers**				
	Reservations				
	Inquiry				
	Airport				
	Tele Check-in				
	Staff efficiency				
	Staff courtesy				

contd. ...

Airport Services	Check-in procedures				
	Ease in finding the check-in counter for this fight				
	Time taken to queue to reach the counter				
	Grooming of the ground staff				
	Staff efficiency				
	Personal attention at check-in counter				
	Boarding procedures				
	Boarding announcements and procedures				
	If your flight was delayed, how well was it handled				
	Your overall satisfaction with out airport staff and services				
	Time taken for baggage screening				
Inflight	Service				
	Friendly welcome/greeting at the time of boarding				
	Help during embarkation phase (guidance, hand luggage & stowage)				
	Courteous and professional service				
	Grooming of the cabin crew				
	Cabin crew announcements: clarity/content				
	Your overall satisfaction with out in-flight service				
	Reading material				
	In flight magazine (jet wings)				
	Selection of newspaper/magazines				
	Cockpit crew				
	Announcements: Clarity/content				
	Temperature in the cabin				
	Cleanliness of the cabin				
	Cleanliness of the washroom				
Food	Type of meal enjoyed on the flight				
	Quality (taste) of the meal				
	Quantity of the meal				
	Presentation (eye appeal) of the meal				
	Appropriateness of the menu for the time of day				
	Your overall satisfaction with your meal				
	Did you receive the type of meal you requested for at the time of making your reservation				

Gap Model of Service Quality

The model is used to understand service quality which can be used for developing marketing strategy for services. Managing the perceived quality of a service means that one has to match the expected service and the perceived service to each other so that consumer satisfaction is achieved. To keep the gap between expected and perceived service minimal, two things are critical. First, the promises about the how the service will perform given by traditional marketing activities and communicated by word-of-mouth, must not be unrealistic when compared to the service the customer will eventually perceive. Secondly, managers have to understand how the technical and the functional quality of a service is influenced and how the customers perceive these quality dimensions. In order to develop greater understanding of the nature of servie quality and how it is achieved in an organisation a Gap model of service quality is developed.

In 1985, Parasuram, Ziethaml and Berry developed the model of service quality. Their model claims that the consumer evaluates service quality experience as the outcome of the gap between expected and perceived quality. The model emphasizes on the key requirements for a service provider delivering the expected service quality refer Fig. 11.7 It is also called PZB model.

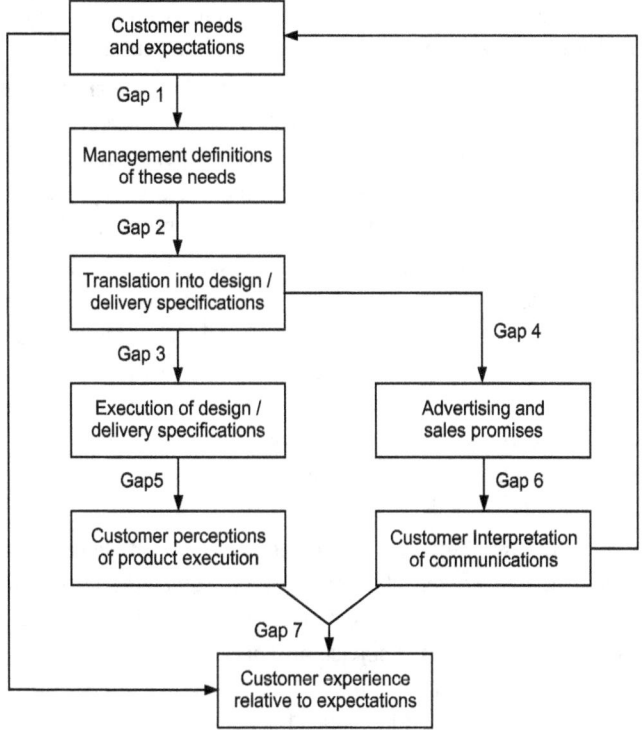

Fig. 11.7: Gap Model of Service Quality

The model identifies five gaps that can cause unsuccessful service delivery. By learning the flow of this model, it is possible to exercise greater management control over the consumer relationships. The study of this model should lead to an improved realization of the key issues at which the service providers can influence the satisfaction of consumers. Consumer's quality perceptions are influenced by a series of five distinct gaps.

Gap 1: Lack of Understanding (Gap between consumer expectation and management perception) – This gap is the result of not knowing what consumers expect in a service. An extensive study by Nightangle (1983) confirms this disparity by revealing that what providers perceive as being important to consumers is often different from what consumers themselves actually expect. For example, management team at a hotel might decide that provision of a newspaper at the bedroom door is not required whereas guest values this addition. The marketers must have a logical approach to undertake research to find out customer expectations.

Gap 2: Lack of Development (Gap between management Perception and service quality specifications) – This is where managers are aware of customer expectations. The management might not simply be committed to implement what is necessary, either through ignorance, lack of vision, limited resources, or adaption of a strategy such as harvesting where management is not concerned with the long-term future. The management might not set quality standards or very clear ones or they may be clear but unrealistic.

Gap 3: Poor Delivery (Gap between service quality specifications and service delivery) – The management understands the levels of service desired by the customer and specifies an appropriate set of standards. However, service delivery may not be of appropriate quality owing to poor employee performance, possibly they are insufficiently trained. Indeed the employees play a pivotal role in determining the quality of service.

Gap 4: Unrealistic Expectations (Gap between service delivery and external communication) – A gap between customer expectations and service provision is sometimes exists simply because pre-purchase promotional material projects unrealistic levels of service which cannot in reality be delivered. This can also be a case with lapsed expectations. A hotel with a great reputation could be bought out by another company which has far weaker standards. Retention of past customers would be difficult in such circumstances. Marketers must pay close attention to ensure consistency between the quality image portrayed in promotional activity and the actual quality offered.

Gap 5: Service Gap (Gap between perceived service and delivered service) – This represents the difference in any given situation between expected and perceived quality. It is a combination of the one or more of the previous gaps and provides a clear indication of the degree to which service quality exists in service organisation. Lovelock a leading authority on services expanded Parasuram, Ziethaml and Berry model to include two more gaps and thus offering total of seven gaps as shown in table 11.6 below. He explained the seven gaps as under:

Table 11.6: Seven Gaps that may lead to Customer Disappointment

Gap 1:	Is not knowing what your customers need and expect. This is really inexcusable. A logical response is to undertake research to find out.
Gap 2:	Is not using knowledge of customer needs and expectations as basis for defining and specifying service quality standards. This is what is called 'father knows best' phenomenon. Even if the kids tell you what they want, you ignore it and prescribe what you think will be good for them.
Gap 3:	Results when execution fails to match the predefined standards. This is the conformance problem and often reflects poor internal communications and lack of quality controls.
Gap 4:	Comes from a failure on the part of advertising and sales people to portray the service accurately in their communications to customers, most commonly they overpromise. The problem could result from being poorly briefed about the service or from a tendency to exaggerate performance in order to capture customer interest. Excessive claims are just asking for trouble, since they raise customer's expectations to heights that cannot be possibly met.
Gap 5:	Results when the customer misperceives the quality of service performance. One of the characteristics of good quality is that it is often unobstructive. A customer may simply not realise the quality work performed, especially with an infrequently used service such as healthcare, consulting or specialized repair work.
Gap 6:	Occurs when a customer misunderstands what the sales executive says or misinterprets the nature of advertising message and expects something different from what was actually promised.
Gap 7:	Occurs when the customer compares what he or she experienced with what was expected (additional expectations as modified by marketing communications).

Their study examined the hypothesised relationship between the organisational gaps and their antecedents and consequences. Key findings from the study have the following managerial implications:

1. Face-to-face interactions between managers and contract employees and reduction in organisational barriers separating the two groups are useful strategies for understanding expectations.

2. To close the standards gap, management must allocate the necessary resources to put in place systematic processes for setting service quality goals.

3. Develop customer trust through long-term strategy rather than a snip-shot superficial programme.

4. Understand customers habits on how they prefer to consume a service, for example, a customer would prefer extended hours for a meal in an exclusive restaurant.

5. Pre-test new procedures and equipments before introducing them. The failure of a productivity improvement programme is more damaging than otherwise, for example, when Indian Airlines introduced computerized reservation system to improve its service, it was found that at most places the system remained down most of the time. It created more confusion, both among customers and employees and proved to be counter-productive.

6. Understanding the determinants of consumer behaviour in terms of their choice, by forece or by any other external forces, for example, shopping behaviours is not even throughout the month. It changes between the first week to the fourth week of the month, it changes between weekdays and weekends.

7. Teach consumers how to use service innovations – most people do not know how to go about treatment in government hospitals – there is a need to make people aware of how to go about from registration to appointment to check-up and treatment, in the same way as changes in traffic routes at India Gate or Connaught Place are notified through press and television before introducing them.

8. Promote the benefits and stimulate trial. The success in innovation lies in encouraging trial by making the benefit obvious.

9. Monitor and evaluate performance. One can learn from experience – good or bad. As one goes along introducing changes, corrective measures should also be taken simultaneously. These measures could be restricted to redesign of facilities and procedures or extending to educating, communicating and promoting the efforts.

The Gronroos Model

This is a consumer oriented approach that recognises the holistic process of service delivery which has to be controlled by taking into consideration the expectations and attitudes of service consumers. Hence the starting point for service provider in the understanding how the consumers judge, their perception of processes as to whether a service is good or bad, how quality can be managed to increase satisfaction.

Gronroos developed a model to explain the 'missing service quality concepts'. The models' centre point is the image, which represents that a gap can occur between expected service and perceived service. The image is created by the overall impact which is summation of different aspects of technical and functional variables. Care that should be taken when you use this model is that you cannot use it in isolation or only with a few variables but on the basis of overall impact of all variables.

The marketer has to find out what are the customer needs and wants, how they are perceiving the quality, how they evaluate quality and what are the means of influencing service quality.

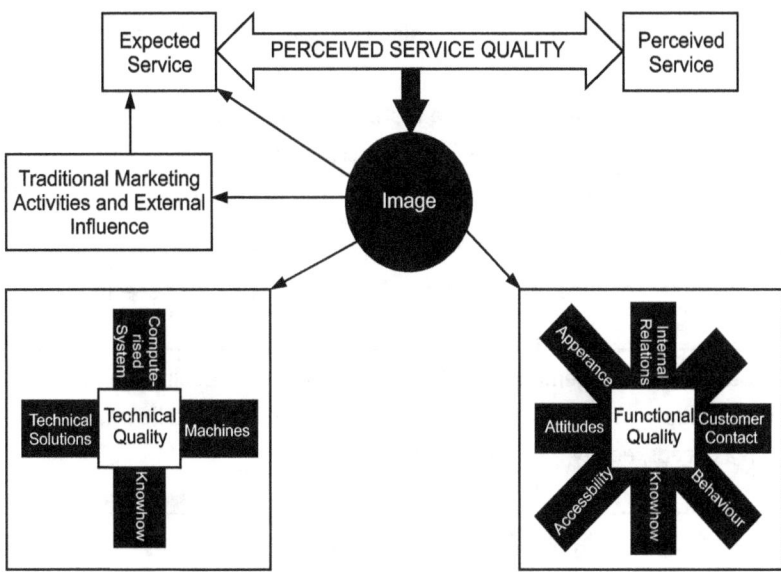

Fig. 11.8

Groonroos stated that 'perceived service quality' is dependent on two variables namely 'expected service' and 'perceived service'.

The technical quality and functional quality play an important role for customers image formation.

1. Technical quality is what the customer is actually receiving from the service and it is quantifiable and can be measured.

2. Functional quality is how the technical quality elements of the service are delivered. This includes appearance, accessibility, customer contact, attitude, internal relations, behavior and service mindness. The culture of management can influence the attitudes, behaviour and general service-mindness of employees. We know that a student in a lecture will evaluate not only the quality of the lecture by content but also the way in which it was delivered in terms of style, appearance, ambience, support of the support staff.

The Distinction between Service Quality and Customer Satisfaction

A review of the emerging literature suggests that there appears to be relative consensus among marketing researchers that service quality and customer satisfaction are separate constructs which is unique and share a close relationship (Cronin and Taylor, 1992; Oliver,1993). Most researchers in the services field have maintained that these constructs are distinct (Bitner, 1990; Carman, 1990; Boulding et al., 1993; Spreng and Mackoy, 1996).

Table 11.7 identifies a number of key elements that distinguish customer satisfaction from service quality.

Table 11.7: The Distinction between
Customer Satisfaction and Service Quality

Customer Satisfaction	Service Quality
Customer satisfaction can result from any dimension, whether or not it is quality related.	The dimensions underlying quality judgements are rather specific.
Customer satisfaction judgements can be formed by a large number of non-quality issues, such as needs, equity, perceptions of fairness.	Expectations for quality are based on ideals or perceptions of excellence.
Customer satisfaction is believed to have more conceptual antecedents.	Service quality has less conceptual antecedents.
Satisfaction judgements do require experience with the service or provider.	Quality perceptions do not require experience with the service or provider.

Source: Adapted from various sources (Taylor, 1993; Oliver, 1993; Rust and Oliver, 1994; Spreng and Mackoy, 1996; Choi et al., 2004; Grace and O'Cass, 2005)

11.12 Service Quality Performance

1. **Service Quality Performance is the best competitive weapon:** The best way to build quality and competitive advantage in global markets, and to grow profits, is by being better than competitors in providing service/quality. Excellent service quality performance, tailored to local markets and cultures, and even individual customers, is the best way to differentiate one's consumer benefit package(s) from those of competitors. The old paging 'think globally but act locally' is even more true for using services as a strategic weapon. Excelling at service quality is the most difficult strategy to implement but impossible for competitors to duplicate.

2. **Service Quality Performance is more difficult to manage than product quality performance:** Service quality performance is more difficult to define, measure, and consistently execute than product quality performance.

3. **To truly understand service quality, one must truly understand service management:** Service management is the bedrock of ideals, principles, and philosophy of management upon which to base an effective service quality

improvement effort. Service management thrust must be imparted and ingrained in all employees. Service management, and its approach to service quality, is one competitive advantage US companies still enjoy.

4. **Think Service Management:** Orient management and worker thinking, style, and action to shift from a product' or functional-perspective to service-management-perspective. This change must be made quickly in the organisation to compete in the Service and Information Age.

5. **Use time based competitive strategies:** Service and information based processes consume majority of the time to get something done. People, information, paper, equipment is always waiting. Primary and supporting service and information based processes and service encounters offer the greatest opportunities for executing a successful time based competitive strategy. A time based competitive strategy is not complete till it reaches the service encounter level. Time compression and service quality will increasingly dominate product quality as key to competitive advantage for the firm. Thus package consisting of time, information, entertainment, and service with tangible attributes with consumer benefit package (CBP) is the key to gain competitive advantage.

6. **Use interlinking to excel at service quality performance:** Data analysis tools and methods applicable to services must be developed to build quality and competitive advantage. Interlinking can help managers design CBPs; service encounters, reward and recognition systems, and service processes better and quicker than competitors do and with less risk of failure. Interlinking can help managers segment markets and allocate process resources better and more efficiently. Interlinking can help reduce the firm learning cycle. Management by fact can replace management by opinion, and strengthen management and employee intuition and decision-making powers. Data analysis capabilities and information intelligence become the key assets in the Service and Information Age.

7. **Understanding personal relationship and different cultures:** Providing services, whether they be primary or supporting services, usually involves a relationship between the customer or customer's group and the service provider. Subtle differences in consumer benefit package design, service process design, and service encounter execution are all dependent on understanding group culture, values, norms, behaviours, and service styles. The success of service process performance not only depends on CBP attributes but also how they are provided. Firm should take advantage of regional, national or group differences to increase market share and profits.

8. **Make quality improvement a way of life:** The organisation must truly integrate quality improvement into all organisational systems and management decisions. Quality includes all product and service features of the consumer or employee benefit package as well as the time to develop them, fully deploy them and modify them for local conditions. Quality improvement becomes an integral part of the firm's strategy and decision cycle to generate revenues, lower costs, and grow profits.

Questions for Discussion

1. Explain: monitoring and measuring customer satisfaction.
2. Explain the concept: service guarantee.
3. Explain: customer's expectations in services marketing.
4. State the reasons: why do customers of a service organisation leave?
5. State the measures used for handling the customer's complaint effectively.
6. Explain: service failure and recovery.
7. Explain: unhappy customers.
8. State how contribution of services facilitates customer satisfaction.
9. Discuss the relationship between customer satisfaction and customer retention.
10. Explain the concept of service quality state the various dimensions of service quality.
11. Explain the various 'gaps' in service quality.
12. Explain various factors affecting service quality
13. State the various factors affecting the delivery quality.
14. Explain service quality model.
15. What is SERVQUAL model of service quality? State its objectives.
16. Explain the Gronroos model of service quality.
17. Explain the Parsuraman-Zeithaml-Berry (PZB) model of service quality
18. Describe how customers evaluate service performance.
19. Explain the various ways of classifying services failures.

■■■

Chapter **12**...

Technology and Service Strategy

Contents ...

12.1   INTRODUCTION

12.2   TECHNOLOGY IN THE SERVICE SECTOR

12.3   E-SERVICES

QUESTIONS FOR DISCUSSION

12.1 Introduction

In the recent years much attention has been focused on the structural changes technology has brought upon in the manufacturing industry. But technology has created even more dramatic changes world over in the services sector. The shift towards services has been a long term trend in all the major industrialised countries of the world. Over the last decade the Services sector has become the biggest and fastest-growing business sector in the world. It now employs by far more people than any other sector and forms 64% of the world-wide GDP, twice that of the Industry sector. For this growth to continue, this sector is faced with unprecedented pressure to make services more widely and easily available and to yield higher productivity.

The rapid development of the Internet, both in speed and in capabilities, enabled this re-engineering of the service industry. It relies on very sophisticated architectures and supporting tools, and intelligent devices that create a whole new and innovative market for new services for sensing and reacting to the physical world (medical, agricultural, environmental, energy-related, etc.).

What is the Service Sector?

The service sector consists of the "soft" parts of the economy such as insurance, government, tourism, banking, retail, education, and social services. In soft-sector employment, people use time to deploy knowledge assets, collaboration assets, and process-engagement to create productivity (effectiveness), performance improvement potential (potential) and sustainability.

Typically, the service sector includes industries like:

- Hotels & Restaurants
- Communication (Post/Telecom)
- Banking & Insurance
- Education & HRD
- Consulting
- Business services
- IT/ITes
- Tourism
- Transport & Storage
- Healthcare/hospitals
- Real estate

India's service sector is larger and growing faster than that of economies with higher per capita GDP. The rapidly increasing two-way trade in information technology and information technology enabled services (IT–ITES) and other high-end services sub-sectors has been a critical factor in India's improved economic performance. The service sector recorded a robust 9.1 % average growth, while total GDP grew at 7.0 % in the first four years of the tenth Five Year Plan (2002–07). India's large pool of engineering talent and its rapidly expanding telecommunications sector - IT–ITES - has in recent years been the key catalyst of growth. Growth and improved efficiencies have also been observed in other key areas, such as financial services, transportation and transport infrastructure.

Subsectors within the Service Industry

1. Information Technology Industry

The Information Technology industry has achieved phenomenal growth after liberalisation. The industry has performed exceedingly well amidst tough global competition. Being a knowledge based industry; India has been able to leverage the global markets, because of the huge pool of engineering talent available and the proficiency in English language among the middle class.

2. ITES sector

The ITES sector has also leveraged the global changes positively to emerge as one of the prominent industries. Some of the services covered by the ITES industry would be:

- Customer interaction services – Non-voice and Voice.
- Back office, revenue accounting, data entry, data conversion, HR services.
- Medical Transcription.
- Content development and animation.
- Remote education, market research and GIS.

3. Retailing

Prior to liberalisation, India had one of the most underdeveloped retail sectors in the world. After liberalisation the scenario changed dramatically. Organised retailing with prominence on self service and chain stores has changed the dynamics of retailing. In most of the tier I and tier II cities supermarket chains mushroomed, catering to the needs of vibrant middle class. This indirectly contributed to the growth of the packaged food industry and other consumer goods.

4. Financial Services-Banking And Insurance

Prior to liberalisation these two sectors were controlled and regulated by the government. Nationalised banks and insurance companies had a firm grip over the market. After liberalisation, the banking and insurance domain opened up for private participation.

5. Banking Sector

The three major changes in the banking sector after liberalisation are:

1. Step to increase the cash outflow through reduction in the statutory liquidity and cash reserve ratio.

2. Nationalised banks including SBI were allowed to sell stakes to private sector and private investors were allowed to enter the banking domain. Foreign banks were given greater access to the domestic market, both as subsidiaries and branches, provided the foreign banks maintained a minimum assigned capital and would be governed by the same rules and regulations governing domestic banks.

3. Banks were given greater freedom to leverage the capital markets and determine their asset portfolios. The banks were allowed to provide advances against equity provided as collateral and provide bank guarantees to the broking community.

6. Insurance Sector

The Insurance Regulatory and Development Authority Act 1999 (IRDA Act) allowed the participation of private insurance companies in the insurance sector. The primary role of IRDA was to safeguard the interest of insurance policy holders, to regulate, promote and ensure orderly growth of the insurance industry. The insurance sector could invest in the capital markets and other than traditional insurance products, various market link insurance products were available to the end customer to choose from.

Some of the prominent insurance companies are Bajaj Allianz Insurance Corporation, Birla Sun Insurance Co Ltd., HDFC Standard Insurance Co Ltd., ICICI Prudential Insurance Co Ltd., Max New York Insurance Co Ltd., Tata AIG Insurance Co Ltd etc.

12.2 Technology in the Service Sector

By and large, the service sector is a consumer of technology rather than a developer of technology. National statistics describe the steady growth of technology internal to the service sector -increasing from less than 5 percent of total R&D performed 15 years ago to 26.5 percent in 1993. IT accounts for more than 80 percent of the technology purchased by service sector firms and is the predominant focus of service sector staff. While some level of technology development is occurring throughout the service sector, it appears to be technologically diffuse and quantitatively modest.

This said, however, Information technology has now become a crucial part of the business world. Electronic transactions now dominate the services sector. These transactions range from banking and other financial services, to electronic purchase of goods and services. There are two major trends in this trajectory in the use of IT. The first relates to business to consumer (B2C) transactions and the second, business to business (B2B) transactions. Both these transaction types are encompassed within the broader term, e-commerce. B2C revolves around the web storefront with which consumers interact while B2B involves all transactions between corporations and their suppliers or partners such as banks, vendors and distributors. B2B transactions have generally dominated the trade and investment domains where companies deal with one another to reduce transaction costs. The more recent phenomenon is that of the growth of B2C transactions and this has meant the collapse of distance and geographical boundaries, and increased transparency of pricing.

The extensive use of IT has been made possible by several important factors. These include:

(i)   Better and cheaper telecommunications technology,
(ii) More sophisticated and cost-effective computing power,
(iii) Increasing PC literacy and user-friendly software.

These factors have further been strengthened through deregulation of telecommunications markets and the advent of internet service providers (ISPs) who have reduced barriers by providing low-cost entry into the world of e-commerce.

This evolving onslaught of changes in technology can have an enormous impact on small economies with few factors for sustainable growth. When factors such as skilled and cost-effective labour can be created, these economies can take advantage of fitting into the value-chain of global economic activity by providing specialised service capabilities.

In this wider context there are several services such as offsite accounting and back office operations of banks and credit card companies, insurance claims processing, translation services, medical transcriptions and the like that can and are being done in remote locations. But exploiting this niche requires capital investment in high quality infrastructure for telecommunications, uninterruptible power supply and, equally important, in developing the quality of flexible skills. The table below shows the different kinds of services where technology plays a major role, and the projected offshore markets for year 2010 for each of the services.

Table 12.1: Projected Offshore Services Market in 2010

Projected Offshore Services Market in 2010	(USD billion)
Customer Interaction Services	42
Market Research	5
Website services	7
Network consulting and management	8
Remote education	19
Data search, integration and management	20
Finance and accounting services	20
Animation	3
Translation, transcription and localization	1
Engineering and design	6
Human resource services	50
Total	**181**

Source: McKinsey & Co. in Far Easter Economic Review, September 2, 1999

Applications of Technology in the Service Sector

Technology can be applied in various ways within the Service Sector. In-fact, technology has given birth to many aspects of the service sector. Indian businesses are changing to deliver better value to customers and maintain their position in a fiercely competitive scenario using information technology. Some of the major applications of technology within the service industry include:

1. **Customer Interaction Services:** Customer interaction services give their subscribers access to a wide variety of information, data, entertainment, and others which are packaged for ease of use. Internet shopping is one such activity. There are also other similar services such as advertisements, personal finance, electronic publications, online gaming and the like.

2. **Consulting and Management Services:** Network consulting and management companies provide value -added services such as electronic data interchange (EDI), electronic mail delivery (e-mail), file transfers, and electronic funds transfer. They also provide access to databases and electronic bulletin boards, and customised research (Search engines).

3. **Data and System Related Systems:** Data search, integration and management include systems integration, custom computer programming, consulting, training, disaster recovery, and facilities management. Some of the most highly coveted and value-added jobs now being provided through the internet relate to systems integration and computer consulting in an environment where security and control are critical.

4. **Banking, Finance and Accounting Services:** The broad term, finance and accounting services encompasses services such as data entry, transaction processing, credit card authorisation and billing, invoicing and payroll processing amongst others. Technology is used in banks now for instant updates, transactions and data generation – via net-banking, mobile banking, ATMs etc.

5. **Telecommunication Services:** The use of internet services has reduced telecommunications costs considerably, making it easier for companies to outsource back office operations to lower cost locations.

6. **Outsourcing solutions:** Several processes are being outsourced other than the financial and accounting services. These include business process in areas like legal processes, email answering services, travel and ticketing services, medical transactions etc.

The table below shows some of the different types of services being sent offshore.

Table 12.2: Outsourcing of Services to Asia

Company	Location	Numbers Employed	Sector
America Online	Philippines	600	E-mail answering service
Andersen Consulting	Philippines	515	Software customisation
Caltex	Philippines	120	Accounting and financial services
GE Capital	India	800	Financial back office processing
British Airways	India	750	Airline ticket coupon processing
US Hospitals	India	300	Medical transcriptions
Signapore Airlines*	China	600	Airline ticket coupon processing

Source: For Easter Economic Review, 2 Sept. 1999; STA Company sources.

There are a number of key factors that a location must have in order to attract these offshore services. These are:

1. An adequate supply of skilled, English speaking workers.
2. Reliable and cost -effective telecommunications.
3. Reliable power supply.

In order to sustain and keep the comparative advantage provided by these key factors, countries must also provide tax and other incentives to support the service sector. For example, incentives such as simplified tax returns, tariff-free imports of capital equipment and special economic zones dedicated to the service sector can be instrumental in supporting the growth of digitally deliverable offshore services.

The boom in the services sector has been relatively "jobless". The rise in services share in GDP has not accompanied by proportionate increase in the sector's share of national employment. Some economists have also cautioned that services sector growth must be supported by proportionate growth of the industrial sector, otherwise the service sector grown will not be sustainable. In the current economic scenario it looks that the boom in the services sector is here to stay as India is fast emerging as a global services hub.

The use of information technology can overcome the limitations of size and remoteness but it requires flexible and skilled labour with good quality, reliable, infrastructure.

12.3 E-Services

Until recently, the Internet was about the creation of e-business and e-commerce systems, and it was dominated by websites and store fronts. The spread of electronic networks continues to transform business, marketing and consumer behaviour. One feature of this transformation is the appearance of the e-services phenomenon that arises at the border of two business domains of study: services marketing and e-commerce. Although some think about e-commerce in terms of the marketing of tangible goods (books, clothing etc.) online, a growing proportion of online activity is strictly devoted to the consumption of experiences – both pleasure-seeking, as well as utilitarian.

E-services is the idea that the World Wide Web is moving beyond e-business and e-commerce into a new phase where many business services can be provided for a business or consumer using the Web. Some e-services, such as remote bulk printing, may be done at a Website; other e-services, such as news updates to subscribers, may be sent to a user's computer. Other e-services will be done in the background without the customer's immediate knowledge.

"E-services are modular, nimble, electronic services that perform work, achieve tasks, or complete transactions." – Hewlett Packard. Almost any asset can be turned into an e-service and offered via the Internet to drive new revenue streams and create new efficiencies.

Using HP's e-services concept, any application programme or information resource is a potential e-service and Internet service providers (ISPs) and other companies are logical distributors or access points for such services. The e-services concept also sees services being built into "cars, networked devices, and virtually anything that has a microchip in it."

HP notes three trends:

1. The increasing availability of "apps-on-tap" - for accounting, payment systems, purchasing, and enterprise resource planning (ERP). (HP offers several of these services.)

2. An increase in the number of specialised Web portal sites such as www.yatra.com (travel services) and Amazon.com's e-procurement services.

3. More on-the-fly handling of service requests that may require handling by several companies.

What is an eService?

E-Services have previously been defined as "those services that can be delivered electronically," (Javalgi, Martin, and Todd 2004, p. 561) and similarly as "provision of services over electronic networks" (Rust and Kannan 2003, p. 38). Boyer, Hallowell and Roth (2002, p. 175) use the definition, "interactive services that are delivered on the Internet using advanced telecommunications, information, and multimedia technologies."

The first two of these definitions focus on the fact that delivery is electronic, and answers the question "what is a service?" or "what benefits are expected by the customer?" The third definition is concerned with the infrastructure necessary to deliver an e-service, but still does not define the term. Thus, it is important to clarify what we mean by "e-service" before we continue.

Lovelock and Wirtz (2004, p. 9) define service as "an act or performance offered by one party to another...an economic activity that creates value and provides benefits for customers...by bringing about a desired change in, or on behalf of, the recipient." This definition brings out both the process by which the service is produced and the outcome, in the form of benefits, that the customer receives.

Both the service production processes and the outcomes are relevant when we consider e-Services, as well. Regarding the service production process, an e-service is created and stored as an electronic code comprised of binary numbers, because it exists in a digital environment. Building on this, it can be observed that, by definition, the result of translating an act or performance into binary numbers is called an algorithm. Hahn and Kauffman (2002) have also identified e-Services with algorithms.

Using this idea, an e-service can be defined as: *"an act or performance that creates value and provides benefits for customers through a process that is stored as an algorithm and typically implemented by networked software."* This definition highlights the distinction between service production (a stored algorithm delivered by software) and service outcome (the desired benefit received by consumers). The flexibility of algorithms and networked software combined with the requirement imposing structure on the service experience are distinguishing features of e-service which help to define the opportunities available to marketers.

As an illustration, consider Yahoo!, which offers a calendar service to subscribers. The service production process begins with Yahoo! programmers who create and store the algorithms (procedures stored on computers which can be used to accomplish a task) that produce the calendar service. These algorithms can be programmed to behave in millions of different ways, producing different features, appearances, interactions and benefits, all of which might differ considerably from a physical calendar. Visually maintaining the metaphor of a paper calendar allows the consumer to have a similar "calendar" experience during the service experience. The benefit sought by a user of this service might be a reminder of an important birthday; thus, she creates a calendar entry for the date of the birthday either through her cell phone or Web browser. Before e-Services were available, such a benefit might have been provided by a human personal assistant. Today the consumer might decide to have that Yahoo! reminder delivered to an email inbox or to a phone number, or she might receive the reminder through a cell phone, PDA, laptop or desktop machine. An e-service is logically independent of the devices that create, store, and deliver it. This logical independence of the service delivery process creates an additional level of flexibility.

Familiar e-services are online banking or online retailing (e.g., www.Amazon.com). Other types of e-services are e-learning such as courses offered online, e-health such as online medical advice (e.g., www.netdoktor.com), e-government (e.g., online government services such as tax information online), e-libraries providing electronic access to journal articles or book chapters and information and location services.

Characteristics of E-Services

The basic characteristics of e-services include that service is accessible via the Internet or other electronic networks, the service is consumed by a person via the Internet or other electronic networks and that there might be a fee that the consumer pays the provider for using the e-Service.

However, there are six characteristics that distinguish e-Services from traditional IT services and information systems. The e-Services are specifically characterised by (Tiwana & Ramesh 2001):

(a) **Application Centricity:** The core service provided is the software application/system itself. This is different from consulting which focuses more on design of a custom solution or outsourced programming or IT outsourcing, infrastructural services.

(b) **Contractual nature of performance and reliability:** The Application Service Providers bear the responsibility for service level agreements and performance of the services provided to the customer, irrespective of whose software is deployed on the supply end.

(c) **Centralised Management:** Applications are centrally managed rather than at the each customer's site and access is provided through the internet.

(d) **Application access is sold:** Customers gain access to new applications without making any other upfront investments in software licenses, hardware, additional staff etc. The ASP adds value to their service through contractual arrangements with software vendors or through ownership of the application.

(e) **One-to-Many:** An ASP provides a customised set of application from a common set of modules/subsystems to a number of different customers. This implies selling modified versions of the same e-Service to a set of multiple clients.

(f) **Mass Customisation:** Due to its one-to-many nature: there might be a certain level of customisation available for individual customers.

Properties of E-Services

This section establishes four commonly-cited properties of services and their managerial consequences: intangibility, heterogeneity, inseparability of production and consumption, and perishability (see Zeithaml, Parasuraman, and Berry 1985). They are useful in distinguishing e-services from more traditional services. Lovelock and Gummesson suggest identifying services as those purchases that do not result in ownership for the buyer; rather, benefits are obtained through access or temporary possession. This "non-ownership" dimension is helpful in identifying e-Services as a unique product category.

(a) Intangibility

It can be assumed that an e-service is less tangible than the same service delivered in person. However, in cases such as continuously delivered services (insurance), services which involve processing possessions rather than people (package delivery), or where there is an important symbolic component (plane reservation, ticket to a play) an e-service delivers increased tangibility.

The specific delivery mechanism (DVD, kiosk, hand held device, personal computer) and format (web page, email, video, text message, voice menu) also offer an important contribution to tangibility. Although an e-service designer has considerable choice and flexibility in terms of delivery options, an e-service consumer has only a fixed set of senses and limited information processing capability. Thus, choice of channel should take into consideration the specific type of intangibility.

(b) Heterogeneity

Heterogeneity represents variability in the quality and essence of a particular service. Given the error checking capabilities of networked software, an e-service is likely to be far more homogeneous than other services because it is not labour intensive, and so therefore does not incur as much risk of human error. In fact, upon production, an e-service is more homogeneous than a typical physical good.

(c) Inseparability of Production and Consumption

Because "place" is not a property attributable to networked software (Kobrin 2001), e-Services are highly flexible in terms of physical separation between consumer and producer. A musical band can record a song, which is an experiential product, and sell it on a website. We might determine that the service production (performing the song) and the service consumption (listening to it) have been separated in both space and time. Of course, the same song can be copied by the consumer to different media or played on an MPEG player or the car or home stereo system, or sampled and used in creating a new work of art. This example shows that the flexibility of an e-service can render it more separable than a physical good. However, if we consider an online music retailer that offers a variety of access methods, including downloading, we might classify that as a case where the consumer must be "present" on the website in order to consume the service.

(d) Perishability

Vargo and Lusch (2004b) argue that, in some cases, services are not perishable and can be inventoried. An e-service, being an algorithm, offers an excellent example of just such an exception, as it can be stored indefinitely by the firm (server disk) or consumer (CD or other media). We conclude that e-Services are not necessarily perishable, as a consumer who has enjoyed a downloaded copy of *The Iliad and the Odyssey* might confirm. Unlike goods or offline services, binary numbers delivered by software can be consumed over and over again without being used up. Further, unlike offline services, an e-service such as the downloaded song mentioned above can be copied and given to someone else and yet still be retained.

(e) Non-ownership

Lovelock and Gummesson (2004, p. 34) propose that nonownership uniquely identifies services, which is to say that there is no transfer of ownership in services. This is true for both offline services and online services. Also, in e-Services consumption can occur simultaneously without reducing the other consumer's utility.

Categories of E-Services

E-Services is a highly general/generic term usually referring to the provision of services via the Internet (the prefix 'e' standing for "electronic", as it does in many other uses). It is true Web jargon, meaning just about anything done online. It can cause confusion when used in conjunction with "Support," as who knows the difference between "e-Services" and online Support. It is often best to be avoided for this reason, especially in Website navigation. e-Services include "e-commerce," although they may also include non-commercial services. Non-ecommerce e-services include (at least some) "e-Government" services. E-services are real and they are available today. They can be used to rethink a business process, deploy an application, collaborate in a new way, or to plan a trip.

The following diagram gives a broad overview of kinds of e-Services available today:

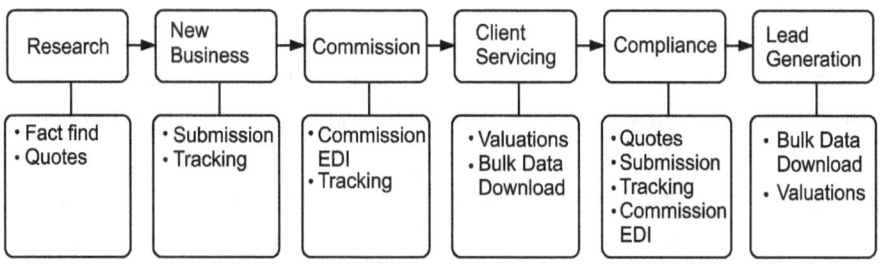

Fig. 12.1: Various kinds of e-Services

E-services come in many shapes and sizes and can be divided into the following categories:

- Consumer Portals
- Employee Portals
- Trading Portals
- Publishing
- IT Infrastructure
- General Business
- Vertical Industries

1. Consumer Portals

It's not all business in an e-services world. E-services, targeted at making the lives of consumers easier, more efficient and more fun are beginning to emerge.

2. Trading Portals

E-services on trading portals deliver a wide range of functions such as the dynamic aggregation of hundreds of thousands of products from thousands of different vendors. They provide advanced market-maker e-services such as bidding, reverse auctions, and collective bidding. Some provide direct e-service to e-service connections, so that business ERP systems can connect directly to portal-based procurement services. Others replace traditional manual business processes for purchase order routing and approval with completely automated e-services. Trading portals that deploy e-services deliver a long list of benefits to businesses - streamlined supply chains, lighter IT, faster reaction times, and reduced costs - to name just a few.

3. Portal Solutions

There are portals that enable customers to host their own URLs/portals and this eService is broadly classified as Portal Solutions.

4. Publishing

Publishing has come a long way from the days of letterpresses and typewriters, and today is being increasingly automated and expanded with digital printing solutions that integrate new technologies and capitalise on the explosive growth of the Internet and mobile devices.

For publishers looking to meet consumer demand for mobile news and information, media publishing services enable the delivery of customised publications to wireless Internet appliances such as Web-enabled phones, hand-helds and laptops.

5. IT Infrastructure

Businesses now have a new opportunity to rethink fundamental aspects of IT. One of the key capabilities within e-services, apps-on-tap, can also be applied to elements of a business' IT infrastructure. For example, messaging/email can now be provided to the employees of an enterprise using an 'apps-on-tap' model. This frees time and money for the IT organisation to invest elsewhere - into areas that can better serve their customers and their partners.

6. General Business

The world of e-services enables businesses to be more nimble and cost-effective. E-services are available in a number of forms to help one streamline supply chains, automate business processes, and ultimately, better serve one's customers. Some e-services are available as apps-on-tap to give a more efficient method to deploy applications. Other e-services are available on business portals that enable new ways to improve efficiency. Business-oriented portals can be found in areas such as ERP, sales force automation, engineering automation, and training.

7. Vertical Industries

E-services solutions exist that are tailored to meet the needs of specific vertical industries.

Challenges to E Services

The future of E-services is bright but some challenges remain. The first challenge and primary obstacle to the e-services platform will be penetration of the Internet. In some developing countries, the access to the Internet is limited and the speeds are also limited. In these cases, firms and customers will continue to use traditional platforms. The second issue of concern is fraud on the internet. It is anticipated that the fraud on the e-commerce internet space costs roughly $3 billion. Possibility of fraud will continue to reduce the utilisation of the Internet. The third issue is of privacy. Due to both spyware and security holes in operating systems, there is concern that the transactions that consumers undertake have privacy limitations. For example, by stealthily following online activities, firms can develop fairly accurate descriptions of customer profiles. Possibility of violations will reduce the utilisation of the internet. The final issue is that e-services can also become intrusive as they reduce time and location barriers of other forms of contact. For example, firms can contact people through mobile devices at any time and at any place. Customers do not like intrusive behaviour and may not use the e-services platform.

E-services encompass all informational services (data, information, and knowledge) and software delivered on digital networks to users. However, not all e-services are commercial. Presently, there is a range of digital applications, which are provided by the users and are put at the disposal of other users for free. Some of the most important conditions for the development of e-services are concerned with the codifiability of knowledge. However, even if knowledge is codifiable, it does not necessarily follow that it can be entirely digitized or that it will be interpreted in the same manner in different contexts. Digitisation and a common interpretative context is, therefore, also important for the development of e-services.

Whether the development of e-services leads to more specialisation or convergence in the production and marketing of informational services is an open question. However, the likelihood is that the production and marketing of informational services will develop in a manner similar to other production areas.

Finally, it should be emphasised that the development of e-services not only depends on the potentials in terms of digitisation and with respect to codifiability. It also depends on the actual demand of users and customers. And, it depends on the incentive for producers to digitally market their services. In some cases, producers prefer and give emphasis to a direct and personal relationship for business reasons.

Questions for Discussion

1. What do you mean by 'applying technology to services'?
2. Explain the various technological service processes.
3. Explain how technology can be used for core and supplementary services.
4. What is e-Services. State its features.

■■■

Case Studies

CASE STUDY 1

Mumbai Nutan Tiffin Carries Ltd MNTCL, comprises around 8000 semiliterate 'dabbawalas' of Mumbai, every day deliver more than 8.00 lakh tiffin boxes to working people across the city and later return the empty tiffin boxes to their respective homes same day.

A meagre amount of ₹ 300/- p.m. is charged for this indispensible service, providing homecooked food to working people at their work place. In spite of problems, hurdles of transport system and adverse climatic conditions, the quantum of error is as low as 1 error in 8 million deliveries.

The modes of conveyance used are bicycles, manually driven trollies and suburban local trains. The entire process of giving / taking delivery is carried out with the help of 3 different sets of carriers.

With the help of a unique colour code system, sorting of thousands of tiffin boxes is carried out within few minutes, at the destination, thanks to the splendid team spirit and meticulous timings.

Although the common working Mumbaikar is getting home cooked food at all nooks and corners of the metro city due to efficient system of MNTCL, off late, there has been a marked decline in the business, on account of changes in working and eating habits. MNTCL is showered with sigma (σ) ratings and affectionately called as 'Management Guru. At premier institutes, the office bearers deliver lectures on managing operational hurdles and sustaining high quality of services.

Questions:
   (a) Critically examine the factors which have led to achievement of excellence in the service provided by MNTCL.
   (b) Suggest suitable measures for improvement in business growth and higher profitability for business continuity in the years to come, for MNTCL.

Ans.: (a) Factors that led to Achievement of Excellence in the Service Provided by MNTCL:

   (i) Effective marketing planning;
   (ii) Effective distribution system;
   (iii) Effective use of various modes of conveyance available in the Mumbai City;
   (iv) Committed and motivated workforce;
   (v) Use of effective unique colour code system;
   (vi) Splendid team spirit and meticulous timing followed by the workforce;
   (vii) Effective time-management techniques followed by the company.

(b) **Measures for Improvement in Business Growth and Higher Profitability for Business Continuity in years to come:**

   (i)   Providing training to the workforce of the company to satisfy the wants of the customers more efficiently.

   (ii) Strengthening the distribution network to be followed by the company.

   (iii) Raising the price / charges for the services to be provided, (say from ₹ 300 p.m. to ₹ 400 p.m.).

   (iv) Increasing the strength of the workforce of the company.

   (v)   Adjusting the company service to the changes in working and eating habits of the customers.

CASE STUDY 2

Sandeep is a young man who operates newspaper lines in the suburbs of a majority city. He distributes a large variety of English, Hindi, Gujarati and Marathi newspapers and periodicals. His customers appreciate his 'service with a smile.' They also appreciate his punctuality and prompt delivery, through all the seasons of the year. However, since last 5-6 months, Sandeep has been in the company of Kiran, another newspaper agent. It seems that Kiran has several short-cuts to easy money. Under his influence, Sandeep has started selling special supplements like Ascent, Dossier, Strides etc., separately from the main newspaper, that too at a higher price. Obviously, such supplements are snatched from the daily issue to his regular customers. A senior newspaper agent, has recently cautioned Sandeep, about this malpractice, saying "This is surely going to prove a bad long-term policy". Sandeep, however, is in no mood to listen to this advice. Sandeep believes that he has a monopoly in this area and is confident of fooling them, without attracting their attention or complaint.

Comment on Sandeep's marketing wisdom and business prospects.

Solution:

Business Prospects Comment on Sandeep's Marketing Wisdom: 'Sandeep' has fooled and exploited his customers. But, this activity is never going to last long. Some day one of the customer might notice the tactics played by 'Sandeep' against them. It is not easy to fool everyone all the time. As soon as the 'Customers' learn about the bad tactics of marketing played by Sandeep against them, they will immediately start complaining collectively causing 'Sandeep' to think over his policy again. Even then, if 'Sandeep' does not change his approach, the 'Newspaper Agent' (who already knows the bad tactics played by Sandeep against his customers) will hire another newspaper agent. It is not very difficult for the newspaper agent to break Sandeep's monopoly in the area. Sandeep must understand the fact that in today's world of intense competition, it is only the 'quality service with honesty' that lasts long, if any other newspaper agent starts his activities in Sandeep's area of operation, it will be very difficult for 'Sandeep' to maintain his present customers as he has already lost faith of many of them and one-by-one, all his customers may acquire the services of another newspaper agent. And if that happens, Sandeep will be heading towards major disaster in his business due to his bad services policy.

CASE STUDY 3

You have been appointed as the Marketing manager of a Health Club, having its own international grade indoor Swimming pool. In the last year, two deaths occurred in the swimming pool. Public, at large, doubt the safety provisions at the swimming pool. The membership stands adversely affected. The management of the health club had appointed a fact finding committee. It's suggestions are as follows:

(a) Reduce the membership fee to attract more price-conscious members or increase the membership fee to attract the up-market membership.

(b) Try to hide-out the facts of deaths at the swimming pool from the public's notice or call the Press to convince them the club's management is not guilty. As a marketing manager which suggestion will you endorse ?

Solution:

As a marketing manager, I will endorse the following strategies.

(a) I will reduce the membership fees to attract more members. This will also raises the total revenue of the club.

(b) As in the last year two deaths occurred in the swimming pool, I will firstly arrange the press conference and ensure to the public at large that the management of the club is not totally responsible for the incidents. It is wrong to hide the facts of deaths at the swimming pool from the public's notice.

(c) I will recommend to appoint more life-guards on the swimming pool. These life-guards are well trained swimmers with vast experience.

According to my opinion, the real problem for the club, is the negative publicity created by the deaths incidence. I will try to stop this negative publicity. I will take such necessary steps to increase the Goodwill of the club.

CASE STUDY 4: RAILWAY'S SERVICES MARKETING: FOCUS ON PRICING STRATEGIES

Indian Railways always worked on the premise that there is no competition for their services. They also felt that there is no need for marketing for them as the demand for their services is much higher than the capacity. Nonetheless, Indian Railways is competing with other modes of transport for both – passenger traffic as well as freight.

Criss-crossing the country over a 62,000 kilometer, route having more than ₹ 16,000 crores as capital-at-charge an annual turnover of above ₹ 13,500 crores, and a large workforce of about 16.5 million employees, Indian Railways are the second largest railroad system in the world under unitary management. Efficient management of this gigantic infrastructure plays a vital role in the economic, industrial and social progress of our country. Indian Railways carry over 10.57 million passengers and 0.94 million tones of freight traffic, on an average, per day.

Railways in India are a semi-monopoly as they hardly face any competition from other modes of transport in respect of the numbers of traffic carried by them. Long distance passengers of average means and commuters in and around metropolitan cities have hardly any other choice. Similarly, long and medium distances freight traffic comprising bulk commodities such as coal, iron ore, cement fertilizers, iron and steel etc. also have to depend primarily on rail transport. As far as marketing of Railway's services is concerned pricing is a major element which needs to be updated from time to time. The other elements of marketing, however, have limited scope primarily due to two reasons. First, the semi-monopoly of the Indian Railways and secondly, the demand-supply syndrome. Pricing of Railways services is not guided by competitive market forces but is decided by the government after detailed discussions in the parliament keeping in view the various socio-economic factors and the overall interest of the country. Therefore, rail tariffs in India are, in fact, administered prices. Pricing of railway's services influence not only prices of essential commodities, raw materials and finished products but also a large population of traveling public. The importance of having a proper and rational pricing policy for the Railways cannot, therefore, be over emphasised.

Also Railways have the flexibility of being a discriminating monopoly. They can fix different tariffs for various commodities and passenger services so long as there is no undue discrimination between individuals or specific users. Thus, they can resort to cross-subsidisation of certain services by others. In fact, the passenger services in India are being cross-subsidised by freight traffic earnings.

The Influencing Factors

Keeping in mind the semi-monopolist nature of rail transport and the objectives of a social welfare state, there are four important aspects which have to be borne in mind while devising freight rates and passenger fare structure as shown in Table below.

Table: Factors Influencing Passenger Fares and Freight Rate

• Requirement of the developing economy
• Importance of making the Railways financially viable
• Interest of the common man
• Possibility of increased efficiency
• (and not to have a simple 'cost plus' approach)

Needs of a Developing Economy

Transport infrastructure plays a vital role in the industrial, economic, and social development of a country. It has been emphasised by the National Transport Policy committee and other high powered committees that the transport capacity should always be ahead of the actual requirements so that optimum utilisation of industrial capacity, in which thousands of crores of rupees have been invested, is not handicapped due to a transport bottleneck. Adequate transport facilities ensure proper distribution of essential commodities from producing to consuming areas thereby avoiding unhappy situations of gluts in certain areas and scarcity of the same commodity in other areas in a country as big as India.

Amongst the various modes of transport, our country has to rely more and more on rail transport from an energy conservation, efficient land use and anti-pollution point of view.

Apart from making use of electric traction on their busy routes, the Railways are six times more fuel efficient in diesel traction than road transport. In view of a difficult balance of payments situation and very heavy burden on foreign exchange due to import of oil and oil products to the tune of nearly ₹ 15,000 crores per year, it is obvious that Railways have to play a far more vital role in the transport sector than road or air transport.

The total number includes 541 million non-suburban passengers traveling on season tickets – obviously working in urban areas. Thus, out of a total of about 3857 million passengers in 1990-91, about 2799 million, i.e., about 73 percent were suburban or suburban like passengers.

The remaining so called common men, excluding the upper class passengers and those traveling on business account, undertake rail journey, if any, once in a while when absolutely necessary. Their expenses on such rail journeys are obviously a small percentage of their total annual cost of living. The interest of the common man will, therefore, be served better by making the passenger services pay for themselves rather than subsidise the same to the tune of over ₹ 1800 crores per year. There is, therefore, inescapable need in the interest of the common man for increasing passenger fares and rates for other coaching services on a rational basis so that these services do not run at a loss. This will also strengthen the Railways efforts to provide better passenger amenities and improve the quality of service to its users.

'Cost Plus' Approach

In fixing the administered prices for services rendered by a semi-monopoly such as the Indian Railways the level of efficiency of the organisation cannot be ignored. An organisation should not be allowed to pass on the higher costs of its operations due to inefficient management to its users by hiking the tariffs arbitrarily. It is often argued that before the Railways are allowed to increase their freight and fare rates, they should reduce their costs by higher productivity of resources and by plugging the leakages of revenue from ticketless travel, compensation claims etc.

So far as the Indian Railways are concerned it has to be admitted that they have a very good track record in respect of productivity of resources – their rolling stock and track utilisation indices are one of the best amongst other world Railways. The overall efficiency index has also shown a marked improvement since the overall losses are a minor percentage of the total revenue. Even so, these must be curtailed to the maximum extent possible. However, it should be borne in mind that the Railways are not an island by themselves and while deciding upon the desirable efficiency level, overall social environment prevalent in the country should not be lost sight of. The desired standards should be realistic.

Basic Principles of Pricing

Pricing of Railway's services has to take into account twin consideration – cost of services and value of services

To achieve financial viability, it must be ensured that each stream of traffic meets its fully distributed cost or at least its long-term marginal cost. This, therefore, forms the lower limit that can be attained. Then to generate the requisite surpluses we take into account the 'value of service', or in other words 'what the traffic can bear'. Rates are fixed for different commodities and classes of travel based primarily on the principle of 'value of service'. It is very difficult to estimate exactly the cost of service streamwise, commodity wise and class wise mainly because of the joint costs involved in Railway's operations. These cost comprise terminal, line haul and intermediate marshalling expenses. However, costing methods have been refined to assess these costs as accurately as possible.

Value of service can be determined more easily in respect of traffic when alternative competitive modes of transport are available e.g., road transport for highly rated freight traffic or short distance passenger traffic. However, for captive traffic, the inflationary impact in case of freight traffic and public welfare and reaction in case of passenger traffic have to be duly taken into account.

Important Landmarks

Prior to 1948, there were 16 class rates for various commodities in freight traffic in addition to large number of special rates. There was no concept of telescopic rates and the charge varied. Crawford Committee in 1948 contributed towards first rationalisation by introducing the concept of telescopic rates on a continuous mileage basis and reducing the large number of special rates.

Another Freight Structure Enquiry Committee under the Chairmanship of Shri Ramaswamy Mudaliar examined the Railways freight rates structure during 1955-57. The basis of telescopic rates was reoriented and the concept of class 100 rate was introduced-rest of the rates being percentage of class 100 rates. Minimum weight conditions for wagon load traffic for various commodities were also fixed. Wagon load rates were lower than small rates for obvious reasons.

Freight rates and passenger fares were subsequently rationalised on the basis of recommendations of Rail Tariff Enquiry Committee, 1977-80, which was also called Paranjape Committee. It was for the first time in the history of the Indian Railways that the rationalisation of passenger fares was studied by this committee and its recommdations were implemented in 1983. The fares for various classes were fixed as multiples of second (ordinary) fares as shown in table below.

Passenger Fares as a Percentage of Second (Ordinary) Fares

Second (ordinary)	100
Second (Mail Exp.)	140
First/ AC Sleeper	550
First ACC 1100	

The taper for telescopic fares was fixed as follows:

Distance in Kms	Fares
1-150	100% of basic rate
+151-400	80% of basic rate
+401-750	65% of basic rate
+751-1200	55% of basic rate
+1201 onwards	50% of basic rate

Subsequently, there have been several ad hoc increases in freight rates and passenger fares from time to time resulting in distortion in the rationalised structure.

Railway Pricing vis-à-vis Rise in Cost Index

Railway Freight rates and passenger fares have lagged far behind the rise in cost of inputs. Taking 1970-71 as the base year (=100) the composite weighted index of inputs in 1990-91 was 837.6 while on the revenue side the indices for average receipt per passenger km stood at 425.6 and per tonne km of freight at 644.2.

Raillways have been able to make the two ends meet inspite of prices lagging far behind the rise in the cost of inputs by ensuring higher productivity of resources, thereby passing on the benefit of their increased efficiency to their users.

The Paranjape Committee (1977-80) had recommended that fares and freight rates should be suitably adjusted from time to time to meet the increase in cost of the inputs to the extent of 80 percent and rest 20 percent should be neutralised by increased efficiency. The following formula was recommended by the committee to meet the escalation factor:

Total escalation (%) = 0.80 (0.55s + 0.09c + 0.04e + 0.23os)

Where, s = % increase in staff cost, c = % increase in coal price, d = % increase in diesel price, e = % increase in electricity charges and os = % increase in prices of stores and other materials.

It will be much better to adjust rail tariff annually or so on the basis of the above (or any other modified) formula instead of making ad hoc increases in fits and starts and thereby not only taking the rail users by surprise but also gradually distorting a rationalised tariff structure.

Influencing Demand through Appropriate Pricing

To a certain extent, the traffic offering to the Railways for carriage can be and is influenced by appropriate pricing. For example, it is more economical for the Railways to carry wagon load traffic than small loads which are less than a wagon load. Therefore, tariffs for small traffic are kept higher than wagon load traffic. Carrying freight traffic in full train load is much more economical than piece-meal wagon load traffic. Hence, Railways have quoted train-load rates which are cheaper than the rates for the same traffic to be carried in piecemeal wagons.

In respect of passenger traffic, Railways are finding it difficult and uneconomical to run slow moving ordinary passenger trains on busy routes. Such trains are an impediment to fast moving mail and express as well as freight trains. Very short distance passenger traffic should, therefore, be discouraged by the railways.

Summary

Railways have to play an increasingly dominant role in the transport sector to satisfy the needs of the developing economy. Interests of the common man will be served better if the public utilities are paid for properly by its users and subsiding the same by public exchequer is avoided.

Railway pricing and its operations have to ensure financial viability of the system and generation of adequate surpluses for properly contributing towards the required growth and development of the system.

The freight rates and passenger fares for transportation of goods and passengers should not be less than long-term marginal costs and pricing should duly take into account the value of service with a view to generating the required surpluses.

Increase in freight rates has a multiple inflationary impact on the price index while increase in passenger fares hardly has any such impact. It is, therefore, anomalous to subsidise passenger travel from freight earnings. Keeping passenger fares lower than the cost of service is not in the overall interest of the country's economy. The Railways should not have a 'cost plus' approach and all possible measures must be taken to achieve highest possible efficiency and productivity of resources.

Questions

1. What are the factors that influence pricing decisions in Railway services?
2. What do you understand from the 'cost plus' approach of pricing Railway Services?
3. Is value addition a better strategy for freight transportation? Justify your answer.

CASE STUDY 5: RM ASSOCIATES

Akash is a graduate mechanical engineer from one of the best ten engineering institutes of the country. He is young, energetic and a gold medalist. During the campus interviews he was selected by an industrial house to work in the industrial products division as sales executive. Though he found this job satisfactory he felt this qualifications were inadequate – as all the people superior to him in the organisation were management graduates in addition to their basic qualifications. This inadequacy made him insecure and he soon left his job to acquire an MBA.

He joined the MBA course as a regular student and completed it with distinction. As a part of the MBA curriculum he took up a project work to develop a marketing plan for Autocorp, a small organisation which was producing autoelectric parts for the replacement market. Though Autocorp had established itself as a quality product in the replacement market, the lack of professional competence was a major drawback in establishing its roots in the market. The Organisation did not have a professionally qualified marketing manager to energise its sales team members.

The plan submitted by Akash was based on market analysis, competitor strength and weaknesses in promotional marketing strategies and strategies of various players in the market, after making a systematic analysis he focused on issues related to demand projections, competitive analysis, marketing mix elements i.e., product offering, promotional, pricing and distribution strategies. Autocorp found the report quite useful and could implement some of Akash's recommendations to its benefit. But being too small an organisation it could not absorb him.

RM Associates are consultants in the field of management consultancy and training and provide advice and training to various companies in the area of facilities planning, re-engineering and productivity improvement

- The re-engineering department of RM Associates provides services of psychological testing, total quality management, employee training, efficiency studies, process planning, layout studies and application of information technology in business decisions.
- The facilities planning department of RM Associates have experts in the field of mechanical, electrical and civil engineering. They have provided with the full support of a computer lab, CAD/CAM facilities to optimise the use of facilities. They are fully equipped to provide services related to fulfillment of regulatory obligations, like building by laws, pollution control, environmental issues and land use etc.
- The productivity improvement department is competent to establish PIPs (Productivity Improvement Programmes) establishing and implementing Productivity Measurement System, selecting and advertisisng productivity improvement methods through work redesign, through incentives, through job enrichment, through individual and group participation etc.

Promoters directors and staff of RM Associates are qualified personnel in the area of mechanical, civil, electrical designing and have a long industrial experience. In fact, most of them were employed with reputed companies before promoting RM Associates.

Their client base is very broad and industries served by them include engineering and metallurgical industries and the mining and allied industries. The clients are from the private and public sector. Advisory and training services are also provided to some government departments.

Ram, Managing Director of Autocorp talked to Ritesh, Chief Executive Officer of RM Associates about Akash and appraised him of the good work done by him for his organisation. He requested Ritesh to interview Akash and see if he could be absorbed into RM Associates

Akash was called for an interview with the directors of RM Associates and was appraised of the business interests of the organisation. No one at RM Associates had ever worked in the field of marketing and their total business was based on their contacts. They were facing great difficulties in expanding the business base.

Since Akash had a marketing background and experience in industrial products, he was a suitable candidate for marketing consulting services. As marketing consultancy services is customer-oriented, they felt that hiring Akash will result in winning more customers even in the competitive market place.

RM Associates had a competitive edge because of their technical superiority. Their companies was doing exceedingly well for the past five years. During these five years of operations, three more consulting organisations in the same field had emerged and were establishing their base in the segment where RM Associates had a stronghold. The impact of this was being felt as they were losing clients every now and then. They were not able to win the tenders they used to do in the past. The technical competency of the staff was no more a competitive edge. They were not even able to diagnose the cause of declining sales of the organisation.

To deal with the above situation RM Associates offered the position of Marketing manager to Akash. Akash realised that the combination of basic marketing knowledge (as he has worked as sales executive for three years), his technical background and newly acquired MBA degree will enable him to take on the challenges of marketing consulting services. His marketing knowledge blended with technical expertise of RM Associates will make the organisation proactive in the present competitive environment.

Akash joined RM Associates to take up this challenge. He was assigned the task of making the marketing plan for the organisation.

Questions

If you were Akash—

1. Explain where you will start?
2. What would you like to know about the services business?
3. How would you use the technical expertise of the staff to market consulting services?
4. What marketing strategy will you suggest to promote consulting services?

CASE STUDY 6: GOOGLE MARKETING MIX.

Google is a search engine. Search engines are used to search the Internet. However, Google is much more than a search engine - it's a global company that specialises in innovation and technology. The business focuses on information made up mainly from web pages, although today all information is absorbed by the Google sponge including books, videos and music. Let's not take the search engine for granted - masses of information is available to everyone and we all have the potential to develop our own knowledge and learning.

Google's search engine indexes billions of pages and gives the search speedy results. The engine ranks websites organically regarding links into a page as a positive endorsement or vote. So if people like your pages they will link to them and the page will get a better rank than sites with fewer in-links.

Google was started in 1998 by Larry Page and Sergey Brin with an initial investment of $100,000. The company went public in 2004 and both founders did very nicely. (and became billionaires overnight). At that time the duo employed around 7000 people and grew at a tremendous rate, with some claiming that Google was the fastest growing internet company in the world. In 2008, revenues were more than $21 billion and net profit was $4 billion.

Larry and Sergey are now worth an estimated $6 billion. Their story is synonymous with Google's history. They were brilliant computer science students. They met when Sergey was helping out at a student open day and Larry was one of the prospective students. They became good colleagues although rumour has that they used to debate quite a lot. Eventually, they worked together to build some software that could be used to search the internet. They touted it around the early search engine companies of the time but none of them had the enthusiasm that matched that of Larry and Sergey. So they decided to start their own company called 'Google.' Their competitive advantage was that the search engine would give objective and useful results - quickly.

Product

Google's income is made through advertising. When a consumer types in a keyword such as 'contact lenses' the search engine will display natural or 'organic' results - as it would for any search term. However, you will notice that at the top and/or along the right hand side of the results, there are a series of advertisements. These advertisements are paid for by companies. The advertising programme is called Google AdWords. See 'price' below.

Google has a relationship with a number of libraries around the world. One of its goals is to digitise as many books as possible and to include them in search result. This could mean that all books are available to everybody. The key problem with this initiative (apart from the enormity of the task) is that Google does not own the rights to all books - the writers and the copyright owners do, and they are not happy. One of those participants is Stanford University.

Google is the world's most popular search engine.

Google Earth enables users to view the world from space. That's a real opportunity for you and me to experience something that our ancestors never did. However, there could be security implications. Like any information - it can be used for good or bad. Anyway you'll notice that the pictures are often dated and taken some time ago. Privacy is also an issue - do you want a satellite taking pictures of your home for the world to see? In 2009, they launched a revised version of Google Earth which include the opportunity to view 3D oceans.

Critics argue that Google is a tool for plagiarism. Plagiarism is essentially cheating by passing off the work of others as your own when submitting assessments at school, college and university. It is the same as copying and is often punished.

Google Scholar - which supports a broad trawl of material such as peer reviewed journals, theses and other academic material.

iGoogle - a personalised Google page.

The ever evolving list of products includes Google finance, Google news, Google blog search, Google video, YouTube, Google sites, Blogger, Orkut, Google Reader, Google Groups, Google Calendar and Google Docs.

In 2008, Google Chrome was launched. Google Chrome is an open source browser.

Price

How does Google make money? Through a special advertising programme called AdWords. AdWords (see 'product' above) are keyword-based advertisements that are bought by companies. So if you have a company that distributes contact lenses, you would bid against other distributors of contact lenses for the highest place (or nearby). By bidding for lucrative keywords this raises the price and Google make money. It's rather like selling a rare item on eBay; the rarer it is the more money you make; the more bidders that compete for the item the more money you make. Hence, the more valuable a keyword the more it will make money. Advertisers are making more than their investment in advertising, and this makes it an appealing programme for business. It is measurable using basic software so advertisers can work out how much they are making on their investment, which is more complex to do with traditional advertising media.

Click fraud is a potential problem with AdWords. Every time you click on an advert, Google gets paid by the advertiser. Sometimes, competitors will fraudulently click on your advert and this is theft, or fraud. Google has many ways of tackling this and click fraud is less of a problem today.

Place

The company is located at Mountain View in California. The site looks very much like a university campus with gyms and cafes. The environment enables employees to maximise their time. The Googleplex is the name given to its HQ.

Another way of looking at place is that Google is an online business i.e. it distributes using the internet as its channel.

Promotion

Google uses AdWords itself. Often you'll see adverts with a link to Google's own services. They include flyers inside business magazines.

They use money off promotions to incentivize advertisers to use AdWords e.g. free $20 worth of advertising.

Google Chrome has its own TV advert.

Google has a Public Relations function that it uses to proactively manage media.

Google will sponsor a $30 million competition for an unmanned lunar landing. The winner must land a rover on the moon; the rover should travel 500 metres, and then send back a video to Earth.

Process

Google retains your search term. It collects data on searches to help refine the search algorithm. So don't think that you search anonymously. Google keeps your search terms and can link them to the address of your computer, and then to you. Whilst Google may not wish to spy on you, governments may take an interest in searching habits and this is a civil liberties issue.

If you use Google mail (Gmail) or Google calendar then you are giving even more information about yourself to Google.

Google co-operates with the Chinese government in its censorship of certain search terms and results. Is it becoming a political animal, or just maximising a business opportunity?

Physical Evidence

The name Googol means a number followed by 100 zeros. However, the founders mistakenly registered Google as their domain name.

The company is located at Mountain View in California (see 'place').

People

In 2008 Google employed 20,000 people.

Many of the original employees of Google came from Stanford and other elite US universities. It employs the top brains, and people working together towards Google's innovative business culture. Employees are encouraged to take advantage of 20% time - that's one day every week working on their personal pet project. They play sports at lunchtime, with Larry and Sergey enjoying roller hockey in the early days.

Its motto is 'Don't be evil.' This comes from its informal, collegiate origins. Google can be a success without losing its integrity. However search engines are based upon algorithms which are loaded with choices about what to value and what to include/exclude.

Company Overview

Google's mission is to organise the world's information and make it universally accessible and useful.

As a first step to fulfilling that mission, Google's founders Larry Page and Sergey Brin developed a new approach to online search that took root in a Stanford University dorm room and quickly spread to information seekers around the globe. Google is now widely recognised as the world's largest search engine an easy-to-use free service that usually returns relevant results in a fraction of a second.

When you visit www.google.com or one of the dozens of other Google domains, you'll be able to find information in many different languages; check stock quotes, maps and news headlines; look up phonebook listings for every city in the United States; search billions of images and peruse the world's largest archive of Usenet messages more than 1 billion posts dating back to 1981.

We also provide ways to access all this information without making a special trip to the Google home page. The Google Toolbar enables you to conduct a Google search from anywhere on the web. And for those times when you're away from your PC altogether, Google can be used from a number of wireless platforms including WAP and i-mode phones.

Google's utility and ease of use have made it one of the world's best known brands almost entirely through word of mouth from satisfied users. As a business, Google generates revenue by providing advertisers with the opportunity to deliver measurable, cost-effective online advertising that is relevant to the information displayed on any given page. This makes the advertising useful to you as well as to the advertiser placing it. We believe you should know when someone has paid to put a message in front of you, so we always distinguish ads from the search results or other content on a page. We don't sell placement in the search results themselves or allow people to pay for a higher ranking there.

Thousands of advertisers use our Google AdWords programme to promote their products and services on the web with targeted advertising, and we believe AdWords is the largest program of its kind. In addition, thousands of web site managers take advantage of our Google AdSense program to deliver ads relevant to the content on their sites, improving their ability to generate revenue and enhancing the experience for their users.

What's a Google?

"Googol" is the mathematical term for a 1 followed by 100 zeros. The term was coined by Milton Sirotta, nephew of American mathematician Edward Kasner, and was popularised in the book, "Mathematics and the Imagination", by Kasner and James Newman. Google's play on the term reflects the company's mission to organise the immense amount of information available on the web.

CASE STUDY 7: RYANAIR MARKETING MIX

Ryanair is the European low cost airline. Low cost or no frills marketing strategies are of great interest to marketers since the marketing mix employed tends to run in opposition to what makes a great brand - and Ryanair is a great brand and a very successful business. In a nutshell Ryanair sells the cheapest tickets that you can buy (on most occasions). If you'd like to learn more about this topic then take a look at our marketing mix lesson. Otherwise please read on.

Its charismatic boss Michael O'Leary has a business model with a central focus on cost reduction (and making money of course!). In around 20 years he has taken Ryanair from a single plane company to become the largest airline in Europe. He had a vision and achieved it through masterful leadership. So how did he do it? How does Michael O'Leary retain his narrow cost focus niche strategy in the face of intense competition? The business simply has lower costs and those costs are passed on to their passengers in the form of low fares.

The branded airlines argue that passengers are willing to pay more for a better level of service. You can pre-assign seats. You get food and drink onboard, and can choose a higher level of service e.g. business class. However, the large flag carriers have taken notice of the low-cost model and have employed it as part of their own more differentiated business model.

In 2009 the company settled for 30% of its local Irish rival Aer Lingus after a prolonged takeover bid. Tough trading conditions meant that Ryanair made its first annual loss in 2008-09. O'Leary put this down firmly to rising fuel costs (as did British Airways in the same year). The company also needed to take into account the burden of purchasing its stake in Air Lingus. So in reality things are looking good for Ryanair and its budget operation - since the business aimed to fly double the amount of passengers 2009-10.

Let's take a closer look at Ryanair's marketing mix:

Product or Service

Low cost, no frills air travel to European destinations.

There is no free food or drink onboard. Food and drink are income streams. You buy them onboard, or you don't - take your own food and drink if you like.

There are other income streams - or ancillary revenue. The company has deals with Hertz car rental, and a number of hotel businesses. So Ryanair takes a commission on 'up selling' i.e. ancillary revenue. Other examples include phone cards and bus tickets. About 16% of profit is made this way. This keeps costs lower.

Price

Ryanair has low fares.

70% of seats are sold at the lowest two fares.30% of seats are charged at higher fares. The last 6% are sold at the highest fare

Ryanair occasionally get in trouble with bodies such as the Advertising Standards Authority (ASA) in the UK over differences between advertised and actual price - in fairness to Ryanair these are rare mistakes.

Place

Ryanair does not use travel agents so it does not pay agency commissions. It uses direct marketing techniques to recruit and retain customers, and to extend products and services to them (i.e. Customer Relationship Management). This reduces costs.

You book tickets online. This saves them 15% on agency fees.

They are based in Stanstead in Essex - which is known as a secondary airport. It is new and accessible. It is cheaper to fly from Stanstead than either Heathrow or Gatwick, and since it is less busy Ryanair can turn aircraft around more quickly.

Many of Ryanair's destination airports are secondary. For example, if you fly to Copenhagen (Denmark) you arrive in Malmo (Sweden) - although it is only a short coach trip over the border. Secondary airports, which tend to be smaller regional airports, depend upon this single carrier - some (it is rumored) paying up to £100,000 for each additional new route. Costs are lower and aircraft can be turned around faster.

Keeping aircraft in the air as much as possible is another important part of the low cost jigsaw. However, the company has been challenged by the European Union in relation to anti-competition laws.

Promotion

They spend as little as possible on advertising.

They do not employ an advertising agency. Instead, all of the advertising is done in-house. In fact O'Leary himself overseas much of the promotion of Ryanair. They use simple adverts that tell passengers that Ryanair has low fares.

Ryanair employs controversies to promote its business. For example in 2009, the company reasoned that passengers would be charged £1 to use the toilets on board. O'Leary reasoned that passengers could use the terminals at either the destination or arrival airport.

This would speed things up. It was reasoned that this is what passengers wanted - since they did not want other passengers leaving their seats and walking the aisles to go to the toilet. O'Leary also argued that larger passengers should be charged more since they took up more room - again it was reasoned that this is what the majority of passengers wanted.

Some of their aircrafts are decorated in the livery of advertisers e.g. News of the World, Jaguar and Kilkenny (beer).

People

Pilots are recruited, when they are young, as pilot cadets. They work hard and take early promotions and then move on after 10-years or so to further their careers.

Cabin crew pays for their uniforms to be cleaned. They invest in their own training. They are mainly responsible for passenger safety as well as ancillary revenues onboard.

Physical Evidence

They pay as little as possible for their aircraft. Planes are the most expensive asset that an airline can make. They get big discounts on aircraft because they buy them when other airlines don't want them, for example after September 11th, or on the invasion of Iraq and Afghanistan. Aircraft manufacturers cannot simply stop a supply chain in minutes. If orders are being cancelled or delayed, this is when to buy. It was rumored within the industry that Ryanair was buying Boeing 737s - list price around £40,000,000 (forty million pounds) - with up to a 50% discount.

Process

There is no check in. You simply show your passport and supply your reference number.

You cannot select a preferred seat. It is first come, first served. This aids speed.

There are no air bridges (the tunnel that connects to the side of the aircraft when to board it). You walk or are bused to the aircraft.

Baggage is deposited directly onto the terminal - it's quick. However if your bag is broken don't expect high levels of customer service.

Beyond any doubt, Ryanair is one of the strategic marketing successes of the last decade. Undoubtedly synergised by Michael O'Leary - the low cost strategy that it employs is remarkable and industry changing. In many ways the business has looked closely at all aspects of its markets and operations to remold the industry and customer expectations in a unique way. This is how Ryanair has applied the marketing mix.

■■■

www.ingramcontent.com/pod-product-compliance
Lightning Source LLC
Chambersburg PA
CBHW081141020726

47504CB00009B/1953